Murder at the Flamingo

This Large Print Book carries the
Seal of Approval of N.A.V.H.

A VAN BUREN AND DELUCA MYSTERY

MURDER AT THE FLAMINGO

RACHEL McMILLAN

THORNDIKE PRESS

A part of Gale, a Cengage Company

Farmington Hills, Mich • San Francisco • New York • Waterville, Maine
Meriden, Conn • Mason, Ohio • Chicago

Copyright © 2018 by Rachel McMillan.
Thorndike Press, a part of Gale, a Cengage Company.

Thorndike Press® Large Print Christian Mystery.
The text of this Large Print edition is unabridged.
Other aspects of the book may vary from the original edition.
Set in 16 pt. Plantin.

LIBRARY OF CONGRESS CIP DATA ON FILE.
CATALOGUING IN PUBLICATION FOR THIS BOOK
IS AVAILABLE FROM THE LIBRARY OF CONGRESS

ISBN-13: 978-1-4328-5661-8 (hardcover)

Published in 2018 by arrangement with Thomas Nelson, Inc., a division of HarperCollins Christian Publishing, Inc.

Printed in the United States of America
1 2 3 4 5 6 7 22 21 20 19 18

For Ellie

Then he climbed to the tower of the
  church,
Up the wooden stairs, with stealthy tread,
To the belfry-chamber overhead . . .

— HENRY WADSWORTH LONGFELLOW,
        "PAUL REVERE'S RIDE" (1860)

Love is like a tree: it shoots of itself; it
strikes its roots deeply into our whole being, and frequently continues to put forth
green leaves over a heart in ruins. And
there is this unaccountable circumstance
attending it, that the blinder the passion
the more tenacious it is. Never is it stronger than when it is most unreasonable.

— VICTOR HUGO, THE HUNCHBACK OF
          NOTRE-DAME (1831)

CHAPTER 1

Heartbeat, Hamish. Assess your surroundings. Acknowledge the trigger point. Assure a corner for quick retreat before the symptoms draw attention.

When he could finally blink his surroundings into focus, all he saw were dozens of perplexed eyes studying him concernedly. Others coughed and turned away. The courtroom seemed smaller, suffocating. He loosened his tie with one hand, feeling his heart's rhythm with the other. But it was too late. He was supposed to take preventative measures.

As long as he could remember, and often without rhyme or reason, he would have an episode of nerves. According to his doctor in Toronto, "nerves" accounted for his bouts of panic, tremors, shortness of breath, and a myriad of other things. The doctor had heard of relaxation treatments prescribed to patients who shared Hamish's symptoms.

Other doctors had more advanced treatments, some more drastic than others, including frontal lobe surgery or the shock treatment he had read about in studies reported by the *Telegraph*. He didn't belong in one of the asylums he read so much about by the light of a torch under his quilt when he was a kid, spending a night wide-eyed in terror that he would be locked away. Yet something caused his fingers to tremble and his heart to speed up and his words to trip over themselves — sometimes for no reason at all. Something that turned his first real court case into a waking nightmare. In that moment of humiliation, he would have done anything to get away. But he saw it through: tripping through an apology and sitting back down, the world closing in around him as he studied his shoes, the air so heavy he finally rose and rushed out of the double oak doors, their broad weight slamming behind him.

It would have been all right, of course. He could explain momentary panic and fall back on his proficiency. Most of the time, no one knew. He kept it well hidden.

In chambers, one of the two Winslows (Hamish had trouble telling them apart) stabbed him with the words that set his life in motion: "I hired you as a favor to your

10

father." Of course he could have been angry, but it was the terse inaction that instead startled Hamish. He would have rather been yelled at. The slightly checked anger made Hamish think that he was getting some kind of special treatment.

Hamish barely caught the gulps of breath that had driven him from the floor after the sentence had been read. And that was what clinched it. Hamish's father had gotten him his first real position.

"Cat got your tongue, DeLuca?" said one of the interchangeable Winslows with a snarl.

Hamish thought he had done it on his own. He was top of his class at Osgoode Law School. His grades were impeccable. He was well rounded in everything but sports. When you hid away a lot, you had ample opportunity to refine skills like playing chess and solving math problems. And it still wasn't enough. He hadn't gotten into one of Toronto's top legal firms on his own. His editor father had paved the way.

He went back to the office on nearby Yonge Street and, ignoring the secretary's chipper greeting, wandered in a daze into Mr. Winslow's office on the second floor. No doubt the reporters were having a field day, scratching in shorthand about the young lawyer who froze and panicked in the middle of a case.

But he wasn't fired. Mr. Winslow wasn't even angry. Well, not angry enough anyway. "It's all right, DeLuca. Everyone has a moment."

Hamish didn't remember if he gave his leave or mumbled anything politely before hurrying down the corridor of City Hall and into the sticky June air. The Toronto *Telegraph* office was a quick stretch from the offices on Yonge to King Street West.

As he was more prone to nerves than anger, the heat crawling beneath his collar was an unfamiliar sensation. He gave his father's name and lied that he was expected. As the elevator girl adjusted her small hat and stepped to the side of the sliding door, Hamish's mind buzzed with what he would say the moment he crossed into his father's window-side office.

The chime announcing his arrival at the thirtieth floor came much too early for Hamish's liking. He gave an absent thank-you to the elevator girl, failing to notice how she watched after his mumbling.

Hamish passed reporters, their desks strewn with folders and papers. It was a chaotic space. A noisy one. One that made Hamish tense up, his shoulders rise a little

12

in the direction of his ears, even as he smiled and acknowledged a few hellos from people who recognized him. A constant tapping from a telegraph machine accompanied the rest of his journey.

"I thought I had done something on my own!" Hamish's voice creaked a little on the ascent when he told his father why he was there. "Without anyone. That I had finally conquered enough of . . . enough of . . ." He spread his hands, unable to think of how to describe what startled him from his sleep and hiccupped his voice in anxious moments. That forced him to double over sometimes, trying to catch his breath, trying to focus his eyes on a corner of the wall until his head stopped rushing and the air returned to his lungs.

"I will do something on my own," he vowed. "And I will be good at it. I will prove it! I don't need you to open doors for me. I will rise above this . . ." He raised his still shaking hand. "And I will be exceptional at something."

"Hamish, calm down. I'll get you a glass of water."

"I am not a child." Hamish hated how he stuttered on a statement he hoped would be liberating.

"Don't throw away a good opportunity,"

Ray DeLuca said. "You're smart. You were top of your class. You can still prove yourself. You still *will* prove yourself. You had one setback. I am sure that they would have hired you anyway — or you would have found an equally prominent firm. There is nothing wrong with accepting a little assistance. You just have to believe in yourself the way that I —"

"The way that you believe in me?" Hamish shook his head. "If you *believed* in me, you would have trusted me to find my own way without interfering."

"Jobs aren't falling from the sky like rain, Hamish. You have to think rationally."

"I have thought rationally my entire life. I have never once stepped out of line. I still adhere to the curfew you gave me when I was sixteen years old. What kind of life is that? And now I find out that the one stride I made toward independence — well, that was you at the oar, wasn't it?"

He slammed the door of his father's office and cycled home at a furious pace, wondering if he would have been so upset had he not been so humiliated. He threw his beloved copy of *Hunchback of Notre-Dame* amidst clothes and shoes and left a note for his mother, who was visiting a friend.

So he ran away.

Hamish had a pretty good idea when people were lying. It snagged in his chest the same way the signs of a panic episode did. No, if he had been truly angry and not just miffed, Hamish might have been able to weather it. He might not have tossed all of his clothes in a canvas bag and booked a train ticket to Boston and Luca Valari.

Living in the back of his parents' two-story Victorian on College Street saved money and space. He even had a separate entrance from the backyard. Toronto's boarding houses and bachelor apartments were overrun with men and women funneling into the city to find work that was scarce in rural towns in 1937.

When people had pennies to scrape together, they allotted some for the purchase of the *Telegraph,* maybe to compare their situation with those less fortunate, perhaps to hold on to hope's slippery slope, even as tensions on the other side of the world boiled and brewed. Ray DeLuca, chief editor, was certain that bad news sold as well as good. And so Hamish enjoyed what so many others did not — a safe environment, a roof, a table full of food, and now a train ticket to see his cousin.

Now, staring out the train window at the whir of green speeding him far away from

Toronto and home, he waited for his pulse to slow. It would — eventually. Though he had never done anything so drastic as storm out of his father's office at the Toronto *Telegraph* and cycle at two times his normal speed home to make a long-distance call to Chicago — only to be told that his cousin, Luca — the closest family he had beyond his parents — had relocated to Boston. He frantically stumbled through a few sentences with the operator in hopes of finally reaching his cousin before his mother returned home. Staticky seconds later, Hamish was patched through.

"Cicero!" exclaimed the voice on the other end. Luca was seven years Hamish's senior, but looked — and sounded — younger, especially when he used the old nickname. He didn't seem fazed when Hamish spilled everything. The court case. His father. "You're twenty-five years old. It's about time you ran away from home. What have I always told you? You have to be the hero of your own story! And you will be. Come to Boston. I'm opening a new club. Stay as long as you want."

Hamish rationalized he was merely going to spend some time with his cousin, but he knew it was his pride — and his disappointment that he had failed to live up to expectations. It humiliated him into adventure.

Hamish could be anything as long as he wore a disguise. As if he were in a carnival of people — as exposed as Quasimodo on the Feast of Fools, a hunchback mistaken for wearing a mask even when it was just the vulnerable ugliness he wore. The court had seen the real Hamish then, under the bright lights, the clock above the jury's box ticking loudly and matching the thud of his heart.

In the end it was the feeling of hopeless humiliation that drove him to Luca. Humiliation at a courtroom of his peers and Toronto's legal masterminds seeing him at his weakest when he most wanted to seize the day, like Quasimodo stepping out of the cathedral and into the sun. Humiliation at realizing that his firm had taken pity on him and that everyone knew — that everyone saw — no matter how he tried to iron out his voice, often taking a few ticks before speaking on anxious days, working it into an art so people assumed he was just thoughtful about what he was going to say. No matter how he hid his hand behind his back and monitored his heartbeat as his father had taught him when he was a child. Humiliation at not even being able to get his own foot through the first wide-open door of his life.

He reached into his bag and extracted *The Hunchback of Notre-Dame,* rolling the pages between his fingers.

The book knew where to open as Hamish reached for it, its pages transparent with wear, its words imprinted inside him. He nudged his black-rimmed glasses higher on his nose.

Beside it lay a pair of bellows no less dusty, the upper side of which bore this inscription incrusted in copper letters: SPIRA SPERA.

Breathe. Hope.

When the bells in his mind clanged. When his heartbeat wasn't tempered no matter how often he counted, when he looked out the window for hours, unsure of how to step out into the sun, he would conjure the words and tremulously repeat them. From one of the many chapters in *The Hunchback of Notre-Dame* tattooed on his brain, for when his father compelled him to hide his hand behind his back or excuse himself before his chest pains overtook him and a sheen of perspiration crossed his brow. As long as no one saw. As long as no one knew . . .

He pushed his hair back. "Sometimes stories are in the people whose life's pages no one thinks of turning," his father once told him. Maybe it was time to land *straight* in the middle of the adventure. Not just peer through a glass and count his heartbeat.

If he didn't take a massive step now, he never would.

Hamish retreated to the lavatory and splashed cold water over his cheeks. He combed down his black hair and met his eyes in the gold-plated mirror. He adjusted the buckles on his braces and attempted to smooth out the creases in his shirt. Never possessing anything close to vanity, he studied his visage in the harsh light of the upscale lighting, his hands splayed steadily over the marble counter, lips tightened and accentuating the comma of a dimple inherited from his mother set firmly in his left cheek. Unremarkable blue eyes magnified by his thick glasses.

Would he ever reconcile the Hamish he saw with the Hamish he was trying to be? Luca could help. His cousin had always boasted that under his tutelage, Hamish could have the world — and women — lining up at his door. Hamish wasn't as preoccupied with world domination as he was the potential of life with an easy confidence. He supposed that girls would follow after.

If he stayed with Luca (who always had the world bowing at his feet), maybe some of his cousin's impenetrable belief in himself and his life would brush off on him. Maybe he would become who he was meant to be.

CHAPTER 2

Boston
Three months earlier

Life wasn't like the pictures. With the panache of Irene Dunne, Reggie Van Buren should have been able to merely throw her suitcase out the window and scurry down an old oak after it and into her life of adventure, leaving her would-be fiancé Vaughan Vanderlaan nursing a too-sweet chardonnay miles behind her. But that was the problem with pictures. They never showed what happened en route to the adventure. They only showed what happened when the heroine *arrived* in the middle of the adventure. And the camera lens never panned to routine duties like fixing a clogged sink in the communal water closet or changing a lightbulb in one's new boarding house.

A New Haven Van Buren was not expected to know how to change a lightbulb. Subsequently, every fizzle and snap of the socket forced her into a quick retreat. More than once she almost fell backward over the chair she had scraped across the rickety floorboards to reach the dangling light. She looked at the bulb and sighed, stepping off the chair, and again considered asking the porter in the office on the main floor of Miss Clara's Boarding House for assistance. But every time she considered taking the two strides toward her bedroom door, her stubbornness reined her in. Regina Van Buren would prove herself capable of anything — from recklessly leaving the comfort of her wealthy life to making the bulb stick in its finicky socket. She took a deep breath, stepped back on the chair, squinted her eyes shut, and twisted the bulb in, flinching as it buzzed, not daring to open her eyes until the room radiated and she could see clearly even as dusk fell outside.

"Ha!" she said proudly, wiping her hands on her trousers. Another accomplishment to scratch off in her Journal of Independence. Reggie picked up said journal from the side table and opened it to a creased page, crossing through *Change lightbulb*. Another victory, though not as grand as the one she had crossed off a week previously — *Find gainful employment*. The moment the train screeched into South Station in Boston the week before, Reggie circled three prospective ads in the *Herald*, determined to lug her suitcase across the city until she found a means to put bread on her table and a roof over her head.

Boarding houses advertised as clean and respectable were listed by the dozen, and Reggie secured a room in one across the Charles River in Boston-adjacent Charlestown on Pleasant Street, near a tavern with wooden walls just down from Bunker Hill once frequented by the Sons of Liberty. She'd be able to take a quick elevated ride to Boston's North End if she was in a hurry or a brisk twenty-minute walk if she had time to spare. She emptied bills from a candy tin she had swiped from her dressing table at home. When the landlady pressed as to her being alone and unaccompanied by a male chaperone as reference, she peeled another bill off the wedge and explained her family had fallen on hard times. Her falsehood was thus overlooked and the room secured thereafter, Reggie having shrugged out of pretension and her allowance until all she had left were a few pieces of jewelry she intended to sell should her employment train not screech into the station.

She hadn't supposed her high breeding would be a detriment, but it was. Drat the years of diction lessons. The dancing. The tea parties elongating her spine and teaching her to speak with crisp, clipped consonants. Potential employers assumed a woman of her pedigree must be in some sort of trouble to be circling potential jobs in the classifieds. And not an acceptable manner of trouble either.

The first advertisement led her to an address on Washington Street and into the bustle of newspaper offices and theaters, cafés spilling onto the street, automobiles jamming along in the summer sun. She turned just before a jaunty alley through which she could make out the Common's spurt of green. Inside, she was met by a man on the wrong side of portly, folding in and out of his skin like poorly bound bales of cotton.

She checked the clipping once more then hid it behind her back with one hand while extending the other to match his offered hand. As he walked her into the corridor leading to his office, she felt for the first time she truly knew the definition of *leer.*

Behind the door featuring a frosty glass window with his name, Rod Barlow, in black block letters, she entered an office smelling like it had been stuffed in the back of her parents' laundry.

Her eyes stung with the atmosphere. Nevertheless, she crossed through the room and took the offered chair.

"I am looking for a secretary."

Some of his lunch was still lodged in his teeth.

"Ah."

"And you seem perfectly suited." His gaze lingered somewhere between her collarbone and navel. Reggie folded her arms around her abdomen, the muscles tight from perching there, half on the chair, half not, appearing comfortable while slightly raised, the muscles in her legs cramped with the effort.

"I haven't said anything yet. Don't you have any questions? About past experience perhaps?"

"Your voice, your manner." His tongue found the side of his mouth. "You can tell a lot about the quality of a woman in her bearing."

Reggie shivered. He was looking at her as if she were a canvas and his eyes a paintbrush. He rose from behind the barrier (safe barrier, she thought) of his desk and soon faced her, leaning against the chipped mahogany and staring down at her. The imbalance of power unsettled her and she rose a little higher, her calves burning.

"Everything in this line of work is appearance."

"You're in real estate," she said. Swallowed. Nervous.

"Exactly. Property value." She knew for certain he wasn't talking about plots of land when he reached out with a beefy thumb and trailed it down her shoulder.

New Haven had never seen her recoiling from a man's physical advances. In her silver-spooned sector, if a man said something untoward, a member of her father's extensive house staff removed him. And Vaughan? He was a little boring sometimes but never a cad. He treated a lady like a delicate flower, only . . . oh my . . . what was Rod Barlow doing now? Reggie felt her eyes peel open with surprise because his finger moved lower and lower and — Reggie jumped from her chair.

"Pardon me!"

"Jobs aren't easy to come by in this city, Miss Van Buren."

"So you think you can take whatever liberty you like then?"

"It's my business. I like a pretty face."

"I-I have far more to offer than a pretty face," Reggie shouted before realizing she had given him further bait.

It didn't end well, of course. Reggie had to shove him off, flailing her arms weakly before turning and nearly tripping out the door in her sprint. Panting down Washington Street, she stopped, leaning a moment on a lamppost clock even as the throng moved around her. Her eyes fuzzed it with the towering Old State House in an interesting juxtaposition. She was in over her head. She wasn't ready for the big city. She wasn't Jean Arthur in *Mr. Deeds Goes to Town,* able to hold her own with the other reporters and catch the latest scoop.

A cold perspiration beaded the back of her neck.

She walked onward, first unsteadily, slowly finding a surer pace. The city was beautiful. Her rural life so green now replaced with people and movement like cogs in a wheel picking up momentum with harried speed. A horn shrieked and a church bell chimed the hour.

She sighed and moved to the next notice in her crumpled newspaper: secretarial work for the man behind the Flamingo Club. She had seen advertisements for the club the moment she stepped into the city. It had a fashionable address at School Street and Scollay Square and was set to enjoy its grand opening in a few weeks' time. A nightclub. What would her parents think of her even applying for such a position? Would the devil reach out his scaly fingers and drag her down to the underworld for even daring to meet with its owner? Maybe that was why the position was unfilled by a respectable woman.

Reggie didn't have the privilege of choice when it came to finding gainful employment. Economic times had fallen hard for those with numerous skills she *didn't* possess. But she *did* have resolve and she refused to be taken advantage of. Nor did she want to be leered at. A nightclub owner might be precarious, but he might be a saint compared to that Barlow fiend. She asked directions and wandered past Faneuil Hall and Quincy Market in the direction of the North Quarter. Once across North Street, she found the office easily: adjacent the centuries-old house where Paul Revere had once been a resident. It hugged the wood-slatted building closely even though it towered high above it. Tourists milled about and the neighborhood engulfed her in a parade of tangible senses: smell, sound, and light.

She ascended the stairs to the proprietors' offices on the second floor and read the names on the doors around her. Paul Petrov, General Practitioner and Psychiatry. Jimmy Orlando, Private Investigations. Nathaniel Reis, North End Housing Development. Mildred Rue, Temporary Employment Agency. Here, several stragglers with hollow eyes and worn expressions formed a tired line. They looked at her closely and she lifted her manicured fingers to her hat self-consciously before smiling wanly and pressing on her way. By process of elimination, she selected the last slightly ajar door.

Reggie fidgeted with her netted gloves fusing to her hands in the summer heat. The man behind the door was moonlight and chocolate and Rudolph Valentino. She widened her eyes. He was exceedingly handsome.

"My name is Luca Valari." He extended his hand.

"Regina Van Buren." Her heels echoed over the creaking boards toward him, and she met his hand with her own.

"A New Haven Van Buren?" He raised his eyebrow.

"Yes."

"Which father? William Senior or Thaddeus?"

"William. How — ?" But of *course* she knew how. Everyone knew about the Van

Burens — the society pages in New Haven gave way to the same in Boston.

"I've read about them enough in the paper." He motioned her to take a seat, his eyes looking straight through her. "So you're here to kick off the dust of your past." He folded his long fingers. "I was expecting a young woman who would answer my phone calls and correspondence. But this could be even better. You look like you stepped out of finishing school."

He stretched languidly in the chair behind the desk she assumed would be hers if she secured the position. Reggie was mesmerized by his aquiline profile and sparkling black eyes. His hair glinted purple in the overhead light. Her own was frizzed by the outside humidity.

"My entire upbringing was a finishing school," Reggie said honestly.

"You sound like it too." He lethargically gave her a once-over. She sucked in her stomach and erected her shoulders, and it seemed to have the desired effect.

She was rarely self-conscious about her well-trained Mid-Atlantic, popularized by Katharine Hepburn and Clara Bow on-screen and something she couldn't shake from years of elocution.

If she was self-conscious about a chipped

nail, she could hide it behind her back. If she was self-conscious about a cut of purple under her eye due to sleeplessness the night before, she could use the magic of Max Factor, but her voice? It was hard to erase years of practice.

"I don't have a lot of secretarial experience." She folded her hands in her lap.

"But I bet you have a great deal of taste. My nightclub is going to be the quintessence of good taste." He held her eyes with his magnificent obsidian ones. "I want all business to be done away from the Flamingo, hence my establishing an office here. Never mix business with pleasure. My Flamingo will be the first of many similar clubs throughout America to become *the* watering holes for those who want a nightly escape. The best music. Liquor. Food."

Reggie nodded. "I've seen the advertisements."

"And I am thinking, as well as being the face of my little business corner here, you would know a Beaujolais from a merlot?" He tilted his head.

"I've been to enough parties."

"While I respect your leaving your past behind you — and thus will not require references — I hope you will also allow the door on my past closed. I am recently of

31

Chicago and — how shall I put this delicately? — not all my accounts there are settled. A man, say, rings, asking for me, having nothing to do with the Flamingo, you are just to talk about the Flamingo. Of its advertisement. Of how it is going to flourish."

"Even before it is flourishing?" She raised her chin.

"Exactly. You grew up in a society that is very adept at closing the curtains on some things. This should come easy to you." He rapped the desk with his olive-skinned hand. He had long fingers, carefully manicured. If he was so attentive to detail and class, she wondered, why choose an office where dust specks flickered with each ray of light? With creaky scuffed floorboards in a neighborhood bursting at the seams with life — just life? No cadence of wealth or social graces. Just swinging laundry, discarded vegetable peels, the splash of used water in alleys accustomed to murky rivers, hot and rank in the midday sun. Reggie listened to the music of this world through the open window directly behind Luca. "And I will need someone who will be discreet. I have confidential business here and I don't want it leaking out into the pages of some rag newspaper." Was he looking at her more closely? "But you won't let me down, will you? Young girl out here trying to make it in the world. You recognize a good thing when it crosses your path. Surely you've seen the lines outside of the employment agency."

She took a moment. His eyes were intent on hers.

"I will try," she said. "I have a specialty in social graces."

A specialty in social graces? She might have secured the job, but she couldn't dismiss the stupid things coming out of her mouth when face-to-face with a man who looked like Luca Valari. She didn't know what to think of him, but she wasn't of a mind to set out into the city again and run into another fellow like the one on Washington Street. Besides, a nightclub? It wasn't so scandalous if it was respectable: a high-class watering hole for the city's elite. Vaughan and his friends often went down to the city to try out the floorboards of a new dance hall. Sometimes she went with them. This wasn't any different.

Reggie's Spanish heel caught in the floorboards as she maneuvered her way out of Luca's office with a promise she would start the next morning. She wriggled it out with an unladylike grunt, eager to disappear into the square and count the bills in the envelope he handed her. "For moving expenses." He studied her as if he'd watched her shrug off her old life like a moth-eaten sweater.

In a way, she had. She could pin it on the reckless behavior of one night, but really she was a pot warming to boil. She hopped on one foot, inspecting the scuff on her heel. Had it really been three full days since the fateful night that flung her from her parents' colonial Connecticut bower? It had begun as so many before it with Reggie Van Buren the dandelion at the end of a rose garland of New Haven debutantes. Reggie watched Katherine Harrow and Cecilia Thorne fan out their scented handkerchiefs in an appeal to the variety of slick-haired suitors milling around her parents' annual garden party. If Reggie cocked her head at a slight angle, she could see how the manicured lawn, the sloping curves of the shrubbery, and the sun's buttery tint on the horizon could conjure a million fairy-tale moments. Instead, she was relegated to a too-tight dress her mother insisted accentuated her best assets and Vaughan Vanderlaan's penchant for handing her drinks she didn't care for.

"Another chardonnay." Vaughan handed

her what he'd brought from the bar.

Reggie wrinkled her nose. "Lovely. Thanks, Vaughan." She set the glass untouched on the high table beside her next to a glass once filled with more unwanted chardonnay until she'd tipped it onto the lawn when Vaughan wasn't looking.

Vaughan grabbed her hand and stroked it with his thumb. She hated the sensation but feigned a smile. "Such a luscious night." Reggie hated when Vaughan tried on his romantic hat. It never fit. "Such a night for things to happen, Reggie. Things to change us *forever.*"

"Such a night for you to speak in euphemisms and italics." Reggie stared at the reviled amber liquid in the glass.

"Regina Van Buren, I am the only man here who would put up with your peculiar brand of sarcasm."

"And that's what makes you so special to me."

"Am I special to you?" Vaughan ignored her tone, his persistent thumb-strokes like the flap of butterfly wings.

Reggie looked to the pinpricks of stars for an answer. Finding none, she took her hand gently away. "Sometimes I think we have nothing in common except our parents and your unfailing belief the stars have aligned to see us together for all of eternity."

"I never said that."

"I have half a dozen cards upstairs from half a dozen bouquets of roses proving otherwise."

"We've always been friends. I told you, I will find business in Boston. You want the city. So do I. A planning firm wants to have a conversation. The week after next."

It was more than the city. It was more than her remembrance of the moment Vaughan turned from the most bearable of her parents' friends' children into a young man whose slight touch made her feel like she was the ocean and he the midsummer sun. It was the desire for someone to understand her right through to the core. "I want . . . I want to be someone's Gallagher."

"I hated that picture." Vaughan's nose wrinkled at the recollection of *Platinum Blonde,* a Jean Harlow feature Reggie was besotted with. It took the brash, brainy reporter played by Robert Williams the length of almost the entire picture before he realized he wasn't in love with the beautiful bow-lipped Harlow, but rather the smart, hardworking reporter played by Loretta Young. Reggie was always more Young than Harlow.

"It's because you didn't understand some-

36

times life is more than the glitz of parties and the broad Roman columns of a grand estate."

"Like your parents." Vaughan's tone was rimmed with irony.

"I am *not* my parents."

"With certain breeding comes certain responsibility, Regina."

"Don't call me Regina and . . . Vaughan — Vaughan, stop! Vaughan, what are you doing?"

Vaughan gripped her forearm, tugging her across the lawn to the middle of the looming crowd.

"What are you doing?"

"This is all you've ever needed, Regina, a little shove into the future." Vaughan was radiant. "Dear friends, family, and esteemed colleagues. I am the happiest man alive. Miss Regina Van Buren has just consented to be my wife."

Regina spluttered but no words came out. Her mother gasped with delight. The rose garland of debutantes conjured up smiles to hide their jealousy.

When the applause erupted into the otherwise calm evening, Reggie tried to run but found Vaughan's hold on her stronger than ever. Vaughan's rowing lessons, apparently, were going *quite* well.

Not having a full glass of detested chardonnay to throw in Vaughan's face, Reggie settled for swerving out of his grip, standing back, raising her forearm, and slapping him across the cheek.

Her parents were mortified and the rose garden of debutantes withered. A New Haven Van Buren did *not* slap her intended — even if she had never entered into a marriage contract and intended anything *but* marriage to the man who had just claimed her in front of half of New Haven's most prestigious society.

After an eternity of awkward exchanges with guests who didn't even attempt to conceal their judgment, Regina decided the only thing she could do was run. Jean Arthur would run. Katharine Hepburn would run. Myrna Loy would run. No, Myrna Loy would sprint.

Moments later, guests spared the Van Burens further embarrassment by leaving in cars waxed to a shine they could catch their reflection in and Reggie fumed safely in the confines of her childhood bedroom. She threw stockings, dresses, hats, gloves, her journal, and a threadbare teddy bear in a poor jumble into a suitcase and arranged for a maid to assemble a trunk to be sent to General Delivery, Boston, all while attempting to ignore the rising voices of her parents from the foyer below.

"A Van Buren does not treat a man that way regardless of what a Van Buren thinks might have been done to slight her!" Reggie's mother's voice intersected desperation and fury.

Her father was a different kind of angry: the patronizing tolerance he used when proudly asserting his position before a board of directors. "We must respect Regina is still learning."

"She was to marry Vaughan Vanderlaan." Her mother was at the end of her rope. "She doesn't have the social graces of the other girls. She has too much rattling in that brain of hers and Vaughan never seemed to mind. Vaughan seemed to like that. What more could she possibly ask for?"

The end sentence was uttered at an amplified volume and Reggie knew her mother had moved directly under the landing so her words would certainly creep through the crack under Reggie's closed door.

In the end, and rather devoid of grace, Reggie tumbled out the window and scrambled down an old oak, snagging her nylons and scuffing her saddle shoe, then ran panting in the slick gray cold of a misty morning to the train station. She found a milk-run train at dawn.

When Claudette Colbert spent a night on a bus with Clark Gable, she had been able to keep her mane perfectly intact. Not Reggie Van Buren. She looked like some strange drunken raccoon arisen from poor sleep, navigating the sudden glare of sun as her heels clopped over the cobblestones of the city.

Yet soon enough, she had replaced the small talk about boats and varsity tryouts and stocks swapped at her parents' garden parties with celebrity gossip at the communal dining table until the landlady barked it was immoral. She saw *Platinum Blonde* three times at the Royal, liking more than ever the way Loretta Young could fit into any situation, even as she was just one of the guys: Robert Williams's reliable Gallagher and the smartest girl in the newsroom.

Reggie didn't dry her stockings on the radiator or let her kettle boil long enough for it to screech a vehement protest that could be heard across the hall. No, she colored inside the lines as much as possible for a girl who had left all she had known (including her parents' good opinion) behind.

She used the contents of Luca Valari's

envelope for new oxfords — so she wouldn't have to take the jagged North End stones in heels — and drug-store lipstick. Then celebrated with ice cream and the pictures. Imagine! A young woman unescorted sliding down into the red velvet of RKO Keith's on Washington Street, snickering over an Irene Dunne double feature. In the shadows cut through by the projector, its beam lighting little dust specks around her, Reggie was suddenly aware of the absence of someone beside her, the whisper of Vaughan's tailored shirt over her bare arm. The scent of him. Vaughan . . . Vaughan wasn't to blame for the world that bred him. Regardless, she fell under the spell of the story soon enough, and the feel of Vaughan's fingers intertwined with hers was just a phantom sensation. Was she really trying to escape him, or was she using him as the catalyst needed to break free of her parents' world? Maybe it wasn't Vaughan. Maybe it was his association with a world she wanted to leave behind.

41

CHAPTER 3

Poach an egg. Surely one of the easier tasks to fulfill in her Journal of Independence.

Easier said than done, Fanny Farmer. Eggs were sticky and runny. She was proud enough she had secured a hot plate that she, like many of the other girls, kept in a box she slid under her bed, disguising the burned attempts of her culinary efforts with spritzes of rosewater.

Back home, eggs arrived like fluffy white scoops, perfectly rounded. Here, they ran over the side of the pan. Reggie straightened her shoulders in combat mode and sucked at the red mark on her pointer finger. She slid the gummy disaster into her waste bin and cracked two more eggs into a mug. Then she filled the pan with the requisite amount of water, added the recipe's dictated amount of oil, and tried again. And tried again.

And then again and again until they were

more than congealed globs. She added a pinch of salt and scooped the eggs from the pan to her now-cold toast, watching the yellow liquid spread over the bread. Her hunger pangs had been replaced by the incense of frustration, but nonetheless, she scooped a small bite.

Cold toast . . . poached eggs that looked passable on the outside but were a little overdone on the inside — it wasn't perfect. But never mind! She crossed it off in her journal. Then she fixed her collar and smoothed her hair and collected her fare for the train.

Out the train window, boats gulped in from the Atlantic beyond and the dimpled ripples of water winked in the morning sun. She pressed her nose to the glass, drinking in the sight. When the train shrieked over the tracks and stopped, she disembarked at North Washington and joined the pulse of the city. The North End awakened with the scent of baking, lines of laundry strung like monochrome rainbows conjoining brick buildings snugged together over the warped cobblestones. Her flat oxfords were a welcome reprieve from years of calf-straining Spanish heels, especially over the uneven stones of the North End.

Children free of school for the summer

jumped rope, scattered jacks on the red-bricks, rimmed the fountain with arms outstretched for balance, and exchanged secrets under the border of trees.

Freedom yawned over the jutting balconies and sighed with the scent of fresh pastries wafting from Leoni's.

Finally, she reached the North Square and the office came into view with a now familiar cacophony of sound and bustle from slightly opened doors. Luca Valari's name sat boldly on the frosted glass. She reached into her handbag for her keys and jiggled the correct one into the knob.

Reggie hung up her bag and hat on the stand, then smoothed her skirt. She wanted to prove worthy of the inflated salary he offered her, but answering the occasional phone call from Chicago was not enough to earn her keep. Her enamel file was worn down from midday filing. She had finished three novels, and a new Packard Bell model radio was still warm from her constant spin of the dials until *Winchester Molloy: New York Gumshoe* crackled over the airwaves at three in the afternoon. Luca had a wireless in case she found herself in need of entertainment beyond her duties. As her duties for the past few weeks had been little more than fretting over the arrival of her parents' inevitable response to the letter she had sent them after she half tumbled out her bedroom window, the radio had proven a much-needed reprieve. She had been staring at her nails for hours. A knock at the door and a shadow beyond the milky window stirred her.

Reggie looked up. Through the crease in the half-open door, a pleasant-faced young man with a *kippah* over his dark hair peeked in.

"Well, you are not Luca Valari," he greeted, strolling in, a paper package in his right hand.

Reggie rose. "I am his secretary, Regina Van Buren." She extended her hand.

"Nathaniel Reis." His fingers were chalk-dust light over her palm. His smile was bright, eyes sparkling. "North End Housing and Development. No one calls me Nathaniel but my mother, and only when she is angry with me. It's Nate."

"And no one calls me Regina but my mother's bridge club. I'm Reggie."

"I was hoping to find Luca and bribe him with cannoli." His eyes roamed up to the ceiling, over to the window, and down to the cracked wooden baseboards where they met the horizon of peeling wallpaper. His eyes crinkled. "Reggie." He tried the name on for size. "I will just give it to you instead. You probably deserve it more. I've heard that you can't buy Luca with money. He gets suspicious. But cannoli?"

Reggie reached out and accepted the gift. The closer the package, the more acutely the smell of fried dough and cream filling infiltrated her senses. "Thank you." She smiled. "Why would you want to buy Luca?"

Nate shrugged and took a beat. "Oh, you're pretty," he said, not with a cadence of flirtation, but rather of certainty. "Of course you're pretty."

Reggie laughed awkwardly and looked into the package. "You want one?"

"Mrs. Leoni's kitchen is far from kosher," he said, a glint of humor in his eyes. "But please, indulge. A North End bouquet." He smiled. "She's the nicest lady. Her bakery is just at the corner of the square. By Prince? You've seen it, I'm sure. Yellow awning. Hard to miss."

Nate's eyes sparkled with kindness. She pushed through a curtain of pretension and found that speaking with an open, smiling human with no expectation rimming the conversation was a fresh delight. "Been here for two years," he continued. "Seen so many people come and go and come and go. But

I know the ropes. Hot out today. Do you smell it?"

"Smell what?"

"The molasses. From the factory disaster back in the olden days. On sticky hot days the ghost of smell wafts over our little neighborhood here."

Reggie reached into the bag and extracted an oblong pastry. It looked and smelled divine. Her upbringing, however, prevented her from tasting it in front of a new acquaintance, so she held it out to him in a slight toast before setting it on the desk behind her.

"If you need anything, just let me know," Nate said. He pressed the crook of his finger to his temple. "I'll see you around then."

"See you around." Reggie smiled even after he had left, his friendly face reminding her she might not be so very alone here after all. Then she turned back to the pastry. It would be difficult, she deciphered, looking at the cream filling spilling out the sides like clouds, to taste the cannoli daintily. Like a lady. She dipped a manicured finger into the filling and lifted the soft concoction to her tongue. It was a subtly sweet explosion of cheesy fluff. Reggie melted. She peered over one shoulder and then the other. Assuredly alone, she lifted the pastry and took

47

a large bite, her teeth cracking the fried dough, the icing coating her mouth and wreaking havoc on her lipstick and face powder, she was sure. Reggie finished the dessert much too quickly and reached for a handkerchief. She dabbed at the sides of her mouth and inspected the damage in her compact mirror. Then she sat back in her chair, let the sun stream through the blinds, and smiled. Mrs. Leoni's cannoli — if nothing else — was worth uprooting from New Haven for.

CHAPTER 4

When the train finally pulled into Boston's South Station, Hamish startled straight. He had ripped a paper napkin to shreds. He was really doing this. He wasn't somewhere in the in-between. He was in another city in another country. In Luca's world.

Centuries-old ghosts hovered over the red-bricks and flickered in the dance of the sun's rays as Hamish stepped into Boston for the first time. Hamish had the propensity to connect with places easily. He supposed it was his desire to immediately find safety and familiarity in the unknown. He waited for Luca at the appointed spot and the city introduced itself to him in waves of people coming and going. Hamish fingered the handle on his suitcase. A girl smiled at him in passing and he gave her a quick smile in return. He studied the streetlights and memorized the span of Atlantic Avenue, cramming as many details in his brain as he could, from the neoclassical grandeur of the golden-bricked station to the towering buildings in his line of sight. His father had told him that the moment he first saw Toronto from the deck of a boat, he knew he had found his world. His home. Hamish stared at the dulling sun spreading over his first view of Boston and wondered if he felt the same.

"Hamish DeLuca?" A broad-shouldered man strode toward him.

"That's me."

"Mr. Valari sent me. I've a car waiting."

Hamish picked up his suitcase, but the man stopped him and tugged the bag away with a strong grip. Hamish thanked him, hiding his disappointment that his cousin wasn't there to greet him in the unfamiliar city. *Not unfamiliar,* Hamish coached himself as he followed the man to a sleek car nearby. Hamish looked around again, his eyes settling on buildings he had already seen until the surroundings were less strange. He smiled as the man opened the rear passenger door.

Hamish slid in. The driver was silent, giving Hamish the opportunity to study the city outside the window. Washington Street, with its snail-slow traffic and bright marquees, reminded him of Yonge Street. Imparting some of his own city's characteristics into this new place would help with familiarity. And soon it would feel comfortable and he would breathe a little easier and the fingers clenched into his palm would fall into repose. The driver sped up and turned rapidly at a traffic light, slowing only for a crossing pedestrian then pressing harder on the gas, swerving from Winter Street to the corner of Tremont. Outside the window, Hamish could make out the great golden dome of a nearby building.

"What is that?" he asked the driver, pointing from the back seat through the windshield.

"Massachusetts State House," the driver said in a tone that forbade any further questions.

"And what is —"

"I drive. I'm not a tour guide. But that's the Common." He inclined his head toward the large span of green, a fountain erupting, people scurrying from the subway below the Park Street Station.

The driver helped him with his suitcase, transferring it to the doorman. Inside, the concierge told him he was expected in the penthouse.

Of course. Hamish's eyes widened at the sleek foyer, tall walls, and marble columns.

He had stepped into Luca's world and, not for the first time, hoped he could learn its language.

Hamish followed a bellboy with his luggage in tow to the lift. Encased by the mirrored cube, he took a moment to inspect himself: tousled black hair, pale skin, and a slanting nose. He hadn't removed his thick reading glasses after the train ride and they magnified his bright blue eyes.

The elevator dinged. Hamish crossed the tiled floor to the penthouse suite. If there was a doorbell, he didn't see it, so he knocked instead.

He was greeted by a woman who might have been attractive had she taken the time with a little makeup or curlers in the limp brown hair peeking out of her cap. Hamish thought her features looked soft — and the way she smoothed her skirt as he stepped through the door made him think she did care about the impression she made, or at least she once had. She was an odd contrast to the grand entrance and the strange, framed swirls of color that probably cost a fortune adorning the foyer where he stood.

Luca approached and threw his arms around Hamish's neck. "Cicero!" His voice was bright. He stepped back, his hand still crooking the back of Hamish's neck. He looked like he had stepped out of a collar ad in the Sears and Roebuck catalog. Hamish's smile spread wide.

"It's been so long," Hamish said. "Christmas last year, wasn't it? I didn't even know you had moved." Luca's eyes looked a little tired and his face was thinner, but he still had his characteristic charm; it hung off his shoulders like a cavalier embrace.

"Cic, this is Fidget." He indicated the lady who answered the door. "She keeps me in line."

"You need it!" Fidget swatted Luca. She turned her attention to Hamish and smiled kindly. "Ah. Yes. *This* is a nice face." She grinned up at Hamish and patted him gently on the arm. "You are a good influence on this rapscallion here."

"I hope so, ma'am." Hamish inclined his head in a respectful bow.

"No! No 'ma'ams.' You must call me Fidget, and I shall call you —" She looked away. "Luca! What is your friend's name?"

"Fidg, this is my dear friend and cousin. Almost a brother, really. This is Hamish De-Luca."

Fidget's crooked smile widened. "You are most welcome, Hamish. I mean to spoil you immediately. Come, come." She waved the men out of the hallway and into the main apartment. "I will make you sandwiches and milk for a snack. You look hungry!"

"That's why I hired her," Luca said once Fidget had retreated to the kitchen. "She bosses me around something fierce but feeds me all the time. She makes the best egg sandwiches this side of heaven."

Luca strolled to a bar caddy in front of a large window compensating for a wall. "A toast?" he asked Hamish, holding up a martini mixer.

"A Coke for me," Hamish said, watching his cousin mix several splashes of gin in a glass. "Luca, honestly, it's so early."

"It's nighttime somewhere," Luca said flippantly, assembling a few olives on a stick.

Hamish took in the living area, which proved an exercise in keeping his jaw from slacking. It really was something out of a picture set on the Warner lot. Framed splashes and scrawls of art that he would never understand but were undoubtedly priceless were featured on three of the four walls. The grand window was canopied by modern black blinds. The furniture and ornamental statues were sparse in their grandeur, everything precisely selected from the year's most elegant and modern offerings. The entire room was designed to highlight its focal pieces: a sleek grand piano in one corner and a long leather sofa in the middle.

Onto said sofa Luca plopped a moment later, extending a Coke to Hamish with the hand not holding his strong martini.

"Chicago, Chicago," Luca droned after Hamish asked what had inspired his move. He reached over to a side table and presented Hamish with a folder. "I had worn the town out. Was getting bored."

Hamish opened the folder, filled with numbers relating to the Flamingo: a place to Hamish as mythical as old Atlantis, such was the hyperbolic mist of enchantment surrounding Luca's every written and verbal description. Luca's eyes followed Hamish's across a few mockups of newspaper ads.

"It will make the Palais Royale seem an oversight." Luca drew on their shared point of reference: a club they sometimes went dancing at in Toronto. "It will seem like a little hiccup by Lake Ontario. Count Basie. Ellington. Porter. They will all be tripping over themselves to play my joint." Hamish had rarely seen his cousin so animated. "And it will be attended every evening by the most prestigious Boston has to offer." Luca beamed. "But why stop there? People will train in from miles and miles to see it for themselves."

"It's a club."

Luca dismissed him. "No, Hamish, the Flamingo is not some run-of-the-mill club. The Flamingo is a bottled experience ready for the making. The Flamingo will change everything."

"What needs to be changed?" Hamish asked.

"Nothing. I just mean it will change the way people *experience* a club."

"Oh."

"What did you think I meant?" Luca swished his martini.

Hamish shook his head. "Nothing."

"Because the Flamingo, Cic, is all about the experience —" Luca broke off before giving another embellished recitation of the club's positive attributes and the optimal experience it would provide.

Hamish studied the room around him. There was nothing homelike about it, and his trick of finding familiarity to fend off later anxiety failed. Something about this place tightened his chest. He sipped his Coke. Often his anxious episodes were the result of internalizing the projected worry of another. While Luca appeared as he always did — dressed to the nines, with perfectly smoothed hair and an easy smile — something in Hamish twitched.

"Empathy is the greatest gift," his father had often told him. There was no divide in empathy. It transcended race and class and gender.

"I got you a bicycle," Luca was saying.

"You did?"

Luca nodded. "I want you to be at home here, Cicero."

Cicero. Luca had used that nickname for as long as he could remember. Even before Hamish had gone to the library and picked up an encyclopedia that nearly dragged him down with its weight. Cicero, who refused the magnanimous invitation to join the First Triumvirate on account of his fear of undermining the Republic in Caesar's time. *Cicero.* Named for his proficiency in all things legal, philosophical, and academic.

"Thank you."

"And I want you to not feel guilty for leaving. You needed to break out on your own for a bit."

"I don't feel guilty."

Luca chuckled. "Cicero, do you remember that one Christmas when I told you I was late because my train had been held up and you saw right through me? You did. You stared at me intently and then you called me out for lying. Which I certainly was. And I said —"

"That I had an amazing gift." Hamish remembered the incident clearly. "That I could tell when someone was lying."

"And in this case" — he squeezed Hamish's shoulder — "so can I. Now! I propose a toast." Luca's smile was broad and his eyes glistened under the white lamp beside him. "I actually can't believe you're here." Luca shook his head with delight.

"Is that the toast?" Hamish inclined his Coke bottle.

"No, no, no. It's just that . . ." Luca stopped.

"Are you misting up?"

"Stop mocking me!"

"I wasn't mocking you."

"And bottoms up!" Luca insisted, chiming Hamish's glass and taking a long sip.

Hamish gulped a welcome swallow of cold soda. Then he laughed. "That was a terrible toast."

"Yes, maybe." Luca swished his martini. "But it's going to be an absolutely dazzling summer."

CHAPTER 5

Reggie blinked away the mosquito-like persistence of Vaughan's memory. Why was he still in her brain? She was angry with him. He really was the springboard that catapulted her to Boston, wasn't he? Yet his looks, his smiles, and his easy way with her spun through her mind like a record skipping on a phonograph. New details and remembrances sent her off-kilter. Had she overreacted? Had she made a mistake? Would she ever truly be able to survive beyond her parents' wealth, or was she only playing at independence?

Yet she was sure she had never felt freer than when skipping over the stones of age-old patriotism en route from Miss Clara's to Luca Valari's office in the North End. Church steeples scraped the sky and old bells chimed their authority over cobblestones once prodded by the hooves of Revere's legendary ride, just like the poem she had learned in school, now slick under her oxfords from a recent spurt of rain. The promise of the city rose up and pulled her close, becoming more pronounced as she neared the oldest part of the quarter with taverns and houses sloping into little alleyways, nooks and crannies with secrets extolled by a harvested heritage.

Luca's office was on the second floor with just the right vantage point to see the uneven rooftops for miles out the grainy window.

With *Winchester Molloy: New York Gumshoe* on the wireless, unwrapped cannoli at her elbow, and the bells of St. Stephen's tolling the hour, Reggie couldn't think of anywhere she would rather be. Boston intoxicated her imagination. Every time the church bells pealed, she conjured the outline of the bell tower over a century before. A swinging lantern. One if by land. Two if by sea. Galloping hooves and derring-do pulled her from the routine of ledgers and books and phone messages from men with deep voices who always spoke to urgent Chicago business for which she never had an answer before reciting the grandeur of Luca Valari's new club. More than one morning she wondered if she would see her employer again. She dusted and filed and tried her best to take messages — leaving out the inevitable cursing when she was yelled at by investors and creditors, a past now nipping on Luca's heels. She also heard from the offices of several men whom she mentally described as Luca's entourage. Men who buzzed with enthusiasm, as excited for the opening of the Flamingo Club as her new employer had been when she signed her work contract.

Reggie knew little about business beyond the endless hours around the dinner table with her own father speaking to the fluctuation in current markets and Vaughan's father agreeing with a sound intersecting a wheeze and a snort. These men sounded similar. Their alma mater was probably Harvard and they would probably say it in a tone making her wrinkle her nose.

Reggie's confidence grew with these interactions; yet the Chicago calls persisted and her employer was often nowhere to be found, telling her he was busy on location at the soon-to-open club.

While her head told her she was probably tying herself up in an unstable business, she had few other options — and when Luca was around, she fell under his spell.

"Good morning!" she said delightedly when he walked through the door ten days before the club's official opening. She slightly adjusted the flowers she had picked from Copp's Hill Terrace on her morning walk and arranged in a chipped blue vase.

Luca smiled down at the bouquet and grabbed a daisy, turning it over in his hand. "This is sweet. Love these little feminine touches." The comment might have sounded patronizing if his voice wasn't so dazzling.

"There have been a lot of phone calls from Chicago, Mr. Valari," Reggie said. "Should I tell them something specific?"

"Reggie, if we spent all of our time being tugged into the ennui of old business, we would not be physically, mentally, and spiritually prepared for our next big adventure." He cocked his eyebrow expectantly and his whimsical smile sparked one of her own.

"The Flamingo." Reggie played along with heightened enthusiasm.

"Precisely. Chicago is in the past. Whenever you are in any kind of business" — Luca ran his fingernail over the side of the desk — "you doubtless have some leftover strands. But I am starting something new here, and your job, as you recall, is to be discreet. To answer phone calls and be here if anyone — the press, a rival like that fellow at the Dragonfly, a potential investor —

calls wondering about the progress of my club."

"Yes, Mr. Valari." He had written a type of memo about her duties the day she started and her eyes flickered over it. What would he think if he knew her daily routine included slamming the receiver on angry cursing men from the Windy City and listening to *Winchester Molloy: New York Gumshoe* with Nate, who had started to make daily visits to listen to the serial?

"And call me Luca, for the love of the angels," he said. "I am *not Mr.* Valari. I don't even think my father was *Mr.* Valari."

"All right, Luca."

"You won't have to spend all your days in this dusty hovel alone. I will be needed more and more at the location while we prepare for opening." Luca reached into his lapel and showed her a new advertisement introducing Boston's newest supper club at Scollay Square. "And soon I'll want you along."

"It's gorgeous." Reggie appraised the art deco lettering and the careful precision of the club's expected grandeur.

"I'll need you to free up a few evenings as well. If you are to represent my club here, you should have firsthand experience. Plus, you're a Van Buren. You have taste. You can help me decide what we should steal from our rivals and what to leave behind."

Luca hopped on the edge of the desk and leaned toward her. "My cousin is visiting. He's a little bit bookish. A bit shy sometimes. Especially around members of the fairer sex and . . . say . . . is that a new lip color?"

Under Luca's attentive eye, Reggie self-consciously worked her teeth over her bottom lip. "I thought I needed to start looking the part if I am going to be the face of the Flamingo's headquarters. No more roses and white gloves for me." Reggie strung anecdotes of her debutante life like beads. Some flourished for Nate, some for Mrs. Leoni. Now for Luca.

"Yes!"

"And a bit more the style of the North End," Reggie concluded. "It's strange you chose this location. I thought a man like you would want some busy glass sky-scraper."

"We can't always get what we want," Luca said. "Besides, isn't being so close to Paul Revere's house good luck?"

"I certainly think so."

"Schultze is one of my investors, as you know," Luca said easily. "And he thought the cost of rent here would allow me to spend more on my club."

The phone jangled and Reggie moved to pick up the receiver.

"Good to see you, Reggie," Luca whispered, leaving her to business and handing the daisy back to her with a playful bow.

Reggie smiled and tucked the receiver under her chin. "Luca Valari's office, Reggie Van Buren speaking."

The man was yelling so loudly words spilled into one another. Reggie placed her finger in the opposite ear to block out any slight noise so she might better focus on the jumble of angry syllables. Close, but no cigar. All she heard was "Chicago," trailing into a sentence about a clip joint and a bunch of sums. Luca owed someone something. She could make that much out. She should also shake a leg because "whoever you are, girly, he's beat. He'll bleed you out and leave you by the roadside."

"Thanks for the warning." She held the receiver away, inspecting her chipped manicure while the voice ebbed and flowed in a wide range of expletives, looking through the door Luca had just exited. Then she carefully placed it back in the cradle, wondering how Luca seemed to disappear the moment angry people wanted him. She wondered how they found his new office number in the first place. If Luca wanted to escape these incessant phone calls, he was doing a poor job of it.

The one reprieve was the eventual appearance of Nate. Who seemed to know everything and everyone in the neighborhood, including Luca's investors.

"That would be *Tom* Schultze." Nate gritted his teeth, answering her question about the fellow who prowled about rapping a walking stick over the floorboards. "He owns several properties in the area," Nate explained. "A sort of side business to whatever he does the rest of the time. Loud talker. I hear everything he says outside the door. And the landlord and property manager? Mr. Edwin Baskit. Yes, funny name. Edwin Baskit squeezes everything he can from property laws. But I always figured there was more than one egg in that Baskit." Nate laughed at his pun. Moved closer. "Our little North End community has changed a lot in the past few years. The powers that be — the Lantern League as they so like to call themselves, committed to the glorious cause — gutted some of our housing in pursuit of light and fresh air and gardens. And to preserve the beauty of our Old North Church. The preservation of the past ironically means the displacement and discomfort of the present."

"My father is on a similar committee," Reggie said.

"Not like this I don't suppose. They slotted several 'undesirable' houses for demolition. Turned Webster Street into the Prado and a grand open space. They just didn't take into account the people who would have to uproot their lives. Again." He smiled ruefully. "Considering so many of us were uprooted in the first place."

"And this Mr. Baskit?"

"He's good to ignore leaky faucets and demand rent weeks early and hike up fees with little notice. But I try to keep things fair. Or at least let the neighborhood know someone is in their corner."

Reggie bit her lip.

"And the Temporary Employment Agency." Reggie recalled a sour reception from a middle-aged woman whose figure was so broad, the violets on her flimsy dress wilted under her arms and under her bosom. "Mildred something?"

"Rue. Mildred Rue."

It was a hodgepodge of people; but so far it was safe, if a little dull. Reggie's skin still prickled remembering Rod Barlow's advances on her first day in the city.

Nate misinterpreted the look. "Fair Regina, you needn't worry about some slithering old man with a walking stick. I will protect you from any dragon. Even if that dragon is Luca Valari. Or Tom Schultze."

"What do you know about Luca Valari?" Reggie leaned her chin into the heel of her palm.

"May I sit?"

Reggie nodded and Nate sank into a chair on the opposite side of the desk and turned his head over his shoulder a moment.

"I sometimes wonder if there's something just in front of me that I'm missing." Reggie spread her hands on the desk. "But maybe that's just because I've seen *The Thin Man* too many times."

"I personally don't understand why a man like Luca Valari — obviously of means — decided his office should be here." Nate waved his hand toward the window. It was slightly open and the bustle of a sunny afternoon in the North Square filtered under the pane: children laughing, tourists milling around the Revere house.

"I thought the same thing," Reggie said.

Nate continued, "On one hand, it takes the space from someone who couldn't afford the lifestyle Luca Valari appears to live. We have little space as is and people need to be able to afford rent. So I wonder what he and Schultze and their ilk are doing here."

Reggie bit her lip. "Capitalizing on cheap rent?"

Nate shrugged. "I think there are bigger forces at play with some of these men."

Reggie felt a shiver slide down her spine. "You mean organized crime?"

Nate nodded. "I don't want to scare you. I like having you around. There are good people here, Reggie. Even Mildred Rue. Mrs. Leoni. Others who just want to help and make something of a community here. But times are tough and money is nearly impossible to find and some people are desperate enough to do anything. And there are always people who know where to find desperation and how to use it."

"Luca?"

Nate rocked back in his chair. "I am thinking aloud."

"I don't want to be involved in anything that isn't aboveboard. My parents would think it was scandalous enough that I found a job with a nightclub owner."

"Then maybe you can turn the experience into something good."

"How do you mean?"

"Find out what Luca wants. Why he's here. What those phone calls are all about."

Nate's eyes drifted toward the wireless. "Be the best Winchester Molloy that you can be."

With Nate, a new world opened up. As did the power of perspective. The side of life bordered by her parents' insistence on society functions, dances, and parties. Nate translated the lives of the people who were experiencing a world flipped upside down. The safety of their houses and jobs shattered by an economic downfall. Their pride depleted by waiting in line for hours for the Temporary Employment Agency to open. Nate did what he could. But his job was to ensure that the North End was functioning and habitable. More than once he had remarked on why Luca Valari was there in the first place. "Men like him don't usually take the time to drive over Cross Street into our quarter."

Reggie never knew what to say in response. She answered more phone calls and was pleased to have the opportunity to practice what she had learned about the specifics of the Flamingo with an eager reporter. Outside, the evening was lemony light, serenaded by the laughter of kids spilling out of the Prado and diners in the open windows of street-side cafés. A thought of Vaughan pinged her. She almost missed having someone to rush home and apply red lipstick for. Someone to turn in front of a mirror and adjust her skirt for. Someone she would watch the clock to be fashionably late for, sitting on her made bed, picking at her nylons.

The world beyond her seemed to be made in pairs. Like Noah's ark. Two by two by two by two . . . and then Reggie. Reggie sporadically reporting her whereabouts to her parents. Reggie working a far-too-easy job for a whimsically absent employer. Reggie who now, alone, was taking the North End in stride. She tucked her train fare back into her purse. Why rush over the tracks to Charlestown? She could afford the time and the stroll over the bridge, the ramshackle tenement buildings sloping behind her. She had nothing to do and no one to rush back for. But maybe she had something better. She thought about what Nate said. She could be the eyes and ears to determine whether her employer was, as he said, an innocent businessman opening a new club — or involved in something darker.

CHAPTER 6

Settling into Luca's apartment was not unlike trying to fit into an oversized sweater. Hamish wasn't used to being waited on or demanding things: Luca's method for gliding through life with his usual ease was a surprise to him.

But Luca wasn't without his positive qualities. He was genuinely fond of Fidget and he spoke of his employee, Reggie, with the highest esteem.

"Honestly, Cic, never underestimate a proper upbringing," he said, speaking of Reggie. "There is something about cordiality and professionalism that stretches so far. It makes clients die to work with you. Raises the bar!"

Luca had visited the office earlier that afternoon, telling Hamish to enjoy himself and not worry about anything but unpacking and tasting Fidget's cooking.

"Make everything to his specification!"

72

Luca had instructed the housekeeper the previous night. "My tailor will be by tomorrow, Cic. He'll see to everything appropriate."

Hamish pulled at a thread on his cotton trousers. "I don't need —"

"You will represent me," Luca said. "And I need to put forth an image of confidence and professionalism. Don't look at me like that. You look fine. It's not like you're a cat I found under a newspaper near Mystic River. No. And I want to treat you."

He treated Hamish immensely — to several new pairs of pants and suspenders and short-sleeve polo shirts, a few tailored jackets, and silk pocket squares.

Hamish stared at the stranger in the mirror. His hair trimmed and slicked to the side, his eyes brighter with the effect. The new suit jacket hung perfectly tailored on his slim shoulders and gave him a command he usually associated with men like Luca. "Clothes make the man," Luca said while Fidget dragged a full-length mirror into the sitting room and Luca consulted with the tailor, refilling the man's empty whiskey glass.

Hamish's two-toned shoes were scuffless (something rare considering the amount he cycled), and his trouser legs brushed the tops of his shoes in perfect measurement. He was presented with an array of silk kerchiefs and cuff links in an open mahogany chest. The tailor grabbed at a burgundy scarf, which he affixed as a sort of cravat at Hamish's collarbone.

Hamish scratched at the unfamiliar sensation.

Attentively, the tailor detached the cravat at his neck and held up a variety of bow ties in silk and brocade. Happier, Hamish selected one. Luca was across the floor in two long strides and selected four more. "We'll take the lot of this," he said, his finger moving liberally around a selection of shirts and pants and shoes.

Hamish shoved his hands in his pockets and swayed a little. He didn't want to see how much this was costing Luca, who easily put it on credit.

"And you must come to the Flamingo," he cooed to the tailor as he walked him to the door of the penthouse. "Opening night. You come and bring your lovely wife and we will see you have the most magical evening of dancing and the best wine. Or this." He gestured to the empty tumbler Fidget was taking from the tailor's steady hand. "More of this gold, eh?"

When the tailor left, Luca turned back to

Hamish and clapped his hands. "Well! That's settled. What else do we need to see to?" Hamish dropped onto the sofa, surrounded by carefully laid-out clothing.

"You could show me where the Flamingo will be," Hamish suggested, itching to be outside. The window spread out over sunshiny Boston, and while he was excited for the opportunity to test his bicycle wheels through it, he would settle for a stroll.

Luca consulted his watch. "We have just enough time."

"Do we have plans tonight?"

"If plans mean the Red Sox versus Chicago . . ."

Hamish beamed. "Really?"

"I told you I had season tickets, didn't I? Wasn't it part of my grand plan to lure you here? We have great seats," Luca said as they stepped onto the elevator.

Hamish checked his reflection in the elevator's mirrored wall: casual slacks and one of the collared cotton shirts his cousin had purchased for him that afternoon, hair slicked to the side. He thought the style made his ears stick out a little, but Luca waved away his insecurity.

Hamish knew Luca didn't care as much about baseball as he cared about being seen at a baseball game. It was the same when they went to the Maple Leafs Baseball Club at Bathurst Street in Toronto. Luca had splurged on seats behind the first baseline. Baseball visibility was to Luca as opera boxes were to characters in an Edith Wharton novel.

"One stop first," Luca said as the bell dinged and they exited the elevator. "Let's check on my Flamingo."

They took Tremont at a fast stride, the sun splashing over the tall buildings and spreading over the grand entrance to the Parker House Hotel like an outstretched hand. They turned on School Street and crossed in the direction of King's Chapel, slowing before City Hall, which towered in Empire style, domed windows under frowns of gray stone, columns colossally joining one embellished layer with another like a cake. Josiah Quincy's statue stood sentinel, umbrellaed by a tree whose branches curved down to the manicured lawn. They crossed beside it in the direction of Scollay Square. Luca was silent, but Hamish could feel his eyes drift toward him.

"You're watching me a lot," Hamish said.

Luca laughed. "I'm practicing. I want to make sure I see you seeing the Flamingo for the first time."

Scollay Square assaulted their view with

garish neon lights, automobiles, and a large pedestrian walkway populated by women and men who looked like they had stepped directly from the pages of a Sears catalog. They jogged over the stones and ascended from and descended into the subway kiosks, bordered stairs to an underground world below Washington Street. Large advertisements for cigarettes and Coca-Cola hung from buildings facing off on either side of the hurrying droves.

Hamish's hand shook slightly: an involuntary response to multitudes and sound. Luca noticed the slight change. "You grew up in a city just as large."

"And crowds have the same effect on me there." He tensed.

Luca didn't respond, just grabbed Hamish's arm and dragged him across the street like a kid spotting a candy shop.

And there it was: not as large as Hamish had conjured in his mind, but an exclamation mark in a row of cafeterias, small hotels, liquor stores, penny arcades, and burlesque theaters, lights winking down even in the cotton candy light of early evening.

The russet awning over the door clashed with the bold, bright cursive announcing "The Flamingo" and the club's saucy fluorescent emblem, one leg lifted, beak drooping down to meet the sign's flashy o.

Luca's eyes were on Hamish's profile. "What do you think?" he asked, intently surveying. "Do you see that?" Luca stretched his hand out over the red carpet leading to the club's revolving door. In the center, in mock gold, was the same flamingo emblem. "Soon, when we get this one off and running, I want to open more! Luca Valari's Flamingo Club." His hand gestured on each syllable. "Luca Valari's Russet Robin!"

"Russet Robin?" Hamish chuckled.

"I'm still thinking of other bird themes." Luca led Hamish to the front door.

Hamish peeked inside, holding his hand up over his eyes for a better view. "Luca Valari's Painted Ostrich." His delivery was deadpan, his eyes bright. "Luca Valari's Precarious Pigeon. Luca Valari's Blusterous Blue Jay."

"You mock now, Cicero." He swatted Hamish's arm.

Hamish looked up at his cousin's face, painted with sheer childlike delight, and smiled.

"It's really beautiful, Luca. It truly is. Looking inside, I can just imagine what it will be like with all the press here: the bulbs flashing, you making your grand entrance from a shiny Rolls. People dancing and drinking."

Luca's eyes shone with satisfaction. "You really think so, don't you? It's grand, isn't it? I have my bandleader, Roy Holliday. We'll get Maisie Forth out here for a weekend. Let her rip up the dance floor."

Hamish smiled, thinking of his best friend and sometime dance partner from back home. "Your ship is coming in."

Luca laughed. "Oh, Cic, it already docked."

They turned from the empty club and Luca acquired a cab. The world at his fingertips. Soon Hamish was watching Boylston Street through the taxi window as they entered Back Bay. Though less convoluted than the bustle of Scollay Square and the four-way traffic jams of Tremont Street at the Common, it still reflected one of its earliest names: Common Street. Copley Square and the Public Library were visible over the manicured green. Traffic moved slowly toward Fenway Park between streets rimmed with craggy tall buildings, steeples, and clock towers. Each building was rutted with bobbling brick. Telephone wires sagged over high awnings blurting from ornamented windows. Hamish squeezed his eyes shut, taking a mental photograph of everything around him. Making this new stretch of this new place familiar.

While Luca continued to talk excitedly about his plans for the club, the car swerved onto the Emerald Necklace where Hamish watched the fens span wide around a bubbling brook rimming the path to the stadium.

Then Fenway Park sprawled like a leviathan with its tall stadium wall: a metal sheet that, when surmounted by ball, was a point of pride for every slugger on the field. The lights of the neon billboards streamed popping rays onto everything below: trattorias, ice cream stands, hot dog vendors, and gas stations.

The taxi maneuvered carefully through the crowds and vehicles, depositing Hamish and Luca as near to their gate as possible.

Wandering through the stadium for the first time, Hamish experienced the contrast of reality to what he had imagined listening to recorded games on the radio. Peanut shells crunched under his shoes, the salty smell of popcorn mingled with the yeasty smell of foamy beer. Press bulbs flashed and rowdy fans squirmed in their seats, cheers mounting even before the first pitch.

Luca and Hamish sidled to their prime

seats directly behind the first baseline, Hamish blinking at his proximity to the green turf.

Luca removed his hat for a moment and ran his fingers through his hair. "I told you I have the best seats!"

And Luca's name was on the lips of the other men and women in their direct vicinity. People of the same status, season ticket holders accustomed to the proximity to the field. The first baseman so close, Hamish could reach out and almost touch him. He watched Luca a moment, surprised at his cousin's celebrity at first.

"You're popular," Hamish said, rolling his eyes.

Luca gave a strained side smile. "Can't go anywhere, can I?"

An announcer with the buoyant inflection of an auctioneer announced the starting lineup of the Red Sox, and uniformed men took to the field to rapturous applause. The rival White Sox took their positions and the first pitch was tossed.

The thwack of the bat's belting power shuddered through Hamish.

Luca passed him a bill and motioned to a vendor weaving through the stands.

Hamish purchased two cartons of popcorn and Cokes, nervously perspiring but holding himself together.

While he was passing Luca the change, he was interrupted by a smallish silver-haired man, accompanied by a buxom woman smacking gum.

"Schultze!" Luca lit up, exclaiming a name Hamish had heard several times since his recent arrival. "Cicero, you must meet Tom Schultze."

"Ah! The cousin." Schultze's voice was nasal. "I heard you were in town."

Hamish set the snacks on the empty seat beside him and extended his hand. "Hamish DeLuca." He wanted to be polite, but he ensured one eye was peripherally watching Grove toss a smooth pitch.

"And this is Mary Finn." Schultze nudged the pretty woman at his arm, the age disparity between them leading Hamish to think the man was old enough — with crinkly eyes and receding silver hair — to be the woman's father. He took the offered hand politely.

"Very nice to meet you, Miss Finn."

"Miss Finn!" Mary smiled. "You're a gent."

Luca leaned forward, took Mary's hand, and kissed it. "Here you are, lovely Mary, with this brute who would drag you to a baseball game against the White Sox of all teams rather than show you Boston's sparkling nightlife."

"I'm going to work at your club, Mr. Valari." Mary giggled. "Schultzie here said I could be a cigarette girl." She smacked her gum. "You have the cutest outfits."

Schultze's fingers worked up Mary's arm. She tittered. Hamish averted his eyes.

"You don't mind, do you, Valari?" Nothing in Schultze's tone made this seem like a request.

"I need all the pretty girls I can get." Luca's tone was gracious. "Welcome to the Flamingo."

Pleasantries aside, Hamish was eager to turn his attention back to the game.

"It comes with the territory," Luca said out of the corner of his mouth once Schultze was out of sight. "An investor with a mistress and you have to put up with her." Luca ran his palms over his kneecaps.

As the innings slipped by, Hamish sparkled with the possibility of the night. The stars winked happily in the navy canvas above them as the pipe organ belted out riffs in major chords to rally the crowd. The popcorn left his tongue parched enough to order more Cokes, and Luca stretched happily beside him. Having been acknowledged early in the first inning, he was satiated enough to fall into the ease of the game and Hamish's company.

Hamish realized, stealing a sideways look at his cousin before turning back to the game, that this was the perfect sort of evening. No expectations. Just snickers of laughter and too many bottles of soda. When the ninth inning gave way to celebratory shrieks, they made their way out of the stadium, Luca throwing his arm around Hamish's shoulders, more relaxed than he had been in an age.

But unlike their transportation to the stadium, they weren't in search of a hired cab. Instead, Luca pointed toward a large man standing under a streetlamp, solid like a tree trunk, arms crossed to exaggerate his biceps.

"Phil." Luca stepped toward him, tugging at Hamish's elbow. "Hamish," he said as they approached the man, "this is Phil, and he is part of my . . . well . . . how would we say it? My team?"

Phil didn't extend his hand, but he did nod in Hamish's direction.

Hamish nodded back with a slight smile of recognition from their meeting (if it could be called that, so silent and terse was the driver) at the train station.

"If you need anything, you call Phil. If we

are out late at the club and the liquor has flown a little too freely, you find the nearest phone booth and call Phil. If you need a ride anytime, Phil will be there. We will arrange it. You'll be seeing him a lot." Luca squeezed Hamish's elbow. "You don't need to navigate this city at night, Cic."

Hamish wasn't sure what to say. Fortunately, Phil was a man of no words. He was, however, a man who could part a crowd easily with his size and intention, and so they found their way with ease back to Kenmore Square.

"Is he your bodyguard?" Hamish whispered once they were settled over the slick black leather of the back seat.

"Phil is to ensure I can open my club without a hitch."

Hamish swallowed. "So you think you need protection?"

Luca smiled confidently. "Don't worry, Cic. It's partly for show. I want everyone to know I have an entourage of people. I am untouchable." He tapped Hamish's kneecap. "And so are you."

Hamish worked his tongue over a kernel of popcorn still wedged in between his teeth and concentrated on its excavation as Phil wove them through the postgame traffic. Was there always to be a part of Luca he could never understand? Hamish couldn't reconcile the Luca he wanted riding beside him in the back seat, laughing and talking about the rises and falls of the baseball game, with the prickling feeling his cousin was like the gargantuan wall barricading the field and stands.

Luca stayed relatively silent the rest of the ride home. Hamish thanked Phil for the ride and was met with a stony gaze. The man still had not uttered any words, merely acquiesced to Luca's requested time for the next day with a nod.

The elevator bell pinged at the penthouse floor and Luca rummaged in his pocket for his keys. The door opened and Hamish was welcomed with the bleach-clean scent of an apartment in perfect, glistening order. There wasn't a single piece of furniture that sighed easily under his weight or had the worn-around-the-edges comfort of home. No errant magazine or newspaper slouched half-read over the sofa.

Luca crossed to the bar near the window and fixed himself a martini. Hamish declined.

"I loved seeing the Flamingo today," Hamish said as Luca joined him on the couch, the cushion shifting with the added weight.

"It will be exactly what I hoped it would be."

"You know I'll do anything you need to help it get running. Make up for my room and board."

"I told you. We don't need to worry. I want you to relax this weekend." He checked his watch. "All right. Get dressed, Cicero. The white, I think." He narrowed his eyes at Hamish. "The red bow tie."

"Going where?" Hamish took a furtive glance at the clock. "Luca, it's 11 p.m."

"This is when the night is coming alive." Luca's grin spread.

"Where could we possibly be going?"

"How sheltered you are. This is when the bands are just tuning and the champagne is popping. This is when the city finally wakes up. I have meetings."

"When everyone else is going to bed?"

"I knew I needed to see to your education." Luca chuckled. "The Palais Royale is a huge disappointment if you think 11 p.m. is lights-out."

Luca rose and retreated to his room, returning several moments later dressed in a smart tuxedo, wings of ebony ornamenting his jacket. "Ticktock, Cicero," Luca said impatiently.

Hamish was still adjusting his cummerbund. "I don't wear things like this." He frowned.

"You do now."

Hamish carried his shoes to the sofa and sat down, tying the thin laces. When the phone rang beside him, he reached for it.

"Luca Valari's residence," he said. Polite. Official.

"Where is it?" a voice hissed on the other end.

"I'm sorry, I —"

"He sold me out."

Hamish looked up at Luca, who crossed his fingers. "I'm not here," he mouthed. "We have to go."

"May I take a message?" Hamish asked, watching Luca intently.

"He knows the message." The line clicked and Hamish listened to a dial tone.

Hamish followed Luca to the elevator. "You sold him out?"

Luca laughed. "I don't sell people out, Cicero."

Phil drove them the short distance to Scollay Square, its eponymous sign flashing neon, demanding immediate attention, a magnet. Signs and bulbs glimmered off the car windows and Hamish could almost be convinced it was daylight. But it was night: muggy and pitch, the lights lingering over the tarmac, deciding where to settle before spilling on the ground in bright reflection.

Boxes of newspapers outlining the headlines of the day were ignored by pedestrians skipping up from the direction of the subway while other more affluent patrons were escorted from the backs of sleek black automobiles.

Hamish tugged at his bow tie and smoothed down his hair: it felt gummy under his touch, but Luca insisted he use pomade to tame it.

Hamish ignored him and smiled at the doorman who ushered them into the cacophony of people and the rising height of the music: brass and cutting through the smoke of the crowd, the laughs, and the bustle. He shrugged off the fact that since he arrived, he could more than count on his fingers the number of times Luca had begun often unsolicited advice with *can't*.

Inside, Luca beelined for the bar, cutting through a cluster of laughing girls.

"Ladies." He parted their sea of silk and satin. "Thirsty gentleman here."

Hamish stayed to the side. If sidling through ladies to secure a martini was part of his education, he wasn't sure he wanted to be schooled.

"The cousin." Hamish turned at a nasal

voice undercut with irony.

"Mr. Schultze." It was hard to see the man under the low lights. Trailing near was the young woman he recognized from Fenway Park, dressed in suspenders and boy shorts, a box of cigarettes in her hands connected around her swan neck by a thick strap. It was the only thing thick about her. Her torso and shoulders were on full display when she laughed, which Hamish discovered was quite often. A pillbox hat cocked to one side of her tilted head.

"You're cute." She stepped toward Hamish in her heels. "Chesterfields?"

Hamish shook his head and smiled while his eyes followed a sudden tapping. Schultze employed a walking stick Hamish didn't remember from before. Or maybe he just didn't hear it among the sounds of the baseball game. Or, more likely, he was too busy hoping the introductions would end so he could turn back to the game. The head of the stick caught the lights, casting a bright orbit across the dance floor.

Hamish leaned in for a closer look at the insignia carved atop it.

"Ah, this interests you, Mr. DeLuca." He obliged Hamish by tilting the stick toward him.

The top of the sterling head bore the

insignia of a carefully crafted rattlesnake. It was obviously expensively intricate work and the symbol was somewhat familiar to Hamish. Though he couldn't immediately recall why.

Luca returned with a laugh and a fresh drink. "Schultze." He noticed Mary Finn in her red lace and corseted romper. "You were right. She looks perfect. You'll be great at the Flamingo, darling."

"Bob's a nice old fellow," she soothed. "But the Dragonfly is nothing compared to your club, Mr. Valari."

Hamish followed Mary's eyes to a short, balding man holding a drink in a toast their way.

If that was Bob, the proprietor, Hamish could see why she preferred his dapper cousin.

"She laughs too much," Luca said quietly, passing a martini to Hamish as Mary strutted away for more cigarettes. "I don't like women who laugh too much."

"The Dragonfly has potential. We could think of buying it out if the Flamingo goes according to plan," Schultze said just as the bandmaster was announcing another set after a ten-minute break. Hamish, Luca, and Schultze strolled away from the sudden barrage of dancers forming a sloppy line at the bar.

"It's too crowded." Luca's eyes scanned the bar. "I want to make sure the dancers have the space they need and a walk to the bar to take a deliciously short effort. They'll work up a thirst dancing and drink more." He searched and calculated. Hamish watched the slow movement of his cousin's face. It was steady but something danced in his eyes like a teetering flame. He saw everything at once and was committing it to memory.

"Only you would want the bar to take effort." Schultze snorted. "You want people to stumble into more purchases."

"I don't want my club filled with intoxicated ruffians who spill out onto Washington and into police vehicles. It's going to be a classier joint than this. The magic is what happens en route to the bar." Luca warmed to his theme with a wide smile. "The magic is the little conversations, brushing shoulders with a stranger."

"You're a romantic underneath it all, Valari."

Mary returned and Schultze tapped his stick with finality. "My lady awaits. We have some business next week. And I'll need that payment for MacMillan."

"I know."

"And I am hoping you'll take my advice and hire some legal counsel." Schultze's eyes dragged over Hamish a moment.

"I told you, I still have some guy on retainer in Chicago and my cousin here is a lawyer. He'll go over anything I need at a moment's notice."

"You're still too loyal to Fulham," Schultze said.

Hamish fingered his pocket square.

"Who is Fulham?" Hamish asked Luca once Schultze had left.

"Old lawyer. In Chicago. Let's find you a partner." Luca's eyes circled the room.

"Mr. Valari." The balding man who had toasted them earlier edged in.

"Bob! The Dragonfly is in its prime."

"I worry about your Flamingo stealing away my clientele." Bob didn't possess Luca's confidence or swagger. His eyes beaded a little as if he was always adjusting to the dim light.

"You could use a better band," Luca said easily as a trumpet riffed on a discordant note.

"Are you looking to buy me out?" Bob's voice picked up speed. "Because word on the street is that you are. That you know things. About numbers."

Luca grabbed Hamish's elbow. "Meet my cousin here. Take a breath. Bob Miller, this is Hamish DeLuca."

"Pleased to meet you." Hamish shook his hand and gave Bob a half smile. How much of this business of Luca's would he be expected to know? Luca couldn't enter a room without having a connection with at least one person therein. Luca lingered in a place like a trail of liberally doused cologne.

"Why don't we go to the bar and talk?" Luca peeled a bill off his clip and handed it to Hamish. "Buy a girl a drink. Take a spin, Cicero. Don't crowd here in the corner."

They disappeared.

Hamish folded the bill in his slightly trembling right hand.

"Chesterfields?" whined Mary Finn, wiggling her hips by him.

Hamish smiled. "I don't smoke."

"What did Luca Valari say your name was? Cicero something."

Hamish extended his hand. She snorted, reaching and taking it around a pack of cigarettes. "You're the polite one, Cicero something."

"Hamish DeLuca," he corrected.

"I have a break in five. Save me a dance?"

Hamish agreed and a few ticks later nudged his glasses and followed the trail of her heady perfume to the smoke and light of the dance floor.

Her hand was clammy in his, her breath close. She'd changed, and the cotton of her dress fell like water through his fingers when he brushed his hand over her shoulder. The first measures of an Ellington tune ricocheted and Hamish's heartbeat matched the pound of the drum. His feet did the work while his eyes moved past her, over the crowd, his brain anticipating the next turn. Then he did something reckless: he switched his brain off so all around him was silky light and the ashy tang of secondhand smoke, and her perfume tickling his nostrils. His hand unshaking in the curve of her outline and his smile wide. The girl noticed the change and brightened. "You're swell at this, Cicero." She fell into him, her footwork not as sure as her hands moving up his shoulders.

The band slowed and stilled, the last note lingering in the close air. Hamish smiled. "Wanna dance another? Do you have to get back?"

Mary's eyes were over his shoulder and locked with Schultze's. Hamish felt her tighten slightly. He turned and followed her gaze a moment. Even in the dark of the club, Hamish could make out the whites of

Schultze's eyes.

"I'd better get back," Mary said softly, disengaging herself. "Thanks for the dance."

"Are you frightened of him?" Hamish asked.

"You're nothing like him, are you?"

"Who, Schultze?"

"Your cousin." She bit her lip.

"I don't know —"

"Thanks again."

She spun away on her heels. Hamish felt the back of his neck, working through the odd interaction. He caught the eye of a girl with bottle-red hair and bright cherry lips and followed her lead, compensating for her enthusiasm with every drum roll and her tendency to drag him across the floor. *Just like Maisie.* He missed the familiarity of the Palais Royale despite the new faces. The pretty girls.

Hamish took his time on the way back to the bar, sidling close to where Luca leaned, whiskey glass dangling from his hand, his laugh rising over the bass line. The band had slowed to a thrumming number in three-quarter time, the dancers' heels scraping over the floor in a slow waltz.

Hamish ordered a Coke from the bar.

"There's no such thing." Hamish heard Luca's voice gather authority.

"Mr. Valari. I have heard that you have influence. That you have ways of solving problems."

"Bob, I am just trying to open a club."

"But Schultze said . . ."

"Don't believe everything you hear." Luca cursed under his breath. "I'm empty." Luca rapped his fingers on the counter and another whiskey appeared. "And what does he know? He just rents me that office of his over in the North Square."

Hamish swooshed the ice in his Coke glass. Luca's back was to him, the hand not holding his drink in his pocket. He leaned in. Part of him wanted to give his cousin the privacy he needed, but the other part of him was intrigued. Bob was pleading. "I can't afford to keep this place if I don't have some help. I heard you could help. You never just hire someone. You are too careful. People talk about you."

Luca chuckled. "I am just trying to open a club."

"I'm sorry, Valari, I thought . . . Chicago said . . ."

Luca lifted his drink and drained it. "The Flamingo. I'll send you and your charming wife an invitation." Luca turned and Hamish saw he was annoyed.

Hamish stepped back, swishing his Coke

and pretending he hadn't heard.

"Did you dance, Cicero?" Luca didn't look back at the club owner.

"With Mary Finn," Hamish said quietly, not wanting Bob to hear. "She was on a break."

"She's a bit of a flirt, isn't she?"

"I think she's scared of something," Hamish said, keeping his voice low. "She tensed up a lot. When Schultze —"

Luca squeezed his shoulder tightly. "Not everyone gets anxious in crowds," he said lightly.

"This was more than that."

"Stay for another set? Or should we head home?"

"Whatever you want, Luca."

"Off we go. Our business is done." He directed this to Bob, while his smile stayed on Hamish. "We'll see you at the Flamingo."

Hamish and Luca stepped into the night, Hamish stretching his arms out to the fresh air: still warm, but without the mix of perfume, alcohol, and smoke found inside.

"I don't see how you can frequent these places every night," Hamish said as they walked to the edge of the block where Luca said his driver was waiting.

"Ha! You love them just as much as I do. Do you remember that night at the Palais

Royale . . . when was that . . . last year? Last Christmas, wasn't it? You and Maisie Forth and I. We wanted to go, but you wanted to dance all night."

"There was a pretty girl there."

"Pretty but a few sheets to the wind if I recall."

Hamish shrugged, studying his two-tones a moment.

"But you were so bold that night, Cic!" Luca continued. "You strolled right across that floor just as Maisie remarked that the girls might have thought you were a wall sconce."

Hamish cracked a half smile. "None of them dance like Maisie."

"How is she doing, anyway? She's a bit in love with me I think."

Hamish laughed. "A bit? She's fine. She —"

"Valari!" Hamish and Luca turned at Schultze's voice.

"We should have walked faster," Luca said under his breath.

"You have Bob in a fix."

"Not now, Tom." He dismissed Schultze with a wave and shuffled Hamish toward the car. Hamish looked over his shoulder, puzzled at the exchange. How many conversations did Luca leave in the middle of?

■ ■ ■

As he had only swirled the martini glass Luca handed him before asking for Coke, Hamish was awake and alert long before his cousin. He smelled coffee under his door. Luca had left him a silk robe and he tied it over his pajamas, tucked his feet into mule slippers of the same fabric, and reached for his glasses and *Notre-Dame*. The night before when he jolted awake thinking about the fight with his father that brought him to Boston, he normalized his heartbeat by peering into Pierre Gringoire's first encounter with the beautiful Romany girl Esmeralda. He thought of Esmeralda in poetry. Familiar words on familiar pages: a safety blanket, something bringing him home. Wherever home was. At night, sometimes it was up in Quasimodo's bell tower overlooking medieval Paris. Maybe home would be here.

Fidget was in the kitchen attempting to be quiet, but she peeked her head out after he settled on the sofa.

"You read your book, Hamish. I will bring you something to eat. You are too thin."

The something was piles of eggs and cinnamon rolls. Hamish smiled and tucked in with an appetite he hadn't had in a long while. After she cleared his plate away, he quickly dressed, eager to have the city's roads and alleys introduce themselves to him.

His bicycle leaned where it had taken temporary residence, outside the front door of the penthouse, and he wheeled it to the elevator. Once on the main floor, he walked it by the concierge and maneuvered it at an angle through the revolving door.

The day was overcast with low clouds billowing with the threat of rain. The sun struggled to lighten the hovering gray and its effect highlighted the tarmac and rooftops with the possibility of light. Hamish loved mornings like this because they framed the world with possibility. He flung his leg over the crossbar and kicked a few times for momentum, leaning over the handlebars a moment and pedaling off into the city.

Hamish didn't think he could belong anywhere he didn't know intimately from the friction of rubber and pavement. He pedaled across Tremont after the Temple and in the direction of Park Street Church. He smiled without inhibition, quietly acknowledging the restraint he had shown in not pursuing this activity — gliding and swerving through a new world of paths and streets, growing accustomed to the bike Luca had bought him.

He promised himself his quick slide through Boston Common and the Public Garden would be one of many, opting instead to pedal through as much distance as possible. He leaned up a little to gain traction up a slight hill and turned on Washington Street, avoiding pedestrians as the Old South Meeting House and the Old State House whirred by. A quick familiarization with Boston from a map Luca had left in his bedroom allowed him to recognize Faneuil Hall below him with Quincy Market straight beyond. The Custom House announced itself. Then, beyond, the type of monument he always chased when on his bike. Something to work toward: a landmark so he could find his way back. The arrow of a compass pointing north when you most needed your bearings. Chasing markers had introduced him to many nooks and crannies of Toronto. Now, in Boston, he used the same skill: weaving past the farmers hawking their wares, the horse-drawn carts, the butchers and tailors, the automobiles and gas stations and billboards of Haymarket Square, sliding to a halt at Cross Street and looking beyond to an uneven line of brick, signs for markets and restaurants in his father's first language, fire escapes skittering down and crisscrossing between closely connected buildings.

The North End, he surmised. Maybe he'd find Luca's office before his first formal introduction.

He pedaled to Hanover Street, keeping the tall steeple in his sight. Skidding over the uneven bumps of the cobblestones, he swerved to avoid heavy pedestrian traffic. Flags spliced in the colors of his heritage adorned storefronts, awnings, and signs in an eruption of Italian. Hamish smiled at an exhale of something so familiar meeting him in a place so far away and trained his mind not to think about home. His parents. His note.

Around him, people spilled from indoor cafés. Banners announcing summer festivals draped between tenement-style buildings. Hamish dismounted his bicycle and walked it to sidestep children dashing through the road and around carts and cars, their mothers shrieking at them in a variety of languages. Men languorously puffed at cigars. Through windows sheltered by candy cane awnings, beefy arms threw dough in the air while women with straggles of hair escaping from loosely tied buns bagged pastries with tight-lipped precision.

The atmosphere was a carousel of natural music and color, rotating through the magic of an ordinary morning. Hamish smiled as he rolled his bike away from a girl with pudgy pigtails, sticky ice cream streaming from her cone down her chin and over her forearm.

He turned through a slight alleyway: fire escapes laddering up russet brick, window boxes displaying all manner of pinks and purples between laundry strung across and drooping. On the other side of the alley, he turned again, his wheels catching in the ridges of the stones, his eyes darting around the new neighborhood, so like Toronto in its Babel-like explosion of dialects, yet so new. The rims of some roads were turned inside and out, construction churning. And then he found it: the church with the compass steeple. He edged near it, rolling his bike across the street and dodging a gray automobile in pursuit.

Hamish monitored the lugubrious sky, moody with a few fickle drops of rain, before following his nose into an open door boasting the neighborhood's best cannoli.

Chapter 7

"I am putting Aaron Leibowitz in his place," Nate explained when Reggie showed up at his office door wondering why he was shouting so loudly. He held up the *Jewish Advocate.* "This is the incriminating evidence. Reggie, we have never once seen eye to eye on an issue, and this is the last straw. And you know my mother — *my* mother actually suggested we invite Leibowitz to Shabbat dinner this weekend to *bury the hatchet.*" He adjusted his voice femininely on that last phrase. "As if I could stand being in the same room as a man who clearly thinks the Mishnah is just a plaything for his primitive ideas."

Reggie smiled. She had just met Nate, had just learned about his rivalry with Leibowitz, and though she knew little about the specifics, she couldn't help but be on Nate's side. "Sounds intense."

"It's life or death. We will battle an eternity."

"You're quite passionate."

He grinned. "How should I put this? Sometimes you can't verbally die on the hills on which you want to die." He reached out to the open door. "My community. My home. We are uprooting and making it something new. But it is changing and people are being forced in and out. Tugged rather like the tide that pulled them in here from all corners of the world in the first place. And I will die on this hill for people from all corners . . ."

Reggie enjoyed watching his eyes light up with his indignation. "From everywhere."

"Mostly the Irish," Nate continued, "then they moved out. Then my people. Then the Italians. Now we are a bit like my Bubbe's patchwork quilt. And —" Nate's phone jangled. He excused himself and answered it. Reggie studied her cuticles. Years of professional treatment had given way to small little slices of skin at the ends and uneven nails. She would just buy a kit like Olive down the hall of the boarding house had and do her own.

Nate's voice was quiet and steady as he assured the talker on the other end of the line he was doing everything he could.

"Does your son have a trade?" he was saying. "What kind? Electrician. Carpentry. Ah! Your daughter. She is educated in music." Nate opened a file on his desk and scribbled something with a pencil. "That is just what we need. No, no. There is an opening. My absolute pleasure, Mrs. Corcoran."

He clicked the receiver, then exhaled and scribbled a few notes. Reggie wanted to ask what music lessons had to do with North End development, but she didn't want to be rude.

"Sorry, Reggie," he said, looking up at her.

"This is your actual business, Nate. I am just in the way." She shut the door behind her after flashing him a wide smile. He was so open and friendly. And happy too. So different from the men back home. Men who would never allow themselves to speak with unbridled passion unless it was for something acceptable: boats, regatta day, football clubs, automobiles. If she could but bottle one tiny ounce of the passion Nate had when speaking about Aaron Leibowitz! If she could care but a margin he did when he wrote incisive editorial letters contradicting Leibowitz day after day —

When was the last time she had done anything of significance? Other than running away, which, of course, only benefited herself. She stalled outside of Nate's office. On the staircase and landing below, people were lined up for Mildred Rue's assistance. The days stretched on and the lines never ended. She answered a phone call, listened to an angry voice, then hung up. She sometimes wondered if she was working at an actual office or merely a placeholder for calls never to be returned by their intended receiver. What use was she here?

She turned on the wireless and fiddled with the knob, trying to find some soothing music. Or something to distract her from thinking of that long line. How hopeless. It sometimes stretched out the building's main door. Reggie reached for her handbag and counted out several bills. So used to putting things on her parents' credit back home, she was still unsure how much cash a person needed to carry. What a rare problem that was. Reggie grabbed her hat and tucked her handbag under her arm and locked the office door behind her. She passed several men and women leaning and shifting tiredly outside the Temporary Agency. Then Mrs. Leoni's beckoned from under its yellow awning, wedged in the rectangle of brick buildings, interrupted by the green-tinted copper of ornamented windows.

"Mrs. Leoni," she called just as raindrops

hurried their pace and the sky exploded.

She swerved around a bicycle leaning against the wall and ducked inside, nearly bumping into the store's sole other customer. Mrs. Leoni's kerchiefed head disappeared into the back room.

Reggie shook out her hair and smiled at the other shopper. The smile in return was a small half-moon one. He shoved his hands deep in his pockets and shifted down the side of the display case to give her more room. He was wearing suspenders and a bow tie and his pant legs were rolled up a little over his two-toned shoes. A book was peeking out of his pocket.

"It's raining now." She smiled. "Your book will get wet."

He nodded and pulled out a battered paperback of *The Hunchback of Notre-Dame.*

Reggie surveyed the labels in front of the carefully arranged cookies. She'd make her way to cannoli after *Reginele,* little oblongs dotted with sesames; *Pignole,* soft, chewy almond cookies shrouded in pine nuts; and assorted tri-color butter cookies and meringues.

Mrs. Leoni returned a moment later with a steaming fresh tray. "Here you are, young man. The batch was just ready." Then she burst into Italian, which the young man matched, animation lighting his face. Barricaded from the conversation, Reggie leaned in for a closer look at the arrangement on the tray. Lumpy, wrinkled-looking cookies with brownish chopped nuts filled the tray haphazardly, countering the uniformity of the other displays.

The stranger was following her gaze. "Bruttiboni." His voice stalled a little on the first syllable.

"I don't speak Italian." She shrugged.

"Ugly but pretty." His smile, like a little thumbnail of moon, creased into a dimple on his right cheek. Reggie looked for its match on the left side, not finding one, deciding she liked the irregularity. He was handsome. But also a bit like a puppy dog with black hair tumbling over his forehead and wide eyes. He leaned toward the display case again and spoke in Italian, pointing at several options, Mrs. Leoni smiling intently in response. The young man rocked a little on his two-tones. He was lanky but his arm muscles were outlined by his cotton shirt. She wondered if the bicycle leaning outside was his.

"Ugly but pretty," she laughed.

"V-very pretty," he stammered, adjusting black-rimmed glasses over large blue eyes, illuminated under the overhead light.

"For your book." Mrs. Leoni handed him a bag. "And for you, Miss Regina?" Mrs. Leoni asked.

"Cannoli. And these cookies. Whatever he said and enough to take back at least . . ." She checked the money in her wallet then handed the wad to Mrs. Leoni. "Whatever this will buy."

"Having a party?"

"It's raining. It's drafty in the office building, and I am having a crisis of conscience for sitting there answering phone calls while people stand around the Temporary Employment Agency waiting for appointments they might never get." Reggie exhaled.

Mrs. Leoni smiled. Reggie shifted her gaze to her shoes then slowly looked up at the young man beside her. Something in his expression had changed. She couldn't say what — just that the moment their eyes met, he turned quickly away.

"I have lots of pistachio," Mrs. Leoni said.

"Yes, please. And whatever you bring me at the office."

Mrs. Leoni lit like a lightbulb and turned her bulk toward the kitchen.

Reggie smiled. Mrs. Leoni spread wax paper into a box and carefully arranged her assorted order.

Reggie looked outside. "It's pouring now.

I should run back."

Mrs. Leoni didn't turn from her work. "You need an umbrella, Regina?"

"I'll make it quick. Easier with these packages."

"And you, young man?"

"I have my bicycle. It'll be a bit of a squeaky ride." He was looking at Reggie slightly from under long lashes. "The wonderful thing about being caught in the rain is how good you feel when you are finally dry at home. It's almost worth it — getting soaked — for that first feel of a dry shirt." His smile flattened. "You need help with those?"

Reggie finagled the pastries. "It's a short walk." She smiled and the bell over the door chimed with her departure. She stopped under the awning a moment to tighten the twine on one of the boxes, sneaking a peek at a deformed brown meringue. She thought of the man's voice. The man's blue eyes. *Bruttiboni,* she remembered. "Ugly but pretty." She'd think of him every time she saw this cookie, she decided. His unexpected coloring: black hair and bright blue eyes. No, that wouldn't work. He wasn't ugly at all.

Reggie shook the rain from her hair, enjoying its cool sensation against her legs as she handed off the boxes of sweets to a man she had seen almost every day, trusting him to see the bounty well distributed. He looked at her appraisingly, from damp hair to squeaking shoes. Doubtless he noticed she wasn't wearing stockings. Her mother would likely throw a tantrum. She was surely condemned to a special circle of hell reserved for women who showed bare legs.

Back in her own office, she unwrapped a sandwich from wax paper. Deciding she wasn't hungry, she watched the rain awhile before pulling a paperback novel from her bag. She had just begun reading when the telephone rang. "I'm sorry, may I take a message?" But the line was fuzzy. She returned it to its cradle.

She sat back and stared at her cuticles until voices from outside drew her attention.

One clearly belonged to Schultze, Luca's accountant who often dropped by the office even though her employer was rarely there. The other was of a higher pitch.

Reggie had watched enough movies to determine the dynamic between them. He was the older one — probably married with a family at home. She was the younger, prettier one who kept him on a leash. Used his money. Was draped in his diamonds. More than one Winchester Molloy serial painted this scene.

The voices drew nearer. Reggie erected her spine and pretended to reach for the phone just as the door opened.

"Miss Van Buren."

"Mr. Valari is not here," Reggie said plainly, looking beyond Schultze's shoulder to the pretty piece of fluff behind him. She was more Jean Harlow than Greta Garbo, exaggerated lips, heavily lidded eyes. "I would assume, as an investor, you would know when and where to find him. And he doesn't frequent this place."

Schultze approached the desk. His companion's silhouette darkened the doorway, but she didn't move forward. Reggie focused on Schultze. "Maybe I came to check on you." He leaned forward, and Reggie straightened.

"To see I am shuffling his papers and answering his telephone?"

"Is that all you're doing?"

"Secretarial work? My job?"

Schultze's gaze narrowed, his eyes locked on hers, scanning for something. He obviously didn't find it because he broke their gaze and shifted. "Very well. You keep shuffling papers and answering telephones."

"And you keep patronizing me," Reggie

114

muttered under her breath.

"I'm sorry, Miss Van Buren?"

"I said and you have a nice day, Mr. Schultze." She enunciated each word.

"I will." He swerved on his heel. "Mary!" He called after her as one might a canine companion. What else could Luca possibly expect her to be doing? Watching Schultze eye Mary as he walked behind her, she had a pretty good idea. She thought back to the man at Leoni's. The smiles through the employment agency line welcoming the distribution of the pastries had nothing on the shy one that curved his mouth up into a dimple. Imagine him strolling in as brash as Schultze. She couldn't! But then again, the man at Leoni's would probably never be found in the same vicinity as a nightclub owner. There was something . . . she searched the lexicon of her mind . . . genuine about him. Yes, genuine. That was more than she could say for Schultze! She fingered the phone wire. Or herself.

CHAPTER 8

Hamish couldn't stop thinking about the girl from the bakery counter. No, not girl. Woman. The woman from the bakery counter. If ever a person was worthy of the word *woman,* it was she. The universe of her face, the galaxy of stars freckling over her nose, the brightness of her eyes. He thought about her as he wove his way back from the North End. He thought of her as a turning automobile and a jut of a pothole resulted in a sheet of water over his left side. He thought of her as he discarded his bike and entered the apartment, shaking water droplets from his hair. Luca was draped over the dining table in a red silk dressing gown, downing a cup of coffee and pouring another from a carafe so shiny Hamish could make out Luca's face in it.

"Ah, Cic. Rest up. And dry off. We've the Stardust tonight. And the Ivy tomorrow."

Hamish rolled his eyes. "I am beginning

116

to think your work is just drinking and flirting with women. What *would* my father say?"

"That's why you're here. So you don't have to find out. What I am accomplishing is part of my work," Luca said without looking up from his newspaper. He exchanged the sports section for the society pages.

"How?" Hamish asked.

"Making sure I am seen and people want to be seen *with* me. I will sup with them. Dance with them. Drink with them and slyly ensure they will follow me like bees to honey."

"So this is part of your plan?" Hamish cleared the tone of incredulousness from his throat with a strangled cough.

Luca shrugged. "And I'll snatch the best people and transfer them to my club."

Hamish cocked an eyebrow. "And can you do something for them?"

"Besides providing the best drinks and the best dancing with the best band and making sure they enjoy the experience immensely?"

"Mary Finn and that club owner seemed to think you had . . ." Hamish stalled to choose his words carefully as Luca's eyes intensified on him. "Had some sort of influence. Something beyond just a club."

"Nonsense."

Hamish thought about pressing further, then stopped himself. "Well, one of the things I didn't account for when I stupidly hopped on a train was how many days I would spend being idle on your couch."

Luca chuckled. "Maybe I can rustle up some contracts for you to look over. I technically have a lawyer on retainer. But I trust you more."

Hamish lightened. "Really? I would love that. I'm not as experienced as one of the lawyers you are used to working with. But I would really love to be useful."

"Hamish, you need to have a little more confidence in yourself. See yourself the way I do."

"Which is how?"

"Kind of remarkable. It's in your name, isn't it? With a name like Hamish DeLuca, you're destined to do something memorable."

Memorable? Hamish rolled the word over in his mind as he retreated to the guest room.

Most men didn't reach a quarter century barricaded in the pages of a book, still unsure of the moment when their careful armor would fall away and a member of the opposite sex would catch them unawares.

Men like Luca Valari could teach school on it. Hamish aired out the soggy pages of *Notre-Dame* that the paper bag didn't protect and flopped back on his bed. He was starting to shiver through his wet clothes but convinced himself he didn't deserve dry ones. Not after his pathetic attempt at talking to the pretty young woman at the counter. He should have said something suave or startling or smart. Hamish planted his palm over his eyes. He didn't come from a lineage of shyness. His mother had proposed to his father. She'd told him a million and one times about how she had fallen in love with him at first sight.

Hamish smiled at the story. He had asked her to tell it again and again. It sounded a bit like poetry. Like some of the prettier lines in *Notre-Dame* before Paris burned and Quasimodo turned to dust. Epic and lasting.

Hamish finally turned the tap on the claw-foot tub in his bathroom and promised himself he would try harder. He wasn't Toronto Hamish who tucked his knees to his chin in a corner of the library or kept his black head over his books at school so he wouldn't have to make eye contact. He was in a new city. He would just become a new person.

Look at a girl. Approach a girl. Talk to a girl. It seemed so easy. Luca did it all the time. He, too, when on the dance floor. He whispered to the ceiling, "Fall in love with a girl." He investigated the slight moon scars on the palm of his hand, from years of digging his nails in. The trick was to have the girl fall in love with him too.

What he was falling in love with was the city. Just as he had hoped when he first stepped from the station and began imprinting it on his brain. Hamish was someone who liked to find the affinity in places. His father had told him that a person could usually know within a short amount of time if a place would be something special — something familiar — or if you were destined to always be a visitor. But Boston wore at the seams like a stretched sweater. Luca took Hamish to another game at Fenway, Phil's car rimming the Emerald Necklace in the hazy dusk, Hamish navigating the packed stadium to their seats. He pedaled through the Common and the Public Garden, swerving into Beacon Hill and over the fragments of cobblestone between stately brick houses holding hands in a narrow barricade. Many of the homes dripped red, white, and blue with f lags draped patriotically, catching the tickle of the summer breeze. There was a pattern in stalling outside of the Paul Revere house, sloping into it, dismounting his bike, steadily climbing while the clouds puffed out in the sky over a towered building blending with many of similar breadth and height rising up along the North Square, all the while hoping to see her again when he stepped into Leoni's for cannoli.

CHAPTER 9

At night, the cares of the day unraveled with the pulse of the clubs. Prohibition was still on the lips of the teetotalers in their Salvation Army uniforms hoisting up signs of prudent disapproval in front of the bronze doors. Inside, of course, awaited a world of sheer abandon: far from the soup kitchen lines and the panhandlers in the Common, the headlines from Europe growing bleaker by the day.

The moon rose and life began, as it would soon underneath the garish pink and green flash of the flamingo, cocky beak in the air, one leg raised saucily.

Sweat and gin. Smoke and bright lights. Voices raw from rising over the din of the music and the unending wail of the trumpet. A corner of the world protected from figures and numbers and the ennui of the day. And Hamish DeLuca adjusting his braces and counting his heartbeat, which pulsed in time to *Go home.* He ignored its thrum. He had spent enough time with his cousin to know that even he was not immune to the Valari charm. If Luca decided to freefall off the Grand Canyon, Hamish had no doubt he would spread his arms as wings and pretend to fly.

"When I am not around, you will be my extension at the Flamingo." Luca clutched Hamish's lapel. "And so you need to see as many clubs as possible to give you an idea of how we want to run our joint." But Hamish was bored of clubs. Tired by the late nights. Most excited at the prospect of kicking his bike into gear, throwing his leg over the crossbar, and taking Boston in stride. Every day it became more familiar as he had hours at his leisure. Sure, Luca passed a few of the promised contracts to him and he was asked to go through catering and pay lists line by line.

Yet when Luca referred to "our Flamingo," something buzzed inside of him. He had never thought of the club as theirs. It was Luca's club. Luca's affair. Luca's conclave of men like Tom Schultze and Brian MacMillan — who was far brighter and more engaging than the taciturn patron of the MacMillan family, or so Hamish had learned the day before.

Luca knew all of the city's watering holes. The ones hidden in back alleys people would never think of entering, others flounced proudly out on Washington Street, contributing to the waterfalls of light cascading from the theaters and billboards to glisten the tarmac. And in all of the clubs the owners would immediately cross their floors to welcome Luca and ensure he had a drink in his hand. While they shot the small talk of the day and pandered to Luca's incessant need to list the Flamingo's virtues, there was a tightness in their spines and a slight uneasiness in their eyes. Hamish assumed it was because of the way his cousin carried himself. Luca Valari made a room smaller just by entering it, and with his silver-screen good looks, deep voice, and charm, Hamish supposed the rival club owners found themselves in immediate competition.

Luca subsisted on black coffee, which he indulged in from the time he woke late in the morning to the first peals of the afternoon bell from Park Street Church at a diagonal from the penthouse at Tremont and Winter streets. Then he leisurely explored his liquor cabinet. Hamish furrowed his brow every time his cousin took another sip from a glass. It wasn't that his behavior changed — Luca was too in control of himself to let his habit overtake him — but there was a tiredness in Luca's eyes. As excited as he was about his new business venture, Hamish wasn't sure exactly how set up he was for taking this plunge. His accounts looked good to Hamish's amateur eye — he always could put a few figures together — but were augmented by investors. Hamish didn't know how much capital his cousin had or where it came from. There were baseball games and nights out and a beautiful apartment as well as the rising costs in preparation for the club's grand opening. Hamish's presence added expenses.

Then phone calls and Fidget attentively seeing to their laundry and food. One night she set shortbread on a plate before him and Hamish felt such a pang for home that he nearly leapt for the phone to call his mother. But as he nibbled, the pastry melting in his mouth, Fidget surpassing her skills yet again, he stayed strong. The attendant had posted a letter for him the week after he arrived, leaving his parents Luca's address and contact information at both the penthouse and the office. He knew he would hear back eventually and that he would finger the letter guiltily before opening it when he did. Then there was the young woman he had met at Leoni's, gathering pastries to give to the people waiting outside of the Temporary Employment Agency. At least working for Winslow, Winslow, and Smythe, he had the opportunity to do some pro bono work.

Spira Spera. As long as he breathed he could find a new way to approach this new adventure. No chain was tugging him back, just the promise of a summer to finally move his grip off the handlebars. And if that meant following Luca to clubs night after night until the Flamingo opened the week after, then so be it. It was the finish line in some way and Hamish mentally looked at it as a crossing point. After, he would decide what to do. But he was so invested in seeing his cousin succeed that he wouldn't make any sudden plans until then: either to return home or to stay.

CHAPTER 10

They arrived at that night's chosen club, Luca parting people like Moses the Red Sea. "Let's find the owner." It was Luca's usual habit: show up, charm the attendees, sweet-talk the owner, and then have Hamish survey everything about the dance hall. Hamish didn't think he was at all qualified, but Luca waved away his concerns.

"I'm going to take some of the pressure off." Luca smiled and led Hamish toward the bar. "I've invited my secretary. She comes from a long line of class and will be helping me with last-minute preparations. She's pretty too. You'll want to take her for a spin. Though this band leaves something to be desired."

Several murmurs around the bar resulted in the appearance of a balding man in a slick suit, the easy smile on his mouth not reaching his watery eyes. "Mr. Valari, I hear that to welcome you is a first-class honor." He gave a little bow. "I also hear that you are poaching for your Flamingo and that I'm to keep an eye on you." He looked over his shoulder in the direction of more murmurs.

Luca's smile stilled them into silence. "Nonsense! Charles Galbraith, right?" He shook Galbraith's hand. "What is a bit of healthy competition? As you know, I am new to this game and I want to learn from the professionals. I also" — Luca extracted his gold money clip — "want to throw money on wine, women, and song. Or, in this case, the best martini your man can rustle up."

Galbraith rapped his knuckles on the bar. "Wet Mr. Valari's whistle." He put his hand around Luca's. "No payment needed. What are a few drinks between friends?" He noticed Hamish for the first time and sized him up with reptilian eyes.

"This is my cousin, Hamish DeLuca," Luca was saying. "Oh! And here she is now looking rather remarkable! I say, Regina Van Buren!" He gave a low whistle. "What a vision!"

Hamish turned as the rhythm of the upbeat Cab Calloway number pulsed through the dark and found himself face-to-face with an apparition in cranberry tingling his tongue and widening his eyes. "It's you."

She smiled at Luca and Charles Galbraith and then at him. "Bruttiboni," she said by way of greeting, shaking his hand.

She looked remarkably pretty under the lights of the bar. Her hair rich in finger waves, her brown eyes bright orbs in their lining. Her lips were cranberry like her dress and an interesting contrast to her powdered ivory face and hair.

"You two know each other?" Luca asked.

"We met over cannoli. Well, we didn't *actually* meet because we were never introduced."

"Then allow me." Luca was watching Hamish intensely. Hamish tried to avert his eyes politely, but the woman in front of him was a magnet, her dress knowing just where to curve in and where to flounce out. "Regina Van Buren, this is my cousin, Hamish DeLuca."

Hamish took her hand lightly. "Hello, Regina."

"Please, my friends call me Reggie."

"Does that go for me too?" wondered Charles Galbraith, eyeing her with an intensity that made Hamish finger his bow tie.

"Of course." She took his hand and gave it a firm pump. Galbraith turned to the crowd then, excusing himself.

"I've a few people to see." Luca laughed quietly. "Actually, a few people I want to see me. Remember, you two. Dance, drink. Assess the band. Assess the cigar girls and see if we should snatch anyone up for my club."

Luca squeezed Hamish's forearm and leaned into his ear. "Dance with her, Cic. Don't just gape at her like a lost puppy."

"Well, Quasimodo," Reggie said once Luca had left. "Are you going to ask me to dance?"

"Quasi —" Hamish started, then smiled. "Ah. My book."

"Looked like it had been read to within an inch of its life."

"It has."

They stepped to the side of the throng, watching Luca command the room, shaking hands and moving in to sprawl his arm around someone's shoulder. He was accessible and smooth, taking the floor like an elaborate dance of which only he knew the steps.

"He's something. And you're sure he's your cousin? Oh, I'm sorry. Don't look like that. I just meant, there's not really a family resemblance. He's very handsome and . . . well . . . Regina . . . put your other foot in your mouth, why don't you? I just mean

130

that in a way he's aware he is very handsome. You . . ." She looked him up and down, Hamish's eyes widening under her scrutiny. "You are a different *flavor.*" She warmed to her assessment.

"Flavor?" Hamish chuckled. "Like cannoli?"

"Exactly! If he's all pistachio crust and icing sugar, you're . . . well . . ."

"Bruttiboni?"

"Ha! No!"

Hamish raked his fingers through his hair. "I have absolutely no idea what to say to that. Thank you, maybe?"

Reggie had a clear, alto laugh. He wanted to hear it again. And again. It lifted him a little. "Would you like a drink?"

He led them to the crowded bar. He waited for a few patrons to finish, not having Luca's ability to part crowds like a stream, and handed her a requested Coke.

"Nothing stronger?" he asked.

"I'm on the clock." She took the glass and sipped. "Working for your cousin."

"My cousin seems to work best when he has had several martinis." Hamish studied the fizz in his own Coke glass.

"Hamish DeLuca. What a name. Where are you from?"

"Toronto."

"And do all Canadians have names like Hamish DeLuca?"

Hamish grinned. "When their father's Italian and their mother's Scottish, they do."

"Canada! Maybe that's what's so different." She narrowed her eyes in concentration, studying his face. Hamish willed himself not to blush or avert his gaze. "You all live in igloos, don't you?"

"Of course."

Reggie sipped her Coke. "So I suppose I should start work! Let's see." She gave the room a once-over. Hamish followed her eyes over the well-dressed crowd and in the direction of the monogrammed bandstand. "On a scale of one to ten, how would we rate this joint?"

"We?"

"Well, if you're Luca Valari's cousin, you must have some semblance of taste. You're certainly garnering attention."

Hamish tried to see what she was seeing. "Attention?"

"I am spotting . . ." Her eyes swept the room. "One. Two . . . Oooo, no, four! Six! And . . . ah yes, one more. There. Seven! Hamish, I spot seven women who are dying to dance with you."

"How can you tell that?" He traced her visual path. There were pretty girls all over, leaning into their friends, inspecting their pocketbooks, some with long fingers embracing the stems of cocktail glasses. Many on the dance floor or at its edge, tapping their feet and watching the ebb and flow of the movement from its shore.

"When you aren't looking, they look at you. And their looks become a little more attentive the closer" — she shrugged closer to him — "we" — closer still — "stand together." Now even their shoes were touching. "I bet, Hamish" — she tipped her chin up and looked into his eyes — "that if we started dancing we would have their rapt attention."

"I don't understand."

Reggie tugged at his shirtsleeve just above the rolled fabric at his elbow. "Not every woman wants to dance with Luca Valari." She looked at him expectantly and, when he didn't answer, continued. "You have lovely hair and a dimple when you smile and those blue eyes. There" — her laughter was a glissando — "there's that smile. Smile more often. Really, truly smile. It illuminates your whole face like a lightbulb."

Hamish stretched the smile a moment then scratched at the back of his neck. If he were to return the compliment, he'd tell her she was radiant. He liked the way her hair brushed over her shoulders and the way her neck curved gracefully like a swan's. He liked the way she held herself and the way her painted nails caressed her glass. "Thank you, Reggie. That's very helpful."

She laughed. "Hamish, you are deliciously hopeless." His heart started up. He absently moved his palm over it as it thrummed and quickened. "If you were William Powell and I were Myrna Loy, we would be on the floor already!"

Hamish studied his Coke glass.

"Do you ever go to the pictures?"

Hamish looked up. "Sometimes." He hadn't been to a theater in months.

"What's your favorite?"

"Oh, I don't . . ." He trailed off. Suddenly self-conscious at what she had observed. Were all these women watching him? He scratched the back of his neck again, suddenly feeling exposed. He knew she was just being playful and nice, but he felt a quickening in his heartbeat. Was it something that needed to be monitored? A harbinger of an episode? Or was it just *her*? "Did you ever see the Robert Young picture *Death on the Diamond*?"

"Is it a heist movie?"

"It's a baseball movie. St. Louis Cardinals. A fellow tries to figure out who is killing his teammates." Her eyes were saucers on him. "There's a wonderful girl in it," he added for her. "Madge Evans."

"So you like murder mystery stories?"

"And I like baseball." He shrugged. "This movie has both."

A girl sidled past with a smile and Hamish returned a half-moon one, keeping his attention on Reggie.

"Cicero!" Luca's voice was an unwelcome barrage. Next to his cousin, a young woman with rosy cheeks and chestnut-brown hair giggled and bopped, her drink casually tipped a little too steeply, its lapping liquid about to spill onto his shoes. "I brought you a dance partner just in case you hadn't asked Regina to dance yet. This is Ethel. She was asking about you."

"Cicero." Ethel's voice was shrill. "Such a funny name!" She gripped Luca's bicep. "Cicero."

"Cicero?" asked Reggie.

"Nickname," Hamish said.

"That's a funny name. Hamish Cicero." Ethel's voice climbed higher.

Hamish shot Luca a look. Luca's smile spread. "Cic, Ethel is eager to dance and I told her that you were waiting for an absolute vision before you stepped to the floor."

"Thanks for the crumbs from your table,"

snorted Reggie.

Ethel was a vision all right — buxom and red-lipped, curving in at the right places and out at others. He set his Coke on the bar. Hamish DeLuca was many things, but never impolite. But just as he was about to accept, Reggie stopped him.

"I'm sorry, Ethel. But his dance card's full."

Reggie tugged Hamish to the crowded floor as a spotlight crossed over the crowd and the band swung into a three-quarter tune.

"Now let's see how you dance." He was a little stilted at first, taking his time and measuring, but once he started, *really* started . . . He was different when he was dancing. Something happened to him that made the shy man from the cannoli counter seem miles away as he held her waist and pulled her assuredly into a spin.

Reggie was delighted. "You're a wonderful dancer."

"You sound surprised."

One bar. Two bars. Three and four. Their movements a whirling dervish of weight released and pulled back — in and out. Full count and the rumble of the drums, Hamish setting their pace while her brain drifted to Vaughan. He didn't dance like this. Not

136

with this uninhibited smile that pressed a dimple and the world wrapping around him. Hamish letting it. Reggie couldn't take her eyes off him. Then, as was her custom, she looked to see who was watching her watching him: a defense she learned long ago, knowing that staring at someone or something too long was just more fodder for speculation and gossip.

"I guess we should tell your cousin the band is pretty good," she said, as the music slowed to a stop.

Before Hamish could answer, a girl cut in. "My turn," she said with a sly smile at Reggie. Mary Finn. Yes. Schultze's girl. She recognized her from the office.

Hamish looked at Reggie, who shrugged. "You go on. I can't keep you all night." She picked up her pace before another man could step in and found herself back at the bar ordering another Coke.

"On Luca Valari's tab," she said with a twinkle as Luca stepped toward her.

"He's a lawyer, you know. Graduated top of his class."

Then what is he doing here? "He's a wonderful dancer." They watched him a moment. Mary spun out and Ethel finally broke in.

The skirts got shorter as girls spun into

him; their lips grew redder and their laughs louder. "And they're talking to him and laughing at him over the music and he is trying to think of what to say." She felt unsettled but wasn't sure whether it was the prickling feeling that his business ventures dabbled in something darker or her annoyance that he'd pulled Hamish from her and thrown him into the arms of a fluff-head on the floor. "I don't think I've ever met two more different people belonging to the same family."

"And you're like your parents?" Luca's charcoal eyes bored into hers, startling even in the dim light.

"I just meant —"

"You speak your mind, Reggie. I like that. But I don't think I require your opinion on my cousin." He brushed his thumb over the rim of his martini glass.

Then he tapped the bar and another drink appeared. He indicated a refill for Reggie. "You're Johnny Wade. I know you. I've seen your band."

The bartender leaned into the light. Reggie saw his fine features clearly.

"You're Luca Valari."

"I am."

Johnny handed Reggie a drink with a smile, then turned to Luca. "It's an honor to have you here, Mr. Valari. All my friends are talking about the Flamingo. You got Roy Holliday. He's the best in the city. Hey, how did you know I play?"

"It is my business to know the lineup of every club in the city. And you? I hear you're the best tender in Beantown. Can whip up a martini in seconds flat and have the art to an alchemy." Luca peered closer. "You're a looker too. Girls in my club would frequent a bar tended by a movie star face." Luca took a long sip then gave a decisive nod. "I'll pay you double what you make here. And maybe audition your band on an off-night. Can't promise anything, but we'll need an alternate for Holliday."

"Are you serious?"

"I don't throw out jobs like confetti, Johnny Wade. I want the best. If you're the best . . ."

"They say that if people get in with you they're golden. Even from the ground floor."

Luca feigned modesty. It fell as flat as a fizzed-out Coke. "We open a week from tomorrow. We're hosting a little warm-up the night before. The staff, the band, my illustrious secretary here."

Reggie took this as a cue. "Regina Van Buren." She shook Johnny's hand.

"Pleased to meet you." He flashed her a

million-watt smile.

"I'll expect you there at six thirty. Gives you time to give your notice and transition." Luca rapped his fingers on the bar, demanding something other than a drink. "Don't let me down."

You couldn't scrape a smile off this fellow's face. It was like his ship had come in. No, his fleet.

"Well, just you and me," Luca said a moment later. "A pretty dame like yourself. Want to take a turn, Reggie? Nothing untoward. We're friends."

Reggie took a sip and shook her head. "I like watching."

"Don't think I don't appreciate your caring for dear old Cic like you do." Luca raised his glass slightly in her direction. "He needs someone to care about him."

"Does he?"

"He's just a little shy."

"You truly do care about him, huh?"

"You sound shocked."

Reggie shrugged. "I am just trying to understand your . . . what's the word? Dynamic."

"Our dynamic." Luca whistled. "You need another drink." Luca rapped the bar.

Reggie put up a staying hand. "Does secrecy run in your family, Luca Valari?"

140

She was trying to put her finger on Hamish from their two meetings. Confident on the dance floor, but like a poor lost puppy out of the rain at Leoni's. Showing up in Boston just as his cousin's club opened. And not to practice law either. Reggie had the name of a lawyer above her desk at the office.

Luca laughed it off but his eyes intensified a little. "I think —"

"Who is this vixen?" Reggie recognized Schultze's voice through the film of smoke. The incessant tap of his walking stick followed. "Ah!" His eyes trundled over her with recognition. "Your little secretary cleans up quite nicely."

"Pick your jaw off the floor, Tom," Luca said lightly.

Reggie watched another man join their conclave, making the room smaller with his height and breadth. Reggie smiled at him, but his face was stone.

Schultze ignored his companion, painting Reggie's figure with watery eyes. "If you can spare us," he said, locking eyes with Reggie. She broke her gaze. "They're here."

Reggie looked from Schultze to Luca. Luca, for all his Clark Gable charm, faltered.

"Reg—"

"What's wrong?"

"Nothing's wrong. Business."

His voice had a strange note to it. He reached into his pocket and pulled a bill out of a gold clip. "For a taxi home. See Hamish home, too, when he's finished dancing. We might be a while." His eyes fixed on her and in them she read a thousand words. He was putting his cousin in her charge.

Reggie accepted the money but only because she wanted something to distract her from Schultze's unwelcome stare and the big man's lumbering gait. The trio slipped past the bar into a hallway beyond.

"Anything you want, Miss Van Buren, on the house," the bartender was saying. "I get to work for Luca Valari! We get to work for Luca Valari."

Reggie blinked a few times. "Imagine that."

The evening pulled toward midnight, the liquor loose and the band in a heated fervor. Just as she wasn't sure she could handle the suffocating rise of echoed trills and thumps and riffs, they took a break and the waves of sound gave way to laughter and raised voices.

Reggie was about to make for the coat check to collect her wrap; for every moment that ticked on, men forgot to look at her eyes, their own drifting to the cut of her dress.

"Hey, Reggie." Hamish's tongue tripped a little. His hair was dampened with a glisten of perspiration, his eyes radiant with exercise. His glasses were falling down his nose. He took them off and ran his hand over his face, then repositioned them.

"See? You were the most popular man here!"

"I saw you talking to Luca. And I saw Tom Schultze and Luca's driver. Phil." Hamish looked around him, as if his cousin might materialize.

"Phil? That's the name of that lug of a man?"

Hamish nodded. "He's from Chicago. I think Luca uses him as a kind of bodyguard."

"Why does Luca need a bodyguard?" It was a more innocent question than the dozen she wanted to ask about Chicago.

"More for show than anything." Hamish paused, panted.

"You're exhausted." Reggie looked him over. "Your cousin gave us cab fare. We can split. Would you like a nightcap?"

Hamish shook his head, dabbing at his forehead with his sleeve. His eyes moved in the direction of the back — beyond the bar

— where Reggie had watched Schultze and Luca and that man Phil disappear earlier.

"I am sure he is fine, Hamish." Reggie smiled, squeezing his arm. The cotton of his shirt was damp and stuck to the sinewy outline of his forearm a little.

"Something isn't right." Hamish sounded distant.

"Chicago?" wondered Reggie.

Hamish shrugged. "I just get an uneasy feeling."

"I'd say you watch too many pictures; but that's me."

"You want something on the house?" Johnny leaned toward Hamish. "You're a friend of Luca Valari's, right? He just hired me. For the Flamingo. Do you work there too?"

Hamish exchanged a glance with Reggie.

"This is Johnny Wade, the best tender in Beantown." Reggie pulled out her familial knack for pleasantries. "And this is Hamish DeLuca, Luca's cousin and" — she winked at Hamish — "right-hand man."

"Geez. You're related? Is he really as high life as they say he is?"

Hamish stole Reggie's earlier line. "He's something, all right."

Johnny was lured by a voluptuous blonde and Hamish looked over the sea of heads.

"Did they go to the back or something?" He searched the crowd. "If it's business and the two of us are here, he would want us nearby."

"You really are worried."

"Just an instinct." His hand was tucked under his brace and his two forefingers rapped slightly. If she didn't know better, she would say he was counting something. But what?

"Well, you can't go find him by yourself," Reggie said. "I'll come with you. That way, we can say we were on our way to the coatroom or whatever if we're caught."

Hamish smiled. "I think you should take the cab fare." He touched her shoulder lightly. "I have this under control."

"Tsk-tsk, Hamish DeLuca. William Powell would never leave Myrna Loy out of the adventure." She winked up at him. "It's the least you can do after dancing with every woman in the joint and never coming to give me another spin."

"It's not that I didn't want to —"

"I'm teasing you, Hamish. I am glad you had a good time. You *did* have a good time?"

"I don't like trying to talk to these girls. They were pretty but I —" He stopped a moment, then ironed the slight stutter that threatened to hiccup his sentence. "I didn't have a lot to say to them." He shrugged. "That's why I wish I had still been dancing with you."

"And Luca thinks *he* is the flatterer."

Hamish ducked his head a little. The smile whispering over his lips was full enough to tug his cheek into a dimple. "Let's go see if we can figure out what my cousin is up to." His voice was light but undercut by an uneasiness that pricked Reggie. Then he added, "All right, Myrna Loy?"

Reggie beamed.

Reggie walked ahead, parting the crowd with her straightened shoulders and a regal air that evaded her in cotton and oxfords. The dress she wore spilled over her like liquid. Even a gentleman would be hard-pressed to ignore how her hips moved under the sheath of fabric.

When they approached a door with a filmy window, clouding the view beyond, a man with broad shoulders stood with crossed arms beside a sign that said Management.

"My, my." Reggie's voice was crisp glass like Katharine Hepburn's. "And wouldn't you know, Luca told me to just go straight through. Just go straight through is what he said."

The man didn't budge. "I highly doubt

that, lady."

"Well, it's true, isn't it? This is his business associate, Hamish DeLuca. And I swear on my grandmother's grave that Luca told us to meet him down there. He's with Tom Schultze, isn't he?"

"Why should I trust you? You're just dropping names." The man transferred the steel of his gaze to Hamish.

"It's true. I'm his . . . his . . . legal counsel." It was an improvisation.

"Luca Valari deciding to get legal counsel? What kind of counsel do you give? The kind with a tommy gun? A few kneecaps shattered here and there?"

He wouldn't falter. He erected his spine, Adam's apple bobbing over his loosened tie and open collar.

"Where I come from," Hamish seethed, his voice straight and steady, "we mind our own business. I graduated *summa cum laude* from the most distinguished law school in Canada. And I am, I assure you, Luca Valari's legal counsel. Is there a password to get by you, you badgering oaf? Open sesame, perhaps?"

Hamish looked over his shoulder at Reggie.

He could feel her subtle tics and twitches. He inched closer, surging with a need to block her from the odious man. He didn't like the way the man's gaze kept returning to Reggie: to the dress that accentuated her feminine lines, to the crossed-ribbon top of her dress.

"Perhaps" — Reggie opened the clasp of her purse — "we might reach a better understanding." She retrieved a sizable bill. "Might we persuade you now?"

The man uncrossed his arms and took the money. He raised his eyebrows. "Legal counsel?" he said, not meeting Hamish's eyes, instead focused on the stern etch of a magnanimous president on the greenback.

"Legal counsel," Hamish repeated.

And the door opened.

Hamish motioned for Reggie to stay behind him as they descended the creaky stairs. The stairwell boasted an interesting mixture of alcohol and mold. Hamish could hear his breathing and wondered if Reggie, in the sudden silence, only the drumbeat beyond the now closed and still guarded door, could sense its rhythm.

A slow drip percolated from the ceiling as they reached the midpoint of the staircase. Hamish heard funneled voices through the wall. He swallowed and turned to check on Reggie. In the much brighter light, a single bulb extending from the ceiling, swinging and bathing them in its glow, he could make her out more clearly.

Now that she was no longer framed by the entrancing neon lights over the bar, he could see the slightly smudged color over her tense lips, the paleness of her skin more than compensating for the powder that was wearing off, the slight circles under her beautiful, black-rimmed eyes. He conjured a half smile he hoped was reassuring.

In return she reached out her manicured hand and clutched his shoulder.

The muffled voices were growing louder. Harrowing. Angry. Spewing curses. He heard a shrill cry and stopped in his tracks, petrified. Reggie collided with his backbone.

"It's all right, Hamish." Her lips were at his earlobe. "We'll figure it out." She nodded her head, waiting for him to acquiesce.

Hamish clenched his right hand. It was cold and clammy and the nerves in his fingers were aching for the reprieve of a slight shudder. His heart was beating faster now. And its puncturing count took him down to the floor level.

He found his footing and moved slowly toward the noise coming from what he deduced must be a heavily shrouded room. Nearly soundproof.

Hamish exhaled and turned to Reggie.

"Please stay here."

Raised voices, another shout that startled both of them. Reggie jumped slightly, gripping his arm.

"I don't know what you're talking about." It was Luca's voice responding to a man whose tone was like that of a gangster in a radio serial. Before the organ pounded. "I've told you."

"It has to be somewhere." This came from Tom Schultze. "But I don't think he would lie, gentlemen."

"He'd better not lie," seethed another voice. "How many digits do you need on your right hand, Valari? Get this pretty ring after I saw it off."

Reggie swallowed. Hamish paled. "I think that Luca needs his legal counsel now." Reggie shuddered as Hamish swallowed a sudden wave of nausea.

Hamish nodded, his fingers undergoing the slow metamorphosis from loose clench to tight fist. Then he rapped at the door.

The muffled noise beyond stalled. "What's that?" Someone cursed.

Hamish and Reggie awaited the insufferable click of the locked latch.

The door creaked open slightly. A sliver. Hamish frantically looked beyond. He heard Luca more clearly through that teasing slice.

Luca pleading in Italian. Bargaining.

"What do you want?" It was Tom Schultze.

"I was looking for Luca."

"He's in a meeting."

Hamish strained over Tom's shoulder. Tom lifted his walking stick and pressed it into Hamish's chest. "You should stay put. And what's this?" Tom chuckled as he spotted Reggie. "Ah, my little vixen. Well, before we can move forward with the Flamingo, we need your cousin to spill a few secrets. And these gentlemen." Schultze inclined his head toward Phil, then to two figures Hamish had never seen before. One on either side of his cousin, whose hair was matted to his head, his suit wilting around his shoulders, his collar buttons undone. Hamish saw the flash of a blade dangling by one man's pant leg and, squinting, saw Luca's pinky finger tilted back. Hamish blanched.

"I-I can help," Hamish said. "I am sure I can. What is it that you think Luca has?"

One man's menacing smile curved. "What is this? And a girl too." He gripped Luca more tightly. Hamish frantically took in the room with wired eyes. Luca's mouth bled and his arm was twisted at a strange angle by a man who was the same height as Phil. Why wasn't Phil intervening?

"Who is this?"

151

When Luca's eyes met Hamish's, they filled with immediate terror. "What are you doing here? Get out! This is none of your business! This is just my stupid little cousin and his girlfriend. They must have been looking for the coatroom!"

The man to Luca's left looked between them and smiled. "There." He smiled at Luca, whose face was granite. "There it is. A breaking point." He crossed the room to Schultze, commandeered his walking stick, and, before anyone could intervene or Hamish could flinch, pressed it into Hamish's neck, simultaneously knocking his glasses off. Hamish blinked a few times, focusing without the lenses. Then choked, gasping frantically against the pressure. Spots marred his vision and Reggie's voice behind him sounded like it was in a tunnel. Panicked, he clutched the stick tightly, though the tendons in his fingers strained acutely, the nerves in his bicep aching from the restraint of their natural tremor.

He reminded himself, through his fear and his pain, that it was better that it was him — not Reggie, who was now in his periphery, her arm pinned behind her back — and that the man standing behind Luca — Hamish could just see through his squint — had dropped Luca's arm but still kept a tight grip on his cousin's shoulder, pressing him down as if he could shove him into the floor.

He saw Luca's mouth move and he supposed it was emitting a few words in a colorful language, but it sounded farther and farther away.

His eyes watered and he felt unbearably hot. He wondered what was rattling and realized it was the wheeze from his truncated windpipe.

He tried to fight through the black but the spots persisted and became larger and he wondered if this was like falling . . . like dying . . .

He closed his eyes and went limp, felt every tendon in his fingers loosen. Then the curtain behind his eyes fell over splotchy kaleidoscope colors.

He looked dead. Hamish looked dead. Reggie panicked. She wriggled and wriggled then finally gained enough liberty to wrestle her elbow out and drive it into the thug's ribs. She quickly stomped on his foot with her Spanish heel and heard a crack over his exclamation of pain. She flew at Hamish.

"He's still breathing," she reported from behind Hamish's limp figure. He looked younger in this repose with a single swath of his licorice hair over his forehead.

"You've made your point," said the big man Reggie had heard addressed as Phil. "He doesn't have the file. He proved that to you when you tried to kill his cousin."

Reggie looked up from Hamish's still form a moment to watch Luca. "I swear to you. It's not in Boston. I don't have what you want. So don't hurt my cousin!"

"Then it's in Chicago. With Fulham. Another loose end. You've got quite a reputation for loose ends. At least we know your breaking point, Valari. If we don't come for you, we'll come for your pretty friend here . . . or your young cousin." He motioned for his partner to join him and they slammed the door behind them.

Tom Schultze followed, speaking in pleading tones. "I am only investing in the Flamingo. I have nothing to do with him."

Reggie brushed Hamish's hair back from his forehead. Its texture was finer than she imagined when she'd examined its swerved sheen earlier in the club.

When she looked up, Luca was beside her, the blood at his lip congealing, rubbing at his arm.

"You almost got him killed." Her palm was up to Hamish's slightly parted lips. His breathing became stronger but was accompanied by a wheeze of a whistle.

"He needs to wake up," Luca said through gritted teeth.

To his credit — his brief and wavering credit — Reggie noticed that Luca's face had taken on an ashen hue she didn't think possible due to his dark complexion.

"I can't work for you!" Reggie's voice hit a hysterical height. "What are you involved in? It's one thing for these men to accuse you, but what if it's true? What if —"

"Not now, Reggie." Luca cursed. "You have no idea what you're talking about."

"Poor Hamish," was all she could think of to say. "Wake up." She rubbed his shoulder. "Luca, what happened in Chicago? All those calls."

Luca ignored her. "Phil? Phil!" The large man was still on the sideline. "Go get the car and bring it up, and if that doorman gives you a hassle, shove him through a window."

When Phil was gone, Reggie sneered at Luca. "He could have died! What is it they think you have? Don't drag him into this, Luca, I beg you."

"I care more about him than I do myself! And I always will."

"Then give them what they want and send him home!"

"I need him." Luca's teeth were clenched.

"You can't lift him. That man nearly ripped your arm off."

Finally, Hamish opened his eyes a little. They were so blue — and wide too. Uninhibited by his glasses. Reggie saw the glare of a lens out of the corner of her eye and reached for them. They were unharmed.

Luca's handsome face softened into a mask of vulnerability. "You alive, Cic?"

Hamish nodded slightly, which hurt him greatly. He winced. He tried to speak but coughed instead.

Luca used his good arm to prop Hamish up. "We need to get you home." He looked around.

"I can help," she said, gently taking Hamish's elbow. "Come on then." He was a little unsteady on his feet, but he started walking.

Luca kept a bracing arm around his cousin's back, and Hamish seemed happy to fall into the crook of Luca's shoulder. Reggie placed his glasses on his nose, took a step back, and adjusted them. "Better," she said, with a smile that Hamish tried to return. It barely got up the side of his mouth. She leaned in to the ear farthest from Luca and whispered, "Thanks for the adventure, William Powell."

The small smile stretched a little and she led them out of the open door.

Hamish's head hurt when he woke. Even prying his eyelids open stung. At first, he was displaced, unsure where he was and how he got there, but then he recognized the quilt over his legs and the décor of Luca's living room. He was still fully clothed, his tie loosened, lying on the couch.

He felt at his neck. It was still raw and bruised from where the walking stick had jammed. Swallowing would be hard for a few days. Fidget must have peeled back the curtains, for the broad windows showed Tremont Street waking, parishioners and tourists mulling outside the Park Street Church and the Granary Burying Ground. He knew the sun would inspire droves to the Common and the public park for a lazy afternoon. The familiar sights of Boston through the glass and from his vantage point did wonders for smoothing out the terror from the night before.

"Hamish!" Fidget peeked in from the kitchen. "I thought I heard you rustling."

Hamish looked down at his motionless form.

"Can I get you something to drink, dear?"

"Bit of a sore throat this morning."

"Might make you some cocoa. Or tea with honey? Sip it slow, help you feel right as rain."

Hamish nodded. "That'd be fine. Thank you, Fidget."

Fidget crossed the living room and smoothed back his hair. "You are a good boy, Hamish. A good boy."

The motherly gesture touched him. For a moment he felt a pang of homesickness. His mom checking in on him when he was ill, smoothing back his hair and kissing him on the cheek. He could almost detect the faintest scent of her customary lavender with the memory. But then there was Reggie. He certainly warmed to her quickly. But his mother had always told him that the first time she saw his father, it was the same. Maybe Reggie was like Boston: something he wanted to trace and study and find familiar so he could draw some kind of strength from her. She was the kind of girl you knew quickly, if you knew what to look for. Just like Boston was beautiful to those who knew what to look for: what cobblestoned alleyways to turn down, what tree in the Public Garden afforded the best view of Boylston Street. He chuckled darkly. Just like him to think about a girl when Luca had a much bigger problem on his hands.

Whatever Luca's business was, it was more than a club.

Hamish checked his watch. It was only half past eleven. He assumed Luca was still fast asleep. He was almost glad. His cousin's eventual appearance wouldn't stop the flow of a thousand and one questions. What was Luca involved in, and why was Hamish stupid enough to think that his cousin had changed? His father was right: Luca always ended up in someone's web. That was what he had been telling Hamish for years, trying to keep him from Luca's influence — despite Hamish's protests and the fun they had at a dance club or a ball game.

"Cic!" he heard a few moments later, though not from the direction of Luca's bedroom, but the front door.

"Luca —" Hamish's voice croaked.

Luca proudly held up a package tied with white twine. "Lemon cannoli. Got it myself. Walked all the way to Prince Street."

"You didn't have to go all that way, Luca."

"Yes, I did. You have no idea how sorry I am." Luca dropped the box on the table and sat at Hamish's feet on the sofa. "No idea. I can't even . . ."

Hamish was used to Luca's easy strings of hyperbolic reassurance, but he also knew when his cousin's sincerity poked through.

Luca's eyes told him everything his words assured.

"I'll live," Hamish said. "But I need to know what happened. What did those men want from you?"

"They thought I had something. I don't."

"Luca, I am involved now. I live here. I see Phil block the door every night. Reggie and I walked in on a violent meeting that could have gotten worse. That man was going to sever your finger." Hamish felt his stomach turn.

"They know you're off-limits. They know that. They know." Luca's nod was frantic and unconvincing. "I told them. It was an accident." He patted Hamish's arm. "They won't touch you again. They needed to make a point. To me and to Schultze."

"An accident? Luca, what were they doing to you? If Reggie and I hadn't shown up, if that man . . ."

Luca's red-rimmed eyes shut. "He was just going to rough me up a second. To show face in front of his goon."

"Is that what you really think?" Hamish's voice scratched and he welcomed the hot drink Fidget brought him. Luca gave her a quick smile and shooed her away. Hamish studied his cousin. He was remarkably calm. Especially for having slept so little and having almost lost a finger the night before. He blinked and refocused. Something in his chest sped up, but he ignored it. A ripple. An aftereffect of the trauma of the night before? Or perhaps . . .

"I am so naïve," Hamish said after a few ticks of silence. He tried to sit up but the blood rushed to his head. He grunted and put his head back down on the sofa cushion. "I thought you were doing this right. Everything I had seen so far showed me that you were doing this right. Bank loans. Cosignees. Associates. No tommy guns or broken kneecaps."

"Don't be ridiculous. What am I, an accountant? I just happen to work in certain circles that attract the type of people who want to squeeze a buck."

"Luca, what are you doing? Have I been stupid? Is everything my father has always said about you true?"

Luca darkened. "You are part of the Flamingo, Hamish. That is all you are a part of."

"I can't be a part of one aspect of your life without being a part of all of it, it seems. I want to help."

"You can't help." Luca's voice rose. "How could you possibly help? You're here for a lark because you got it in your innocent

161

little head to run away from home. I'm putting you up in my gorgeous apartment and introducing you to pretty girls and —"

"This isn't about me!" Hamish raised his voice, but the effort made his throat raw. He reached for his mug and sipped slowly. "This is about being called all the time. Here and at the office. This is about Phil trailing you. Whatever you left behind in Chicago. Whatever is nipping at your heels, I want to help you with it. I don't want to spend every night at a different club and half the day waiting for you to sleep off martinis from the night before."

"Don't judge me. You are free to leave at any time."

Hamish put his hand over his eyes. "I can't leave now. I can't. I was going to wait until the Flamingo opened and see what to do. But now I have to protect you."

Luca laughed bitterly. "How could you possibly protect me? Some anxious kid from Canada who can't even see his way through his first real trial."

"That's not fair."

"I don't want to fight with you, Cic, but I am giving you a chance at a life here."

Hamish motioned to his tender throat. "Some life. Luca, those men wanted to do a lot worse to you." He was sick of talking.

162

He was sick of looking at Luca too. His cousin's eyes were red-rimmed. Luca hadn't slept at all.

"Let them try," Luca said. "I have a club to open and a business to run and I was going to bring you into it. I am giving you a chance to be something more than you thought you could be. Don't you like living here on top of the city? The endless tabs, the girls and the dancing?"

"I could —"

"Don't you like cycling to the North End knowing that you have somewhere cozy to come back to? You want anything, I'll give it to you. We're so close to the opening. Things will change."

Hamish exhaled. He didn't want things to change. Especially if change meant knowing what Luca truly was. He wanted to barricade his thoughts from turning to the worst. He fingered his wrinkled suit collar, almost feeling guilty for having fallen asleep in such a pricey outfit. "Luca, I just wanted to spend time with you. Have an adventure. Go to a few baseball games. I don't care about all this fancy stuff." He blinked away belated tears that chose the most inopportune moment to prick his eyes, after his having survived the hurt of the night before and the anxiety at seeing Luca roughed up by those goons in the basement. The heart palpitations, the hand tremor before he blacked out. "I'm not . . . I'm not good with meeting people. I never had a lot of friends. But you were more than my cousin. You were like my brother. I had no one else and . . ." Hamish swallowed and blinked away a tear. "So I don't care about the parties or the fancy drinks."

"Just don't ask any more questions. I don't need you to protect me. I don't want you involved in anything. I don't want you to get hurt."

"But I was hurt. And that was okay because I knew for a moment I was taking their attention off of you. I thought —"

"Stop!" Luca slammed his hand on the side table, startling Hamish, shuddering the crystals dripping from the lamp, sloshing tea out of the mug.

Hamish stared a moment. His hand was shaking slightly. He tucked it under the blanket.

"Don't you ever, ever, ever think of that again, Cic. All right? My decisions are my decisions and their consequences are mine, not yours." Luca's eyes bored into him. "I don't deserve that kind of loyalty. I certainly don't inspire it. And I am not asking you to do anything illegal. I never would. Ever. I'll earn your loyalty. I'll show you."

"It's not about earning it," Hamish whispered. "You're Luca. You didn't have to earn it, you just had to be my cousin."

Luca blinked a few times then shifted his eyes to the tied package. He tore at the string with his long fingers and creaked back the cardboard. Crisp oblongs stuffed with light green clouds of filling sat in appetizing ovals of grease.

"My favorite." Hamish accepted the pastry Luca offered, finding the cold filling easy on his throat.

"Mine too." Luca's voice was a little uneven.

And Hamish guessed, for the moment, that at least in this they were the same.

CHAPTER 11

Having stuck her finger in the dam of anger with Luca for the moment, Reggie turned her thoughts to Hamish. Hamish with the bicycle and the shy smile. They hadn't known each other long. But in that moment she felt strongly. Like she would peel herself from the goon holding her and throw herself in his place.

She reached instinctively for her Journal of Independence. Beyond the sundry accomplishments of grocery shopping and cooking and installing a lightbulb and sewing a button, it lapsed into pages of the romantic. Of moonlight and sonatas. Of dancing under the drop of stars in an endless sky and stealing a moment and a breathless kiss that wrapped around her and sparkled down to her toes.

The memory of a moment surged . . . of her pressing into his back as they descended the stairs to the bowels of that club. Feeling his staccato breath, his thumping heartbeat.

Reggie corked her thoughts before they ran any more freely. They had just met. She at least had known Vaughan for more than half her life. But when did Vaughan dance with her like that?

Reggie slid out of her nightgown and pulled a green cotton dress over her head. She smoothed her curls and stared at the leftover flakes of mascara sticking to her eyelashes from her careless bedtime routine the night before.

She couldn't work for a man clearly involved in something illegal. She knew that from day one, but there had been Nate and cannoli and Winchester Molloy and Mrs. Leoni and now Hamish. Maybe she could find some way to stay attached to the North End. Maybe Mrs. Leoni would hire her. Or she could work at the Temporary Employment Agency. Ha! Ironic. Reggie out of a job and finding employment at a place that had little to dole to anyone, let alone an entitled rich girl like herself.

Reggie ran her fingers through her hair, still wavy with the extra attention she had taken in curling it the night before. She figured if she didn't show up at the office, Nate would worry about her. He was becoming a dear friend. And while she knew

Luca lived in a penthouse on Tremont near the Common, she wasn't sure *which* penthouse, and the news of how Hamish was faring was best learned at the office.

She walked slowly to the elevated train, took a seat, and leaned her head against the glass as it trundled over the tracks above the Charles River.

When she finally got to the office, her cotton dress sticking to her back, she set about dusting the office and answering phone calls and pretending she cared about the stupid Flamingo.

"You look tired," Nate said, popping his head through the door. He meant it kindly.

"Late night. Luca had me check out a club."

"So there are more perks to your job than making your own hours and having nothing more pressing to do than write hypothetical situations for Winchester Molloy to get out of," he said with a teasing wink.

Reggie faked a smile. "Deciding whether I should write my resignation letter."

"Oh, don't do that. I have half a mind to take a break at 3 p.m. and find out what Boots Malone is up to. Will Molloy foil his villainous plot?"

"I won't do anything rash then."

"Glad to hear it."

At lunchtime Reggie left the office and went to a delicatessen on Hanover Street to buy a sandwich. After settling on a bench outside, she took her Journal of Independence out of her bag and creased it open to a new page. *Phil. Schultze. Luca.* How were they connected? What about Chicago? It was easy enough if they were on the trail for some owed money, but Luca was too meticulous for that. She couldn't see him being roughed up for a few dollars. He never would have let his suit get wrinkled that way. He was suave, yes, but smart too.

Thinking of Luca made her think of Hamish. Her parents would be appalled at the easy familiarity she was showing with Nate and now Hamish. But she wasn't used to meeting people who didn't want anything in return.

"Miss Van Buren." Brian MacMillan, the accountant, was removing his hat and tipping it toward her in a way decidedly like Vaughan Vanderlaan. Reggie closed her journal and folded the sandwich she was eating back into its paper. Quickly swallowing, she made to rise.

"No, please don't let me interrupt your lunch. May I?" With her assenting nod, he lowered beside her. "I was hoping to find Mr. Valari. I need to assure him everything on our end is looking right as rain."

"You're welcome to follow me to the office. I can give him a ring."

He smiled. He had such a pleasant face, she decided. One of those kind faces with smile lines like loose commas on either side of his thin mouth. And while he treated her with the utmost respect and looked at her appreciatively, he never flirted.

She wrapped the rest of her sandwich, unable to eat it with him beside her, and tucked it into her handbag.

"You're sure you're finished?" he asked as she stood to leave.

"Yes. But thank you."

They rambled by St. Stephen's and in the direction of the North Square. "A beautiful day." He let her walk ahead as they sidestepped children single file on the stones. Their teacher was illuminating the night of Revere's famed ride. Some children giggled. Others gasped with delight at the rise and fall of his voice.

"I think it's odd that an office for what Mr. Valari hopes will be a long chain of nightclubs is here in the North End. But I am happy it is." She smiled at him as he reached and pushed open the front door of the office building. "I love how alive it is here. And the cannoli."

He let her lead them up the stairs to the second floor. En route, they passed a buxom brunette woman on the descent. She had a swing in her step, her generous hips swaying with intent when she made out Brian MacMillan.

He smiled. "I know you."

"Sure," she whined nasally. She sounded like a girl in a picture, Reggie thought, one of the actresses who was always trying to steal the love interest back. One of the actresses who made you wish you could retreat to the days before talkies.

"From where?" he hedged. "Oh! Wait. I've seen you with Tom Schultze. You sometimes pedal Chesterfields at the Dragonfly."

"Schultzie! What a gent. I'm going to be at the Flamingo now." She noticed Reggie. "Oh, hello."

Reggie's smile was tight-lipped. "How do you do?"

"Just waiting for Schultze. But he has a real wreck on his hands." She sighed, looking around the building, appraising it as she had doubtless seen Schultze or men of his standing do in the past. "The staircase in the back is falling apart. My heel gets stuck." She gave MacMillan a long look — one Reggie recognized from several pictures — usually from a girl with heavily lidded eyes and bright red lips and the ability to turn an entire room with the swish of her skirt over her hips. She playfully brushed past them and out the door.

"Schultze's mistress," Brian MacMillan said once they were inside Luca's office. Reggie noticed he watched her retreating figure for several moments. "I wonder how long she'll last. She isn't the first."

It was the first almost indelicate thing the man had said. He took a seat and Reggie offered him a copy of the *Globe* she had pilfered earlier that morning from Jimmy Orlando's office mailbox. The private detective hadn't been seen for days. And one of the things she was proudest of during her idle days in Luca's employ had been securing printed ads for the club's opening. It was still open at that page when she provided it to her guest.

When the phone rang, she answered it presciently, delighted that it was Luca's housekeeper informing her that Luca and Hamish would be by later that afternoon and that if she had the opportunity, she should start drafting a new memo to the Flamingo's investors. Reggie scribbled some of the instructions, distracted by the realization that Hamish must be better than she had anticipated if he was well enough to come in today.

"Mr. Valari will be coming to the office." Reggie smiled brightly as she set down the receiver.

MacMillan looked up from the paper. "Wonderful!"

Reggie couldn't keep from turning her chair in the direction of the window behind her and looking down to the street below for a sleek black car to court the curb. When it finally did, she smiled.

A moment later, Luca and Hamish walked in, Luca looking tired but still as if he had stepped out of a cigar ad in a magazine. Hamish smiled to see Reggie and merely clasped Brian's hand warmly as Luca prattled on about the latest baseball scores as if they were the new accepted social greeting.

When Luca politely asked if he could make use of her chair to speak to Brian, Reggie happily took the opportunity to stand and stretch and join Hamish by the door. It was far enough to convince Luca that they had privacy but not far enough that she couldn't steal a furtive look or snatch of a sentence now and then.

"How are you?" She leaned into Hamish.

"Tired. And sore."

"I'm surprised you're here."

His eyes drifted toward the tête-à-tête

173

Luca was having with Brian MacMillan. "And I am determined to figure out what is actually going on. I'm worried for Luca." His eyes fixed on hers and she knew he trusted her. That their shared experience the night before had earned his trust. He lowered his voice so it was barely more than a whisper. "I know you might not feel comfortable working here. I feel I should have been smart enough to know that . . ."

He shrugged. Reggie filled in the blanks to mean something in the vein of *wherever Luca is, trouble follows*.

"I should have been able . . . I thought it was different." He shrugged. "My fault."

"You aren't to blame at all," Reggie whispered with conviction. "We're *both* to blame then. I've enjoyed having rent money away from my parents and twiddling my thumbs and listening to the wireless."

Hamish nodded. "Luca thought I should stay home today." His eyes were drifting to the conversation by Reggie's desk as often as hers were. "But I wanted to let you know that I'm all right. And I wanted to let you know I am determined to figure out what is really going on here."

"If you truly think your cousin is innocent . . . ," she hedged.

"I wanted to let you know that I am

determined to clear Luca of whatever it is these men think he has done. He told me he is in the clean. Whatever he did in the past . . ."

He shrugged again, but his eyes were serious. They both knew Luca had a past. Heck, anyone seeing that suave Valentino gait would know Luca Valari had a past. And probably a present.

Reggie nodded. "Well, I have to at least see this through the Flamingo's opening. You too, I assume. Since you're here."

Hamish smiled. It almost reached its full stretch, but she wouldn't push further. She knew he wasn't at his prime, and he kept feeling at his neck before wincing. He was still in a lot of pain.

In her past, such an intense reaction to a new acquaintance would be seen as a weakness. Her mother had taught her that women were floral music boxes with keys that turned slowly and secrets they should always keep inside. That smiles should never reach their eyes. That everyone should be held at arm's length as propriety and decorum dictated. But her mother must never have felt the jolt of connection. Dwelled on the ampersand when Luca (as he did at that moment) leaned toward them with a quick "Cicero and Reggie! MacMillan here wants to ensure all books are in order for the Flamingo's first months' expenses."

Reggie moved to retrieve a ledger from a filing cabinet near the window. MacMillan was questioning Luca on Hamish's nickname. As in most things, the questioning brought out Luca's evasion. He flitted around answers with a precision and skill that took years of practice. She should have noticed that too. On the first day. But her heart hopped with the idea of unraveling Luca's mystery with Hamish.

Luca's conversation with the accountant — up until this point a low murmur — had taken a different timbre. Luca's voice rose.

"Arrangement?"

"I wondered about the *arrangement.*" Brian uttered the last word in italics.

Luca laughed him off. "Arrangement?"

"My father and I . . . You must know that I know there are others who look at the Flamingo as a unique opportunity. That . . ." He coughed. "Father is getting older, and our clientele is not as robust as it once was. I am here to let you know that I am completely dedicated . . ."

MacMillan stopped. He followed Luca's gaze, which was wide and aware in the direction of Reggie and Hamish.

Luca slapped him on the back with a

laugh. "Don't believe everything you hear. Don't let my young friends here think that the Flamingo is anything but what it is." He was speaking in a firm voice for their benefit. "An opportunity to show Boston what class is."

Reggie caught Hamish's eye. Luca could change the subject with that ease of his, but they both knew that something was ticking. Some people had access to an aspect of the Flamingo that others did not. And Brian MacMillan wasn't given leave to cross the threshold. Luca walked Brian MacMillan out just as Mrs. Leoni's shadow curved through the doorway.

She looked at Luca apprehensively, reserving a smile that spread wide for Reggie and wider still as she remembered Hamish from her shop.

"How can we help you?" Luca asked with a slight bow.

"I brought some cannoli for your secretary."

"Don't let me disturb you." Luca flashed a smooth smile. It didn't melt Reggie or Mrs. Leoni and he ironed it out. "Cic, Mr. Baskit is expecting me. Schultze has encouraged me to invest in another property in this area. And he needs the rent." Luca's eyes swept the office then settled on Mrs.

Leoni a moment. She was perspiring and her mouth wavered. "If you want to stay here with Reggie for a while? I'll meet you outside with Phil in an hour, say?"

Luca left and Mrs. Leoni uttered something under her breath that no lady should say. Even though it was in Italian, Hamish recognized it from one of his father's tenser moods.

"My cousin, Mrs. Leoni," Hamish said softly, leading her to a chair.

"He owns the office. He works for those bad men."

"He doesn't work for anyone," Reggie said.

"My niece's husband was told that he has to vacate his apartment." Mrs. Leoni crossed herself and lapsed into Italian. Hamish leaned closer, listening, nodding.

He sighed and leaned back.

"What is she saying?" Reggie whispered. Hamish was pale, which made the broad red stripe on his neck stand out even more in the crevice of his open collar.

"They signed a year lease. The owner wants to renege."

"Oh."

Reggie looked toward the open door. Hamish followed her train of thought. Luca was meeting with Mr. Baskit. They had some time to themselves.

"If you like, I can take a look at her lease."

"Hamish is a lawyer from Canada," Reggie explained.

"You would?"

"I'll do what I can."

Without the previous night's makeup, Reggie looked just as she had before Hamish knew her name. When she was just the girl with the intelligent eyes and flicker of a smile he saw in the cannoli line. She was more on his level like this. Not some girl out of a picture and out of his reach. He opened his mouth to say something but was waylaid by another party: a young man Hamish supposed to be about his age whose face broke into an easy smile and a comfortable familiarity with Reggie. Hamish looked between them.

"Sorry I missed the last few days. Do clients not realize their property problems are of secondary importance to Winchester and his femme fatale Veronica? They —" Seeing Hamish, he stopped, extending his hand. "Nathaniel Reis."

"Hamish DeLuca." Hamish judged the man to be a little older than he was. He had a pleasant face — like a book knowing what page to open and stay on. An Action Comic was tucked under his arm.

Nate discarded the comic on the side of Reggie's desk. "It's dull as tombs here."

"Oh, I've told him." Reggie sparkled today. Did she fancy this Nathaniel guy? She lit up when he entered the room. Women were a crossword puzzle: the seemingly perfect word was met with too many letters.

"So I hear you're from Toronto. Tell me, do you all live in igloos and ride moose?"

"He's joshing you. Nate, be nice."

"I'm just breaking the ice." Nate scraped a chair next to Reggie's desk and sank into it.

"Do you want your magazine?" Hamish asked, holding it up before returning to the seat behind his own desk.

"That isn't a magazine, Hamish," Nate reprimanded, but his eyes twinkled. "That is only the home of the most exciting new comic I have seen in an age." His voice ebbed and flowed dramatically and Hamish smiled despite himself. Nathaniel had a way of putting others at ease. "There's this fellow, Clark Kent." He held up the comic. "He's a human, right? But he has these superhuman powers."

Reggie snorted. "Superhuman powers? Like a fairy tale? Like magic?"

180

Nate rapped at the comic. "He can leap over tall buildings. Bullets don't hit him."

Hamish chuckled. "Bullets hit everyone."

Nate shook his head and warmed to his theme. "Not him. Not this super-man. He's a man but isn't. Any fear you have. Anything you wish you could do: amazing speed or strength. He has it."

"I know a few guys from the Harvard varsity team who would like to *think* they are super-men." Reggie rolled her eyes to the ceiling.

"There is nothing he cannot do." Nate narrowed in on Hamish as Hamish's faltering smile stayed a moment. "Nothing."

Hamish looked down at his right hand. It should have been involuntarily shaking a little with new talk with a new person. But it calmly rested on his knee. His eyes darted up to Nate and then to Reggie. He wasn't reacting the way he was used to reacting. Happy, he listened to Nate describe the new comic.

"But he's not really human." Sensing Hamish's waning focus, Nate turned intently to Reggie. Even his chair had shifted on a diagonal in her direction. "He's from a planet called Krypton."

Reggie shushed him. Her long finger turned the dial on the wireless. "We can talk about super-men later," she said, her eyes meeting Hamish's. "It's almost time for *Winchester Molloy.*"

While an Ovaltine jingle filled the office, Reggie reached into the top drawer of her desk.

"Almond cookies from the delicatessen. Perfectly kosher." She extended them to Nate, who eyed them happily.

"You're a wonderful woman." He opened the paper parcel, inhaling. Hamish could see he liked what was inside.

Reggie beamed and held up a second bag to Hamish. "And for you and me, Mr. De-Luca, the most uniquely named cookie in the whole bakery. Pretty but ugly."

Winchester Molloy was plagued by a pretty client whose voice reminded Hamish of Mary Finn's. She was kept by a wealthy man who had ties to New York's criminal underworld. Just as Hamish was beginning to think it all sounded a little too familiar, the phone jangled. Reggie turned the volume dial on the radio and reached for the receiver. "Luca Valari's office, Regina Van Buren speaking." She squinted and held the receiver away from her ear so Nate and Hamish could hear the loud and angry voice on the other end. It droned on and Hamish could make out some of the words in heightened volume. Reggie animated her face in exaggerated responses for their benefit, and Hamish, watching her, felt a little spark of something deep inside. "Yes, I hear you." She put the receiver back against her ear. "No, Mr. Valari is not here. He is very busy with the Flamingo." She had a recitation of the Flamingo's charms down to an art form. "The most popular club in Scollay Square. Already the rage. Mr. Valari is too busy fighting off reporters who want every last detail for the society pages." The voice erupted again and Reggie tilted her head, puppeting her hand for Nate and Hamish's amusement. Finally, she hung up.

"Well."

"That happens every day?" Hamish looked concerned. "You would think they wouldn't talk to a woman like that."

Nate guffawed. "Hamish, Hamish, Hamish. What rabbit hole did you crawl out of? Someone controls the North End."

Reggie and Hamish leaned forward. Nate took another bite of cookie, this time not bothering to swallow before he answered. "There is a theory. Just a theory, mind you." His voice was muffled. He swallowed. "That there is someone who controls everyone."

"For what purpose?" asked Hamish.

Nate shrugged. "Clearly something sinister and untoward." He laughed. "There are layers and layers of crime here. You'd think it was a chocolate cake."

Reggie worked her teeth over her bottom lip. Hamish watched her eyes sparkle. She was suddenly far away. "And this man from Chicago must think Luca has something to do with it."

She turned to Hamish, who raised his hands innocently. "Don't look at me. Sometimes I think my cousin is on the *fringe* of the law. But I don't think of Luca and *sinister* in the same sentence."

"He's too good-looking to be sinister," Nate reassured with a wink at Hamish. "Besides, he doesn't have the right mustache."

"That's right." Reggie picked up on Nate's cue. "Winchester's nemesis, Boots Malone, is always twirling his mustache."

Hamish grinned, tucking Nate's theory in his pocket. Nate may have been playing laissez-faire, but he heard something serious in his tone.

CHAPTER 12

"I don't think Mr. Schultze is aboveboard, Luca," Hamish said as he slid into the back seat, meeting Phil's dead-set eyes in the mirror a moment. He was empowered by his afternoon with Nate and Reggie. Back in Toronto, Hamish wouldn't have fathomed contradicting Luca for any reason.

"Oh heavens! Is anyone aboveboard? I thought you would like the fact that I am bringing money to this community. To these people."

Hamish watched the North End out of the pristine window of the car. Kids with scraped knees and matted hair stopped a game of stickball to gaze at its shiny hubcaps and peer through the tinted windows with smudged faces. "We *are* these people," Hamish said. "Your mother and father and my father came over on a boat from far across the sea to this new promised land to eke out a life. Just like these people." He emphasized it the way Luca had, but without the clip of derision. These people. Settling. Redefining themselves. Finding their Court of Miracles in the haven of a city of liberty, just like in his favorite book where Clopin and the band of gypsies hid in a refuge for migrants. Far from the toll of Notre Dame's bells, beggars who faked injuries by day for a scrap of bread were miraculously healed at night.

"So you ran away to become a philanthropist?" Luca said.

"Why is your office smack in the middle of the North End?" Hamish didn't want to break his train of thought.

The tires wobbled over uneven stones warped with time and tread until the smoother pavement. Hamish rubbed at his sore neck.

"I never should have let you come. You're tired and flustered now. You probably just wanted to see Reggie, didn't you?"

Hamish's ears tingled. He shrugged.

"Of course! You have a little crush."

"I hate when you're patronizing."

"And I hate when you keep things from me."

"What am I keeping from you?"

"That woman was not there to give Reggie cannoli. And that man from next door. The

186

land development one —"

"Nathaniel."

"My office is for business for my club, Hamish. Not for you to listen to little old ladies eliciting your good nature."

"I understand her. I can translate. This neighborhood is not always kind to her. I should do what I can. So should you."

Luca touched Hamish's kneecap. "But tonight no clubs. No baseball games. You can listen on the radio. You need to take care of yourself."

Funny that coming from Luca. Hamish nodded distractedly. He was still mentally piecing together a puzzle missing some pieces. He remembered how he had once owned a little set of unevenly cut pieces that, together, formed the picture of a sailboat. He always started with the easiest pieces first, working them into each other in a perfect fit. And the lapping water with its foamy milk crust began to take shape. But other pieces, carved and etched irregularly, were harder to fit into the picture's scheme. Luca was a locked vault and so Hamish would need to learn the combination another way. Having Reggie agree to stick by him was a relief. He tugged at his collar.

"You're still in pain." Luca broke his reverie.

"I thought I was going to die," Hamish said evenly. "I couldn't breathe, Luca. I couldn't see except these explosions of color. I was terrified. What do those men want from you?"

Luca gently gripped the back of Hamish's neck. "I'm sorry, Cicero. I nearly lost my mind when I saw what he was doing to you. I —"

"I know you're sorry." Hamish checked his tone. "I *know*," he repeated more softly. "But I wish I knew how . . ." He didn't finish. They were on School Street, the old School House squat in its old brick, City Hall grand and filled with people mulling under the trees and around the statues. Out the window just over Luca's shoulder, well-dressed patrons stepped out of the attended Parker House doors. Some hailed cabs, others took to the city streets in their fashionable shoes. Such a change from the vision of the North End still impressed on his mind. A different line of music, just as exciting, just as new.

Fidget took extra care with dinner that night: minestrone soup for Hamish and a plate of soft gnocchi. Luca kept the conversation light. Speaking of baseball and bicycles and chiding Hamish to write another letter to his parents. Later, Luca slipped out

188

to a club to meet a date.

"Her name is Louise. She has the prettiest eyes." He fixed his tie in the mirror in the front hall. Hamish had a clear vantage point from the sofa. "But you're to stay here and rest. There won't be business like last night," Luca assured. "Just dancing and a few too many drinks. So don't wait up and don't worry. I don't want to come home and find massive welts on your palm."

Hamish smiled and creased a book with his fingers. "I'm going to listen to the game and read a bit."

Luca moved to open the door then turned. "I'm glad you're all right, Cic," he said in a voice stripped of charm or pretension or his usual lightness.

"Me too."

"You don't regret coming?"

"I was pretty angry at my father."

Luca turned. "Then I'll see you tomorrow."

When Hamish did fall into bed, a million bells tolled in his head and he couldn't escape the sound. His pajama shirt stuck to his back. His chest panged and blood pulsed. He rolled onto his stomach and tried to fluff his pillow. He cracked open the window. It did little to help. Hamish exhaled. Then he opened his eyes and stared at the ceiling in the dark and cursed his eyes for watering. Why did he revisit that feeling again and again when he tried to sleep? He was miles away from Toronto, from the dark corridors of Osgoode Hall. Far even from Maisie who tried to cheer him up. Far from his mother who hadn't ever known what to say, though he adored her for trying. He could smell her perfume now. Now in this new world where Luca offered a new platter of complications. He touched his neck in the dark.

After tossing and turning, he climbed out of bed and into his mule slippers. He could warm a cup of milk. Or make a sandwich. Retrieve his copy of *Notre-Dame* from the front room. He blinked to adjust his vision in the dark.

Hamish creaked the door open and wandered into the spacious hall. Everything perfect and shiny and pristine. Like Luca — too calm. How could Hamish still carry the weight of last night while his cousin shrugged it off and went carelessly about his business?

The door to Luca's bedroom was ajar. Hamish took a deep breath and pushed it open gently with a crooked finger. He found the light switch and the shadows striped with the outside streetlights gave way to light. It wasn't as ornamented as Hamish assumed. Nothing hung on the walls. The paisley bedspread was neatly tucked into corners, Luca's dressing gown stretching across it like a colorful ghost. There was a desk in the corner. Hamish tugged on the drawer handle, only to realize it was decorative. The closet was a careful arrangement of Luca's tailored suit jackets and shiny black shoes. Luca was neat, but there was nothing to give any hint of personality.

Hamish tiptoed out. Then he moved in the direction of the study: another room he had seen only when Luca gave him an initial tour of the apartment. He gently tugged the light switch.

Here, there was personality, just not Luca's. Instead, a composite of pretty things perfectly arranged. Hamish squinted. He wondered what a room reflective of Luca would look like and couldn't imagine any picture or decoration that would inspire thoughts of his cousin. Luca liked tasteful things. But Luca was generic. Among art and furniture, small marble statues, draping green curtains, and the polished brass of a room preserved like a museum, he wondered how well he knew his cousin at all.

Luca the enigma. Luca who could not be captured by the perimeters of a place.

Hamish ran his fingers over the sleek mahogany of the bookshelves and wondered what it would be like to step into Luca's shoes for a moment. Wondered what went through Luca's mind. His cousin flirted with every woman in the room but never left with one on his arm: just faint lipstick on his collar. His cousin's office for the first of his many nightclubs happened to be in a building run by a man notorious in the North End for bleeding people dry?

He raved about the Flamingo, but the light in his voice and the smile splayed across his enthusiastic face never reached his eyes. And then there was Chicago, the dog nipping at his heels. And those men . . . the one he might have lost a finger for . . . There had to be something in here.

Hamish inched nearer Luca's desk. He had never seen Luca at it. He wondered how Luca got anything for his business done in the first place, and the untouched blotter and absence of papers or files just emphasized his doubts. Even the telephone didn't have the slightest smudge of a fingerprint. And while Fidget could have dusted it carefully, he felt certain that wasn't the case.

Hamish felt pulled toward the closed drawers like a magnet. But something held him back and he focused on rows of books he knew Luca hadn't read: alphabetized perfectly and lined up uniformly, their gold embossed titles alluring between the ridges of their binding. And yet none of them had been explored and touched and felt and loved. The realization saddened Hamish, as he rubbed his sleepy eyes and squinted at the titles, too occupied to steal back into his room for the glasses discarded on his night table.

"Words are blood," his father had always told him. He certainly felt that way about *Notre-Dame.* His armor. The soft cushion that found his head when the world was clanging and discordant. And these abandoned, untouched words clutched at his thrumming chest.

He had no familiarity with encountering a book and not picking it up, caressing its spine, or teasing open its pages and tasting it a moment: its tangible smell, its musty tang. Its promise of reprieve. He could slip into it and drown in it a moment, momentarily forgetting who he was.

Clearly, Luca had a different relationship with books. They were carefully arranged, a sad mausoleum. He was tempted to duck back into his room and stroke the spine of his *Hunchback of Notre-Dame* as if it had feelings and he had to offer penance. He immediately felt foolish for the thought. But Nate hadn't looked at him strangely. Rather, he said, "Everyone needs a safety blanket. Especially in a book inspired by a summer revolution and written by an author who always uses metaphor to really talk about what's going on in the world." Nate then compared the experience to the Torah he studied and so beloved, leaving Hamish with a strange sense of normalcy, that he could look up and find himself face-to-face with someone who felt the same way. It was a strange sensation and evoked a smile and courage as he headed in the direction of Luca's desk.

He slid open the first drawer, its contents neatly arranged in piles. Nothing of consequence. Bank statements. A few telegrams. Ideas for advertisements. Bold, hyperbolic words in Luca's hand extolling the wonders of the Flamingo. A few unopened letters from Hamish's aunt Viola. His fingers shook as he looked through a sparse bounty that told as little about his cousin as the room surrounding him. What arrangement? Who were those men? Questions pinged his mind. Not because he wanted to judge Luca, but because he needed to protect him. He needed to know, to plan, to pace. He needed time.

The door creaked open and Luca stood behind it. Hamish's already accelerated heartbeat sprung into faster gear.

"What are you doing, Cic?" His voice low and steady. Hamish knew Luca partook in several drinks on his nights out, but unlike Schultze or the raucous boys from his law class, his cousin never slurred his words. He was always in complete, steady control.

Hamish looked up, blinked, and hoped his lie would hold. "I wanted to write my parents. I didn't have any paper."

"You should be asleep." Luca crossed toward Hamish, looked down at Hamish's shaking right hand.

"I-I couldn't," Hamish stuttered. "I keep reliving last night."

Any defense Hamish detected in his cousin melted. "Of course. Poor anxious little Cicero. Your bouts of nerves."

"This room calms me." Hamish breathed in the scent of books, ignoring Luca's tone. It pricked up his spine. "I'm sorry I came in without your permission."

"My house is yours. I've told you a million times." There was a chill in his voice. His eyes flickered over the papers Hamish had in his hands, mostly unopened letters from Luca's mother. "I need to do a better job of writing her." His eyes searched

Hamish's. Hamish nodded. Then he made a display of carefully piling the letters and arranging them neatly back in the drawer. Luca joined Hamish at the desk, opened the second drawer, and extracted a gold-plated pen — one from a set monogrammed with Luca's initials. Also, a few sheets of heavily fibered paper. He pulled the string on the green lamp overlooking the chestnut desk. "You're all set." He tapped Hamish playfully on the head and then turned back in the direction of his room.

Hamish started writing. Pressing the nib into the paper and holding it, the dot of ink spreading while Luca still hovered nearby. Then his shadow disappeared into the low light of the hallway and Hamish set the pen down. Luca had opened the second drawer, and he had found the letters in the top drawer. There were still three drawers and a cabinet unexplored. He told himself he couldn't feel guilty for helping his cousin. If he could figure out what Luca was involved in, he could help him.

Hamish's tongue crept out the side of his mouth and he furrowed his eyes. The top drawer on the right was full of pens and scissors and several expensive necessities of correspondence Hamish was sure Luca had just for show. Underneath, however, was a second drawer. Hamish tugged on it. It was locked. Hamish looked around. Really, if something was valuable, wouldn't Luca keep it in a safe? He entertained often and the men he was with the previous night seemed like the type of men who would stop at nothing to ransack their way to what they wanted.

Convinced that Luca might have something hidden inside — despite his adamant repetition that he hid nothing from Hamish — he was determined to open it. His mother had always told him there were a million and one ways to pick a lock. It wasn't the traditional advice from mother to son, but she was a private investigator and far from traditional. A hairpin. A screwdriver. A paper clip. The latter seemed to be something Luca likely had. Hamish returned to the top drawer and found a small box of triangular clips. He selected one and worked the wire into a spear, then leaned down and worked it into the keyhole with his long fingers. The wire jammed and Hamish licked the salty sheen of perspiration over his lip. He looked up and around but the only noise was the persistent tick of the clock in the hallway. Hamish focused on the slit in the drawer and aligned the clip until he heard a slight *click* and felt it in his slightly shaking fingers. He gently slid the drawer open. And found a pile of telegrams. Many were from Chicago, often with language rivaling the voices at the other end of the phone calls Reggie took at the office. His fingers shook. He flexed them, folding his fingers into his palm and then out again. In and out. His heartbeat a drum. *Heartbeat, Hamish.* He gulped air, tucked the pile under his pajama shirt, looked around, grabbed his unfinished letter, turned off the light, and returned to his room.

CHAPTER 13

Reggie almost collided with Brian Mac-Millan on her way into the office the next morning. "You're here again?" She raised an eyebrow. "You're very invested in the Flamingo."

"Actually, I came to visit Mr. Reis. The development and housing person."

"Oh. Well . . ." She waved into the office. "You're welcome to wait here."

"You're the quintessence of decorum, Miss Van Buren. And, if I may say so, quite fresh and alluring today."

Reggie pasted on a smile. Accustomed to such compliments from a lifetime of knowing men like MacMillan, she should have been used to them, but this one still made her tingle a little. He didn't take her up on her offer, and soon enough Nate's door opened and he smiled out into the hall, welcoming Mr. MacMillan, with a smile over his shoulder for Reggie.

She turned back to a ledger of inventory for the Flamingo's opening. She had to call several grocers and finalize the schedule with the caterer. She tapped her pencil on the desk and pressed the heel of her palm into her forehead. It was more work than she was used to, and men like Brian Mac-Millan exhausted her. She buried herself in numbers for several moments, cursing her well-paid tutors and private school upbringing when her pencil tip broke mid-equation. When next she looked up, Hamish darkened the door that MacMillan hadn't shut behind him.

"Hello." She hid her surprise as he crossed the room and gestured toward the chair opposite the desk.

"Have a seat."

"Thank you." He gave her a half-moon smile that wasn't convincing. It didn't reach his eyes. He was flexing the fingers of his right hand in and out and his pant legs were rolled a little too high up his stockings. He must have cycled over.

The clock on the desk ticked several moments. The crack in the window open over the North Square ushered in the mill of tourists and the laughter of schoolchildren. Reggie wasn't sure what to say, and she certainly wasn't about to fall back on the armor of small talk from her childhood.

"Did you know that listening to Angela from the third floor talk about her two boyfriends — one lives in Quincy, the other in Rhode Island — while giving herself a manicure is even more insufferable than my mother's yearly picnic and quilt auction? I bet you didn't see that one coming."

Hamish reached into his satchel. "What's a picnic and quilt auction?" His brow furrowed.

"No. No. It is best left to your imagination. What's that?"

"I went snooping around the apartment last night. Luca gave me a night off on account of those goons threatening to kill me."

"How benevolent." Reggie leaned over her desk.

He placed an envelope on the desk.

Reggie ran a fingernail over the pile. "He will suspect anyone but you."

His eyes met hers and he blinked to focus. "But we're doing this together."

"Have I earned your trust so quickly?"

"Yes," he said immediately, not faltering on any part of the quick syllable.

"Swell." She smiled, lifting the envelope. "Is this anything someone might lose his pinky finger for?"

"Or his life," Hamish countered sourly.

She made great ceremony in opening the flap, and several telegrams fell out. "That's it? A few telegrams?" She scanned over them. "They're pretty evasive and I have heard much worse on the phone."

"I can't make anything of this." Hamish's voice sounded deflated, and a sheath of black hair fell over his forehead.

Reggie worked her teeth over her bottom lip. "We're not looking hard enough. Everything is a puzzle. We don't have all the pieces."

"Maybe Luca isn't involved."

"Are you trying to convince you or me?"

Reggie leaned forward, and Hamish wiggled his nose to boost the bridge of his glasses higher. Aware of the whistle of his breath, she drew back slightly. He smelled like cotton and lemon with a bit of espresso on his warm breath.

FLORENCE (STOP) CICERO (STOP)

"This is the one wretched thing about the brevity of modern communication." Reggie clucked her tongue. "It just makes it a connect-the-dots — and if you don't have all the dots . . ."

"I flipped through these last night over and over again. Trying to find something."

He chewed his lip. "I can only think that he left something behind. In Chicago. And he moved things around some business or something and it's catching up with him. Someone seems to be in the know. At the center."

"Cicero," Reggie repeated. "That means something to you."

"Other than what Luca calls me . . ." Hamish shrugged.

"Nate mentioned someone who had control of the North End. Well, at least the higher end business of it. It sounded a lot like organized crime." She watched Hamish intently for a reaction.

"If Luca knows about any of that, he refused it. Maybe someone is dead set on seeing that he is a part of the enterprise. Implicating him."

Reggie leaned back. "That would explain their roughing him up night before last." Her eyes held Hamish's a moment. "And you."

Hamish nodded, suddenly far away. His hand quivering with a mind of its own before he had the foresight to tuck it in his pocket.

Reggie surveyed him closely. "What's wrong with your hand?" she asked softly.

Hamish averted his eyes. He was breathing more heavily now, the two fingers of his steady hand tucked in the open slat of his shirt. Counting under his breath.

"You're all white." Her voice quickened. "Hamish . . ."

He slowly rose from his chair, then sat down again. Reggie watched him a moment longer. He was staring straight ahead, his breath coming in gasps. Noting the rope of red around his neck from his run-in with a stick two nights before, she winced at how painful it must have been for him. Yet she knew his current symptoms weren't a side effect of his being nearly strangled. This was something different.

Five minutes later he was much calmer, though he ducked his head low, his shoulders inching toward his ears. A turtle trying to hide in its shell.

Reggie watched him, but when he finally took a tentative look in her direction, she turned back to the telegrams. "Are you all right?"

He waved his steady hand. "I have this . . . these . . ." He stuttered a little. "Episodes now and then." His breath was shaky but evening out.

"I'm sure whatever Luca's involvement, it isn't anything dastardly." She tried to convince herself as much as she did him.

"Luca cares too deeply for you and would never let you come here if he thought you would be pulled into a dangerous business venture." She narrowed in on his face.

"He's not trying very hard to hide, if he is involved in something." Hamish's voice was barely a whisper. "Everyone knows where to find him." He drummed his fingers on the desk. "Luca's always hiding something. But now —"

The phone rang. Reggie held up a finger. "Wait."

"Luca Valari's office, Reggie Van Buren speaking."

"Florence?"

"Pardon? The reception is very bad." The caller sounded distant, his voice crackling as if in a tunnel.

"Is Florence there?"

Reggie's heart thrummed. "You must have the wrong number. I am sorry. I . . ."

But the man kept talking. Reggie plugged her finger in her opposite ear to block out the sound from beneath the window, the slight thud of footsteps overhead.

"Luca."

"No. He's not here." It wasn't the wrong number. "Do you have questions about the Flamingo?"

"I'm in trouble. Tell him Cicero isn't

working out."

Reggie startled at the name. Luca's nickname for Hamish. Reggie tried to listen a few beats more, but it sounded as if someone was holding a sheet of paper up to the receiver and crinkling it in her ear.

"Anything?" Reggie was relieved to hear the question in his regular voice.

"Chicago is following your cousin." She looked at the telegrams.

"I should have known Luca was still involved in something. But he told me this was his fresh start. If there were just some creditors, I could live with that. I thought he'd changed his ways. Become . . . honest." It was such a little word but held so much to Hamish now.

"We'll help him open the Flamingo." Reggie folded her hands, reasoning with herself. "If only to find out who those goons are and why Chicago keeps calling and who Cicero is. Then I'll go find some nice steno pool work and you can go back to Toronto." She smiled at Hamish and looked over his shoulder to the hallway where Nate was locking his office door.

"Nate!" she called. "Come in here."

Nate jogged over. "Can't stay for Winchester today. Have to check out a property."

206

"So Mr. MacMillan found you."

"I won't complain at easy money even if that fellow is involved with the likes of Baskit and Schultze," he said easily.

"You told Reggie that someone owns the North End?" Hamish asked, tracing at a paper with his pinky finger, then scratching at his collar, exposing the red line on his neck.

"What happened to your neck?" Nate's eyes narrowed in. "Looks dreadful."

"Some goon roughed him up at the Dragonfly two nights ago," Reggie said. "Maybe someone is after Luca for not being part of whatever scheme you told me about."

Nate's eyes stayed on Hamish. "It's a myth, maybe. But someone is at the center of — what's the best way to describe it? — a spider's web. Knows who to connect with. Knows where they're going to find the best deals. No one of my level or Mrs. Leoni's would have any access to any information, of course. But if you have someone like Schultze, or even that Brian MacMillan, sniffing out property, you can make a killing. Sniff out cheap rentals and invest the money in a big-time scheme." Nate checked his watch. "I really have to go. Shame about your neck, though."

Hamish bobbed a small nod and Nate was

on his way, leaving Reggie and Hamish to look at the telegrams again.

Hamish ducked his head, embarrassed. "I suppose Luca could have been susceptible to something . . . if he was threatened in Chicago. If he was trying to make a new start . . ."

Hamish was convincing himself more than he was her.

"You needn't worry about me looping the two of you together," Reggie said. "I mean, if that crossed your mind. Because I don't know you that well, but no one can hide being this wet around the ears." She laughed. "No. No. I'm not mocking you. I'm just telling you that I am a Van Buren of the New Haven Van Burens. I'm used to phonies, Hamish DeLuca. And you don't have what it takes to be one."

CHAPTER 14

Help Luca put Chicago behind him. Open the Flamingo. Then return to Winslow, Winslow, and Smythe. It made sense. Stay long enough to see wrongs righted and to ensure that Luca put the past behind him. Hamish nodded to himself, returning the telegrams to their drawer, then he snuck out of the library and doubled back to the main room that was now filled with crates and baskets.

The finest cheeses, jellies, olives, foie gras, and caviar. The choicest brands of cigars that the girls, filling the seams of their high-waisted boy shorts in perfect curves over their polished T-straps, would distribute. Luca had secured a deal for premium cigarettes bought in bulk cases. He stood to the side and demanded and thought and planned and inclined his wrist, the whiskey glass he was holding casting prisms throughout the room.

"We'll get you a new suit!" Luca told

Hamish.

"I was already fitted for a new suit," Hamish countered. The telegrams were safely returned, but his hand still burned with the memory of them. He told himself he wanted to protect Luca from falling into the life he was trying to outrun, but he felt like a traitor nonetheless.

"Not one that will be appropriate for Wednesday evening," Luca insisted, grabbing his cousin's lapel. "Cicero, everything has to be perfect. Just has to be. A stitch out of place is bad luck. I have to get this right."

Hamish worked his lip. His mother had always warned against putting all of his eggs in one basket. He knew he always put a lot of faith in Luca — if for no other reason than Luca never asked him to hide his hand behind his back, or reminded him to duck away before his anxious episodes became apparent to the public around them. Luca's unending faith in his new club, his last shot at putting the past behind him — it was something Hamish wanted to support. If he could. He wanted to devote himself to Luca's cause.

Luca had been rising earlier since the night at the Dragonfly, and Phil had slept on the sofa the past few nights. "Just in case one of the men from the Dragonfly shows up," Luca explained. "It's more for your protection than my own." He looked over Hamish's injured neck, his eyes filled with concern. Luca was living on coffee and half-eaten sandwiches, their crusts hardening under the flecks of dust illuminated by the light from the half-open curtains. Hamish was tired of overpriced food and inventory and contracts that crossed his eyes with their small print. He wanted to take his bike and steal down to the North End. Ignore the people weaving in and out of the pent-house: the flowers and phone calls and raps on the door with more deliveries.

Of course, shipments were also trucked in large amounts to the location in Scollay Square. But Luca wanted to keep a personal eye on the most expensive of the club's accoutrements.

"Do you worry you've spent a little too much capital up front?" Hamish mumbled as Luca continued examining his wares, harried but still perfectly groomed. On Luca, even stress fit like a bespoke jacket.

"What do you mean?"

"Money, Luca. Our penthouse is filled with thousands of dollars of foodstuffs most of Boston can't afford."

"O ye of little faith." Luca's black eyes

sparkled. "To make money, you spend money, Cicero. This is an investment in taste. I cannot possibly fathom opening a club with bathtub gin and candy cigarettes." He swerved back to his bounty.

Tom Schultze arrived with Brian Mac-Millan at his heels. In Luca's presence, Brian turned into a different person; clingy and charming, shrugged out of the shyness from his first visit to the office. Hamish slowly sipped his Coke, wondering what Brian wanted.

Schultze leaned on his silver-tipped walking stick, rocking casually. With the hand not cradling the stick, he was holding up a print. He noticed Hamish watching him.

"Come here. Come see my latest find."

Hamish inched toward him.

"You seem like someone who might appreciate some history. Maybe it's the glasses. More than your cousin here. I'm sure he's told you why I buy so many properties in the North End."

Schultze's gaze moved to Luca. Hamish followed suit. "I am trying caviar." Luca was spreading tiny bubbles of inky garnish onto a cracker. "That's more exciting than your antiques." Luca nibbled at the delicacy. "Your wife's favorite brand, Tom."

"She won't be there," Schultze said. "I

told you, she's visiting her infirm mother."

"Convenient." Luca laughed. "And yet the illustrious Mary Finn will be my star cigar girl."

"And Ben Vasser is your official police detail. That was confirmed this morning."

Luca's look was unreadable to Hamish. "Ben. Interesting."

Hamish took the offered frame and held it up. "I know this drawing," he said.

The sketch was of uniformed men with muskets in detail that reminded him of an old-time political cartoon. If the scene had been in color, Hamish knew their tunics would have been red. "Is this Paul Revere's piece from the Massacre?" His brain matched the grim representation with the stones his bike wheels had glided over a dozen times since arriving in Boston.

"A good eye." Schultze was impressed. "This is the oldest piece in my collection. I was just getting it appraised." He looked up to Luca. "Your cousin is far smarter than you are, Valari."

"I won't argue that," Luca said through a mouthful.

Hamish still looked closely. History told him only five men perished, with six men wounded nonfatally; but the scope of this sketch painted a far grimmer scene. As if the shots and smoke were in the barrage of an intense battlefield. A picture cast in his mind just as Paul Revere had more famously cast it in pewter: men slaughtered on the brink of emancipation.

"It looks a lot like the pewter imprint. Paul Revere's?"

"You know your history." Schultze's small mouth revealed all of his teeth — overcrowded, tripping over themselves for space.

"My father taught me that the stories are always going to be in whatever we have that represents the most public consumption. Newsprints and public bulletins are far more . . . alive . . . than some stale recollection after the event."

"Your father is a smart man. A historian?"

"A reporter."

"Mmm." Schultze absently swung his stick.

"Your stick." Hamish nodded to it. "Another relic."

Schultze smiled like the serpent in the insignia and held it up for Hamish's perusal. "You really do have a keen eye." He tilted the head in Hamish's direction. Hamish adjusted his glasses and peered at the detailed etching. The rattlesnake he recognized from Revolutionary history.

"Join, or Die." Schultze's eyes followed

his track around the artifact. "Become one of our union or perish. The emblem of one of the Gadsden flags. All of the early states are parts of the body of the rattlesnake. Deadly when together."

Hamish ran his finger lightly over the engraved emblem. It was well crafted. He smiled at Schultze, and it was then that he realized the man hadn't once looked him in the eye. Not over the course of their conversation. His father had told him that a real man will look another man straight on. As an equal.

Schultze tapped his stick and moved toward an open crate of cheeses, wood shavings of stuffing springing in all directions.

Luca offered Hamish a cracker with caviar. Hamish, having never tried it, gave it a small nibble.

"I hate the texture." He wrinkled his nose.

Luca chuckled. "I have something more palatable for you. Wait here." When Luca reappeared he was holding a jam jar. "Better?"

Hamish smiled brightly. "Aunt Vi's lemon jam." A prick of homesickness stabbed him. His aunt's careful writing on the label.

Luca stretched his arm around Hamish. "Don't get all misty-eyed."

"I'm not." He blinked and fiddled with

the lid of the jam jar. Luca handed him a cracker and he dipped it in, his mouth watering just thinking about the tart taste soon to be on his tongue. It was better than he remembered.

Later that evening, Phil set out for a cigarette break and to see his girl, and Luca and Hamish stretched by the window, watching the traffic in tiny dots below.

"You feeling better?" Luca asked. He'd sent Fidget home early, so they were gnawing at the end of large Italian sandwiches purchased from a deli a few blocks away from the Common.

Hamish unconsciously felt his neck. "I'll live."

"That I am glad of. I don't want my uncle rapping at my door. He'd throttle me if anything happened to you. Did you send your letter?"

"What? Oh." Hamish had forgotten his excuse for being in the study the night before. "I just have to sign off. Do you think someone would mail it for me tomorrow?"

"Of course."

Luca winked at Hamish. "Just two more sleeps." Something he would say when Hamish was little and Luca telephoned about his arrival. The times when he actually kept his word. "But that's so far away,"

Hamish would whine. "Only a few sleeps," Luca would respond.

Hamish picked out an olive from the nub of the sandwich he couldn't finish and nibbled it. *That Luca.* That was the Luca he would see this through for. "Are you ever worried about some of the phone calls that come in?"

"At the office? That's what Reggie is for. To charm them."

"I just hope you didn't leave things too unsettled in Chicago."

"Cic, we talked about this. The Flamingo will change everything. We are so close." Luca took a long sip of Coca-Cola and bit into his sandwich, a slight smile on his full mouth as he watched the first thumbnail of moon peek through the purple and blue sunset sky.

They were close. And then Hamish would have to reconcile with the inevitable: a life that took him back to Toronto. Away from Luca and the penthouse and the baseball games, yes. But also a life away from Nate and Reggie.

CHAPTER 15

"Reggie, make sure every piece of crystal shines like your mother's cabinet before a DAR tea."

Reggie shook her head. "Very funny."

Promising, thought Hamish. Reggie was a woman who knew how to hold a grudge. And while Hamish was delighted she took his side after the night at the Dragonfly, she wanted him to be on good terms with Luca too. He was completely recovered and all of the last-minute details for the club had been coming together. Now all of the fancies crossing through Luca's penthouse had been safely transferred to the Flamingo in time for the opening the next day.

"You think I hired you for your secretarial skills?" Luca teased. "Darling, you have no experience — save for the most important experience. You have taste." He turned to Hamish. "More taste than you, Cic."

"So it wasn't my glowing references and

personality after all."

"Without me, you would have been charged for eight cartons of canned olives — pitted olives — instead of seven," Hamish said.

"Your eagle eye is appreciated," Luca said.

Their footsteps echoed over the polished floor, ringing up to the rafters. Hamish closed his eyes and imagined the empty space filled to the brim, clouded with people and music and laughter. He was excited to finally be *in* the Flamingo. His cousin's project seemed to be running smoothly with several handymen running the gauntlet on last-minute preparations. Hamish combed his hair back from his face and took it all in. The grand front entrance with its double Deco-style doors whose ornamentation reminded him of the saucy swerve of a flamingo's beak. There was an Employees Only sign opposite the bar on the other side of the dance floor. Another door opened to the back; on their quick tour upon arrival, Luca had shown the alley it led to.

But no office. Luca reiterated his need to keep his paperwork and telephone away from the club. "That's why I have my wonder boy here." He beamed at Hamish. "And his gorgeous right-hand woman."

Hamish couldn't still his nerves. But he

had looked through contracts and signed off on deliveries, ensuring there were no legal loopholes.

"You okay there, Cicero?"

Hamish nodded. "I hope I don't let you down," he said softly. Reggie averted her eyes. Luca met his gaze straight on. "What are you talking about?"

"I don't know. I just hope I didn't miss anything."

Reggie laughed. "Oh, please. Any investor who doesn't want to snatch you up after the club is up and running isn't worth his salt. I know, I know, I haven't spent that much time with you. But I have a good instinct. Call it a Van Buren sense. I sense you would go through anything your cousin asked with a fine-toothed comb."

Hamish ducked his head to the side, hiding his smile. It was stretching wide and his cheeks weren't used to the elastic pull. He would take any compliment from her. Even one about his proficiency.

"And I am smart enough to know that Cicero is one in a million."

Johnny Wade broke into the conversation, striding across the floor with a beaming smile. "Just as you asked, Mr. Valari," he said. "It was swell to open the door while all these people are milling about dying to see what it looks like inside." His blue eyes gave it a swift appraisal. "Classy joint. Much better than old Galbraith's."

Luca pasted on a smile and rose to meet Johnny, shaking his hand. "Please call me Luca." He motioned in the direction of the bar. It was already populated with bottles and glasses of every shape and size. "You should find everything you need. But take a quick inventory and if you find anything missing, let me know and I'll put someone on it. Our stores are in the cellar and they are stocked too. You shouldn't run out of anything." He slapped Johnny's arm. "And be creative. Every Monday when we're dark, you can come in with Bill and a few of the others and stock up."

Johnny nodded, taking the floor in two strides, rapping his hands on the bar and looking as at home amidst the bottles as a scientist might his laboratory. Hamish turned back to Reggie, who was holding a jar of pickled onions up to the light.

"All of these things from my parents' parties always seemed to materialize on the table." She smiled, extending the jar to Luca, who snatched it.

"I have people for this," Luca said. "But I want everything to be to my liking. And —"
He stopped as the front door opened and

Schultze strode in, Mary Finn just behind the gleam of his walking stick.

"Valari! Isn't this just the thing!" the investor boomed.

"Gee whiz!" exclaimed Mary, turning her head around so quickly, Hamish thought she looked like an owl. Her gaze landed on Johnny and stayed. Hamish felt something in the air as she detangled herself from her proximity to Schultze and walked in the direction of the bar. Something palpable filled the air with the hip-swerving strides that closed the space as Mary neared the bar.

Reggie noticed, too, exchanging a look with Hamish.

"All right!" Luca clapped. "Get up off my caviar crates, children!" Hamish and Reggie rose to attention. "Mr. Schultze and I have business. So I need the two of you to inspect the bowels of this fine establishment."

"Aren't there people for that?" Reggie said in her inimitable Reggie way. Hamish couldn't rightly tell if she was teasing or serious. Her tone bordered on a little of both.

"You are to do what young Johnny Wade is doing." His eyes flickered to Johnny, who was dazzling Mary with a smile, while Mary giggled an octave higher than usual. "But I need you." He pointed at Reggie. "For once this summer, you are going to earn your salary." He winked, but they all knew there was truth in it. "And I know you love an adventure."

Happy to have something to do, Reggie and Hamish maneuvered to the Employees Only sign.

Hamish creaked the door open. "I wonder if he'll put a fellow here like that oaf we saw."

As soon as they stepped through, cold air gusted over them. It put Hamish in mind of his mother's pantry under the stairs, heralded by a creaking door. When he was a child, being sent down to the chilly basement for a bottle of vinegar or a jar of chutney always scared him. A feeling that resonated with him now.

"An easy escape route." Reggie's voice was at his shoulder as they stood on the small landing looking down into the dungeon.

"Like H. H. Holmes." Hamish studied the narrow stairs.

"H. H. Holmes?"

"Holmes built a murder castle in Chicago during the World's Fair with all manner of nooks and chutes to dispose of the bodies of his numerous victims."

Reggie shuddered. "Is it necessary for me

to go down there?" she wondered aloud after a moment of dark silence hanging as low as the ceiling above.

"It *is* rather dark." Hamish found the light switch at the top of the stairs. The bulb over the stairwell glowed to life, then fizzled and popped, enveloping them in darkness. Hamish exhaled. "H. H. Holmes's cellar is ever after how this place should be known. Creepy."

Reggie ran her hand over the cold cement; Hamish watched her manicured fingers settle into the grooves. "Old building," she said. She rapped at the pocked cement with her knuckles.

"Bulb's burned," he said, jogging up the two steps he'd descended. "I'll just run and get a new one and a torch."

He left Reggie, noticing the contrast between the coldness of the cellar and the state-of-the-art air-conditioning swirling through the club. After finding a package of lightbulbs and a flashlight, he jogged back to the Employees Only sign, where Reggie waited for him with a broad smile.

"I killed two spiders," she said proudly. "Have to write that in my journal."

Hamish handed her the flashlight and reached up for the dark bulb.

"What is this, Hamish DeLuca?" She

curled a lip at him. "You think I can't change a lightbulb? I'll have you know it is the first skill I accomplished when I moved to this grand city."

Hamish clutched the bulbs to his chest. "Sorry. Be my guest."

"Open the door a little more, Hamish."

He shone the light on her, noting how her freckles diminished with her nose scrunched up in concentration as she licked her lips and widened her brown eyes on the task. He set the bulbs down with the hand not holding the torch. The last thing he wanted was for Reggie to trip over her oxford heels and plummet into the abyss at the bottom of the stairwell. He heard a pop and light buzzed around them.

Reggie bounced elatedly. "There! Reggie Van Buren can change a lightbulb!"

They slowly descended, Hamish contouring the narrow passage with the flashlight.

"Someone's going to kill themselves down here," Reggie said, grazing her head on a low beam. "Why do you think Luca sent us down here?"

Hamish, prickled by a portentous chill that intensified as he looked at the dusty storage, wanted to break and run. Writing briefs for some bushy-eyebrowed lawyer with moth-eaten suits and spittle binding his teeth to his bottom lip as he smacked on about tort law was preferable to a safe haven for bats' nests. "An experiment," Hamish said levelly. "To see if I could be alone with a girl . . . a *woman* in an unexpected place and keep my head. He'll probably have a million questions later."

Reggie gingerly felt her head, then transferred her touch to crates upon crates with shredded stuffing springing out of the side slats. "It's pretty high-end liquor," she observed. It was clear she had little time for Luca's experiments. She crouched beside a crate. "My father's brand."

Hamish flashed the light around. At the back of a cubby, larger crates piled in a lazy tower. Reggie crossed over and Hamish followed suit.

"Champagne!" Her smile widened.

With torchlight, Hamish saw the storage in shadow, but he gauged by her reactions that this cellar held thousands upon thousands of dollars of goods.

The intimidation he felt at fumbling around in a dark basement filled with heaven knew how many priceless bottles of liquor was suddenly replaced with a tiny pang of regret. When had he, Hamish De-Luca, ever been as passionate as Luca was in this endeavor? So in love with his business venture that even the dank basement held a treasure trove of specialties.

"He hasn't just bought things that are expensive," Reggie was saying, untangling herself from behind a barricade of boxes. "He has selected things that are rare and perfect. Like jewels."

She used Hamish's arm to steady herself and he wondered if the tingle above his elbow was from keeping the flashlight extended or her touch. She searched his face. "Look at us! Down here without an escort! My grandmother would screech for her smelling salts."

She brushed by him and back into the thin, dank corridor.

"He needs better lighting down here," Hamish said. "Someone could trip over themselves and ruin those beautiful bottles."

Reggie nodded her head so furiously her curls almost made a sound. "You would think with everything that Luca has planned to a T, he would have seen to the lighting." She extended her hand in the direction of a small lean-to. More crates lined the wall.

"I can see why he didn't want an office here," she said, putting Hamish in mind of the basement office they'd encountered at the Dragonfly.

They started up the stairs again, Reggie's

newly changed lightbulb fizzling pronouncedly before blinking dark.

"What?" she cried. "I know how to change a lightbulb, Hamish! I swear! I . . ."

Hamish edged in front of her and swept the flashlight over the remaining stairs on their slow ascent. "I don't think it's you." He reached up. "There's something wrong with this socket. Luca will need an electrician." The bulb flashed and flickered.

"Let me see."

Hamish moved out of the way. Reggie reached up and twisted the lightbulb again. The light then streamed through, illuminating everything around them.

"Impressive!" Hamish remarked.

Upstairs, the band ran through several scales.

Luca and Schultze were draped against the bar, Johnny Wade passing them highball glasses, Mary Finn turning a carton of cigarettes over in her hand.

She smiled at Reggie and Hamish. "Chesterfields. But we have more brands in the back." She painted Johnny's profile with her eyes. "It's the best stocked in the city."

Johnny assembled two drinks with lemon garnish, sliding them in Hamish and Reggie's direction.

Neither Hamish nor Reggie touched them.

Luca noticed. "How's my stock?" he asked Reggie. "Drink up, children. You've worked hard."

"You need an electrician here, Luca."

"Hamish. Come on. This man makes the best cocktails in Beantown." He raised his glass.

"The lightbulb at the stairs keeps flickering off and there is hardly any light in the basement. Someone could trip and kill themselves," Reggie said heatedly. "Or they could trip and shatter a case of champagne."

Luca narrowed his eyes at Schultze beside him. "You said you had someone."

"I meant to get a contractor from Hanover Street. But there has been so much else and —"

Luca cursed and slammed his glass on the bar. His face darkened. "If you ran out of time, you tell me. If you can't do something, you tell me. I would have done it. It's my responsibility. But *you* specifically told me *you* had someone checking on the club."

"Valari, the air-conditioning is in perfect order. The spotlights. The stage."

"The whole club means the whole club, Schultze." He grabbed his drink and drained it. "I can't have people dying in my basement or wasting thousands of dollars of

229

goods." He swerved back to Hamish and Reggie. "You could have killed yourselves."

"I changed the lightbulb," Reggie said.

Luca cursed again. "You kids shouldn't have had to wade through the dark. Where am I going to get an electrician before tomorrow?"

"Nate will know someone," Reggie said brightly.

"Hmm?"

"Our friend at the office. He can get someone, but you might have to pay for last-minute service."

"Yes, yes. Of course. I'll pay three times the usual service fee. Just get him down here."

"So this is the den of iniquity." They were interrupted by a man who looped his arm around Luca's shoulder.

"Ben Vasser. The best of Scollay Square's law enforcement. How fortunate that you are on our beat."

"My men will make sure this doesn't get out of hand. And I . . . thanks, young man" — he accepted a gin and tonic — "will make sure that you keep to your liquor license."

"We promise to be just as depraved and debaucherous — is that a word? — as every other club on your beat."

Vasser swigged his drink. "I expect noth-

230

ing less. Make me work for my pay. It won't be too hard if the band is this good."

"Roy Holliday is the best. Cic! Take Reggie and give my new floor a spin."

The band rolled the last lazy bars of "Easy to Love." Reggie remembered the way Hamish danced at the Dragonfly. How carefree. How he gave himself to the music. He was stilted now. Holding her, but not too close, as if there were an invisible measuring tape between them. She couldn't blame him completely. They were the only pair on the floor, watched closely by the bandleader and pretty much everyone else. They slowed and stopped and she couldn't admit to herself that pulling away from him felt like swinging her feet out from under the covers on a January morning.

"Take a break, kids!" Luca called. "I ordered cheese sandwiches and Boston cream pie from the Parker House." Luca waved in the direction of the bar. Johnny Wade had deserted it, but a man had brought covered plates full of food for the band.

Reggie lifted a covering napkin and snatched a sandwich and a slice of cream pie.

Hamish followed suit.

"Your first taste of Boston cream pie?" Reggie asked.

"I thought it was lemon at first and was disappointed." A smile danced on his lips but didn't spread.

"You never smile, do you?"

"Hmm?" That slice of smile was still cutting his cheek. They moved to the side of the club and sat on the stairs leading to the fancy doorway.

"You never truly smile." Reggie nibbled a bite of sandwich. "Your cousin, Luca, flashes his bright and brazen. You always just let your mouth turn up a little bit. I think I am going to make it my mission."

"What?"

"To make you really, truly smile."

"I am smiling," Hamish mumbled through a full mouth.

"Ha!" Reggie's mouth stretched wide.

He swallowed, picking ruefully at the crust of his sandwich. "I was smiling when we first danced." Hamish averted his eyes.

"Tell me about your parents."

Hamish paused. "My dad worries about me. About people noticing" — he held up his right hand — "that I'm just a little . . ." He shrugged. "He means well. My mother understands more, I think. She would understand why I came here. She's always

232

dappled in mystery."

"Mystery?"

Hamish nodded slowly. "A lady investigator. A private detective."

Reggie beamed. "That is the most wonderful thing I have ever heard! So adventure is in your blood, then?"

Hamish shrugged and fell silent a moment. Then, "What about your parents?"

Reggie cleared her throat. "My mother thinks I am a disgrace to the family name. I mean, she never said it aloud, but I am sure no amount of damage control can salvage my reputation now."

Hamish's ears piqued. "Is that why you ran away?" he asked, then stopped. "You don't have to tell me."

"It's perfectly all right. It was at an insipid garden party. They throw one every year and I paste on a smile and talk to the silliest women who only think about who will get the fine tea services when they're married and really never see a life beyond the circle of our perfect little world. My boyfriend Vaughan . . ."

Hamish stiffened and drained the camaraderie right out of the conversation. She might just have told him she had smallpox. Reggie continued in a quick jolt. "Yes," she said, her voice resigned. "My boyfriend

Vaughan Vanderlaan — though I'm not sure he's my boyfriend anymore — dragged me to the middle of the party and announced that he had proposed and I had accepted in front of everyone!"

Hamish rubbed the back of his neck. "And you hadn't accepted? You refused."

She nodded. Though the slight movement didn't compensate for the myriad of Vaughan memories suddenly flooding her brain. "Sometimes it seems like a whole lifetime ago."

Hamish looked far away, sounded even more so. "I know what you mean."

They both turned at a slamming knock at the door.

"Oh, it's you," the man storming inside said. Hamish caught his breath, and his hand went protectively to his neck where the same man had pressed Schultze's walking stick into it. "We were never properly introduced." He nudged at a plate of half-eaten cream pie with the toe of his white shoe. "It's very rude to sit when you are receiving company."

Reggie studied his features. He wasn't as handsome as Luca, but the overuse of cologne and pomade, not to mention the cut of a suit tailored to perfection, tried to compensate.

Hamish slowly stood, his arm shoved behind his back — but this time, not to hide its slight shaking, but rather, Reggie deduced, to still her and protectively keep her back.

"Sorry," Hamish said quietly. "My name is Hamish DeLuca." His tongue rippled slightly over the *D.*

"Mark Suave," the other man growled, grabbing Hamish's hand. "And who's your girlfriend?"

"Regina Van Buren." Reggie removed the napkin from her lap, straightened her shoulders, and rose as regally as she could, extending her hand. "And you are a fiend, Mark Suave." She hissed his surname.

"Charming," Suave said, his eyes darting behind him. "Where's Luca Valari?"

"I think you'll find my cousin is quite busy with preparations for our opening tomorrow," Hamish said unevenly.

"He'll have time for me." Suave walked past Hamish, but not before looking him over. "Luca's breaking point. I was worried he didn't have a heart. You know that?" His eyes pinned Hamish. "But seeing the way he went ill at the thought of my hurting you" — Suave stepped forward, leaning into Hamish — "made me think that I have something to bargain with." He gave a stale smile. "I'll go find your cousin."

Hamish sank back onto the stairs, wringing his hands. "This isn't good," he whispered.

Reggie followed suit. "Maybe we should let Luca take care of this? Or phone the police, or — ?" Reggie stopped as Mark's voice shattered the acoustics of the club and startled Roy Holliday's band to silence.

Reggie strained to hear but she couldn't make out the conversation. Only that Luca was as angry as Suave was. Then, roles reversed, Luca tugged the man back across the club toward the entrance where Hamish and Reggie sat.

"I don't know where he is!" Reggie made out. "I told you. You asked me to finish the job. I did.

"I am finished there. I washed my hands of it. I did what you asked and I started over and I suggest you stop following a dead trail. It'll just lead you to Lake Michigan."

Reggie met Hamish's eye. This was more than nightclub business. Hamish's right hand shook.

Suave brushed his sleeves. "Let's hope you're telling the truth." He swerved in Hamish and Reggie's direction. "At least I have bargaining chips." He sneered at the little group, then, parting them before they could rise, he left the way he came.

Luca cursed. Then cursed again. Hamish hopped to his feet. Reggie followed, smoothing the skirt of her dress.

"Don't worry. Sorry about that. Please don't worry."

"What do they think you've done? What does he need? What would lead to Lake Michigan?" Hamish tripped over the sequential questions.

"Cicero! Heavens!" Luca laughed nervously. "Too many questions. Did you have enough to eat?"

Hamish looked at the remains on his plate. He had taken no more than two bites. No wonder he was thin as a rail, Reggie thought. For her part, she stole another bite of Boston cream pie.

"Fidget will have something in the icebox." Luca studied his cousin's face with concern. "Don't look like you've just seen a ghost, Cic. We'll set you right. That man just has a temper. A misdirected temper." Luca turned to Reggie. "And you, lovely Reggie. Shall I arrange for a car?"

"It's okay, I can take the subway."

"Not at this time of night. I'll arrange for a cab. Hold tight."

Moments later, she was in the taxi, fingering the slow raindrops jeweling the passenger window. But a half hour later when she was safe in her room, she switched on the light, finagled for a coin, and pressed it into the meter. She waited for the telltale hiss. Then she took her rickety kettle and placed it over the heating element. Reggie arranged her chipped mug and spooned loose-leaf tea into a strainer. (There were some things that a New Haven Van Buren did not leave in Connecticut, including her outrage over anything but properly assembled tea.)

The kettle whistled and Reggie lifted it carefully. She liked the steam rising from the water as it trickled slowly into her mug. It would fog Hamish's glasses if he were here.

She strained the water over the tea leaves then lifted the mug gingerly to her lips. There was still a stain of pink on them from earlier. She was thinking about Hamish. About his nerves and worries. About all the imperfect smudges that blurred the outlines of his life.

Reggie set the tea on the radiator. She unfastened her garters and rolled down her stockings. She slipped out of her cotton dress and left it puddled in a ribbon of emerald at the edge of her bed. She slipped into the reprieve of her light nightgown and stepped into her mule slippers — the ones with the pink bows her mother had given her for Christmas the year before.

It was strange to have these little mementos of home — her past life — the one she wanted to shrug out of.

She lifted the tea mug and sipped some more, feeling the heat of the liquid mingle with the heat of a muggy Boston evening. If anything, they canceled each other out and a sheen of perspiration over her forehead and prickling under her arms provided a damp coolness. Reggie reached into her nightstand for her Independence book — the list was getting longer with scratches and scrawls and strikethroughs denoting the changes that were slowly shifting her life. And the back held the secret of a list she couldn't make hide nor hair of. She flipped to that page and picked up a pencil from her nightstand. *Florence. Trouble. Cicero.*

Cicero. Hamish's nickname. She wanted to throw at him all the confidence he questioned he had. But she knew he was loved. In the same way she knew she was loved. Her parents had a funny way of showing it, but they loved her. And Hamish? How could anyone not love him? Hamish with his floppy black bangs and brilliant blue eyes. The way his ears stuck out just a little and the way his smile curved slightly like a semicolon, imprinting a dimple into his left cheek.

Reggie sipped more tea and then fell so deeply into the tunnel of thought that she let the rest cool beside her. She flipped to a new page of her journal, away from the unsolved mysteries of the day.

On the first blank line she wrote: *Make Hamish . . .*

Then she crossed it out.

She bit her lip and squeezed her eyes shut and formed a picture in her mind that was at once rainbows and sunshine and promise. Then, opening them, she took pencil nub to paper and wrote in clear, bold print . . . Hamish, whose face had paled when she told him about Vaughan. Who had thrust her behind him again when that Suave fellow got too close. Who was starting to become just as pestering as the looming idea of Vaughan nearby.

Make Hamish happy.

Neither Hamish nor Reggie was required to show up at the office the day of the Flamingo's opening. So Reggie spent the day lazily, painting her nails and strolling in the sunlight to the Bunker Hill monument, prowling around for the first time since she had moved to the city. If she had done the same at home, her mother would have lectured her on the benefits of social recreation. "One can relax under an umbrella at the Cape, love, especially if one is doted on by the Vanderlaans. Have an escape. But make sure that your escape mutually benefits our society."

Surging with a revolutionary spirit that spared little thought for the benefit of any society but her own, she strolled down to the Warren Tavern and ordered a glass of white wine, which she drank while watching the foot traffic on Pleasant Avenue beneath patriotic flags draped and dancing in the summer breeze.

The publican handed her a newspaper. She thumbed to the society pages. Instead of reading of the latest escapades and fashion of young ladies and men she knew personally if not by reputation, she was eager to glance over every last snippet of type dedicated to the Flamingo. Proud of the enthusiasm and anticipation for "Boston's Newest and Classiest Joint," she drained her drink and set out for her apartment and a long bath.

The stroll home to Chestnut Street was a bright one, bricked streets sloping between houses set close together, adorned in a rainbow of colors: blues and reds and bright oranges like autumn's flames. Reggie took the familiar route at a faster pace than usual, her Spanish heels frustratingly finding the uneven seams and grooves of the street.

She wasn't usually home so early, and her landlady, polishing the banister, raised an eyebrow in surprise. Reggie mumbled something that sounded a bit like "half day" and stomped up the worn carpet of the stairs.

In her room, she tugged the blinds down so that the grating sun wouldn't hamper her ability to inspect the lines and shadows of her face. She flopped backward on her bed a moment and closed her eyes. If she thought hard enough, she could transform the empty space of the Flamingo into what awaited her that evening: spilling with light and swathed in music. She caught herself wondering — rising to the small sink in the corner and splashing water under her arms and over her face — if Hamish would leave his glasses at home. And she then caught herself wondering what those eyes of his might look like unfettered by their lenses. She supposed their blue could cut through the throng like a spotlight. She caught herself and splashed more water, letting it trickle over her freckles and the bit of a sunburn just above her collarbone.

Her eyes flittered, rounding in the reflection in the mirror above. A slight pang stabbed when she thought of Vaughan, his memory indelibly stamped on her as she recalled nights she roughed her cheeks and powdered her collarbone and etched her lips crimson and dabbed perfume at her wrists for him. All for him.

She wasn't one of those girls who dressed only for men. But she admitted to herself, running the pad of her finger over her eyebrow to smooth it into a tame line, that dressing for a man certainly motivated a girl. Sighing, she turned from the mirror to her wardrobe. Vaughan or not, she had her employer to impress and, yes, maybe, certainly his cousin too.

As hard as Hamish tried to get him to talk, Luca said nothing about Mark Suave.

Luca retired as soon as they returned from the club the night before and hadn't risen the next morning when Hamish watched the sun slant through the window. Fidget welcomed him with a copy of the morning papers, all brandishing broad announcements of the club's opening. Hamish now navigated the North End. He had long since skidded over the sloping stones of Beacon

Hill and swerved through the Back Bay, stopping to flop on his back at the stretch of green in Copley Square. There was a freedom to the air and the commerce and the weave of pedestrians he would lose the moment he stepped into the wall-to-wall smoke and pulse of the club. Pumping the pedals with his two-tones, leaning over the handlebars, savoring the smooth swerve of the wheels over the stone, he almost unclutched his hands and lifted his arms. It was the kind of day that infused him with a glorious sense of liberty.

He was thrilled by how tightly the past held to the city. The slick cobblestones scuffed with the hooves of galloping horses, the cries of the rebels still echoing. Hamish felt the breath of ghosts on his neck as he cycled along State Street and over the place of the Boston Massacre.

He pedaled slowly here, he supposed out of respect, but perhaps more out of interest. If he truly was to find a home here, at least for the time being, he was determined to learn everything of importance. His father had always told him that the fastest way to understand the heart of a place is to find what its inhabitants valued about it.

He disembarked at Winter Street, a feeling of transition mingling with the late afternoon breeze. His summer to this point, not to mention his snatching at adventure, would culminate in this evening. Luca's success, Reggie's endeavors, his amateurish attempts to keep books and filter through legal contracts for nightclubs all hung in the balance.

The opening of a nightclub wasn't unlike the fall of the curtain on the debut night of a play. By the time the clock struck midnight, you knew whether you would close the next day in a wave of failure or would carry on in a blaze of glory.

The doorman smiled with his customary friendliness when Hamish returned, rolling his bicycle beside him. Hamish took a moment to study it: an open smile he never flashed at Luca. Hamish stopped mid-foyer. Something about Luca kept people in check. Hamish brushed the thought off and crossed to the elevator.

When he arrived at the penthouse level, he took his time striding to the door.

Luca was home, stretched on his sofa with a martini and the society pages. "Cicero!"

"I'm surprised you're here." Hamish unrolled his pant legs, wheeled his bicycle to the alcove.

"I am taking a well-deserved hour of relaxation." He stretched a demonstrative

245

hand over the length of his silk robe.

Hamish smiled. "Did you get the basement light fixed?" The question was a stand in for "Who is that Suave fellow?" and they both knew it.

"Your friend Nate recommended someone and he should be on it." Luca's face was washed of any stress and Hamish knew not to press. "You look tired. Have a nap before tonight."

"I will." Hamish lowered onto the chair opposite the table on which the remaining sections of Luca's newspaper fanned.

"Luca."

"Why the dark tone, Cicero?"

"Do you know anything about a person or organization that links the North End to . . . nefarious purposes? Money laundering?" Hamish studied his cousin's face to see if there was a flicker or switch in his eyes, a tic in his jaw. "Is that why Mark Suave followed you from Chicago?"

"I've heard of it. Same thing you have." Luca's voice was dismissive. "You can't be in this business and not rub shoulders with men who are using it for a different kind of profit."

"So you're not using it . . ."

"What are you implying?"

"You're not using the Flamingo for the

same kind of . . . profit."

"What did I tell you when you came with me? I have a past I am not proud of. Do you really think I would drag you — you, of all people. My cousin! As close as my very brother, into something . . ." He waved his hand. "Nefarious."

"I just . . ."

"I told you. I need you to trust me." Luca cursed in Italian — a word Hamish had heard his father use when his Underwood was out of ink in the middle of a story. "I am going to be tired of explaining myself to you. You would be a fool not to think that such things go on. But I need you to focus on tonight. To come and be my moral support."

Hamish flexed his fingers. Something about Luca made the doorman's sunny smile check itself when Luca passed but spread wide with relief when it was Hamish. Something that rippled in soft tones and under breath when his cousin passed by.

Hamish retreated to his bedroom. Fidget had laid out his tuxedo, steamed and pressed, on his bed. He reached for *Notre-Dame,* clutching it as he turned on the tap to run a long bath.

"When you get an idea in your head, you find it in everything." He paraphrased a line from the book.

He just had an idea in his head. Too many late nights. Too much nervousness about making Luca proud at the Flamingo. He needed to tuck this stupid notion behind his pocket square.

A half hour later he dabbed his wet hair with a towel.

"Be ready in a half hour," Luca said.

"I thought I'd cycle over. Get some fresh air before I'm stuck in a smoky club all night."

"You can't cycle to the Flamingo in a tuxedo."

"I'll sling the jacket over my shoulders so it doesn't crease and fix my tie there. I need the space." Everything felt close. The left-over steam from the bathroom, Luca fastening his cuff links in the front room before stopping at his bar by the window. Hamish smoothed his hair back and nudged his glasses on his nose.

"Oh, leave the glasses, Hamish. For once."

"And be blind as a bat?" They both knew he was exaggerating.

"You're being childish."

Hamish took the glasses off and left them on the table. Then, when Luca turned, picked them up and slid them into his pocket. "Fine. But you're being secretive.

Luca, you can tell me anything. Remember when you had me double-check those contracts?" Hamish remembered when his cousin showed him a lease agreement. Hamish had enjoyed going through it line by line and feeling useful. "I am trust-worthy. You said so yourself."

Luca didn't seem to hear him, focusing instead on rearranging his tie in the mirror and smoothing his hair. "Don't be late," was all he said as Hamish finally rolled his bicycle to the door.

CHAPTER 16

Streams of color pulsed in contrast to the calm of nearby Scollay Square, settled under the blanket of starlit dark.

Reggie took her time with a sleek red satin that accentuated the white of her shoulders with thin, decorative straps and a bodice that clung to her waist before falling away with a delicate, silky flounce. Her lips were outlined in rich cranberry, her face immaculately powdered. Her hair gleamed in its brown finger waves. She turned from side to side, pleased with the effect. The dress fit more tightly than usual, the result of her passion for Mrs. Leoni's cannoli, but rather than flinch at what her mother would say about watching a ladylike figure, she laughed. She had been enjoying life and she had a few new curves to prove it. Rather than traipse to the trolley in her finery, she had accepted Luca's offer for a car to collect her. She gathered her fur wrap and her small purse and stepped to the street, thinking of how her background of finery clashed with the everyday happenstances she was crossing off in her Journal of Independence.

The driver attempted to keep his eyes from fanning over her as he opened the door.

The river sparkled under the last strokes of daylight as they crossed over the bridge. Boston was awakening.

Too soon after, the driver swerved to School Street, the lights of Washington and Tremont behind her, the King's Chapel and the Parker House in their wake. At the garish bombardment of Scollay Square, she waited for the chauffeur to open her door and assist her to the pavement.

Reporters' bulbs flashed and a stream of satin, lace, and sartorial splendor flowed to the double Deco doors under the gaudy neon lights of the Flamingo's sign.

Reggie thanked the chauffeur, who refused her tip, and made for the door. The doorman, recognizing her from the day before, let her bypass the long queue and enter through the doors.

"Miss Van Buren."

That snake, Mark Suave. "Excuse me," she said with finality before he could finish his sentence. She left him leering in the corridor.

She felt the music before she heard it: the beat of the drum and the riff of the brass thrumming through her even before her mind shuffled it into cohesive musical form. Reggie had intended to be fashionably late, and so the club was already an explosion of revelers with dancing and drinking, laughter chiming and catching the echo of the corridors.

She found his rigid shoulders and lanky stature embellished by the tight lines of a finely tailored suit. His ebony hair was shorter over the back of his neck. His right hand — always in his pocket or behind his back — was tucked in the flap between his jacket and cummerbund. Luca was laughing, throaty and deep, hand draping a martini. Reggie smiled away the attention of men on each side, crossing over the sleek tile to where Luca and Hamish stood.

Hamish was laughing at something, she could tell by the slight shudder in his shoulder blades. She grinned, tapping him on the shoulder. He turned and his smile was stretched brightly across his face. Reggie's heart constricted. He wasn't wearing his glasses and his tumbly black hair was smoothed back on either side of his strong profile. She had noticed he was handsome the day they met: his strong nose, that one dimple that now was deep and pronounced with leftover laughter that was, sadly, reaching the end of its ripple. "You look . . ." She blinked and blinked and blinked over the satin wings of his suit lapels and the white of his shirt and the green paisley of his bow tie. He was remarkable.

"You look . . ." She couldn't finish the sentence.

Hamish ducked his head. "Thank you. Reggie, you are absolutely . . ." Perfect. Neither of them knew how to finish a sentence.

What was this man doing to her? Hadn't she just told him a relationship followed at her heels? But he was lovely. She wanted to smooth the sadness from his eyes and pocket his smile for a rainy day.

Luca turned, Clark-Gable-ing the room. "Hamish, offer the lady a drink, for heaven's sake." Unlike his cousin, he had no qualms about letting his eyes linger over her, from her red lips slowly down her dress. "Reggie, you are a vision in red, and the man who is on your arm tonight, which I am very much hoping is my old Cicero" — he draped his arm around Hamish's shoulders — "is the luckiest man at the Flamingo. Thank you

253

for honoring my endeavor by appearing like a scarlet angel."

"Luca," Reggie said, "you are —" Another truncated sentence, but this time not for lack of words. A waiter strolled by with a tray of champagne and Luca grabbed her a glass.

"Your impeccable taste has graced my club. I can only hope our vintage suits your refined palate. Ah! Robert! You're here . . ." Luca turned.

"He lays it on too thick, you know," she told Hamish, watching Luca's retreating figure. "Well, here it is. The fruits of our labor." She raised her glass with an ironic smile, her gaze encircling the room. Luca had ensured that his club would attract everyone it needed to: the cream at the top of society and fashionable bohemians. An exhale for Boston's new set, who wanted to find a club that was on the edge.

Reggie and Hamish stood shoulder to shoulder, Luca's world unfolding in silk and satin. It was everything he had wanted: Roy Holliday bowing again and again to thunderous applause before starting in on another jaunty melody, the liquor flowing, the crystal tinkling, the spotlight haloing in its aimless search over perfectly coiffed hair.

Ask me to dance, Hamish, her heart

throbbed. *Ask me . . .*

Just as he was turning to say something, Tom Schultze appeared at her elbow.

"Accompany me to the floor, Miss Van Buren." Nothing in his demand held even the inkling of a request. He shoved his walking stick at Hamish, who took it, surprised. Reggie gave Hamish one sour look she hoped read, "Thanks for nothing, chappy!"

Hamish passed Schultze's stick over the bar to Johnny Wade for safekeeping, but not before squeezing his palm over the rattlesnake engraving so tightly it left a mark.

"Don't you need that, sir?"

"Not for dancing." Schultze looked Hamish over. "You look happy. You should find a girl. Scare you out of your shell."

Scare. Interesting word. Hamish played along with a smile as Schultze took Reggie's arm and led her to the floor.

Hamish couldn't help but follow Reggie with his eyes. He hadn't known fabric could cling like that. The material of her dress knew what it was doing and how to accentuate every part of a perfect package. He watched until she and Schultze were swallowed in the tapestry of smoke and music, the colorful chaos of the dance floor.

"Another drink, Mr. DeLuca?" Johnny

Wade's voice countered the din. Guests were a tidal wave lapping on the bar's crest of shore. Hamish was surprised Johnny noticed him at all. It was because he was attached to Luca, he surmised. He asked for a Coca-Cola, which he sipped slowly, averting his eyes not out of nervousness but because he was waiting on tenterhooks for the moment he could part a sea of people and whisk Reggie from the floor.

A flash of scarlet, her dress a tipped glass of merlot amidst whites and blacks and sequined grays. And she was Vaughan Vanderlaan's. She was a line he couldn't cross. The sensation of his heart sinking to his knees the moment she casually made that announcement — pulled it out of air — filled his chest again. He was getting so close and she was out of reach.

Mary Finn bubbled beside him. "Go get the girl, Hamish Cicero." Her voice sounded like her throat had been subject to a cheese grater or washing grate. He wondered if she would still have it at the end of the night, having compensated for the smoke and commotion.

"Chesterfields?" Her eyes flitted to a gentleman nursing one of Johnny Wade's extravagant concoctions.

The man refused. Hamish sipped his

Coke. Mary excused herself, edging by him, disentangling herself from the cigarette case strapped around her neck. Roy Holliday sported an affinity for Gershwin, languidly rolling through popular songs. Hamish hoped a string of fast tempos would reign and the band would leave the slow songs for a moment when Reggie wasn't in the middle of the floor with a cad like Schultze — or whoever was currently leading her.

He smoothed his palm over his slicked hair. He was far gone. He knew it even as he should have been swept up in the magic of Luca's dream unfolding around him.

"This is Schultzie's," Mary cooed behind him. She rapped the walking stick on the bar.

"Leave him, Finny," Johnny Wade pleaded. Hamish angled himself so he could catch Mary Finn and Johnny in his periphery, noting the easy way they fell into each other and spoke to each other and engaged each other. A woman could tickle your nose like the bubbly carbonation of his Coke, or she could soothe like liquid satin, like the smooth whiskey of perfect golden vintage that Luca boasted.

"I can't. You gonna keep me in jewels and furs? My ship's come in. But I told you. We'll find a way to be together. I just have to play my cards right."

"He's married," Johnny said. Hamish heard the thud of a glass on the bar. "Married men don't leave their wives for . . ."

Was it just the rising volume of the band, or had Johnny not finished the sentence?

"Don't leave their wives for what?" Mary snapped. "For girls like me? You seemed to think I was just good enough when you proposed in Boise all those years ago."

"Stop rubbing that in my face, Finny."

"I'm only telling the truth."

Hamish ruefully sipped his Coke. The history of the bartender and the cigarette girl. If this were a picture, Reggie would be first in line.

It was quite clear to Reggie, if it hadn't been before, that Schultze's walking stick was purely decorative. He wasn't the best dancer on the floor, but he glided with the same confidence that took him through life.

"Why do you have that stick of yours if you never need it?" she asked, the band lazing through a three-quarter-time tune.

"Power," he said gruffly, spinning her in time with the music.

"Power enough for someone to take it and threaten Hamish with it?" She hated the feel of his clammy hand on her bare shoulder.

"I am an investor in the club. Whatever Luca has following him is none of my concern."

"And yet there you were, watching from the sidelines as men roughed up your investment."

"He sure found a spitfire in you. My secretary is dull as tombs. Moth-eaten sweaters. Talks about her cat a lot."

Finally boring of her, Schultze spun her to Brian MacMillan, who seemed genuinely happy to have her near. He wasn't a fabulous dancer, but at least he kept to the rhythm. Anyway, she was painting in rigid lines, the music not liberating her the way it should have.

"Loosen up, Miss Van Buren."

She'd heard that a million times on several dance floors: varsity parties that Vaughan and his set spun her away to on weekends at Harvard, weekends her mother never would have allowed her to attend had she not made up a safe alibi of a cottage on Martha's Vineyard. She gripped Brian more tightly, mindlessly stepping into his lead while her brain spiraled Vaughan-ward. She even thought she saw him. She blinked away the feeling through the hot lights overhead, the tempo rising and the heat even more so.

"Miss Van Buren, I know that you are Luca's secretary and I know that he trusts you. Luca Valari wouldn't hire anyone he didn't trust. I want to know the real story. If he's involved in anything . . . if he controls anything . . ."

Reggie struggled to formulate cohesive thoughts amidst the pulse and pound of the dance floor. "I'm sorry, you know about as much as I do." She tried to keep her voice to a near whisper, which was quite impossible considering the volume of the band.

Brian's grip tightened slightly, his footing suddenly unsure as they swerved into another coda of another song. "I need his influence. Everyone talks about it. You have to help me. My father . . . He is leaving me with nothing."

"I know more about you now than some people I consider my dearest friends," Reggie said drily.

"Our business is washing up and I don't want to follow my old man's footsteps." His eyes pierced hers, almost ethereally light in the strobe of the spotlight roving over the dance floor. "I would do anything."

Brian halted so quickly Reggie almost tripped over his shoes.

"May I cut in?"

It was Luca. Even at a party he had everyone bending to his will in that soft-spell way

260

of his. Reggie thought Brian looked almost pale under cheeks flushed from their exertion on the floor. She gave him a sympathetic look, one she hoped read, "There's no way he could have heard."

She matched Luca's rhythm, steadying herself with the beat and his presence, his competent movements. Luca never let loose, but the sinews in his arm and the confident movement of his feet tricked everyone around — including her — into believing he had.

He lowered his lips to her ear. "What did Brian want?"

She was aware of his nearness. Very aware, and it wasn't the pleasant sensation that the women looking enviously at them imagined it was. "Everyone seems to think you control a lot of business. They ask a lot of questions."

"I should hope you haven't been putting any ideas in anyone's head. My cousin's, for one."

"I don't need to put any ideas in anyone's head," she said plainly. "Especially not his. He's far too smart as it is. Besides, we both saw you almost lose a finger."

"Talk about more pleasant things," he growled through smiling teeth. She fell into his steps and smiled back genuinely, shelving what she really wanted to say to him, deciding to cut him some slack as this was the opening of his lovely club and, though his hands were sure and steady, even Luca Valari wasn't immune to opening night jitters.

"You want to dance, Hamish Cicero?" Mary's eyes looked over his shoulder at Johnny Wade. Hamish followed her gaze.

"I . . ." He wanted a wink or a nod or a blink or anything from Johnny to solidify a silent contract. He didn't want to stand between any two people who had a past as palpable as they did. Even in the slow few minutes that they ticked through a history, Hamish could feel the pulse of something strong. Maybe it was years of spending so much time alone that made him especially capable of sensing a spark between two people. Maybe his lack of deep personal connections allowed him to see connection between others more transparently. Johnny gave no indication, so Hamish joined Mary.

"You're working!" Schultze bellowed. Hamish hadn't seen him.

"I'm taking a fifteen. Luca won't care."

She strolled from behind the bar and led Hamish to the floor. She smelled like peaches and her hair curled tantalizingly under her ears. *Just take this for what it is, Hamish! Stop thinking that there has to be an intense equation. Just put your arms there on her waist and be grateful that you have a girl in your arms.* Roy Holliday lingered on the first few bars of Gershwin before accelerating the pace. A lover remembering every little nuance. The way she sipped her tea. Almost-love. Hamish would have found it sad if Holliday's band didn't keep the tempo so snappy. As one of Luca's cigarette girls, Mary had traded suspenders and boy shorts for a reddish dress of the same palette as Reggie's. It warmed her cheeks.

"You're good," Mary said happily, holding tightly to Hamish.

"Thanks!"

"How did you learn?"

"I practiced." Maisie. The Palais Royale. Nights of imperfect precision. Wasn't that what swing was? He took a beat. A breath. And she fell into his lead. Smiling. Perfectly trusting him. He smelled alcohol on her breath.

"You're not bad yourself." Somewhere Hamish knew Luca was watching. Happy that he was taking his advice. "Though I wonder what Luca would say if he knew you imbibed on your shift."

"We're celebrating." She giggled. "He

won't mind. Best boss in the city."

Hamish whirled her out a moment, enjoying the buoyancy and pull in his arm as he looped her back toward him. "But he also wants a perfectly run establishment."

"Are you going to rat me out, Hamish Cicero?" Her eyes were saucers as she blinked up at him, stalling their movement for a moment, the crowd around them making him dizzy with the swirl around their pause.

"No." The rhythm found a faster pulse and the trumpet wailed.

Reggie leaned against the bar. Johnny Wade rattled an olive onto a transparent stick and slid the drink to Brian MacMillan.

"Sitting this one out?" she asked, accepting a glass of sparkly wine from Johnny's partner, a blond kid who may not have had Wade's clean-cut looks but had his own rakish, confident charm.

"People keep cutting in on me." Brian's smile was sheepish. Charming, really. "I don't have any of their — how shall we say it — cocksure confidence?"

"But you're in the business of nightclubs." Reggie swooshed her glass up to the light.

"Not just nightclubs. I am learning the family trade. My father is the one who has invested all of the money. I am merely trying on a new profession for size."

"And how do you like it so far?"

"Well, I have been able to visit nightclubs and dance with pretty girls. So I have no complaints in general. Though Luca Valari seems to be more attuned to the success of his club than other men I have met in his position. So many throw hundreds of thousands of bucks around as a bit of a gamble and expect the chips will fall into place." A rowdy couple jostled his glass suddenly. "Mr. Valari assures that even the night before the opening night is planned within an inch of its life."

"Down to the champagne." She raised her wineglass slightly.

"Precisely. A wiser group of investors would have encouraged him to settle for less expensive brands for a trial run."

Reggie's mind's eye sojourned to the dungeon-like cellar and the riches therein.

Brian accepted another drink and then another, and by the time Schultze meandered along asking for Mary, he was talking too loudly about how Luca wouldn't let him in on the ground floor.

Reggie strained to hear, but Schultze was vociferously demanding a drink of Johnny Wade and the band was loud, the drums and trombones in a competition to out-improvise themselves, and she lost the gist of the conversation.

"Do I finally get a dance with you now?" Hamish appeared, his voice slightly tripping over his *d*'s. He looked tired but happy, slicked hair breaking free of its gel, one rebel strand a lazy comma over his shining forehead.

"Finally."

She stepped to the middle of the floor, the clarinet blaring legato through a few perambulatory bars while the drum slowly layered, thrumming softly through a mounting persistence, the trumpeter roaring whimsically overtop even through the modifying effect of its mute. Reggie's smile stretched so wide her cheeks hurt, and not just from the carnivalesque selection on the band's stands. The rhythm and the effect of the wine. Nothing was quite like the magic of an extended hand. Being picked out of a crowd — floral arrangements of girls in silk and shine and dripping with diamonds, lips russet and eyes bright — and led chosen to the middle. And suddenly a song was just for you: matching your passion and rippling through you as you fell into steps you knew but were new, somehow.

She had never danced like this before. The

careful three-quarter world of roses and lace gave way to a pulsating cadence that set her heart on fire and made her think she was floating on air. She was pulled and spun and her head was ablaze. Schultze and Luca and MacMillan made her color within the lines and connect the dots. But with Hamish there was a curious sense of oneness. They were on the same page and she had a preternatural idea of where he was going to step next. He held her so tightly, no shudder through his hands. Just a grip that reassured her as their eyes connected in the firefly light of the dark club that he wouldn't let her go. She closed her eyes, squinting them tightly, and let go — through the smoke and the noise.

It wasn't like dancing with Maisie at all. *At all.* He looked at her. Really looked at her. His feet could function quite well on their own, taking the rhythm in stride, with a confidence he so rarely felt. Real life felt like a sweater with sleeves too long for him. But here, with Regina in his arms, her chin tilted slightly, her eyes closing now and then to taste the moment . . . He wanted to kiss her. He looked around at the explosive carousel of color. Kiss her. No one would notice. He could slow the world and press his lips to hers and make the globe stop spinning. His eyes took a quick sweep of his surroundings. There they were: the men Hamish had seen at the Dragonfly. He instinctively pulled Reggie closer and more tightly than he intended. She gave a little squeal then laughed.

"Any dancing requires a knack for losing inhibition," Reggie said breathlessly as the band broke in between songs. She was clapping but absently. He wasn't applauding at all, just scrubbing at the back of his neck while she wanted the music to keep pulsing. *He almost kissed me.* Or at least she thought he had. Maybe that was just another mind trick, like seeing Vaughan everywhere, the little pings of guilt she didn't quite understand. *Hamish is my friend. I am dancing with my friend. I am dancing just as I did with Luca and Brian MacMillan and that odious Schultze.* And he held her so closely. He smelled like soap and lemons and something else. *Reggie. Snap out of it! There is nothing in your Journal of Independence about falling for another man while your heart is still confused about Vaughan!*
But there was something about the way she felt the sinews of his arm beneath the light cotton of his shirt, the way she sensed

the rhythm of his breathing as they stepped in synchronicity. In time. Swing was a push and pull of buoyancy and athleticism, but also sheer abandon. Abandonment of thought. Abandonment of the conditioned repression starting from your curled-in toes and slipping up the muscles of your calves and all the way into your spine — a straight, spindly line — then up to your neck and over your shoulders. All of it dissolved, a sloppy smile in its stead. You could color inside the lines as much as you liked until the pulse of the drums and riff of the horn pulled you out.

The music started again.

Reggie's hair smelled a little like coconut. He had trouble breathing, but for a completely different reason than usual. He liked how she felt in his arms too. She was just a bit shorter than he was so he could lean protectively over her while allowing her to assert a strength and agility in her movements. And she felt divine. Her soft skin, the satin of her dress, her cheek on his shoulder. He warred between bottling the memory by itemizing every detail and just falling into the starlight of the moment in hopes that it would trail him after. *Kiss her.* Kiss her even though she mentioned a boyfriend from home. Kiss her even though he hadn't kissed a girl before. A reward. For helping. For stepping out. But he didn't. His lips hovered an infinitesimal inch above her mouth before he turned again.

An almost kiss. Quasimodo was only an "almost" in *The Hunchback of Notre-Dame* — maybe he was only an almost too.

Just as he was imagining her in white with a small bouquet and picking names for their children, the band transitioned into a faster tune and a blond man with a stature that towered over them both cut in.

"Regina." His voice cut thick and deep.

Hamish backed up and loosely dropped Reggie's hand.

"Vaughan." Her eyes were wide.

"May I cut in?" he asked Hamish.

Hamish relinquished the floor.

One step and a count and two. Lace curtains wafting with the slightly open window, a world of white and roses. Her mother's condescending tone dripping over the tiles and settling around her, in the wall sconces and plastic plants.

Lift your chin — but not too much. Never let anyone think you are above them. Lower your shoulders. And spin and turn and . . .

Vaughan's embrace took her home. They

270

were chess pieces on a board that instinctively knew their next move. A tapestry woven with years of scrapes and fights and laughs and little moments that veined through her.

It was hard to talk, their conversation relegated to steps on an off-beat. Reggie was sure any words she had would fall to the tile. But she knew that the way she leaned into him was more carefully calculated than the way she had leaned into Hamish.

"You've changed." His lips were at her ear just under the damp curl tickling her lobe.

"I know." *How . . . ? Why . . . ?*

"Dirk Foster has a friend whose girlfriend is one of the cigarette girls. Trust Dirk to find us a swinging party. Who were you dancing with?"

"A friend," Reggie said casually.

Almost. The man with the rower's shoulders and gold-tinted hair was so close to Reggie, almost as close as Hamish had been.

It was wrong for him to think the dance meant anything. Stupid to dream. She had told him about her boyfriend from back home. Still, if Hamish were to kiss her, he would start at her right temple. Flutters of kisses brushing butterfly light over her forehead and over the whisper of her cheekbone, catching a few freckles in soft exploration. He wouldn't press too hard of course. He would treat her like the heirloom crystal vase his mother always warned him to stay clear of. He tingled thinking about it, drew back and worked his teeth over his bottom lip.

She was silk. Milky white. The lithe fall of her arm, the curves shrouded in that scarlet dress spilling liquid light to the floor.

He almost laughed. Absurd! Stammering tongue when he met new people or was caught off guard, heartbeat that didn't need romance to step out of time. What right had he to assume that he could imagine his lips on someone else's? What confidence to think that someone would want to feel the circle of his arms or the tenderness of his touch?

He raked his fingers through his hair. It hadn't really bothered him before. He assumed that he would be alone. He hadn't really imagined a life without anyone, because until this moment, he hadn't imagined a life with anyone. But then, there hadn't been a Reggie before.

An arm stole around his shoulders. "Saw you dancing with Mary Finn earlier. Remind me to dock her wage for the champagne she snuck in the back."

"You saw that too," Hamish said.

"You did your time." Luca's eyes followed Hamish's and landed on Reggie with her new dancing partner. "Tsk-tsk. That really is a shame, Cicero. If I had known she had a young man and he would be prowling around here, I wouldn't have given him admittance."

Hamish grimaced. "Her boyfriend."

"I don't see any ring. Nothing is set in stone. I see the two of you together."

"It's a success, I think." Hamish changed the subject.

"I'm really proud of you, Cicero. Taking a chance."

Hamish smiled. He was happy their little spats and Hamish's suspicions didn't carry into Luca's happy tone. "I am so glad you found something to excel at, Luca."

"Do you need anything? A drink?" Luca dabbed at his forehead with a silk kerchief.

Hamish shook his head. The silver top of Schultze's walking stick caught the transient glow of the spotlight.

"Because Johnny is — Hey! Johnny!"

Johnny Wade was distracted. "We're out of orange bitters."

"I could find someone to run down for you."

"I need a moment alone."

Johnny strolled in the direction of the cellar.

"Was the light fixed then?" Hamish asked.

"You're the height of mystery, Hamish DeLuca," Schultze cut in. "You appear so calm. So innocent."

Hamish didn't know how to respond. So he didn't.

Eventually Schultze moved in the direction of a woman to this point unfamiliar to Hamish: ringlets and dimples and a bow mouth and, like Mary Finn, several years younger than Schultze himself.

Hamish and Luca sidled over, leaving room at the bar for Brian MacMillan, who pushed damp hair from his perspiring forehead. "Where's your girlfriend?" He leaned over the bar into Johnny Wade, who was back and polishing a glass.

"Who?"

"Mary Finn. I saw you getting cozy with her." The longer Hamish listened, the easier it was to make out the fluid slur to Brian's tone. He was a few sheets to the wind by now.

"You're the cousin, right?"

"Hamish DeLuca. We met the other —"

Brian didn't care. "Mary must know something about who is at the center. All of them." He waved his arm. "Schultze, Luca.

They are all in on something. Even Luca's driver. My father made me get involved, and now I want a contingency plan."

"I don't understand."

"Someone is rumored to hold information that could make their lives easier. At the expense of others."

Hamish chose his words carefully. "Certainly if my cousin were involved in some organization, I would have noticed. He's my closest friend and we have been living together for a few weeks now. It sounds as if you are listening too much to what you are hearing. The smoke and martinis might be going to your head."

Brian pounded his glass on the bar for another drink. "You sound so — what's the word? — clinical. I am not visiting my pharmacist!"

Johnny turned to the other bartender, holding up a bottle to show his unavailability.

Brian's glass was filled and Hamish turned away, focusing on the band. He could almost see their outlines through the haze of smoke.

"Another drink?" Johnny Wade asked.

Hamish nodded and held up his empty glass.

■ ■ ■ ■

The liquor flowed as freely as the tongues of men wooing women across the dance floor.

The first bars of "Bei Mir Bistu Shein" sped up. Roy Holliday worked the crowd with the most popular tunes of the day and a band that followed the tone of the evening: one minute setting a furious pace, then swinging languidly into the easy pulse of a slow dance.

The spotlight trailed through the mist of smoke, bringing Luca into focus. Shrouded in shadow, dragging at his cigarette, back erect, commanding the room.

Reggie found Hamish next. His feet shuffled in rhythm with a Porter tune, his hands on either side of a stranger's waist: the dance had all the fireworks of a chaperoned grade school dance.

She joined Vaughan for a drink near the bar. It was the time of night when many patrons trailed out to the square for a breath of air: to laugh and smoke and press close under streetlights.

"You have no claim on her!" Schultze's voice erupted.

"I don't have time for this," Johnny Wade

snarled. He was clearly looking for something amidst the bottles and accoutrements of his trade. "Bill, you have a flashlight? A candle? Anything?"

Reggie leaned over the bar, listening. Johnny was clearly shaken. Perspiring. Frantic.

"Mr. Valari needs me to do one thing and I can't even find a cursed flashlight." He rammed his hand on the bar top, and a few glasses tremored.

"Can I help?" Reggie asked, ignoring Vaughan's look of surprise.

"The lightbulb in the stupid cellar."

Reggie nearly jumped. "I can help! I can change that. We had an electrician." She wasn't sure whether she wanted to prove to Vaughan she was part of this endeavor or felt a personal sense of responsibility for the evening. Johnny Wade, flustered, shrugged. Bill provided the sought-after light. He passed it to Reggie.

"Be my guest."

"I'll be right back, Vaughan!" she said happily.

"You're going to change a lightbulb? Regina —"

"I work here."

"What?"

Reggie waved the flashlight like a trophy.

"Well, I work for the owner. I'm the secretary."

She suspected as she began maneuvering through the crowd that Vaughan's head was spinning.

It was difficult to make the straight diagonal in pursuit of the cellar door. Women and men stood in clusters around the dance floor, chatting in loud voices, bopping to the beat, extending glasses that almost collided with her nose in their general revelry.

The band sighed into a legato rendition of a Cole Porter tune — so different from the Artie Shaw version that was always on the radio — and for a split second Reggie pretended its lazy pulse didn't take her back into Vaughan's arms. It was dirty pool, this song, with its mournful call to reminiscence. As she stepped through the dim magic of the floor, couples losing themselves in the mystery of the pining bars, she felt the music's power wind around her. As she set her mind on the perfunctory task of changing the lightbulb, she recalled Vaughan's cologne tingling her nostrils and his lips at her ear and the luscious tickle of his breath as he whispered the castles that he would build for her in the sky.

Why did music do that? Play on your weakest moments and slip into your veins and your heart and your mind until you couldn't tell where you left off and the longing began.

It swept her to the top of the stairs where the light was, as she and Hamish anticipated, flickering and buzzing its retaliation against the otherwise perfect evening. Reggie sloped onto the balls of her heels just as the saxophone improvised and embellished a verse of the song. She squeezed the lyrics of longing and love from her mind and focused on her task.

"Regina Van Buren!" She heard her name as she neared the staff door entrance.

"Dirk Foster."

"Geez, doll, you look a sight. What're you doing with that flashlight?"

"Fixing a lightbulb." Luca would think her a hero. She'd tally another win for Reggie Van Buren and her Journal of Independence.

"Huh."

"Where's your girl, Dirk?" Reggie asked. "Never saw you without a girl."

"I was just dancing with Mary Finn."

Reggie's ears perked at the name. Was that woman stepping out with half of Boston?

"She's a cigarette girl here. Just haven't seen her. She disappeared on me."

Reggie bit her lip before anything tripped out.

"I'll see you later," she said to waylay his inevitable questions about why she was here and why she left Vaughan.

Reggie excused herself and opened the door to the basement, a glint in her eye that Luca needed her. At previous parties — the ones attended by Dirk and Vaughan — she was as useful as a Ming vase on a doily in the corner. But here? She was part of the inner mechanism that turned the club into sparkling, shimmering life. Luca had told her there were lightbulbs on a shelf at the top of the stairwell. She flicked on the flashlight, humming Cole Porter while she extracted one. Smiling from wine and light and the night and Vaughan seeing her. *"You've changed."* It was the highest compliment he could pay. The new bulb flickered after she installed it, but she bit her lip and fiddled with it, remembering how her trick of loosening it slightly at the top had given her success the night before, and then the dim cellar opened to her clearly. She turned one last time, her smile fizzling. She slammed her hand over her mouth.

The girl was drooling on Hamish's jacket, just over the pocket square. *Look at a girl, approach a girl, talk to a girl.* They were midway through a clarinet wallowing in "Someone to Watch Over Me" and he worried his partner was asleep on his bespoke shoulder. She had been nearly three sheets to the wind when she wound her arms around his neck and propelled him to the floor. He had been midway through a sip of Coke and the surprise fizzed the soda into his nostrils.

"Ssoooo nice," she mumbled into his shoulder. Hamish quivered. He attempted to gently disentangle himself as the trumpet mournfully wailed the last bars. The applause began, Hamish faltering through a clap, hands still full of the sleepy girl. The next number began, and even though it was of a faster tempo, she clung to him, swaying. Hamish let his eyes roll. Revelers bordered the walls like an extravagant garnish, their baubles and beads catching the light. He thought he saw two familiar faces during his scan. His throat stung involuntarily. The men from the office at the Dragonfly: Mark Suave and the other one. He wanted to storm over and run Mark into the wall for the way he had startled Reggie. Hamish bit his lip and tightened his grip on the girl, if only to keep his hand from shaking. When he heard his name over and over again, he wondered if his mind was playing tricks on him. The lights were low and the music could swoon anyone into believing things. But then there was a flash of scarlet from the direction of the Employees Only staircase, and just as Hamish untangled himself from his dance partner, Reggie took her spot, throwing her arms around him and holding tightly.

She sputtered his name a few times.

"Reggie, what happened?"

She mumbled something into his lapel.

Hamish's chest constricted. If it was that fellow with the rower's shoulders . . . If someone had . . . He couldn't even mentally finish the train of thought. He held her a moment. She was smaller than usual, curling into him like a tiny bird, and he wanted her to stay safe and sheltered in his arms forever if need be. Finally she pulled away, face splotchy, makeup smudged with the intensity of her tears. It was an inopportune time for him to realize that even in this state she still outshone every other woman in the club.

"C-come here. Y-you have t-to . . ." She sniffled the end of the sentence, her composure gone.

She held tightly to his arm with both hands, dragging him in the direction of the

Employees Only sign. She waited for him to push the door open, cowering into his shoulder. The light was flickering again.

Hamish reached up and held the bulb in place to stop the blinking. Reggie's grip tightened, her nose soiling the fabric of his shirt with sniffles. He morbidly spared a thought for the cleaning and pressing it would need after not one girl but two made a damp impression on his shoulder.

Then Hamish saw. At the bottom of the stairwell, Mary Finn sprawled at an unnatural angle, haloed by a growing pool of blood.

Chapter 17

It had to have been adrenaline. There was no other way Hamish was ready to sprint down the stairs. Hamish fully expected his hand to shake and his chest to tighten. When his nerves didn't react, he figured Mary Finn's corpse had startled them still.

He didn't want to leave Reggie in case whoever had done this was still in the area. He dragged her whimpering down the stairs, stopping two steps before the floor, eyes lingering on the corpse, his arm tightening on Reggie as he surveyed Mary. She'd fallen backward or else she would have been facing the other way. But there was blood underneath the pantheon of curls over her forehead.

The muted footsteps overhead and Reggie's sobs sparked him into action. They couldn't be here. But he wanted a closer look.

"Wait," he said.

"What?" She shuddered.

"Oh heavens," he breathed. Though the most injurious impact was at her head, Hamish saw a raw band of pink straight across her neck. He used his free hand to rub against the same still-tender spot on his own neck. His thoughts spiraled to the men he'd noticed on the dance floor.

"Hamish," she squeaked. "There's someone —" Reggie's grip tightened. Tighter. Tighter. Footsteps, and not from above.

Hamish felt ill when the shadow became recognizable. And two figures behind him. One that startled Hamish: *Luca. With Schultze's walking stick and Mark Suave not far behind.*

Hamish kept Reggie close as they tiptoed upstairs to the sights and sounds now gaudy and garish. He was in shock. Or else he would have flown down the stairs and ripped the stick from Luca's clutch.

"The police!" Reggie shouted to the milling group smoking and reveling nearest the now closed employee door. "Someone has to call the police!" Her voice compensated for the din. "The police! Call the police!"

Hamish was nauseous. They would call the police, and Luca was there, and —

"I should have . . . I should have . . . ," he

repeated into Reggie's ear.

"What's this racket?" Tom Schultze limped over.

Hamish looked at Schultze, then in the direction of the door. There was a dead woman at the bottom of the stairs and Tom Schultze was without his cane because Luca had it.

When Reggie detached herself, he felt it before seeing it, a damp spot on his shoulder imbued with the impression of her. She blinked around.

"She's dead!" she told Schultze blandly. "And your stick! Your stick!" She didn't mention Luca at all.

"Shhh, Reggie."

"Dead? Who's dead?" a bystander said far too loudly, and soon they were flooded with slurred questions and stirring commotion.

"Mary Finn," supplied Hamish uneasily, her name recalling a life drained of blood.

"What?" Schultze whitened.

"Don't tell me you didn't know!" Reggie jabbed at his shoulder with a weak index finger.

"Get the police!" a man shouted. "Some-one is dead!"

Hamish's shoulder might as well have been a magnet, she was so reluctant to be pulled from him. But when Vaughan parted the crowd, something stirred inside her and with it the safety of home. She let his broad shoulders engulf her, tasting the tang of his cologne as he led her away, forcefully working his way through the milling crowd in pursuit of a glass of water.

"Let's get you home."

Reggie surveyed the bar with swollen eyes. Johnny Wade had been replaced by a short redheaded man whose proficiency made up for his lack of Wade's beguiling charm. *Where is Johnny? He'll be devastated by the news of Mary. If I hadn't offered to go and check the lightbulb, then . . .* Vaughan handed her a glass of water and commanded she sip slowly.

"Dirk." The name bubbled from her suddenly.

"What?"

"Dirk Foster. He knew Mary."

"Reggie, this is hardly the time."

"When *is* the time, Vaughan? A girl is dead at the bottom of the stairwell. Dirk was *just* there."

"You've suffered a shock, darling."

"Hamish!" She looked around for him. Hamish would be wondering about it. He would know.

"Let's get you a taxi."

"No. I should stay here."

"Darling, the police and the press will overflow this place, and you don't want to be caught in the middle of anything."

"But I am in the middle of it," Reggie said tremulously. "I f-found her."

"You're a Van Buren. There is protocol. I am sure any upstanding officer will recognize a woman of your breeding cannot be interrogated like some riffraff. You require delicacy." His fingers gently cupped her elbow.

Reggie shook her head. "I'm going to stay."

"Vaughan!" Dirk Foster cut through the commotion. "We have to leave. I'm already on shaky footing with my father, and a nightclub with a murder —"

"But you knew her." Reggie sounded like a ghost of herself.

"What? Reggie, what are you saying? Dirk . . . she's in shock."

"The police will need to see you, Dirk."

"Is she serious?" Dirk laughed darkly. "Come on, if Reggie wants to stay here and pander to the coppers, she's welcome to it. I will spare myself the notoriety."

"You go," Reggie said, a wave of exhaustion overtaking her.

"Reg, I can't leave you."

"My friend Hamish will see me home. I have a car waiting. Honest, Vaughan."

Vaughan seemed unsure and she was gifted a look familiar from the near past. "You're coming with me," he said with finality.

Reggie pushed him back. "No. I am not." A memory surged through her. Vaughan tugging her into the middle of her parents' party. The same familiarity that tugged Vaughan at Dirk's insistence.

Hamish banged his head against the wall. He only had a small space of it, just to the side of the Employees Only entrance. The nightclub sounds shifted and stretched. After the din of the band, the relative silence was louder than the previous noise.

Luca appeared then. Hamish's heart sank. There was blood on his hands, and he was trying to wipe it off with his kerchief.

"L-Luca, what happened?" His voice wouldn't rise above a whisper no matter how he forced it.

"Wrong place at the wrong time." Luca fashioned a smile that again failed to reach his eyes. He was clearly shaken, his dark skin unnaturally pale. But he would play Luca, ever the consummate professional. Unfazed.

"B-but you have Mr. Schultze's walking stick and . . ." Hamish looked around. "Where's Mark Suave? He was with you. His friend too. Luca! You have to say something. Where did they go? Did you try to stop them?" Hamish grabbed Luca's sleeve and held tight.

"Not now, Cic. When the police come, you stay silent," Luca growled.

"I can't do that." Hamish ground his teeth. "I went to get Reggie and both of us saw . . . We were . . ."

"Well, Valari." Ben Vasser's unmistakable baritone rang out and he appeared at Luca's elbow. "Fine kettle of fish. First night of your club and already a disaster." Hamish followed his study of Luca's pale face and then the blood streak on his bespoke jacket and then the smear of blood on his hand.

"I didn't do it, you know."

"It looks like something else entirely." Vasser's long nose pointed in the direction of an officer carrying out Schultze's bloody walking stick.

"Accidents happen," Luca said shortly.

"We're going to have to take you in."

Hamish wanted to intervene. To do something. To run downstairs and uncover whatever had truly happened. But he froze.

One of Vasser's men approached, detaching his handcuffs from his belt and linking Luca's arms behind his back.

"Go home, Cicero. Answer their questions and go home. Get a good night's sleep. Take care of my club. It'll be all right."

The cops edged Luca along, but he looked back over his shoulder. "You're fine, Cic. Trust me."

The crowd parted, spreading around and past him while he stood in place, jostled a little by the river of satin and silk, gossip and laughter still ringing out in little spurts. Then Luca was gone.

"I have the car, Mr. DeLuca." Phil materialized.

Hamish felt seasick with the sudden wave of people whooshing by him in the direction of the exit. "I-I have to find Miss Van Buren and —"

Phil turned abruptly. "I'll be outside with the car."

Hamish ran his shaking hand over his face. Was this what he got for leaving home? For being foolish? A disaster of a summer, complete with the opening of a club with underhanded investors, his cousin's probable involvement with a criminal organization, as Brian MacMillan had hinted, and now his cousin's arrest?

"Hamish?" Reggie's voice shuddered

behind him. He turned and saw her, face white from more than powder, wringing her hands, the red manicure of her nails blood-like against the ivory of her fingers. Where was Vaughan Vanderlaan? Shouldn't he have been pressing Reggie close and comforting her?

"Reggie." Her name was all he could muster.

"I'm sorry, Hamish. Is there anything I can do?"

"You just stumbled on a corpse," he blurted. "I should be asking you the same thing."

"Well, you look like one." She took his right hand and squeezed. "I'm sure Luca didn't do it."

"Of course he didn't do it."

"I'm just trying to —"

Hamish exhaled. "I know." He retrieved his tuxedo jacket he'd removed for dancing and handed it to her. She draped it around her shoulders.

"So?"

"So what?"

"What are we going to do about it?" Her voice dropped to a whisper.

"You're shivering."

She pulled his jacket more tightly around her dress.

"I think I should have Phil drive you home. Or perhaps you arranged transportation with Mr. Vanderlaan?"

"I'm not going home tonight," she said with finality.

Hamish startled. "Is Mr. Van—"

"Vaughan left."

Hamish felt a stir of rage. Didn't this Vanderlaan fellow want to protect Reggie? She had just witnessed something awful. Hamish reached out and tugged at the sleeve of the jacket around her shoulders. Her blood-red nails gripped the lapels.

"My landlady won't accept my showing up after one in the morning." She shivered. "I could scale up the drainpipe, but it wouldn't be easy in this getup." She gave a weak smile.

"You can come home with me," he suggested.

"Even after the shock of tonight, trust Hamish DeLuca to fall back on his gentlemanly manners."

Hamish gripped her arm on an impulse. "I have another idea. Come on." They walked a few steps before he reached behind to brush her arm and make sure she was behind him. They escaped through the back door and into the alley where he had leaned his bicycle. Hamish stretched one leg over the crossbar.

"Hop on," he said, while Reggie's jaw dropped.

"In this dress?"

"I can't leave you here and I don't want to talk to Phil. There's no way I'll sleep tonight and I doubt you will either after what we just saw. We'll go to the office."

"Are you sure?" Reggie looked around.

"It's just a dress, Reggie. Do you really want to stay here?"

She shrugged. Then assessed the width of the handlebars. "You're going to have to make sure I don't fall off."

"I won't let you fall."

Her shivering had subsided. Reggie wriggled out of Hamish's suit coat and laid it across the front bar of the bicycle. She smoothed her satin skirt beneath her then hopped on before promptly sliding back off, her shoe catching in the spoked wheel.

She looked back at Hamish and exhaled. "Well."

"Sorry. We can —"

"You just put this idea in my head, don't take it back out again." She stepped out of her shoes and dangled them from her two forefingers, then she hopped back on, holding tight, latching her feet on either side of the front wheel and turning her head over her shoulder so the lights from the busy street outlined her high cheekbone and bright eyes. "Just don't let me fall," she breathed.

Hamish could almost taste her breath. She smelled like peppermint and the cigarette smoke they both trailed from inside. For a moment the world slowed to a halt: no Luca, no murdered girl. Just Reggie and Hamish. He blinked a few times, then reached in his pocket with the hand not steadying the bike and settled his glasses on his nose. Then he pushed off. Her extra weight made the ride slower, and her nearness forced him to concentrate twice as hard. He had pedaled Maisie home dozens of times, but Maisie never made him forget his way like Reggie, with her little shrieks and laughs that bubbled above the tragedy of the night and the slight wind they created with the whoosh of the wheels.

When they made it to Cross Street, leaving the dim lights of Haymarket Square behind, the only stragglers on the dark street a meowing cat and a man walking a large black dog, Hamish slowed to a halt.

Reggie followed his lead and hopped off. "Oh!"

"What?"

"Cold cement." She adjusted her dress

and finagled her shoes on, leaning on the unbalanced bicycle. It teetered and so did she. Hamish's reflexes were quicker and he caught her around the waist, letting the bike clang to the ground. The black dog howled. Reggie smoothed her skirt.

"Well, see? I needed my smelling salts after all. Weak in the knees after stumbling."

Her attempt at lightness didn't work. He leaned down, picked up the bike, and rolled it beside them the rest of the way to the office.

It was highly inappropriate. Her father would have polished his hunting rifle, her mother wringing her ivory fingers and bemoaning her "thankless child," wondering, "Where did I go wrong to have a girl . . . my Regina . . . who would stay an entire night alone in a dingy office with an unmarried man?"

They would pray for her on Sunday. The minister more than happy to make it a declaration from the pulpit with the other requests. The people surrounding the family pew eyeing Reggie as if her rebellion might be contagious and shoving their daughters against the hard wood backs of the pews so they wouldn't catch it.

Hamish was rolling up his shirtsleeves and

loosening his collar. His hair was damp from the warm night, and when he ran his fingers through it, it stuck up a little. Reggie smiled. She sank into her usual chair and stretched out her arms.

"Well, this is a scandal. Me alone with a handsome young man." Hamish looked up quickly, sending his glasses down his nose. "Yes, Hamish, handsome" — she smiled at him — "and after finding a corpse at a nightclub."

"I guess it was an impulsive suggestion." Hamish took two steps so far backward she was worried he would tumble into the wall and the bicycle he had leaned there.

Reggie laughed. "Come on, Hamish. I know you don't bite." She motioned toward the chair opposite the desk. Hamish sat and she noticed how tired he was under the lamp above the desk. He nudged his glasses up and ran his hand over his eyes. He had long fingers. Had she noticed that before? They were rather graceful. She yawned. She was clearly exhausted and her mind was focusing on the wrong things . . .

"Why didn't the police detain us for questions?" Hamish asked. "The only person Vasser was interested in was Luca. Not Mark Suave."

Reggie picked at the corner of the desk

with her finger. "Maybe they set up Luca to take the blame?"

Hamish nodded. "Crossed my mind."

For someone who had recently encountered a corpse, Reggie was surprisingly calm. She supposed she was still in a latent state of shock, more worried for Hamish in the moment than she was about herself. He went silent, staring at the window above her shoulder, his face a cross between worry and sadness. "Luca will be fine, Hamish," she said quietly. "He's probably charming the prison guards into a comfortable suite at the Park Plaza."

She felt terrible for him. More so than she ever would for Luca. Luca would find a way out of jail, but Hamish couldn't find a way out of his mind, or his loyalty to his stupid cousin.

She must have fallen asleep eventually, for when she woke in the predawn, rubbing her stiff neck, her head had been cradled in her folded arms and Hamish's jacket was around her shoulders. She sat up, remembering where she was and what had happened. The memories sleep had dulled. She looked around. Had he left her there alone? She shivered and blinked. He had switched the light off and the only light seeped in from the streetlights through the window.

298

She looked around in the shadows.

"Hamish," she whispered, her voice uneven. She leapt up and dashed across the floor in her bare feet, slowly opening the door. The hallway was dark and silent, save for regular breathing below her.

Hamish was slumped beside the doorway. Arms folded over his shirtsleeves, black hair over his forehead, glasses folded beside him.

"Now there's a gentleman," she said softly, impulsively leaning over and brushing her lips over the top of his head before retreating back into the office until dawn.

CHAPTER 18

Throughout the night, Hamish could sense her — on the other side of the door. He wondered what she looked like in sleep. If her lips curved a little or she sighed every time she moved. Reggie kept his thoughts from casting out to Luca like a line to water when he drifted in and out of sleep. And the corpse. Of course, the corpse. No. *Mary.* The giggly, bubbling girl: flirtatious, pretty.

It wasn't Luca who ended her life, of course. Luca could never shove a woman down the stairs to her death. It was Schultze. He was sure the papers would confirm it. All of the evidence lined up. It was his walking stick. The one with the rattlesnake, dormant and convicting. His fingers trembled a little. But he had nothing to worry about. Nothing. Or maybe it wasn't Schultze. That Mark Suave fellow knew how to press a stick against one's neck to cut off the circulation and damage the windpipe. Maybe it was him? Hamish yawned, but his mind was racing. Even when his body was tired, his brain found new levels of worry to exercise. But he would reserve the worry for sleep. He would train his mind to focus on the facts of tonight's events while he was alone, the door barring him from the office and from her. He would use this time to revisit every last detail, because once the morning came and Reggie awoke, he would be what she needed.

When he finally opened his eyes to the sunlight, Nate was standing over him. "What have we here?" he asked with a smile. "You look like a lost puppy." He reached down and helped Hamish to his feet. "It was all over the wireless this morning," Nate said brightly. "You hiding from the police?"

"The papers?" Hamish's voice cracked sleepily. He focused on the noise of the long line on the floor below. The Temporary Employment Agency must have opened. "What time is it?"

"Eight o'clock. I figured I'd better get here early in case Reggie needed a shoulder to cry on." He looked over Hamish's rumpled clothing. "But you might already have that covered?"

Hamish ignored him, rapping on the door before entering. Reggie was awake and playing with the radio dial.

"Only Luca Valari could be detained for murder while his name is lauded," she said sourly.

"Regina Van Buren, I suppose I could come up with an even more scandalous headline," Nate teased. "Society girl found in North End office all night with young Canadian lawyer."

"Oh, hush up," Reggie snapped, then yawned. "You know nothing happened. Go be useful and get us coffee, anything from Mrs. Leoni's, and the papers." She looked over her creased satin dress. "Come to think of it, can you ask Mrs. Leoni if she has anything from her daughter that I can wear?"

Hamish looked tired but a little less conspicuous in his evening wear. Removed of his bow tie, cummerbund, and jacket, his glasses on and his braces snapping beneath his crooked fingers, he wouldn't stand out as quickly.

Nate returned several moments later with two bags from Leoni's. "Mrs. Leoni heard about what happened. She says it is all on the house."

Reggie pounced on the packages of fresh

bread and rolls. In the other bag Nate handed her was a dress several years out of date but sure to serve its purpose until she was able to get home and change. Something she was in no mood to think about now.

Soon Reggie excused herself to the lavatory down the hall, and when she returned, her face was completely devoid of the previous night's makeup, her hair was repinned, and her figure was hidden in the folds of a too-big dress.

Nate was reading the headlines aloud to Hamish, who had used the sink in the corner of the office to slick his hair back from his head. "Club Owner Suspected in Murder," "Cigarette Girl Found Dead," "Corpse at the Flamingo." But the headlines weren't nearly as catchy or memorable as the purple prose embroidering the success of the opening night. The scandal and the passion surrounding Mary's death, the eyewitnesses who recognized the free-spirited cigarette girl from similar establishments (including an interview with Charles Galbraith from the Dragonfly), the sizzling mystery — all framed the club in glittering allure. If Luca wanted publicity, he got it. And then some.

Later, after leaving the office to get coffee at a nearby shop, Reggie and Hamish returned to find Mrs. Leoni waiting outside.

"Nathaniel is not here now. My friend Mrs. O'Connell, she has been turned out of her house."

Reggie swallowed. She was tired and even Mrs. Leoni's voice was like nails on a chalkboard.

The phone's jangle welcomed her through the door. A stack of telegrams may as well have been gift-wrapped on her desk, so neatly were they piled.

Hamish's eyes were glazed. "If we stay here, we'll fall asleep," he said, watching Reggie blink the telegrams into focus. He read a few of them over her shoulder: many praised Luca on his publicity; others quoted headlines. He stretched. "Let's go back to the club." His eyes had snagged on a telegram that hyperbolically used *salacious* and *duplicitous* in the same line.

He shoved his hand in his pocket and retrieved a fistful of bills, handing them to her as he suggested they hail a cab. "You pay. Luca's been footing the bill for almost everything and I am still learning to use

American currency."

In daylight, the Flamingo sighed like the wrapping and bows beside an open Christmas present. Unsparkling, the magic of the night replaced by littered newspaper, sandwich wrappings, and cigarette butts. Reggie was at Hamish's shoulder, feeling the tension in his muscles when her arm brushed his. Men with press cards tucked into their hatbands smoked and talked and draped over the red partitions encircling the club.

The large bulbs on their cameras winked in the sun.

"In *Winchester Molloy* policemen and investors can be bought," Reggie said in a sly undertone. "Surely reporters can."

Hamish aligned reporting with a high standard of ethics introduced to him by his father. Ray DeLuca never would have accepted money under his journalistic oath. But this was a new world spreading before him — far from the confines of Winslow, Winslow, and Smythe. Anything could happen. Anything would happen.

Schultze spotted them and waved at them to come through, so they finagled through the reporters and the two police officers barricading the street.

"Hey, who are you?" A man with a fedora more off his head than on smacked his gum at Reggie and Hamish.

"We're affiliated with the F-Flamingo." Hamish tripped over an evasive sentence. He was exhausted and nervous and sad. Her heart tugged.

"Well, then you won't mind answering a few questions."

Hamish shook his head. "I have no comment."

The reporter stopped him by moving his foot in a swift, practiced step. "You mean you weren't here?" *Snap, snap* went the gum in his mouth.

"I have no comment," Hamish repeated a little more forcefully, though he was sure it sounded like little more than a kitten attempting a roar.

Reggie, more accustomed to nosy society reporters, squirmed ahead. "He said no comment. I say no comment." She waved her hand.

The reporter crossed in front of them. "Interesting. You're hiding something."

"Be gone, you odious, gum-smacking toad," Reggie snarled.

They pushed through a few other reporters and made it inside. A few police were prowling and one photographer had been granted access beyond the border. Ben

Vasser recognized Hamish and waved him over.

"You're Valari's cousin or something? Very well. This place will be ready to open again tonight. Can't do much with an unfortunate accident." He flipped his notebook closed. "Unless either of you saw anything suspicious?" He asked the question in such a tired, plain voice that Hamish wasn't ready to present anything to him. He wasn't taking this seriously. Just another through-the-motions day on the job. Hamish looked at Reggie. She gave the slightest ghost of a headshake before averting her eyes. She didn't want anyone to know what she suspected.

"It's a tragedy," Reggie said. "She was such a free-spirited girl."

Vasser nodded and let them through. "We've covered about as much as we are going to here."

Out of his sight line, Hamish and Reggie exchanged a glance. The Employees Only door was open a smidgeon and they crossed in its direction. Hamish felt Reggie shiver beside him.

"What's wrong?"

"If it isn't an accident," she whispered, "then maybe whoever did it returned to the scene of the crime."

Hamish took a quick glance around the club. Roy Holliday was just moving his band in for a quick rehearsal before the night set. Schultze was now engaged in a solemn discussion with Vasser, eyes narrowed. Schultze looked over Vasser's shoulder and his eyes caught Hamish's for a moment.

"I don't recall my cousin passing the torch to you in the event of an unprecedented circumstance." Hamish was careful with his words.

Schultze snarled. "You sound like a lawyer, you know that? Should've stayed where you were. I invested a lot in your cousin, so with or without him, we'll keep this show going. Even if Vasser and his men want to sniff around for a while."

"Then we can sniff around too." Reggie brushed by.

"We'll be quick and careful," Hamish added.

Once they were standing on the small landing on the other side of the door, he steadied Reggie with a soft grip on her elbow. "Guess they didn't need to keep Schultze's walking stick for evidence," he whispered.

"No one is treating this as a crime." Reggie shuddered, her face white.

"I'm sorry, Reg," Hamish said. "I should

have realized this would be hard for you."

She shook her head. "It's all right. We just need to find out what happened."

Reggie turned to the wall and ran her fingers over the pocked cement.

"Wait, what's that?" she asked. Hamish followed her sight line to a speck of blood tattooing the wall. "So she was bleeding before she fell, or else . . ." Reggie gave a low whistle.

"How likely is that?" Hamish pressed his fingers into his hairline. He should have been paying closer attention. Last night — last night he was watching Reggie when he might have seen someone with Mary. Mary with Schultze. Schultze leaving his walking stick. Mary having words with Johnny Wade. Schultze. Hamish following Mary to the dance floor.

"I danced with her," he said gently.

"I saw."

Hamish clenched his fist. He could still see the gruesome angle and blood from the impact of her head on the cement floor when he closed his eyes, the way her neck was turned and surely broken. The raw ribbon against the white of her skin impressed by force. Nothing about her neck injury could possibly allow anyone to think it was just an accident. She'd felt so nice in his arms. Warm and alive.

"In the pictures," Reggie was saying, "something means everything."

"This isn't a picture. One of your movies," Hamish said shortly, too tired in the moment even to check his tone and filter it through politeness. He turned toward the stairwell. Then looked back, his face softening. "I'm just going to go and take another look."

"I'll meet you outside."

Hamish was right. It wasn't *The Thin Man.* It wasn't the pictures. Even in the pictures there were suspects for every mystery. Some usual. Some unexpected. Some like the villains Winchester Molloy apprehended, twirling their mustaches and working for their own nefarious gain. Others the least likely to be suspected.

"You all done here, miss?" Ben Vasser mopped at his brow with a handkerchief.

Reggie nodded. "So the investigation is closed then? Business as usual?"

"I never should have let you kids in here. But Valari is fond of his cousin. He talks of him all the time."

"You seem to hold great regard for Luca Valari."

"He's a powerful ally for us. I don't want

to bring any more notorious attention to his establishment than is necessary."

"How is he a powerful ally?" Reggie asked, wondering what Luca might have that the police could possibly want.

"My colleagues in the Chicago department cite more than one occasion when he was able to help them apprehend a shady businessman or two. When we detained him, he merely had us make a few phone calls and it was confirmed. If some crazy girl wants to drink too much and fall down a flight of stairs, then I'm not going to implicate Luca Valari. We asked him some questions, I am doing a thorough follow-up for the paperwork, and that's that."

Reggie laughed bitterly. "How wonderful to have the world on a platter."

Vasser lowered his lids. "As I understand it, you're Regina Van Buren. All over the papers. A girl of your breeding" — he seethed the word — "would know quite a lot about having the world on a platter." Vasser turned. "I am sure you can see yourself out."

Reggie strolled over the echoing floor. Just because you had the opportunity for entitlement didn't mean you should take advantage of it.

She crossed through the open doors to

wait for Hamish and ran straight into a swarm of reporters: fidgeting with their camera bulbs, spilling out to the street.

"Miss Van Buren!" called the first to recognize her, adjusting the press card tucked in his fedora. "Miss Regina Van Buren. You're a long way from home. What are you doing returning to the scene of the crime?" His questions and recognition perked the interest of his friends, who soon flocked to her. Even as she studied them in the glaring sun, she imagined what would happen the inevitable moment her name graced the pages of a paper in New Haven, ensuring her parents were mortified and angry. He told her he was from the *New Haven Chronicle* covering the Boston beat — but he started in the local society pages. Blanketing the comings and goings of the suave set, her parents included. She thought of Robert Williams's character in her favorite picture, *Platinum Blonde.*

The door opened a crevice behind her, and as she turned, dozens of expectant eyes looked over her shoulder. With the first bulb flash, Hamish blinked. She gave him a signal behind her back. They were too thrown off by a Van Buren to wonder about him. He was reluctant to leave, inching closer to her.

"Follow my lead," she said through the

side of her mouth. She noticed his hand was balled at his side. The last thing he needed was this new round of questions and scrutiny.

Reggie smiled at each and every one of the tired, anticipating faces. If she couldn't escape, she wouldn't. She would clutch at the moment and give the tea parties and DAR committees something to talk about. She would straighten her shoulders and play a part so ingrained in her makeup it felt like she was a wound-up phonograph knowing exactly what song to play. While Hamish escaped.

"Who's your friend?" bellowed one reporter.

"Driver." Reggie hoped that with his glasses on and his tousled hair over his downturned face, no one would take the time to recognize them from coverage of the club the night before. Her answer satisfied them.

"Were you there when the girl fell down the stairs?"

Reggie let out an exaggerated snort. "Ha! That's no way to talk to a lady!"

"You're no shrinking violet!"

"The police seem to think that Mary Finn's death is best treated as an accident." Reggie didn't wait for a question. "I believe it is best treated as a murder." She conjured a new brand of charm.

Her bold statement erupted their bulbs, and she blinked at the lights popping around her, raising her hand to visor her eyes.

"And what are you going to do about it?" One cheeky journalist tilted his pencil above his notepad.

She added a little giggle. "Why, solve it of course."

CHAPTER 19

Get the girl. Solve the murder. Be the hero of your own story. Over and over again, the words cranked through his mind like a stuck gear. There was a dead girl at the bottom of the stairwell and Hamish had mystery in his blood.

As a kid, Hamish was interested in logic and riddles. He liked puzzles. And now he was faced with one.

Hamish stepped out into a curtain of heat, humidity dampening his collar. Walked and walked down Washington and passed the dome of Faneuil, heading in the direction of the river sparkling under the bridge. Boats bopped in the harbor and their horns mingled mournfully with the usual bustle of a Boston day. The North End embraced him with uneven charm.

What if the ties binding him to this new place with these new people meant something more than just shenanigans with his cousin? What if he was slowly turning the pages of his life to learn the story of these people and this place? His father pulled stories out from their shadows, flashing a light so everyone could see the misfortune and avoidance. Hamish should have done the same for Boston. He *would* do the same for Boston. Perhaps that was why he was there in the first place.

He moved from the North Square and down Hanover Street, which teemed with color and streamers and light, the fountains reflecting prisms of sunlight, the calls and shouts and Babel of dialects echoing around him. Soon he was in the Prado, that red-bricked stretch of solace sandwiched by St. Stephens and Old North Church, and he realized that perhaps in this snug haven of Boston he had found a Court of Miracles like in the book. A place for people establishing a new world — even as men like Schultze and Baskit drained them of what little they had. It was one of the virtues of having lived in a book for so long: his imagination painted its perimeters everywhere. He worried about Reggie, but what was it his father once said about respecting his mother enough to let her choose her own battles?

He picked up his pace, not watching

where he was going and parting a few kids aligning their jump rope for another bout of double Dutch. Laughing and whispering secret jokes to themselves. A language he didn't speak from a world he never knew. He kept his curtains drawn.

One little girl tugged at his sleeve and he looked down with a smile. She waved. He waved back. She asked him his name in Italian. He answered in the same.

Cicero. Cicero. Cicero hiccupping the telegrams. Hamish pressed his fingers to his temples. Then looked up and around with a sudden shudder in case a rogue reporter had trailed him. It was what his father would have done back on the city beat — seeing past the charms of distraction like Reggie and going after the real story.

Luca would eat up the attention. He would have the reporters eating from the palm of his hand and spinning the story in his favor. "It's easy to make people believe you, Cicero. As long as you believe you're the hero of your own story, others can't help but believe it too."

Beneath the office door a sheet of paper peeked out.

Hamish bent and picked it up. A telegram:

FLORENCE (STOP) HE'S BEEN LO-

Cicero.

Hamish settled into Reggie's chair and ran his hands over his knees. He closed his bleary eyes a moment before realizing that if he left them in that state, he would fall fast asleep from the near sleepless night before. He opened them again. There was always more than one explanation for something. That was something he had learned from his mother's occupation. She would sometimes tell him little tricks and tips from her trade before tucking him in. One was that there was more than one path to the same answer, more than one interpretation to any event.

Cicero wasn't just a nickname, nor just a Roman politician from Caesar's time. Hamish recalled his father's newspapers from all major cities fanned over the dining room, Hamish slowing his step on his way to his room after a late night at the library. Al Capone hid in Cicero. A suburb of Chicago. Hamish could almost pinpoint it on a mental map. Wondering why his mind hadn't made the connection earlier.

If Cicero meant the city, then maybe that was the key to unraveling what Luca had left in Chicago.

Luca. He didn't want to think about Luca. But he was everywhere. Even in this office that he left Reggie in for hours every week.

What a horrible mess of logical thinking! For as soon as his mind spiraled out in one direction it snagged on Reggie — Reggie with the button nose and beautiful figure. Reggie with her summery alto voice and her freckles and her smile. Her laugh and her brain and her kind heart. The way her fingers butterflied through his hair, stirring a sensation that offset the chest pains and thumping nausea. But what right had he to assume someone would feel this way about him? Hamish with his shakes and his insecurity.

He belonged in his tower with the bells clanging in his mind. He couldn't offer her protection. He couldn't hope that she would turn to him in trouble when a man like Vaughan Vanderlaan filled any room he entered. There was a chance, his mind chimed, that she felt the same way. That he hadn't imagined her leaning into him with silky smooth eagerness the night they danced. That when she looked his way she did so with the same wistful delight. That when she caught his eyes, she might feel the same aching heart-drop.

He didn't deserve the attention of someone so remarkable. He was awkward and odd and his mind caught in a million directions before tripping through his uneven voice. But that was where the true grace of the matter intervened. If she cared, what was undeserved was a by-the-way.

Winchester Molloy would have gotten the girl by now. Hamish crooked his fingers in his braces.

Reggie arrived, finally, panting but smiling. "Well, I lost them," she said proudly, closing the door behind her. "At least for now."

"I'm sorry for leaving you there."

"Are you kidding? I was just about to thank you."

"Thank you?"

"For letting me fight my own battle. For not jumping in my line of defense. For trusting that I could handle this on my own." She flung her arm out to the office. "I told those reporters I meant to solve this murder." She emphasized the last word while their eyes met. "And I mean to." She swept the room with her gaze. "So this office will now double as the office for a scandalous nightclub and a headquarters for our deduction."

"You mean —"

"Were you not serious last night when you

were telling me about your intrepid private investigator mother and your need to see your cousin's innocence?" She raised an eyebrow.

"Knock, knock." Nate peeked from the open door.

"Hello, Nate." Reggie was catching her breath.

Hamish raised a hand in Nate's direction.

Nate studied him closely. "Glum?"

"My cousin was arrested, they're now writing off a murder as an accident even though I know in my soul it was more than that, and my name is associated with notorious nightclub scandals." Hamish was angry, but not at Nate. He was tired and burned out like a popped lightbulb.

"Is that all?" Nate grinned.

Hamish laughed despite himself. "Petty problems, aren't they?"

Reggie stretched then peered out the window. "They followed us!"

"What?" Nate looked over her shoulder. "We'll go out the back way. Come, come. Nothing that can't be solved by a trip to the top of the world."

"Pardon?" asked Reggie.

Nate didn't respond, just led them through a hallway they had never turned down and then out a back stairwell. "There are rumors Cyrus Dallin's statue of Revere is going to grace our dear Prado." Nate was like a kid on the morning of his birthday. He snatched at any moment to talk about his beloved neighborhood. "Can you imagine, they thought of putting it over in Copley Square! Copley Square, of all places. Tell me, on what part of the great Revere's legendary ride did his steed's hooves ever traipse over Copley Square?"

"I don't know," Hamish said.

Reggie smiled and soon they were in the sunshine and a safe distance from the office.

"Here." Nate grabbed Hamish's elbow and pointed to the mall before them. "Just behind the North Church. It would be glorious. We deserve it. Over here in our little conclave of brick and rubble. To redeem what they tore down a few years ago as 'undesirable.' "

"Tenements, you mean?" Reggie recalled an earlier conversation, her pace matching Hamish's.

Soon the rear of Old North Church was before them, its steeple stabbing the sky. Hamish thought back to his early days in the city — to using it as a compass.

A man stretched his crooked smile wide when Nate approached the front of the church. He waved them in through the grand doors leading to rows and rows of box pews. At the front, an altar was bathed in summer light through the stained glass, teased by the reflection of the overhead chandeliers.

"I want to take my friends upstairs, Harold." Nate's eyes sparkled.

"Anything for you." Harold pointed the way to the staircase. "After what you did for my Mary."

"It was nothing." Nate shrugged.

"You're not afraid of heights, are you?" Nate asked with a wide smile, first to Hamish, then to Reggie. "You just turned green." He nodded at Hamish. "Just take it one step at a time and watch your head." Nate led them up a steep stairwell cloistered on either side by russet brick. Hamish kept his eyes on the back of Nate's head, the pins holding his kippah in place sparkling in the light. Reggie's heels were a light tread behind them.

"Paul Revere was a bell ringer here," Nate said. "They brought all these bells here but no one knew how to ring them or had the time. So there was Revere and the other neighborhood kids."

Hamish watched his shoes a moment. The stairwell grew narrower and higher and the sun blasted from the narrow window on the precipice of another level. He felt more like Quasimodo than ever. He breathed in and out, two fingers wedged in the slight part between the buttons on his shirt. But he kept going.

"There!" Nate said, turning to them both.

Reggie, on the other hand, had no hesitation with the height, sidestepping Hamish and immediately walking out into the sunlight.

When Hamish finally stepped out, staying as near the door as possible, the North End spread before him in tiny flecks of color, pinpricks amidst the rambling red and black shingles, and the tall tower of the Custom House and the cathedralesque dome of Faneuil Hall broadened into the squat grandeur of the State House and the steeple of the Old South Meeting House. Hamish forgot himself a moment, shoved his trembling hands into his pockets, and drank in the city. It elated him. This city. This wonderful city. This canvas of grime and light, of bustle and promise. His breathing steadied.

"You can imagine them swinging a lantern here, just so." Nate stabbed through Hamish's thoughts. "One if by land. Two if by sea."

Hamish nodded. "Your sanctuary?"

Nate smiled and tapped emphatically at his kippah. "Some sanctuaries are for all, wouldn't you say? No matter what religion or race or creed."

Hamish took the vantage the height afforded him. He nodded. "Yes. Sanctuary."

"I know everything about this place." Nate leaned over the rail, startling Hamish.

"Everything looks different up here," Reggie said from beside Nate.

"You're like me, Reggie. You're good at watching people. But I believe in every thread of life's tapestry being sewn in for a purpose."

"You need to come closer, Hamish!" Reggie chided.

Hamish leaned over the rail. Seeing the straight, steep line to the ground, he felt a sudden panic and backed up a step.

"Inside are change-ringing bells. The same bells that live in Notre Dame in Paris.

"It's beautiful, isn't it?" Nate had turned from the Charlestown side and was peering down over Salem Street. "This is my little corner of the world. And from up here you're not really close enough to see the little problems plaguing each and every person. You just see a community."

"You belong here too, Hamish." Hamish

felt a warm light move through him. The side of his mouth turned up an inch toward his cheek.

"Take it from me. You do." Nate opened his arms out to the city as if he could tug it into a tight embrace. "This neighborhood and I are longtime friends, and I can always tell a good apple when I see one. And I can always tell when someone needs a trip to the top of the world." He tapped Hamish's shoulder. "I'll leave you here to conspire." He raised his voice a little. "Reggie, take your time.

"You need to learn how to find your way out." Nate always had pragmatic advice. "So you can always come here if you need to escape."

Hamish took in the view of the city a little longer. He saw one large perspective and not the little nuances of people's ordinary day.

"Penny for your thoughts?"

Reggie was leaning over a little too far and Hamish resisted the urge to reach out and pull her back. "It's funny how you think you know something. You get really familiar with it and then, when you suddenly see it in a different way, it's like you're meeting it for the first time."

She turned, the breeze catching a bit of

her pinned hair. It tickled over her forehead. One strand he wanted to reach out and touch fluttered over the freckles of her nose. She brushed her hair from her face. "Nate loves this neighborhood. He knows every nook and cranny. I had some time to get to know him. Before I met you." She walked over to him and joined him, leaning against the wall. "He loves his history." She looked up at him expectantly. "Does Luca? Is that where you got your nickname? We studied Julius Caesar in school."

Hamish shoved his hands into his pockets. His right fingers were starting to tingle, as if they might begin to tremble. "When I was a kid, I was made fun of a lot. The glasses. The fact that I kept to myself. I don't blame the kids." Hamish dug his shoe into the concrete. "I was always in my own little world. For extra protection. I would memorize all the paragraphs in *Notre-Dame* about the structure and the gargoyles and I would picture myself hidden up there. Protected by the monsters and the saints and the stone. I would imagine what would happen if I stepped out and joined the other kids. Playing stick hockey in the street. And I would imagine them thinking I was nothing but a Quasimodo. I would embarrass myself somehow, or trip over a sentence, or start to panic." He buried his hands deeper in his pockets. "My parents thought it was odd. They tried to force me out of my shell. But Luca . . ." Hamish turned his face up to the sun, past Reggie and over the rooftops and the glistening water. "Luca thought that I was smart. That's all he thought. He was never around enough to see me be awkward or not fit in. He just knew I got good grades and could be anything I wanted. A doctor . . ."

"Or a lawyer," Reggie said softly.

Hamish nodded. "And so he started calling me Cicero. He had heard about him once. Probably, like you, studying Shakespeare." Hamish paused then let out a low breath. "If we are going to confront him, we need something concrete." He didn't know why, but he trusted her. Trusted her enough to tell her his misgivings about his cousin. "Luca can't stand for people to hypothesize. And he remembers everything. We would need a clear strategy."

Reggie pursed her lips. "A long memory?"

"Oh, the stupid things he remembers. From Sunday school. Roman history. The entire roster of the Red Sox." Hamish focused on the rooftops below. It almost felt like he was leaning above the summer and taking a look at it from beyond.

"So someone who would know where all the pieces fit. To ensure that anyone who wanted to take advantage, to use a scheme like the one Nate thinks Baskit and Schultze use to keep slum tenements running . . ."

"While making investments clean through clubs." Hamish hated her train of thought, but he couldn't deny it.

"A good memory would serve someone involved in this kind of thing well."

"And keep it from having to be transferred to paper."

"No paper trail." Reggie whistled.

"No paper trail."

Hamish's pace was slower than usual as he pedaled Hanover until the Custom House and Faneuil Hall and Quincy Market spread familiarly before him. He picked up speed, pumping up the slight hill to Washington Street, holding tightly to the handles. Maybe he was empowered from the perspective high above the city, but something surged through him and he lifted his hands off the bars. The wheels fluttered a little without the usual balance. But soon he grew used to it and spread his arms out a moment. A passing motorist yelled out his window but Hamish ignored him, speeding up. The city was as glorious down here as it had been from up in the steeple, and Hamish smiled despite himself. Despite the night. Despite Luca's arrest.

He put his hands back on the bars just as he swerved past the Parker House, slowing to a gradual stop outside of Luca's building.

Hamish fell asleep the moment he sat on the couch in Luca's sitting room. A deep sleep. When a hand grasped his shoulder, he leapt up, heart racing.

"Easy there, Cicero." Luca plopped at the end of the sofa.

Luca looked tired but relieved. With no pomade in his hair, his black locks fell over his forehead and made him look younger, though Hamish could swear his eyes had aged. He forgot for a moment his anger and suspicion. Instead, he was just Hamish again, Luca showing up when he promised and taking him to a baseball game. His grin spread wide.

"I was so worried. I saw that police officer, Vasser. Reggie and I went to the Flamingo to see if we could find anything that could help you."

Luca chuckled and patted Hamish's arm. "You know I can take care of myself, Cicero."

"I knew they couldn't keep you long. They had no motive or concrete evidence."

"Funny." There was a darkness to Luca's voice. "That almost sounds like a question. Even if they had either, they couldn't keep me."

"Are you out on bail then?"

"Eh? No. Not required." He patted Hamish's knee before springing from the sofa in the direction of his liquor trolley. He poured himself several fingers of whiskey and lifted it to his nose. "Two dry days does not make for a happy Luca." He swirled and sniffed, finally tasting. His face relaxed and a true smile stretched. "Join me? Toast my release from the clink?"

Hamish shook his head. "Publicity has been through the roof."

Luca sipped silently. "Never should have picked up that stupid stick. Schultze! I wouldn't have shoved his mistress down the stairs."

"I know that."

"Of course you do."

"Do you think one of your rivals wanted to see you fail? Charles Galbraith, maybe. From the Dragonfly?"

"You're thinking too much."

"I don't think it was an accident, Luca. When Reggie and I were at the Flamingo, Ben Vasser just let us in. To a crime scene!"

"You look like you slept less than I did."

He smiled distractedly. "Thinking too hard. Let's just go with the police on this one. It was an accident. Don't get your chest all in a knot. I don't want a stuttering, shaking cousin on my hands."

It stung, but Hamish ignored him. "Reggie and I saw her neck, Luca. You were there too. There was some kind of struggle. We went back today and there was blood on the wall. Just at the top of the stairwell. You saw the gash beneath her hairline and the red mark on her neck."

"Cicero."

"You sound tired. I shouldn't have sprung this on you."

"Don't try to placate me."

"I'm not! I just think you must be tired. You were in jail, for heaven's sake. You should go to bed."

Luca was up and refilling his glass. "Don't tell me what to do. And leave this alone. You're not a detective, for pity's sake."

"I just think I could help. If I can help. Reggie and I found her. And I want to solve this. I don't like people linking your name with it." Hamish pulled one of the piled newspapers from the side table.

CLUB OWNER ARRESTED, IMPLICATED IN FLAMINGO MURDER

Hamish held it out to Luca.

"Well, what is it your father always says? A poor headline is dead in the water the moment it drops. I am not implicated at all in an accident."

"An accident!" Hamish spat. "An accident? You can't believe that."

Luca's eyes were bleary. He rubbed his palm over them. "Clearly our electrician wasn't up to the task." He yawned. "It was a quick job. I don't blame him. The girl tripped and fell in the poor light."

"That's your story?"

"I didn't kill her, if that's what you're implying."

"That's *not* what I'm implying. You know that. But I saw it, Luca. I was there. She was injured *before* she fell."

Luca laughed darkly. "You're not a detective. And you're repeating yourself. It's what you do when you're trying to convince yourself of something. Leave it to the professionals."

"The professionals aren't doing anything about it." Hamish folded his fingers into his palm. Luca noticed and raised an eyebrow.

"Now you're just getting yourself upset. You're not good to anyone when you're like that. It's just easier when you have nothing muddling up your mind."

"Easier." Hamish blinked. How did Luca know to cut right through to his heart and twist?

"What?" Luca's voice was stale, fuzzy with another long lap of liquor.

"Easier!"

"Look at you go on. See, this is exactly what I meant. You start worrying about something and it topples over and you have another bout of nerves."

"You're just like my father."

Luca froze, his glass midway to his mouth. "I am not."

"You are! Embarrassed. Look at you. Uncomfortable. Not sure what to do with me."

When Luca spoke it was in a voice softer and sobered. "I'm just trying to help."

"Just like my father was trying to help when he told me to hide my hand in my pocket or check my heartbeat every blasted second!" Hamish's voice rose.

Luca cursed under his breath. "I never should have said anything." He reached over and cupped Hamish's neck. "I . . ." Luca flashed a small smile but his eyes were dead set. Something had changed between them. Luca rose and padded in the direction of his room, saying over his shoulder, "I just don't want you to worry."

Hamish heard Luca slam his door. He fingered the discarded newspaper. A dead headline. There was a fine balance between immediately capturing supposition to sell a few papers and circulating a headline that would fall dead immediately.

Hamish reached for a pencil beside a half-finished crossword on the coffee table. He smoothed a section of the paper and over a pomade ad wrote:

The men from Dragonfly: Mark Suave and other.
Johnny Wade — also from the Dragonfly but now attached to Luca . . .
Schultze
Luca

All of the men who might have had a reason to see the end of Mary Finn. *Luca.* He looked up and around frantically as if his cousin might barge in. That name had been hardest to write. A betrayal in the shaky slant of his right hand. Luca wouldn't kill. Luca didn't have a reason. But Luca was so deeply involved. He was not innocent, regardless of whether he was responsible for Mary's death.

CHAPTER 20

"You should feel bad," Reggie told the reflection in the cab she'd splurged on to transport her to her boarding house so she could slip out of the dress she had borrowed from Mrs. Leoni and take a quick shower before dressing again with the intent of returning to the office and making good on what she had told the reporters. She would solve this murder. Even if it was late afternoon and her fuzzy head had taken more time than it should have to wake up and perform the menial tasks separating her from returning to Hamish and adventure. The sun was butter over the window and when she exited at the corner of the North Square, she had a skip in her step. Adventure! Adventure! Despite her tiredness. And a juicy bit of news to tell Nate with the latest papers.

Turned out, he awaited her arrival, rocking back and forth on his heels outside her office. When she crossed over the creaky floorboards, he immediately gripped her forearms. "Are you all right? You should try to take a nap."

Reggie rattled in her purse for her keys and turned the lock. "I can sleep when I am dead, Nate! I am on an adventure. Besides, you wouldn't sleep either if your name were in all the papers. I keep expecting telegrams from my parents. They'll show up eventually."

"Do they have your address?"

"They have something better." Reggie ran a fingernail over the edge of her desk. "Vaughan Vanderlaan." She told him who he was and how he was at the club that night.

Inside, Reggie exhaled and sifted through the mail. Telegrams tucked under the door. Luckily, none from New Haven. The afternoon edition of newspapers with headlines about the Flamingo in bold, along with pictures of Luca, who, even under custody of the police, looked like he stepped off an ad in *Photoplay*. The phone ringing off the hook.

Reggie dove for it then clicked it down again without answering. "Reporters."

Nate picked up the rolled newspaper near the door, unfolding it. "An accident." Nate clucked his tongue, shaking his head at Reggie. "This won't be the first time or the last. It's amazing what certain police officers can swear on at a crime scene."

"Crooked?"

"Tampered evidence. Eyewitnesses who come out of nowhere." He shrugged. "If you know where to go." He rolled the top of the newspaper with his finger. "Who to bribe. Which cops will turn a blind eye."

Reggie slumped into a chair. "I suspected as much. He just let me and Hamish in." She turned the radio dial through the static of commercial jingles and news broadcasts. Valari's name was mentioned. More than once. Then her name. She exchanged a look with Nate.

"Reggie Van Buren of the New Haven Van Burens." Nate scratched the back of his neck. "Never really gave a hide for any Van Burens before, but assume that your parents won't be thrilled to have the family name associated with a scandal in Scollay Square."

Reggie flicked the switch to silence. "I've done a poor job of maintaining contact with them this summer." Reggie felt a strange sense of empowerment by not caring.

"I doubt that will help." Nate looked at the radio.

"There was a gash on her head. A bloodstain on the wall. A red mark on her neck. She fell backward. If she just tripped on her way down, why would she be walking backward? Wouldn't she have fallen face first?" Reggie squirmed. "She had a rather annoying laugh. It's cruel to say so, but true. And now it's turned off forever."

Nate met her eyes but didn't attempt to fill the silence with a throwaway line. One of the reasons Reggie liked him so much. The phone rang again and Reggie prepared herself for slamming the receiver. She had no patience for Luca's cryptic phone calls. Or reporters. She sighed with relief when it was Hamish.

"Hamish!" She looked at Nate, who smiled.

"I don't want to talk there," he said, his voice tired and raspy.

She hopped up. "Where, then?"

"Union Oyster House. It will be loud."

Reggie nodded, folding her journal into her handbag.

"I suppose this means there isn't only one gumshoe in the building." Nate smiled, thinking of Jimmy Orlando down the hall.

"We won't keep anything from you," Reggie said.

"I should hope not. Though, Reggie, to be a detective, you maybe shouldn't be so trusting with your top-secret information."

"It's you, Nate. You're our ally. Like that doorman in Winchester Molloy's building."

"I don't know whether to take this as a compliment."

"Yes! Our ally!"

With a last smile, Reggie hopped out the door and down the stairs, tossing her hair a moment as if she were Irene Dunne and the camera lens was following her fluid movements. She quickened her pace over Hanover, swerving on Marshall Street, her flat oxfords long accustomed to the grooves and stops of the cobblestones.

Hamish was easy to spot at the oyster bar, book open in front of him. *Notre-Dame.* Of course. A safety blanket or good luck charm. She wondered if he kept it tucked in his breast pocket. She sat beside him on a rickety stool. He was studying the shells of raw oysters amidst squares of ice. Nearby, a man was shucking the sea creatures from their half-shells, spinning a yarn about a man who ate plates and plates full of oysters daily, between gulps of brandy and water.

Reggie wrinkled her nose. "It's smelly in here."

"It's busy and no one will look for us here." He looked at her pointedly. "Not even Vaughan Vanderlaan."

340

"Don't sulk, Hamish."

"Luca doesn't care. I mean he *cares*. He says a tarnished reputation is part of the sacrifice of fame."

"He's so insufferable. Sorry. I know he's your cousin. It's just if it were *my* club . . ."

"What would you do?" Hamish looked up, his eyes wide.

"I don't know." She wrinkled her nose. "But something. I would *want* to do something."

Hamish reached for a napkin, hand grazing a basket full of condiments. The man behind the bar scooped more oysters. "What will you have?"

"Fish sandwich." Reggie knew she wasn't hungry enough to eat it.

"Sir?"

Hamish hemmed and hawed through the menu before settling on crab cakes and a tomato juice.

Reggie turned a napkin over in her hand. "We're agreed on one thing, Hamish. Publicity or no publicity, that was no accident."

Say something clever. Say something clever to this clever girl. "To solve a mystery, my mother said, you just have to cut open the human heart and find its darkest corner."

"Perfect!"

"Morbid, actually." Hamish raised an eyebrow at her excitement.

"It still saddens me." Their food had arrived. Reggie stabbed a bite of coleslaw. "To think that the police are so easy to bribe."

"Not all. My friend Maisie . . ." His thoughts caught on Maisie a moment like a snag in a knit sweater. "Her father was on the police force. Now she's a dispatcher. I just think you can find a few shady characters in every profession."

"If it was someone like Schultze, he probably knew which ones to put in charge of the Flamingo."

"Notice he was there when we went back?" Hamish said, playing the sun's reflection off the end of his knife handle. "They always say people return to the scene of their crime. But" — he snickered — "it was an accident."

"I hate that odious man." Reggie clenched her fist.

"If they're not going to pay attention, then we are. Luca may not mind having a trail of suspicion after him, but I do."

"You're very loyal."

"He's innocent." Hamish looked at his untouched plate. "I know he is." Hamish wasn't sure he knew anything at all. He reached into his pocket and extracted the list of names he had scribbled at Luca's. "Here." He passed it to her and stabbed at a crab cake. It was fluffy and soft, and if he'd had an appetite, he would have found it tasty. "Have you ever solved a mystery before?" he asked, watching her eyes focus on the names.

"Other than Jenny Wyatt's runaway kitten?"

"There is a 98 percent chance that we will fail miserably."

"So there's a strong 2 percent chance we won't. And I get to play Myrna Loy."

Hamish's responding smile stifled his yawn. "So there are several reasons someone might kill Mary Finn."

Reggie reached for her notebook and pen. "Schultze's jealous wife!"

"His wife wasn't at the Flamingo." Hamish leaned back from his plate, played his fingers over his forearm like piano keys. "That we saw."

She continued scribbling. "It doesn't rule her out."

"Crime of passion," Hamish said. "She fought with Johnny Wade." He recalled overhearing their passionate exchange behind the bar. "Hand me a piece of paper, Reggie."

Reggie tore a sheet from her notebook and

slid it across to him with a pen. He flexed his fingers and picked up the pen, drawing a large square.

"What's that?"

"The Flamingo." He leaned into it, drawing. "Every exit and entrance. We need someone who had the opportunity as well as the motive."

"Dirk Foster." Reggie scribbled the name underneath the list Hamish had made.

"Who?"

"Friend of Vaughan's. When I was on my way to change the lightbulb, he was nearby."

Hamish felt a strange satisfaction hearing her say Vaughan's name so passively. "Oh."

"I don't think he could be a killer."

"Anyone can be a killer." Hamish drew a circle on the table with his finger. "We're all driven to things we didn't think ourselves capable of." He was thinking of Luca again. Luca and his club.

He leaned away from Reggie and opened *Notre-Dame*. It fell on the chapter where Esmeralda gave Quasimodo a drop of water after his whipping and public ridicule in the stocks. Hugo spoke of the port of union of two scenes: the chapter began, developed in parallel lines at the same moment, each in its particular theater. Then the two adjacent storylines met at a point of intersection. Two seemingly separate things conjoining in the middle.

"What are you thinking?" Reggie broke his reverie.

"I've read *Hunchback of Notre-Dame* too many times."

"Tell me."

"What if someone wanted to set Luca up to take a fall?" He held out his pinky fingers. He shrugged. "Just something in the book about two separate events meeting in the middle," he finished lamely.

"With Schultze's walking stick the murder weapon?" The oyster shucker looked at Reggie. She lowered her voice. "Wouldn't that be a setup for Schultze?"

"He left it behind the bar when he went to dance." He rubbed his head. "Maybe Mary took it. I don't know — because she was angry with him?" He rubbed his hand. "Besides, it wasn't the murder weapon. Not that we know. It was just used to rough her up."

"Maybe he was tiring of her? Or his wife found out . . . ?"

"Or maybe she was a pawn." Hamish dragged his knife over his plate. "If she knew who knew what strings to pull . . ."

Reggie picked up Hamish's lead. "She

may have known. Always around. Hearing things."

"Someone wanted her dead."

Reggie mussed her hair. "That still doesn't explain why Luca was there. Or Suave."

"Mark Suave and the other man from the Dragonfly. Luca may have been meeting them. I didn't see them leave, but I saw them throughout the night."

"So they could have killed her?"

"I don't know why they would want to." Hamish folded a page of *Notre-Dame* absently with his finger. "Whether or not the murder was committed by my cousin" — Hamish's voice was sad — "I can't help but suspect him."

"What would his motive have been?"

Hamish shrugged. "I don't know . . . but I don't know him at all, do I?"

CHAPTER 21

Sadness swirled through Hamish after Reggie left him for the office. He didn't want to return to Luca's penthouse and wondered if he should just start sleeping on the floor of the office. A prickle in his brain reminded him that he wanted to retreat homeward and shake the summer off, leaving it far behind until it was just Hamish and Luca again without secrets or corpses or telegrams. "Scandal sells," Luca once told him, and the club that had seemed a success at its opening was now near legendary. Brian MacMillan had rung the penthouse earlier to say that people were already lining up hours before dusk. The police said that since it was a contained incident, there was no need to block the entirety of the premises.

"There has to be something I missed when we were there," Hamish explained to Reggie when she asked why he was going back to the club. "Why don't you go to the office and see if anyone calls with anything and I will try to go over everything we may have missed." The reporters probably would have moved on by now and Hamish knew that the club was intended to open per usual that night. Maybe Schultze would be prowling around and he could read him more closely.

He wondered if his stomach would ever stop flipping. Luca was in the basement that night. And if he was innocent, why didn't he just say, "I had no idea. I just ducked downstairs to get some vintage champagne"? Luca didn't think he owed anyone any explanation. Why would he? He was sent home without even a warning. An accident.

A girl falling backward down the stairs. Confronted at the top, terrified. Two of the men who'd assaulted Luca and Hamish at the Dragonfly several days before hovering nearby.

And no one would have heard her scream. Hamish recalled Mary's cheese-grater voice, raspy from her boisterous laugh and the noise rising around her. She flailed with no witnesses, she screeched with a lost voice. The noise on the floor was overpowering. But Luca would have heard her.

Hamish walked through the ornamented doors, looking around. The club seemed so stale in daylight, devoid of the magic that set it alive at night. A uniformed officer was lighting up near the bar and a few vendors were delivering the usual shipments.

Schultze was indeed there, unmoved. Hamish avoided him and walked to the bar. Johnny Wade wasn't there yet and standing behind it gave him the best vantage of the world of the Flamingo in daylight. A different perspective. The bar was slightly curved, and Johnny could easily ease down and take in the whole of the action in front of him.

When the phone jangled, he considered letting it ring and ring and ring into oblivion. Instead he picked it up, fully prepared to slam it down again if it were a reporter.

He didn't know how to answer. "Flamingo Club."

"Hamish."

His father's voice was half-frantic and half-angry. Hamish listened silently through the barrage of Italian, tempted to follow the instinct to listen to his father's advice and buy a train ticket back to Toronto. Of course the headlines had reached Toronto. The ordeal had the right ingredients for a top story: A promiscuous woman. A dashing club owner. Music and madness and blood and passion. Hamish's father doubtless had heard the take that Mary was entangled in an ill-fated love affair with his nephew. Hamish placated him as best he could then dropped his head on the bar top. What wasn't he seeing through his cataracts of loyalty to Luca?

"He was arrested and let go," Hamish explained when there was a break in his father's words.

"Arrested? And you?"

"I found her. Well, Reggie and I found her." Then remembered his father had no idea who Reggie was.

"You found a corpse? You found a corpse. Hamish. You can't even find a dead bird on the lawn without retreating to your room for a week. Are you all right?"

"I am trying to be."

"I will wire you money. Buy a ticket. Come on. There's still a chance, you know. Harry Winslow was by the office the other day."

"I don't need you smoothing things over for me. I make my own decisions."

"You're still playing this game? Don't throw away your life for Luca, Hamish."

"Throw it away there instead?"

There was a crackle of silence on the other

end of the line. "What do you mean by that?"

"I don't know if I'm cut out for law. I don't know if I'm . . ." He waved his hand, not sure how to explain himself, knowing there was nothing but static silence on his father's end of the line. So much had happened. He felt different. He tangled his finger in the phone cord.

"This is hardly the time. You're tired. Anxious. Come home, we can talk here."

"You've read the papers. You know that the police have written the incident off as an accident. I don't believe it is. I can't go anywhere until I find out what happened."

"You sound like your mother."

"Thank you!" Hamish knew his dad's statement wasn't a compliment, but accepted it as one nonetheless.

"Hamish."

"I'm fine. I promise you."

"I . . ."

"You know how you used to tell me that you just *knew* . . . about Toronto? That the moment you saw the harbor and the skyline you knew it was where you were supposed to be?"

"Yes."

"That's Boston for me right now. It's all right," Hamish said, knowing as the words

351

left his mouth he was trying to convince himself. "It's all right," he repeated, starting to believe it.

He clicked the receiver and narrowed his eyes out on the floor again.

"Well, look at you, taking a serious interest in your cousin's endeavors," Schultze said, approaching the bar. "Are you going to mix me a drink?"

Hamish leaned forward. "It was you, wasn't it?"

Schultze straightened his tie. "If it were me, wouldn't I be settled in a prison cell by now?" He waved toward the empty club. "I am just an investor making sure my capital won't be lost due to an . . . unfortunate . . . scandal."

Hamish seethed inside, clutching his fingers tight. "How long have you been associated with my cousin, Mr. Schultze?"

"Not long. Since he moved here. You always go to Luca Valari before he comes to you. Something I learned early on. Edwin Baskit knew his name."

"He has a reputation," Hamish said casually, hoping his tone didn't specify what kind. "But I know he didn't kill Mary Finn. So who did?" He kept his eyes on Schultze.

"That's the question. Or she fell down the stairs. She was a clumsy girl, Hamish. I know better than anyone. Ah! Good!" Roy Holliday strolled from the entrance across the dance floor. "At least we have our bandleader. We can turn a better profit than Luca would have expected. This will help him when he opens the next one."

Hamish recalled Luca talking enthusiastically about several of the same type of clubs. "And I suppose you'll be involved in that?"

"You suppose right. Men like Luca are the same in every city. And the sooner you find one, the sooner you're set."

Hamish studied Schultze. The man made him uncomfortable, but nothing clicked in his chest. There wasn't anything inauthentic about him. What you saw was what you got: selfish, secretive, treated everyone but Luca as if they were below him. But a liar?

Hamish took one more stroll down to the basement, not even registering the ease with which he explored the space where Mary had been sprawled lifelessly. If Hamish stopped to think about it — which he did once he was outside and walking in the direction of the North End office — he would notice that he wasn't reacting the way Hamish usually reacted. He had nearly forgotten about his father's phone call. He had walked into the club and behind the bar without permission — with a kind of command he assumed since Luca had called it "their" club. Men like Luca might have stayed the same, as Schultze said; but men like Hamish? The longer he stayed in Boston, the harder it was to recognize himself.

Reggie couldn't keep the image of Mary Finn suddenly pale and motionless from appearing behind her eyes as soon as she closed them. The calls she received the moment she picked up the jangling phone in the office were all reporters. It was a break from the usual Chicago calls, at least.

"I spent my life saying, 'My apologies, no comment,' " Reggie told Hamish the moment he walked through the door, explaining how reporters liked to shadow her parents' parties and poke at the probability of scandal to serve up on the platter of the society pages. "Find anything at the club?"

Hamish shook his head. Then yawned. "And I spent my life learning that a good reporter will get around 'no comment' and leave the scene with more than a scoop." Hamish sat on the edge of her desk, swinging his long legs. He had become more and more comfortable, or else his brain was too tired to notice his proximity to her. "No comment often means someone is scared of something. You just need to know how to draw out the truth."

"Well, no good reporters are calling here then," Reggie surmised, clicking the receiver on another one.

"My father called."

"Oh?"

"The Flamingo. I just happened to pick up."

"I suppose he realized that would be the best place to reach you."

"I meant to write him and give him Luca's number . . ." Hamish trailed off. Then he studied a note she had written to herself. "Dirk?"

"During one of our dances around the Flamingo, Vaughan told me he was staying at the Park Plaza, as was Dirk. The papers mention him, but he is no longer an interesting link now that the police under Vasser have named it an accident. He answered their questions when someone said they had seen him with Mary."

"And . . . ?"

Reggie sighed. "Maybe I've seen *The Thin Man* too many times, but I am willing to bet that a girl didn't bash her head unevenly on a wall and fall backward. No one showed real attachment to Mary, did they? She had made strong impressions on several men.

Johnny Wade the bartender. Dirk . . ."

Hamish picked up one of the rolled newspapers on the edge of the desk and unfolded it.

"Johnny went on record with the *Tribune.*" He showed her. She nodded.

The headline and the rows of print about his loyalty and passion for Mary showed a man gutted by the loss of his onetime girlfriend. Very sensational, and the shot they used of him captured the height of his cheekbones and the sensual upturn of his lips. Reggie inched the paper toward her once Hamish was finished and read it again and again, trying to find something that would suggest a motive. Something between the lines.

Though favorable, the story gave a different slant from articles about Luca. Luca was quite popular in most of the papers, having breezed into the city with his dark good looks and modern club. Why, a society writer said it was even better than the Stork. More sophisticated than anything in Manhattan. Roy Holliday's band and the selection of liquors had something to do with it. But it was clear that Luca was a part of the ambience and the success.

Reggie rapped her pen over her open journal. She'd told the reporters she was going to solve the murder. How splendid would it be if they actually did it?

"I don't see the *Herald*," Hamish said, leafing through the papers.

"Nate has that one."

Hamish rose. "I'll be back." He ducked out of the office.

Reggie was inspecting the black ink on her finger pads from hours of leafing through the papers when she heard someone approaching.

"Miss Van Buren."

"Mr. Suave." She made his name sound as ironic as possible.

He looked around, hands behind his back, brow furrowed. "So this is Luca Valari's office."

"Any and all business pertaining to the Flamingo happens here," Reggie said evenly. Suave's voice prickled her neck and tingled down her arms. Even his hello had her on guard.

"I need to take a look around." He stepped toward her desk. "You won't mind that, will you? Just a little peek?"

Reggie followed his eyes over bookshelves devoid of books, filing cabinets with no files, her flowers wilting in the excitement of the Flamingo.

So intent in watching what his eyes might

see, she didn't notice when he lunged in her direction. And when her arm was gripped white with his strength, she was too startled to do anything but gulp a breath and widen her eyes through the surprise.

"Luca never does anything without purpose."

"I don't know him that well." Reggie's teeth chattered, though she tried to stay them, her eyes darting around the office. He had clicked the door shut behind him, barring easy escape.

"You know him well enough." He grabbed her arm. "You're a pretty one. I noticed it the other night when you were worried for your boyfriend."

"He's not my boyfriend."

Suave reached out his index finger and pressed it to her chin, working up and along her jawline, tracing over her cheekbone.

"Please stop." Her voice shook. Suave stepped behind her desk, moving into the slice of space she still possessed between her desk and the window opening to the square below.

The giggles and shrieks of children, the call of a young woman to her boyfriend, mocked her with their nearness. And worse still, Hamish and Nate were just down the hall. When she tried to conjure a scream, her voice caught in her throat.

His arms were around her now. "An aristocrat, if I am not mistaken." His breath was suffocating. "What do you know about your employer? Does the name Frank Fulham mean anything to you?"

Reggie shook her head, fighting against him, shoving him back, arm muscles stretched and taut with years of tennis lessons. But he was stronger and the walls closed in around her.

"I don't know anything. But you do. *You're* the one who had him in the b-basement of that club that night."

He laughed lowly then began to say something as the door opened and Hamish returned.

She breathed a sigh of relief as Suave turned, still gripping her but without his sour breath at her neck.

Hamish registered the scene and his voice was immediately masked in anger. "Get your hands off her!" He crossed the room. "Do I need to call the police, Regina?"

"Hamish," Reggie breathed, relieved.

Suave backed up then, looking Hamish over, Reggie wondering if he would move in his direction. Not worth it, he apparently decided. He swerved back to Reggie and with a cocky glance at Hamish stroked her cheek down into the swoop of her neck between her jawline and collarbone. "You really are quite striking. I will be back. Tell your boss. I am this close to closing in on him, and I won't be as lenient." He stabbed Hamish with a glare then shoved out the door. "I know his weakness."

Reggie crumpled over a little. Hamish was in front of her in a moment, putting his hand on her shoulder.

"Are you all right?"

"If you hadn't come." She blinked sudden tears as the realization of her situation hit. Hamish's hand shook a little — but this time she was sure it was from anger more than anything else. "Can I get you something? Water? No? Oh, Reggie, I hate that he touched you."

Reggie shook her head. "If I was smart, I would pick up my hat and gloves and never return here. But we're going to solve this." She held on to that. "We are going to solve this murder." She gestured between them. "You and I. And I don't care if it implicates your stupid cousin." She watched his face for a reaction. He still seemed to be processing the close call with Suave.

Livid and unable to stand still, he rocked back and forth on his heels. "I want to find a nice column to shove Suave into. I should

360

have . . ." He fingered the last whisper of a red mark over his neck. "I'm so sorry."

Reggie gave him a weak smile. "It's okay. I can't have you arrested too. We just need to find out who Fulham is and where the file is and solve the murder." She ran her hand over her face. "It's a lot. But, Hamish, Suave isn't against using force and hurting people close to your cousin. What if Luca's next?"

"Just take a breath, Reggie," he said, evening out his own.

CHAPTER 22

Hamish chewed his lip. Yes, but Luca brought it upon himself. Reggie was innocent and just in the way. He was innocent and just in the way. He blew out a long whistle of a breath.

Reggie rose. "I don't know what I would have done if you hadn't been here."

Hamish swallowed. He didn't know either. Reggie was quite formidable — but when overpowered?

"Well!" Reggie clapped, sounding more like herself. "William Powell. We need to start solving our murder."

"Are you sure? We could call it a day. Get a cup of tea? You had quite an ordeal, Reggie."

"I like to think that I am prepared to handle anything —"

Hamish anticipated a rousing proclamation of strength to follow, but instead she broke off, looking out the window to the square below.

She shrugged. "So let's start with Dirk Foster." She rose. "He's at the Park Plaza." She reached for the phone. "I can call a taxi."

"Or we can enjoy a bit of sunshine." His mouth tipped up a little while his eyes looked in the direction of the bicycle leaning against the opposite wall.

Once they exited the building, Hamish motioned toward his bike and moments later she settled on the handlebars as if she had been doing so her entire life. She glanced back at him with a laugh, and while he could hear a tinge of nerves in it — something he could detect in a stranger as well as someone he had spent as much time with as Reggie — he sensed she truly had returned to herself. Hamish balanced her and they set off. They drew a little more attention in the daylight than they had returning from the Flamingo, but Reggie didn't care. The breeze whooshed away the nightmares and the confusion since Vaughan had returned — and with him barrels full of expectation and memories that took her home.

Hamish swerved with ease through Washington Street, turning on Tremont, the Common a sweep of green on their left, then taking a sharp left on Hadassah, while the triangularly shaped Park Plaza featuring hundreds of windows sweeping up several stories stood out grandiosely in contrast with the bustle of vendors hawking flowers and kiosks selling snacks.

"Regina!" Vaughan's voice was unmistakable as she hopped off the bar and smoothed her skirt beneath her. "Regina!" he repeated, jogging from the direction of the Common to reprimand her. "What are you doing on the front of this man's bike?"

"Vaughan!" Regina composed herself and blew a strand of hair from her forehead. "I believe you have yet to meet Hamish De-Luca. My colleague from Luca Valari's office."

Hamish disentangled himself from the bike, and it wavered underneath him as he decided how to balance it properly and take Vaughan's extended hand. He finally stayed it with his left and reached out his slightly trembling right. "H-how do you do?" He gave a weak smile.

"Do you make it a habit of parading women around on the front of your bicycle?" Vaughan looked at her as if she had sprouted wings and flown over from the Back Bay.

Reggie smiled. "It's the fastest way to get

from the North End."

"Are you here to see me?" Vaughan fix-ated on Hamish while talking to Reggie. "Because I was just out for a stroll. Dirk and I have been conducting business. An architect uptown wants to see some of our building plans."

"That's wonderful. You've worked so hard to get someone here to look at your work," Reggie said. "But we're actually here to see Dirk." Reggie's cheeks were a flattering pink from the wind in her hair and on her face.

"What do you want to see him for?"

"Hamish and I have a few questions about his connection to Mary Finn."

Vaughan took Reggie's elbow and turned her from Hamish slightly. But Hamish could still hear. "Regina, you are not in one of those gumshoe pictures you like. The police learned all they needed to know from Dirk. He's a friend. My friend and my business partner. He has to be fresh for our meetings on Monday. You have to understand that. You and your friend" — he stopped for an emphatic moment and shot a grating look in Hamish's direction — "would best leave this to the professionals. Your name has been splattered around the papers enough. Your parents are mad with the notoriety. In fact, they demanded that I keep an eye on you and I mean to."

Reggie smiled and gently put her hand over Vaughan's. "I know you're just trying to protect me. But look at me! I am here in this big city! Found employment of my own means! Can change a lightbulb and poach an egg. I know what I am doing. Hamish and I aren't placing the blame on anyone." She smiled in Hamish's direction. He was rolling the bicycle back and forth slightly, his knuckles white on the bars. "We just think the police could be a little more thorough." Reggie leaned up on her oxfords and placed a kiss on Vaughan's cheek. "We appreciate the concern."

"Dirk won't take kindly to being pestered about this. A girl he stepped out with was just found dead."

"We'll be compassionate and discreet. Have a lovely afternoon, Vaughan. Are you headed in the direction of the Public Garden? Seems lovely there in the sun." She flashed him a dismissive smile.

Hamish fought the urge to laugh. For some reason this exchange resonated through him like a victory.

Don't do what Vaughan tells you to, even when he uses his business voice. Another line to record in her Journal of Independence. Hamish rolled his bike silently toward the grand awning and the doormen standing at attention on either side of the monogrammed carpet, ushering guests into the broad marble foyer of the Park Plaza. He parked his bike to the left side of the gold-rimmed revolving doors and promised to collect it shortly. The doorman gave him an odd look. Hamish smoothed down the hair tousled with the exertion of their trip. Reggie pulled at her hem. Funny, the statues and fountains and perfumed air of the Plaza were more second nature to her than the convoluted cubes of the North End. At least they had been. Now, she fingered her hair and looked up at Hamish, who was silent as a morgue.

"Sorry about Vaughan," she said as they approached the concierge, sidestepping a bellboy rolling a cart full of luggage across a floor she could see her reflection in.

"He's just being protective." Hamish smiled. "You want someone who will look out for you."

Reggie shrugged. "I suppose. I sometimes wonder if I wouldn't rather have someone who appreciated how I could look after myself." Reggie leaned on the concierge's desk and pulled out her perfectly clipped New England charm. A voice so crystal glass it summoned ghosts of the glorious revolutionary dead.

"Mr. Foster would be delighted to see you in the lobby bar, miss," she heard a moment later after a quick telephone call.

"Thank you."

Hamish and Reggie sat at the bar, Reggie ordering lemonade for both of them. A moment later, Dirk appeared in a white suit, a fedora dangling near the pleat of his impeccably pressed pants. The dark blue of his tie sparked his eyes. "Regina!" She rose and he pecked her on each cheek. Hamish rose as well and accepted Dirk's handshake with a smile that tugged wide enough to present his solitary dimple.

"A shame you missed Vaughan." Dirk raised his hand and snapped until an attendant arrived to take his drink order.

"We passed him. He told us about your meeting on Monday. That's wonderful."

"You're not the only one relocating here." Dirk turned his attention to Hamish. "And who are you? I remember your face from the club the other night."

"Hamish DeLuca."

"Funny name. But that's what I am learning here in Boston — always a new set. Your voice is different though. I don't recognize it."

"Hamish is from Toronto," Reggie said, swallowing a sip of lemonade as the waiter presented Dirk with a fizzy beverage adorned with a lime wedge.

"That explains it. I suspect, then, that this isn't a social call, Regina. Unless your Canadian friend is here to play chaperone."

"Actually, Hamish and I have a few questions about Mary Finn."

"What?"

"We think the police may have dismissed the case too quickly," Hamish said softly, tripping a little on the *d*.

"You've a stutter," Dirk said brashly. "My brother had one of those. My mom was always trying to shove marbles in his mouth and all the latest treatments. Have you?"

"Have I what?"

"Ever shoved marbles in your mouth?"

"Honestly, Dirk!" Reggie snapped. "We are not here to talk about Hamish. Mary Finn was most likely pushed to her death. She can't have fallen. Both Hamish and I saw the corpse, and it was too unnatural to have been an accident. We just wondered if you could tell us anything about your acquaintance."

"I was hardly acquainted with her. I just knew her from when I came to the city on weekends. She was a laugh and good for a spin. I didn't want to kill her, for heaven's sake."

"You weren't jealous?" Hamish asked, his voice calm.

"Why would I be jealous of some cigarette girl?"

"Because you weren't her only dance partner."

"I never wanted to marry her. You have rather old-fashioned notions. Is that the Canadian talking?"

"You're being awfully rude, Dirk," Reggie said. "No need to take that tone with us."

"Forgive me if I don't enjoy Sam Spade here and my best friend's girl interrogating me. A girl died. The police had several questions, and I was cleared."

"We're not saying you're guilty of anything," Hamish said. Reggie watched him closely. Dirk was getting to him. Under his skin, reflected in his big blue eyes. But he was composed nonetheless. She straightened her shoulders.

"I just wonder if anything seemed strange about Mary the night of the opening. Was she flustered or upset? We believe she had quarreled with another young man, Johnny Wade."

"That slick bartender?"

"Yes."

Dirk was still testy, but he exhaled a little, loosened his tie, sipped at his drink. Exhaled again.

"I didn't really notice anything different about Mary." He closed his eyes a moment. When he opened them again, they were filmed with something. Sadness? Confusion? Reggie leaned closer to him. "Except I sensed something was going to change."

"How?" wondered Hamish.

"If Vaughan and I move here and she was going to be easily accessible, it ruined some of the . . ." He shrugged. "I don't know. Allure? Mystery? I guess I have been feeling guilty about that. I didn't know I would never see her again."

"Did you tell her that you were considering moving to Boston?" Hamish stirred his lemonade with his straw.

"I didn't get a chance. We had one dance and then that Schultze fellow needed her for something. And her break was over and Luca Valari was sniffing around." Dirk combed his fingers through his hair. "Come to think of it, she did seem a little distracted. I mean more than usual. She was never the sharpest knife in the drawer. But Schultze had a woman who said something that seemed to upset her." He snapped his fingers. "Lily something. Because he was making up some rather ridiculous compliments on her name." He took a moment to slug the rest of his drink. "Gardner, I think. Geez, don't know why I remember that."

Dirk raised his empty glass, rattling with the dregs of ice, in a salute. "You seem to be having a bit of a lark, Reggie. But knowing Vaughan, he'll want you to consider how your name has already ended up in the *Tribune* and the *Times.* Be careful." Dirk excused himself without bidding Hamish good-bye.

"Friendly set we have back home," Reggie said sourly while Hamish insisted on settling the bill.

"Dirk didn't have anything to do with it," Hamish said as they collected his bicycle and he rolled it in the direction of Tremont Street. "He just didn't."

"I know. Did you see Tom Schultze with another girl?"

Hamish thought back. "There were so many people. The whole night is a bit of a blur."

Reggie nodded. "All until it came crashing down." She yawned. "Let's go to the Flamingo tonight. No! Don't give me that wounded bird look. That's where we're likely to learn something. I just need a few hours of sleep." She looked him over. "So do you."

CHAPTER 23

There were worse ways to spend an evening even in the pursuit of a killer than listening to Roy Holliday's swing band. The selection became more and more playful each night since the opening. The nightly crowds were steady, and any air of scandal following Mary's death didn't seep through the front door or across the dance floor latticed with careful light.

Reggie was happy she'd had the foresight to bring several dresses with her the night that she shoved half her closet into an open suitcase and scrambled down the tree to her freedom. She thought she looked pretty in a green number that now stretched a little tightly across the bust and in the waist on account of too many cannoli. But rather than worry, she accepted that her new curves lent something to her figure she hadn't seen before. Probably because her mother was always reminding her to be careful, that her figure was one that could easily be on the other side of fashionable, especially with the year's penchant for backless dresses and bare arms. Hamish looked at her a moment, and when she caught his gaze, he turned away.

Bill was minding the bar at the moment, as Johnny had a gig with his band at another club. Hamish and Reggie made their way in his direction.

"Your fellow was here last night," Bill said, sliding two Coca-Colas across the bar.

"Vaughan?"

"He was quite protective of you. Some fellow was going on about seeing you in the paper and said a few . . . untoward things. Vanderlaan would hear nothing of it. Stood his ground."

"How heroic!" Reggie said, suddenly uncomfortable and exposed.

"Haven't seen your cousin tonight." He turned to Hamish.

"I'm not his keeper," Hamish said, and Reggie sensed a bit of bitterness in his tone. He was probably just tired and sick of the crowd. It was the sweet spot — or at least that was what Luca called it — the moment around ten o'clock when those leaving late suppers were eager to dance off their indulgences and loosen their ties and their inhibitions with a few drinks.

"Have you seen a Lily Gardner here tonight? Sometimes shows up with Schultze."

"Yes. She's been in and out. I can flag her down if you two kids want to take a spin. Or have a slightly stronger drink."

"We're fine here, thanks," Hamish said.

"You know the drinks are on the house. Luca Valari's standing order for his favorite cousin. There's a note pinned over there by the brandy glasses in case we have someone fill in."

"That's sweet," Reggie said, playing with a peanut she had snapped from a dish of nuts on the counter.

"There's Lil now," Bill said, wiping the inside of a highball glass with a rag. "Hey, Lily, Valari's cousin wants to talk to you."

Reggie and Hamish exchanged a look. Lily looked a little like Jean Harlow, with thin, painted lines for eyebrows and exaggerated lips. Her dress dipped dangerously low and a fur in direct combat with the heat outside draped low on her arms.

"Well, aren't you a sweetie pie." One end of the fur caressed Hamish's cheek, just below his ear.

"Hamish DeLuca. This is Regina Van Buren."

"Oooo! Fancy." She looked up at Regina after hearing her name.

"Isn't it just."

"G and T, Lil?" Bill asked and on her assent turned to fixing it.

"Lily." Reggie edged closer to her and pulled Hamish in. "We had a few questions about the opening night. When Mary Finn died."

"That poor girl." Lily clicked her tongue. "So young. Don't go thinking it was me. Just because I sometimes let Schultzie take me out. There's no crime in that and I'm not the jealous type."

"We're not accusing you of anything," Hamish said, softening her eyes with his gentle tone. "Were you with Schultze the whole night? Even when Mary disappeared?"

Lily Gardner's nasal laugh rippled. "Schultzie was with me. Of course he was with me. I asked about her. He told me she was done. Told me she was stupid enough to call 'round his place and say that she was going to take her chances with this bartender. I bet they fought about it. She had a rep for being a bit of a snitch. Working these clubs, sidling up to the businessmen peddling her cigarettes and knowing what we girls aren't supposed to know."

"What do you mean by that?" asked Reggie.

"A bit of a spiderweb. Who is connected with who. Who knows who and who is straight."

Lily wrinkled her nose. "I'm bored with all that. I don't pay attention. I just want to dance." She stretched her arms out to the dance floor. "But there's this Suave fellow. Isn't that the funniest name? Schultze talks about him. About Suave also talking about how he wants this Fulham guy, Frankie. He was talking about it that night. Suave was around with his friend Arthur. Boring old name. I tried to call him Arty. It didn't stick. Not like how I stick on Schultze." Hamish and Reggie looked to each other and then to her.

"And the night of the opening?" Reggie wanted to bring her back on track. Schultze.

"He bought me a drink and then we slow-danced for hours before he took me outside for a little tête-à-tête. But he limped a little. He can dance when holding on to someone without that stick of his, but he isn't always right as rain without it. Topples a little. He said that I knocked him off his feet."

"And he didn't go back to the bar to retrieve his stick?" Hamish asked.

"He was too excited to steal a moment

alone with me. That's what he said. When we came back to the club, the police were there and all hades had broken loose."

"And what about Fulham?"

"I hear some of Schultzie's conversations, but I never really listen. You know? You can hear and not *listen*. They're two different things."

"Hey, doll, take a spin?" A man with slicked-back silver hair and an expensive suit approached.

"Sure, baby." Lily wriggled out of her wrap and passed it behind the bar to Bill.

"We have coat check for this," Bill said.

"You're my coat check. Stan, give Bill a bill for his coat check." She laughed.

Stan reached into his pocket and produced a twenty. These men peeled off paper like it grew on trees. But why wouldn't they? Her father did too. Vaughan, though slightly more responsible, was known to splurge too.

"We'll cross Schultze and Lily off the list," Reggie said, looking to Hamish to match her enthusiasm.

Her eyes flitted down to his right hand, clutching and unclutching his knuckles. Then he seemed to abandon the effort. His fingers trembled.

She looked up again, her eyes helpless when they met his. His breath picked up.

She could see the incline of his chest. In and out . . . He placed his slightly shaking hand over his heart, mumbling something under his breath. It took her a moment to decipher he was counting. All the while, a sheen of perspiration coated his face, which was paling under the dazzling prisms of the chandelier light.

He nodded, but his short gulps of breath told a different story. "Just . . . a . . ." He didn't finish. His breathing was becoming more irregular, and Reggie was starting to worry.

"Hamish . . ."

He didn't see her anymore. He focused on counting his breath. Failing that, he bent over and lowered his head between his knees. Then he straightened and pushed past her, past them all in the direction of the door.

Reggie dashed after him, finding him finally in the nearby alley, the light catching his blue-black hair.

His shoulders shuddering a little, he rose up a bit. "S-some detective I make." His voice was low.

"Hamish . . ."

His eyes were glazed and his face was white. "As if you hadn't noticed."

"I was so worried that you were having a

heart attack. But —"

"Regina . . ." He blinked and looked away. "Sorry. I know I should control and count my heartbeat and . . ."

She thought of things he probably recalled and repeated to help him when he was trapped in whatever cavern seemed to be holding him now. He was only just beginning to show signs of life! His hand was still shaking until he sensed her eyes on it and folded his fingers into his palm. "It sometimes just creeps up." His voice hiccupped.

"Your heartbeat?"

" 'Heartbeat, Hamish' — it was all my father told me when I was growing up so I could monitor and keep myself in check."

"I understand." Truth was, she was unsure how she had made it through so much of her suffocating life without some resemblance of the condition now washing over her friend. So many times at her parents' garden parties or shoved into white-gloved high society, she had swallowed down feelings that very well could have reared themselves in a similar fashion. She was just lucky. And the same loyalty that bound him to Luca, bound her to him. They were linked, and it felt wonderful. She stole out her hand and placed it at the back of his neck a moment, whispering just over his hairline. The sensation surprised her, made her fingertips tingle a little. She bit her lip. *It's all right,* she thought, *I'm just trying to help.* Then she tried to blink away the lie. It was more than that, wasn't it? She stepped back. "Do you want me to go into the club and get Phil?" she asked after taking several beats. Hamish seemed calmer now, though he averted his eyes, staring straight at the brick wedging them between the two buildings. The tarmac was slick from an earlier rainfall and caught the shimmer of the streetlights and fluorescent signs in dozens of diamonds.

"No." It took so long for Hamish to answer, she was surprised when his voice cut through the dark. "I'll walk. Good —" He gulped a breath. "Good night, Reg."

Reggie knew he was addled or he would have had the foresight to see her home. He was always concerned. Heavens, he put her on the front of his bike!

She watched his black head disappear into the bustle of the street, then started back toward the Flamingo. On either side of the red ribbon of carpet streaming out to the street from the Flamingo's grand doorway, she saw people step out for air, pull long drags on cigarettes, laugh into the night, trading one club for another, disappear into shiny cabs. Reggie wrapped her arms around her torso. It was starting to get colder. Just a hint of a nip warning that fall was hovering.

"Oh, it's you. Miss Van Buren." Mark Suave was at her elbow; Reggie prickled. "Tell me, when you're playing secretary for Luca's little enterprise here, do you ever hear from a poorly patched number?"

"If you hate Luca so much, just confront him," Reggie said, though goose bumps appeared on her arms.

"I never take a step unless I am absolutely certain of the outcome," Suave said. His features were clear under the tantalizing lights luring guests into Luca's club. "But you are a mystery. A good girl. Good name. Involved in a shady scheme."

"I needed a job and now I have one." She took a deep breath, still ashamed of the way he had cornered her at the office. She wanted to scream and stomp and reclaim her weakness in that previous moment. "Now I want to find out who killed Mary Finn."

"Killed?"

"You were there. Downstairs. Meeting with Luca."

"I don't have time for cigarette girls," he said. "But keep playing Sherlock Holmes."

There was something about him that reminded her of the entitled men at her parents' parties. Something that cloaked him in such arrogance, she was sure anything would roll off him like water from a duck's back. It was only after he left her with a sneer of a smile that ten different retorts pinged through her brain.

The next morning, Hamish arrived at the office before Reggie to collect his thoughts.

A badly formed part of his brain affects the patient's nervous system. It can be cut out. We section the cortex between the frontal and parietal lobes . . . Metrazol and medication . . . Injections of insulin shock the system. Separate a patient's emotional state from their intelligent state . . . Institutions and sanitoriums and experimental treatments. Hamish may as well have gone to medical school for all of the reading he'd done in hopes that medical journals could keep his hand from shaking and his chest from closing in. Quotes from leading psychiatrists seemed to stick in his brain as well as *Notre-Dame* did.

He flushed just thinking about meeting eyes with Reggie again. But the sensation of her fingers in his hair had calmed him.

Her eyes had glistened with panic for him. Hamish rubbed at his collarbone, slow, rhythmic circles, hoping his heart was as tempered as it seemed. Its thuds subsisted and trailed off slowly. He was exhausted, but lighter. And the light through which he saw Reggie softened. This pretty girl with her stained lips and high cheekbones, looking at him not with condescending pity but with blatant affection.

When Reggie appeared bearing a paper bag and a jar of brown liquid she explained was iced coffee, his smile tugged.

"Breakfast!" she announced. "Care of Mrs. Leoni."

"Fulham. Cicero. Suave."

"And a good morning to you too!" Reggie laughed.

"Connecting the dots," Hamish said. "I'm sorry about last night."

"You know you don't have to apologize." Her voice was gentle as she unwrapped the cannoli and popped the lid off the coffee jar. She took two chipped mugs from the side cupboard and poured.

"I just don't know . . . I guess I thought . . . Truth is, it happens. I am just ashamed it happened in front of you."

"I'm your friend." Reggie handed him a mug and lifted her own filled glass in a toast. "Is that why you came here? I mean, you don't have to answer, but . . ."

Hamish held his hands out, studying them. "We have all sorts of medicine for people, don't we? If you have a cold or a cough or influenza. I used to think that maybe there was a pill to swallow to make me like everyone else." He fixed his eyes just above her on the crevice of the window. "And I never know when it is going to happen or why. Sometimes there's no reason. Everything just crowds in at once and it starts in my chest." He placed a hand over his heart. "Really dull at first but then it gets worse and my eyes go fuzzy and I feel dizzy. There's no trying to control my hand at that point." He tapped his fingers over his chest. "My dad was always trying to teach me ways to escape so no one had to see. Well, I did a rummy job of it that morning." Hamish shrugged.

"I'm sorry."

"Can you imagine me in a courtroom?"

Reggie cocked her head a little. "I can imagine you anywhere, Hamish."

"I think my dad might have been disappointed. He'd never tell me. But he had such high hopes. And I can't be a lawyer, Reggie. I know that. I don't want it. I want to be here and . . ." He hoped his eyes didn't give him away. He really wanted to be anywhere she was. She excused herself when Nate asked for a woman's touch on a telegram he was writing, leaving Hamish with the empty office.

Now the dusty morning light striped through the blinds and kissed Reggie's desk. With all of this talk of murder, the headlines and the nightclub scandal, all he needed was a well-dressed woman with watering doe eyes, a pocket-sized ivory-handled pistol, and a few good lines about flatfoots, and he would be in a Winchester Molloy serial. Or Reggie. Yes, she was so alive. Color and warmth and not the black ink bleeding over his memory from the latest headlines. "Society Girl at Murder Scene." Reggie told him she was used to finding her name in the society pages. She had laughed off the front page. He wondered what life would be like if he was forced to be conspicuous. He swallowed just imagining it, the world around him fuzzing until the phone jangled.

"Luca Valari's office," he answered in Reggie's absence.

"I only have a minute. You have to listen to me, Luca."

"This is Hamish DeLuca, sir."

"They're giving me five minutes. They can't know I'm calling. You know why I am calling."

The static crackled. The same tunnel of

sound Reggie must have heard with some of these calls.

"The reception is very bad," Hamish said. "It's a bad connection. A basement I —"

"Who are you? Does Luca owe you money?"

"Where's Florence? He sold me out. I had to . . . I had to get this number."

"Speak up! I can only hear every few words. I don't know any Florence."

"He sold me out. She needs to know I am here."

"I can't understand you. Who are you?"

"Tell him I know everything. And I will tell the moment I get out of here. He threatened —"

"Sir — what's everything?" Hamish's hand shook over the telephone cord.

"She always hangs up on me. Calls me a creditor. I'm not a creditor. I'm Valari's lawyer."

"What?"

"Frank. Frank Fulham. He thought he was sending me away, but I found the number. He always thought I was slow. That I wouldn't find her."

"Find who?"

"Florence."

The connection went dead. Hamish exhaled then stared out the open window. He almost wanted it to be cloudy and rainy to match the mood he was in after the cryptic phone call. Instead, the world outside was a study in sunlight.

Below, schoolchildren tripped over the stones as tourists rummaged in their bags for their box cameras, snapping the Revere House and the neighboring Pierce-Hichborn residence, snippets of pocket-sized history to take home and show their friends in floral albums. Seeing the kids sparked memories he would rather not recall. Besides, Hamish was making his own type of memories: ones that severed him from Luca. Ones with Nate and Reggie manning an office where they did little but listen to the radio and eat cannoli. He would have gone on like that forever.

He nudged the window open farther and a breeze countered the North End mugginess, picking up the familiar scents of laundry detergent, fresh baking, basil, and flowers.

He loved the fresh air now. A far cry from when Hamish was little and stayed in his room, refusing to see any sunlight . . . dragged out the door to school, hiding near the back, begging his teacher to let him spend recesses and lunch hours in the library. He would sit near the drawn curtain and press his fingernails into his palm to stop the shaking. It was his teacher who first noticed. She clucked her tongue and rang his father at the *Telegraph* while he sat outside the principal's office until he arrived.

Sitting in that dark corridor, his chair scraping over the linoleum, a slight movement as he pulled his knees to his chest to make himself into a small little ball, he was certain he had done something wrong. That he was horrible and bad. That the pain and scabs on his right hand were tattooed there as punishment. The principal handed his father the number of a doctor and instructed he take care of "the problem."

The problem, Hamish had learned, was him. He crept down the stairs to the landing when he heard his father yelling, and he knew then that his strange shakes and stutters and his habit of breaking his skin with his nails meant that he was trouble. He was something wrong.

So Hamish got used to hiding. To avoiding people and preferring books. He was an excellent student. He had a mind that could absorb anything. He'd wanted to practice law. It made his parents so proud. Furthermore, he knew he could. He had top marks in high school and university. But every time he spoke in front of people, he was afraid his voice might stutter — as it did with little warning. So he practiced putting marbles in his mouth, avoiding his father's eye contact at the dinner table. But he did go to school and he vowed never to be trouble. He wouldn't be a problem. He would be the smartest one in class. Luca would be proud of him and his father too. As Hamish grew older, Luca moved in and out of their lives on a dime; but when he was there, everything was alive. He took Hamish to baseball games, to his first nightclub, and Hamish decided Luca was some kind of shield. He could be out in the world but still invincible, armored by his cousin's easy nature.

"Look at this!" Reggie startled Hamish from his reverie. " 'With the success of Luca Valari's Flamingo, long-standing clubs like the Dragonfly might find themselves in dire straits.' Your cousin is singlehandedly obliterating any competition!"

"Driving them out of business. Taking their best employees." Hamish blew out a long breath of air. "You coming to the club tonight?"

Reggie tossed the newspaper on her desk. "Dirk and Vaughan want to have dinner with one of Dirk's old school chums. He's finally worked up the courage to ask her out and he wants a chaperone."

Hamish tried to hide his disappointment. "I understand."

"I'd much rather be with you."

"It's best if I talk to Luca alone anyway, Reggie." He rolled a pencil over the desk.

Later, he maneuvered his bike down the staircase. The city embraced him, holding him close, knowing exactly what he needed. As the sunset bathed the rooftops in pink and gold, the bricked streets of Boston unfurled before him, his path occasionally interrupted by children playing or lovers tripping into themselves as they wound familiar streets in pursuit of the pulse resounding from a club's open door.

When Scollay Square exploded in noise and light, Hamish hopped off his bike. The night was humid but there was a nice breeze and he almost looked forward to the beat of the club.

"Cicero." The nickname grated on Hamish now. "You're investing a lot of time in my club."

"I will come every night until I find out what happened to Mary Finn." Hamish tried to keep his voice casual, though his hand was shaking behind his back. "And I want to know who Frank Fulham is and why you hired a secretary just to keep his calls from reaching you. And I want to know why you keep company with Mark Suave when he roughed up Reggie in your office."

Hamish noticed Luca's face darken at the last part of his challenge. His smile shrouded gritted teeth. "You need a better hobby, Cic."

"You're lying to me, Luca." Hamish squeezed his hand. He broke skin and winced. Luca noticed. "You know I can tell when people are lying to me."

"I would never keep anything from you," Luca said evenly. "Go dance."

Hamish shook his head. "I will find out what's going on."

"You're investigating me? Your cousin . . . your best friend?"

Hamish blinked, his nails deeply grafted into his palm. "I would. Because my conscience won't let me do otherwise."

Luca cursed. "Well, I suppose we're at odds, then."

Hamish flinched under the cold spark of Luca's look. "I suppose we are."

"Just don't do anything stupid like run away. Stay at the apartment. I still feel responsible for you. Your father would kill me if anything happened to you."

"Like being roughed up in the basement of the Dragonfly?" Hamish said. "Were you

393

ever in danger at all?" Luca was smart enough to ignore the question. "Where's Johnny Wade?" Hamish looked toward the bar. Something needled his mind, drawing him back to Johnny, but he wasn't completely sure what. Something that made him want to keep Johnny in his sight line. But Bill was washing a glass and a young man Hamish hadn't seen previously was mixing a drink.

"He has his own gig for the next two nights," Luca said passively. "Are you finished with your mystery for the night? Because the fellow from the *Herald* is here for an interview and he's just finishing his dance."

"Yes. I am finished." Hamish didn't smile. "For now."

"Don't do anything stupid."

Reggie felt stupid. Here she had spent months shaking off her old life, and now it stuck to her like gum on her shoe. She had forgotten how Vaughan's snobbery heightened the longer he was around Dirk. Dirk's companion was silent save for a few complaints to the waiter. She preferred to agree with everything Dirk said with a nod of her head. Everything from the workless population showing their laziness to the inevitable rise of their class. Reggie sputtered out several rebuttals only to have Vaughan squeeze her kneecap under the table.

"You know what he's like," he whispered in an aside. "Let's not make a scene."

Reggie wanted to throw her napkin. To use the gold-plated fork beside her plate of obnoxiously small mussels as a projectile into Dirk's left eye. Instead she pinned on a smile and tried to engage Dirk's girlfriend in conversation. Suddenly, she realized she had never gotten the girl's name. She wasn't an individual, rather an ornament.

When the chardonnay in her glass was gone and the main course had been cleared, Reggie decided to throw propriety out with the same easy flick that sent her ivory napkin to the floor.

She rose and shook her head. "I can't listen to this anymore. Dirk, have you been living in a cave? I knew you were insufferable in New Haven, but I thought the city might have broadened your perspective. There are people starving. Lining up at soup kitchens, desperate to find any work for their families. I see them every day. They rise before dawn and wait in the heat in a line for temporary employment that stretches out of my office building." She turned to Vaughan. "And you're making it harder and harder for me to feel remorse for slapping you at my parents' party. I know you don't share his views, so *say something*." She collected her handbag. She had drawn a few stares from onlooking diners but wasn't sure if their collective shock was from her outburst or her recent fame in the newspapers. Maybe both.

Finally, she leaned toward Dirk's date. "And you're nothing but a pretty, silent bobble on a Christmas tree. Not even the star. Speak up, for the love of angels! Unless you honestly agree with every last thing the oaf beside you says!" She walked out of the fancy Beacon Hill restaurant, relishing the first blast of fresh air, and started in the direction of the Common, intent on making it to the club in Scollay Square.

"Regina!" Reggie turned at Vaughan's voice. He breathlessly caught up with her. "I'm sorry. I didn't want tonight to be like this."

"What did you expect, Vaughan? That Dirk would have grown a heart?"

"I like seeing you in your new world. I know I haven't proven that . . . but I think I deserve a second chance."

"Vaughan . . ."

"You don't realize how intimidating you can be."

Reggie softened at the vulnerability in his voice. "I have to go. But —"

"Regina — you're a force of nature. I just thought I had to do something drastic to keep up with you. Do you understand? You can't make me the villain. Maybe I was just the catalyst. You were always going to run, weren't you?"

"Vaughan . . ." Reggie turned toward the Common. Vaughan lightly touched her elbow.

"Please, Regina."

"Oh, fine." She wriggled free and took a few steps forward. Tomorrow she would deal with Vaughan. Tonight she wanted to find Hamish and the Flamingo.

CHAPTER 24

"Hamish knows Luca flits in and out of disastrous company, but he won't see him lined up with any crime he did or didn't commit," Nate had said earlier, Reggie revisiting the conversation trying to make sense of Hamish's dour mood. "It's like he has loyalty cataracts, Reggie. And it probably makes for some awkward dinner conversations."

She had to find him.

"If all murder mysteries include dancing with you, Hamish DeLuca, I am ready to live on the fringe of crime." Reggie tried brightness on for size. His face was morose. She had reached the club, smoothed her hair, and stilled her brain of wandering Vaughan-ward. And then they had set into an easy dance. She was pleasantly surprised at how her heart skipped a beat when she saw him, and the night and Vaughan and his friend fell away with the prospect of

Hamish DeLuca and a dance floor.

Reggie had met him at the Flamingo, where she cut in on a girl who sounded like she had a perpetual cold and was tripping over Hamish's feet. Soon after, they changed location. Johnny Wade's band was at a new club that night, or so Hamish said.

They heard Johnny Wade before they saw him. Reggie stepped onto the floor and couples parted to give her room. Johnny leaned over the piano keys, half off the bench, his charisma matching his fingers over the riffs on the keys, bathed in the searching light of the Butterfly Room. The club was off Washington and Boylston, cradled on a side street, well attended but without the air of exclusivity patrons enjoyed at the Flamingo. The dress code was different too. No silks and satins. No jackets or ties. Just people — honest people — falling into music to shrug off the day. Cotton and sewn homemade lace, oxfords and curls falling from their pins with the athletic movements of swing.

She wasn't sure if it was the night or his pent-up energy, but Hamish was more passionate now. There was a possessiveness in his tight clutch on her waist and she knew he, like the rest of the patrons wriggling out of the week, was trying to forget. Everything was in the feel of his hands on her shoulder and on her waist, the way his feet found the perfect steps. Anyone watching Hamish here wouldn't believe that he stuttered over a consonant now and then and that his right hand trembled ever so slightly even in repose. And the longer they danced, the bolder he became, pulling her along into a confident spin and taking her with him as the tempo sped. Reggie felt as if everything he was feeling and thinking from the past week was manifesting itself in the pulse of a truant beat, the slide of their shoes over the floor, the almost suffocating atmosphere of people and smoke.

When the tune finally dissolved into one lingering note, Reggie was exhausted and exhilarated at once. She brushed a stray curl from her forehead and focused on Hamish. She thought of a book she had as a little girl all about the meaning of opposites: a dinner with Vaughan Vanderlaan and a spin with Hamish DeLuca to Johnny Wade's band would make a stirring example.

The band took ten and Johnny dabbed at his forehead, seeing and approaching them. "Luca said I could play the Flamingo soon." He beamed. "The club is all the rave and I don't mind paying my dues." He focused on Hamish. "When your cousin says something, he sticks to his word, doesn't he?"

Hamish hemmed through a sentence. He'd always thought Luca was trustworthy, but these past few months had showed him a side he hadn't seen before. "I believe he tries as best he can to keep his word."

"We have a few questions about Mary Finn," Reggie cut in.

Johnny paled and it was noticeable even in the dark-lit club. "I miss her, you know. I know she wouldn't give me the time of day while that Schultze was around. But we had a history. Worked at a few clubs together." He mopped his brow with a handkerchief. "She believed in my music." He laughed darkly. "But why are you still sniffing around? The police said it was an accident."

"Because you followed her to the basement and you had Schultze's walking stick," Reggie explained.

"What?"

"Whoever was with her before she fell down the stairs impressed an object into her neck. The police ignored it. We won't," Hamish said.

"And how do you know it was a walking stick?" Johnny tugged at his collar.

"Because a similar injury happened to me." Hamish's hand went to his neckline, under his collar.

401

"And you're implying what, exactly?"

"Maybe you saw or heard something," Reggie said.

Johnny looked over the dancers, to the bar, up and over to the bandstand. It wasn't as fancy as Roy Holliday's: the stands didn't have monograms. "I heard nothing. I saw nothing. Honestly, I'm a little tired of having to relive that night. I am trying to make a life for myself. A name for myself." His eyes settled on Hamish. "Your cousin has everything I want. A club. A name. I just want to prove myself to him while creating my own music on the side. You hear that?" Even without their leader, the musicians had trailed into a slow, steady swing. "I wrote that. Publicity is good. I have had my name in the papers. Not the way I thought I would start out, but . . ." He shrugged. "So was that all you wanted?"

"I know people will do a lot to win Luca's loyalty and affection," Hamish said, though he was starting to wonder why.

"Because he's worth it." Johnny said easily. "He has a lot of connections." He spun on his heel, jogged to the stairs, and ascended to the stage. Soon he was back in the spotlight, ramming his baton on the side of his stand and looping the air with his desired time. The band followed.

"What are you thinking about?" Reggie asked Hamish a few moments later. They were standing there, drawing attention with their immobility. Finally, she tugged his arm and they meandered in the direction of the door.

"I would do a lot for Luca," he said.

"I know. He's your cousin."

"Not just that. There's some magnetism to him. Look at you, you're working for him."

Reggie nodded. "He has this allure. You want him to like you, you know? And then you want to make sure that you're making him look good." She laughed. "Look at me go. Just like Schultze or Johnny Wade . . ."

"But you wouldn't go off the deep end for him." They were outside the club now, leftover strings of music funneling out and around them. The neighborhood wasn't Scollay Square with its fluorescent fever of people and cars and billboards, but it still had a pulse and bustle about it.

"Every so often there's this spark to you, Hamish," Reggie said after a moment. Hamish's profile was strong under the streetlight.

"What do you mean?"

"You're so shy, but there's something else underneath. A guy who will carry a girl home on his handlebars, who gives in to the music, who loves pretty and ugly cookies. I am just getting to know that Hamish and I think he bubbles more closely to the surface than people think. And I feel special for knowing that."

Hamish blinked away the look of surprise on his face. "Maybe I just needed someone special to bring it out."

She smiled and felt it down to her toes.

It was a waiting game. Waiting for something that would step out and flash itself. Some revelation that would prove that their suspicions about Mary were founded. Something. Anything.

Little crescents of red rimmed his palm, some scabbed. When he was little, his mother would file his nails down to nonexistent so he couldn't dig them in. Hamish went over the facts again and again in his mind until the story connected. He was good at this: creating tapestries in his imagination. When you spent your life thinking you were on the outside looking in, you had a long time to sharpen your perception of others. He fingered his braces. When he was a kid, his math teacher always told him he complicated things. Adding steps to an equation. Always thinking there had to be more lines and figures. While, really, he only needed to trust his intuition. There was something simpler here in the two parallel lines connecting the stories, just like in *Notre-Dame*. Hugo's book had a whole chapter about it: different plots intersecting at just the right time. The plot of Esmeralda and Phoebus and the gypsies on the Feast of Fools and the plot of Quasimodo. Hamish just had to figure out what it was. He would use the book that had seen him through days pulling his knees up to his chest and flexing his fingers, the sun hidden through the drawn blinds of his bedroom, for a different purpose. Not to hide, but to solve. What if what he thought was a weakness all these years — living in a book, afraid of getting too close to people or of failing — was actually a strength that would help him?

Hamish walked by Nate's slightly ajar door, and Nate muttered something about that fiend Aaron Leibowitz before reaching for the ringing phone. But Hamish heard something in his voice that didn't ring true. Nate was lying. This wasn't about his editorial letters to the *Advocate* at all. Hamish sometimes wondered if his friend left his door open on purpose so if Reggie or Hamish popped by they were a part of the ongoing conversation of his life.

Hamish stalled, drew a breath, and listened.

"Paul. Yes. Let me see." A shuffling of papers. "I need another electrician. Wiring? Telephone repair? I can put you in and you need . . . A moment. I think I hear someone."

Nate opened the door just as Hamish retreated to his own office. North End Housing Development was one thing. Hamish knew enough from his brief acquaintance with Nate that he was good at his job. Fair too. And from what Reggie said about his predilection for sweets and his ability to keep his own rooms on the other side of the Prado, he made a decent living from it. Sure, Nate cultivated proper housing bylaws, but what had he said about the skim off the top? The residents had to fend for themselves. He could only do so much within the metrics of his business. Were there other strings he could pull or deals he could make beyond the bold block lettering of "North End Housing Development" on his office door?

Hamish slumped behind his desk in an office all but useless, occupied only intermittently by him and Reggie, cannoli, and Winchester Molloy. He had half a mind to give it to a well-meaning entrepreneur who needed a boost for his business. One of the men Nate was always trying to help.

The familiar sounds snuck under the crevice of the open window. Church bells pealing, horns honking, carts dragging, people greeting and laughing and yelling in a rainbow of languages. His very own Court of Miracles. Where miracles could happen when people exchanged goods and thoughts and goodwill. Hamish jolted up. Nate had mentioned that people traded services to forgo the paperwork and reports for landlords who didn't care about tenant laws. *And what if someone arranged it?*

Why else would Nate need to document who taught piano and who fixed telephone wires? Unless he ran a Good Samaritan service . . .

Hamish heard Reggie's whistle before he saw her. It was almost 10:00 a.m. He wondered if she had thought ahead far enough to line up interviews for a new job.

"Any interviews?" he asked her when she strolled in with a smile. He felt a pang thinking of someone else sharing her mornings or looking across an enclosed space and finding her there. Her little hums. Her incessant need to scribble in her journal. The look on her face when she melted at the first taste of cannoli on her tongue.

"Not today." She blew a strand of hair from her forehead.

Hamish's smile matched his relief. "I have a theory, Regina. Look at your influence." He flashed her a look. "My brain is working overtime."

She laughed, though it was somewhat forced as her eyes worked over the slight red marks on his hand. "At least your brain is working."

"It's about Nate and what he does, and it might just help us finish this."

"He works in property development and yells at Aaron Leibowitz at the *Jewish Advocate* over their ongoing theological feud. I want to solve our murder mystery."

"I think he is the middleman for an enterprise that matches people with services. If someone needs their wiring fixed and their landlord is a goon like Schultze, then he has . . ." He arched an eyebrow with a knowing look, waiting for her to catch his drift.

"Someone who can tutor their daughter after school in payment."

"No money exchanges hands. No dirty laundry. Just services."

"Which is why Mrs. Leoni and her friend were so desperate to see him."

"And why he has immediate access to Old North Church."

Reggie sparkled. "He's kind of like Robin Hood. He . . ."

They turned at the sound of Nate bounding in with a copy of the *Advocate*. "This mutt Leibowitz! He thinks I am playing a game of chess. That he can make a move. But it is so much more than pieces on a board. It is . . . What? Why are you both looking at me like that?"

"Sit down, Nathaniel."

"Am I in trouble?" Nate laughed. "You two play Sherlock Holmes and suddenly everyone is a suspect."

"We figured it out," Hamish said.

"The murder? Was it me? Because as exciting as that prospect might be, I was nowhere near the Flamingo that night. I was playing seven-card stud with my Bubbe. I lost, by the way."

"You're the North End Robin Hood," Hamish said. "You broker services."

Nate laughed. "I'm not smart enough. Now, see here, Aaron Leibowitz!" He rapped his paper. "He would have you believe that I was put on this earth just to cross him with theological bickerings. But I will prevail!"

Hamish held up a hand. "Enough of

Aaron Leibowitz. I am starting to question his existence or whether he is just some way you quickly change a subject."

"Ha!" Nate reached into his back trouser pocket for a folded newspaper. He unraveled it and held it demonstratively. Most of it was in a language Hamish couldn't read, but he believed Nate.

"If you're trying to be so sneaky, don't leave your door open."

"And don't take phone calls when one of us is in your office," Reggie joined in, grabbing the newspaper and searching for Leibowitz's name amidst Hebrew characters.

"Fine. I have nothing to hide. Do you need your sink fixed?"

"No wonder everyone loves you." Hamish smiled. "No wonder you have access to Old North Church."

"Everyone loves me because I know the ins and outs of the neighborhood. But mostly because they read my editorial letters to the *Advocate* and Aaron —"

Reggie laughed. "Oh, Nate." She reached over and squeezed his hand. "How many people do you think actually read your letters to Aaron Leibowitz?"

Nate smiled. "What's the point of living in this magnificent city of freedom if you can't help people find liberty here?" he said solemnly. "What do you call it, Hamish? From *Notre-Dame*? The Court of Miracles? If I can make a little miracle happen now and then, it's a heck of a lot more fun than property development." He smiled at both of them. "You're quite good detectives, you know. I mean, on one hand I cannot believe it took you this long to figure it out. I didn't exactly lock myself in a vault and my door was always open. But . . ."

After Nate had retreated to his office, Reggie and Hamish exchanged a smile.

"I am going to buy him dozens of almond cookies," she decided. "Forever. Then subscribe to the *Jewish Advocate*. I can't understand half of what he says, but at least I will root for him against poor Aaron Lei-bowitz."

"Nate is a middleman. He is the one who arranges it all."

"And free of charge." Reggie sparkled. "I like him more and more."

"Yes, well, somewhat free of charge. We both know he actually works at that office of his. That . . ." Hamish felt something stir-ring. A parallel line . . .

"Obviously he doesn't take money for it. He would never . . ."

"Reggie! But what if someone had the same type of setup for a different enterprise?

Who knew who could be bribed and who knew where to launder money? They take their crummy slumlord money and invest it in clubs.

"Nate has a file," Hamish continued. He was looking at everything but her. She could see the wheels turning in his mind. "But at core he is the arranger of his little miracles."

Hamish chewed at his thumbnail. "Someone who gets a cut of everything. Someone who knows everyone. Has ties from back here in the North End to the glitz of Scollay Square. Someone who is always around, tapping his way through every club and baseball game and meeting with people who would use his services." Hamish flexed the fingers on his right hand. "Someone who has a good enough memory not to have to leave a paper trail. So no police officer could ever flaunt a concrete piece of circumstantial evidence. But still convince people that they could have a piece of whatever miracle was on offer. That it was some living and tangible thing. A safety net," Hamish surmised. "Every investor, banker, accountant, property manager, club owner, and police officer . . ." He raked his fingers through his hair.

"A gold mine." Reggie bit her lip. So many phone calls that knew something.

"Someone would kill for that level of power. Or" — and here he thought about Frank Fulham — "be sent away."

"And if Luca has access to this person . . . maybe someone wanted him behind bars. Maybe it was an easy way to lock him away so they could get access. Cut him out completely. One less person to share with. Simple fractions."

"And creditor calls are a good ruse," Hamish continued, "to put people off a trail."

"He was never at the office, though. He just put someone there for people to yell at."

Hamish shot Reggie a compassionate look. "Come on."

Reggie shook her head. "Don't I have to man the fort, sit here, and get yelled at?"

Hamish's mind trailed off. "I couldn't find anything when I went sniffing around his office in the apartment; but maybe I was looking in the wrong place." He darted in the direction of his bike leaning against the wall. "It will be faster." He answered the question in her eyes.

When they reached the sidewalk, Reggie hopped on the front of the bike with ease, and in her maneuver over the handlebars, a tickle of hair brushed his cheek. She was so

413

close these days: her scent, her warmth, the little tics and quirks that made her unique. Wonderfully irreplaceable.

He pushed off, biceps straining on either side of her, flexed with the control of movement and extra weight. His mind was weighted too. Burdened on the precipice of a revelation that would see the summer come full circle. What started with Luca ended with Luca.

Reggie hopped off just as they passed the Granary Burying Ground, catching the wink of the summer sun, soft and a little mournful.

The doorman smiled at him and even more pleasantly at Reggie. "How do you do, young lady?"

Reggie flipped on the switch of her usual charm, melting him with a smile and poised shoulders.

Once in the elevator, he exhaled.

"Something's bothering you? I mean, everything is bothering you. But this is something more." She ran a red-accented finger over the ornamentation of the elevator. The bellboy did well at air whistling and looking up and not directly at them.

Hamish didn't say anything, but his mind was a movie reel. It was as if he was finally able to see his cousin for the first time. It

414

startled him. He wasn't sure how it had evaded him, other than he knew it was his nature to see the best first. Especially in someone like Luca. How could he not give Luca the benefit of the doubt?

They alighted at the penthouse floor and crossed the russet-and-gold carpet. Hamish extracted the key in his pocket and turned it in the lock.

He heard Fidget the moment he pushed the door open. Her usual noises: rattling some dishes, humming something in a voice that might have been sweet if not undercut by the sad songs she sang.

"Fidget. I should probably call you Florence, though?"

She laughed softly, turning to the kitchen. "You'll want tea." She looked at Reggie.

"I don't want tea. I want to know who my cousin is."

"I gotta tell you." She folded her skirt under her and sat in an armchair. "I was surprised when he brought you. Maybe he thought you were naïve. Maybe he thought you would redeem him."

"Redeem him from what?"

"Himself." Fidget shrugged.

"Your husband is Frank Fulham. Luca's —"

"Attorney. In Chicago. And the man he

trusted more than anyone else in the world. His vault."

Hamish cleared his throat. Why hadn't Luca trusted him? "He's in Cicero."

Fidget nodded. "Frank thinks he sold him out, but he doesn't know that Luca was supposed to arrange a far more drastic measure for him. Instead, he made it look like he had finished him."

"Finished him how?" This from Reggie.

Fidget's look told Hamish everything he needed to know. "Your cousin isn't a killer."

"But he's at the middle of something, isn't he?" Reggie asked. "I mean, we have an idea, but I want to hear it from you."

Fidget took a moment to look between them, then settled on Hamish for a moment. "Everyone can be bought and sold. Everyone wants money. Those who have it want to preserve it. Those who don't want to find a way — a way and someone who can act as their guidepost. A way to start nightclubs and enterprises using the right connections."

Reggie whistled. "You mean the right people who will help you find a way to squeeze money out of people and businesses that are easy to squeeze?"

Fidget shrugged. "Not proud of it. But I always thought I was one removed. Luca

416

runs a legitimate business. Frank and I just went over contracts. Lent a legal eye now and then. My husband is a good lawyer. But Schultze was on his tail. Thought Frank was behind the operation. It wasn't the case. I just fidgeted with the books." She looked up knowingly. "It's what your cousin has always called me."

"And Luca knew all of it? Had access to everyone?" asked Hamish.

Fidget shook her head. "I don't know. I don't know." She breathed. "All I know is that Luca saved Frank's life. They told him he had to send Frank away." She paused. "Away." She folded her hands. "Your cousin hid him. Found me a job and safety." Her eyes roamed the penthouse. "I sometimes think he's running away too." She turned toward the door. "But I don't want this life anymore. It was one thing when I could hold on for my Frank. When he comes back, and I mean this with all respect, I never want to see your cousin again."

"I understand."

She reached up and touched Hamish's face. "But you are a good boy, Hamish. And your cousin inspires great loyalty." She shook her head. "If Mark Suave is prowling around here and he knows about Frank, then we all have only a matter of time."

Hamish looked up and over at Reggie with wide eyes. She didn't seem to follow his trail of thought, flashing him a look.

Hamish tucked a strand of hair behind his ear. "Do you think you could ring Phil?" Hamish asked.

"Of course, but I think this is his afternoon at his other job."

"We can meet him. He doesn't need to come to us."

"I wish I could read your mind. I know it's buzzing ahead at a frantic speed," Reggie said once they were in the elevator. Hamish didn't respond until they were under the sunlight of Tremont Street, hailing a cab.

"No bicycle?" she asked warmly as Hamish gave the cabbie the address Fidget provided them.

"We'll visit Phil and then go to the Flamingo."

In the wharf, the boats bobbed red and white and blue. The water licked and lapped, tickling the shore with a glisten. Hamish shoved his hands in his pockets. He didn't want Phil to see his right hand squeeze and relax. Phil's face was stone. "I have a ten-minute break." Phil looked between them, unamused. "I don't just drive Luca, you know. I have another job."

"I know. That's why I was happy you

would meet with us."

Phil pulled a long drag on a cigarette. "It's part of working with Valari. I have to be there for you anytime. Day or night. Lucky you're low maintenance." He looked Hamish over. Then his gaze swerved to Reggie, looking her up and down and up again. "Not sure what you're about."

"Did you drive Frank Fulham too? Did Luca ever talk to you about the extent of his business?"

"You think your cousin talks to me? I just drive."

"But you knew him in Chicago?"

Phil cursed, startling a seagull that shrieked loudly before flying away. "He'll do a good turn by you."

"What does that even mean? Are you capable of completing a thought that doesn't sound like it's made up with leftover lines from a Sam Spade villain?"

"Easy, Reg." Hamish didn't like the way Phil tensed and grated her with a look.

"Your cousin is a powerful person and he inspires great loyalty," Phil continued.

"So you know Mark Suave, then?"

At the best of times, Phil's face never betrayed any emotion. Now it was a sculpture in perfect stone, unetched. "I drive, Mr. DeLuca. I am paid not to listen."

How could you find someone who was so disinterested in everything happening around him? Hamish had inched toward adventure since the moment he stepped from South Station on his first day. He couldn't imagine closing the world out and shutting down when there was so much to see and experience and do.

Hamish spent more time at the office, knowing that was the best place to await another Frank Fulham phone call. He wondered, as did Reggie, how many times this missing link to the mystery of Luca's move to Boston had rung before without her knowing. Frank did call again, and Hamish gave him Luca's address. He wondered if things would have played out differently had he spent more time at the office the moment he arrived in the city. The office — while far away from Luca — was turning into a key way to intercept phone calls and learn the truth about his cousin.

"Your wife wants you back," he said simply. If Frank was the reason Luca left Chicago and the reason Mark Suave and his man were on Luca's tail, Hamish thought it was about time Luca was pulled into the light. "I'll wire the money. No? You have it. You're safe, Mr. Fulham. We'll make sure of it. It's time to come back." He wasn't sure how or when, but it was time to put something right.

As right as the moment Reggie arrived. Yes, *right*. There was something right about the space they shared together, the way her expensive perfume lingered even after her commute from Charlestown. He could smell it now.

"Look at you offering to wire money."

Hamish clicked the receiver. "You know I have none of my own. I'd find something of Luca's to pawn. It's his mess." His neck heated under his collar and his ears twitched. Was this what true anger felt like? His father had always had a temper: yelling and ordering people around, flushing red at an inconvenience. Never anything truly harmful, of course, his bark far worse than his bite. Hamish was certain with his quiet disposition he hadn't inherited it, but maybe Luca was bringing some of it out.

"Well, at the very least, he isn't our murder suspect," Reggie said, drawing him back.

He realized he had been gazing out the window until the light blurred his eyes and she, of course, was eager to get back to the corpse at hand.

"Still could be Schultze."

421

Hamish shook his head and straightened his collar. "No. He wasn't lying to me. I have this . . . sixth sense when someone isn't completely authentic with me."

"And it's not Dirk."

Hamish shook his head. "That fellow strikes me as someone whose only loyalty is to himself — and his pocketbook." *Loyalty.* He chewed on the word. His ears twitched when he thought of how often he and others had used it in the same sentence as Luca's name. Luca inspired great loyalty. Luca was someone to whom one wanted to be loyal — regardless of the cost. It may well have been his cousin's second name for all the times he had heard the two words in the same sentence. "Johnny Wade."

"Johnny had a thing for Mary Finn," Reggie said. "Why would he want to see her dead?"

"Jealousy of Schultze." Hamish felt they were going in circles. He drew one on the desk with his fingertip.

"Imagine being jealous of old Schultze when you have the good looks and charm of Johnny Wade."

"Maybe they argued and he used a bit of force with Schultze's stick and she . . . well . . ." Hamish spread his hands to finish his line of thought.

422

"But why stay around, then?" Reggie put her journal into her handbag and leaned back against her chair. "Why not cut and run the moment the police named it an accident?"

"Because he saw an opportunity?" It sounded like a question and not a statement.

"What?"

"I overheard him talking to Bill about the right kind of exposure for the club."

"How can the right kind of exposure be murder?"

"Publicity sells. Luca's business has been bigger than ever." He thought back to Brian MacMillan and how desperate he was to inch his way into Luca's good graces and wield some of the power he believed Luca had.

"So he did it out of some loyalty to the Flamingo? I know Wade's worked at a few clubs, but it's just that — a club. What made this one so special?"

"It was a chance to start over," Hamish said, remembering the way Luca's eyes sparkled when he talked about his new chance, his new club. The Flamingo represented prosperity — for Luca, certainly.

"And it's not Luca," Reggie said for the umpteenth time. He knew she was just arranging her thoughts by mentally checking off any possibilities.

"No." Luca — *his* Luca — would never just see the end of someone. He didn't do things that way.

Hamish stood and grabbed the back of his hair. "No one else is credible. When you eliminate the impossible" — he paraphrased a line from the Sherlock Holmes stories integral to his childhood reading — "whatever is left is the truth."

"And it wasn't Dirk." Reggie counted with a hand. "It wasn't Dirk or even Schultze. And not Luca. Or Lily."

"Mary could just be a tragic accident. Not the middle of this web at all."

"With no motive. In the pictures there is always a motive. I know. I know what you're going to say. This isn't the pictures."

"An accident gone wrong." He sighed, imagining Johnny Wade confronting the girl of his dreams, attempting to paste on a smile for his customers while the woman who painted the corners of his imagination flirted with a club investor for money. Hamish looked up a moment, startling Reggie.

"What? Your eyes are so intense right now . . . they . . ."

"Close your eyes!" Hamish demanded,

stretching out his hands to map the scene. "Imagine an argument between a handsome bartender and his cigar girl."

"Not hard," Reggie snarked. "I've seen it a million —"

"Hush, Reggie!" Reggie clamped her lips. "Imagine they are fighting about the intentions of Schultze: the investor of this big, sparkly club. But then it turns into an argument about something else." Hamish warmed to his theme. "You see, the girl wanted to break away from this world. Had dreams of . . . whatever girls like her have dreams of . . . Hollywood? Broadway? Kids? Who knows! Johnny promised to save money from his bartending gigs and then he would find a cushy mainstay job. One like Roy Holliday had. Do you see it, Reg? At least nod, for the love of heaven. Good. All right. So Johnny had heard rumblings. He's a bartender. No matter how careful the inner workings of crime are in Boston, lubricated tongues can tell tales. He hears about Luca. Galbraith's a decent enough guy but a bit too aboveboard. Johnny no longer wants to live on tips. He knows Mary hears the same things. She tells him she knows a way to the center. Together, they are the perfect pair — the perfect way to get to the middle of it. Whoever is making

425

money, they will be able to skim from it. Heck, they were both there the night before the opening. You saw the way they looked at each other. The chemistry . . ."

"It was palpable. Like Gable and Colbert."

"Shhh!" Hamish hushed, glad she couldn't see the smile stretch across his face at her equally palpable excitement. "The night of the Flamingo opening, Mary Finn tells him she's sick of waiting. She's had a bit of champagne on her break. Heated from the dance floor. She wants to make a break from Schultze. From this world. But Johnny . . ." Hamish smiled a little as the pieces fell into place. Then he smiled some more. The more he explained it to her, the smoother his voice became, free of ripples or trips. Confident. Like Luca. Like Johnny Wade.

"Johnny wanted to stay." Reggie's nose was wrinkled with her concentration behind closed eyes.

Hamish smiled for a different reason altogether. "Yes. They fought. She fell. She died. Johnny needed to think about himself. He heard — as I have constantly since the moment I arrived in this stupid world — that Luca inspires great loyalty. He could twist Mary's accidental death into something . . ."

Reggie's eyes shot open. "He could pretend that it was for Luca! For the publicity! He had worked at clubs! He had read the papers. He could have a safeguard. Luca, being Luca, would be let off . . ."

Hamish loved matching her mental stride. "And Johnny had the security of having done something to bring business to Luca's club."

"Yet it's been a few days."

Hamish chewed his lip. "Maybe he wants things to settle down. For the books to inflate."

Reggie was almost bouncing in her chair. "We can get a confession!"

"How?"

"It's a gamble. But if you're right . . . and why wouldn't you be right? It's the only thing that checks out and you're brilliant. Hamish, you're brilliant and . . ."

Brilliant? He knew he was book smart. Everyone told him so. But everyone telling him things would never replace the confidence he was only starting to find in himself. He wanted nothing more than for the things he believed his greatest limitations to prove his greatest strength. Would this murder, this moment, be the tip of that iceberg? Hamish scratched his neck. "Reggie, it's hardly decent to be this joyful about discov-

427

ering the identity of a murderer." The seriousness of his statement didn't match his tone.

"I'll tell Johnny we're onto it. That we know Luca appreciates his magnanimous gesture of loyalty."

"You're being hyperbolic."

"Only when the occasion warrants it."

Suddenly the office seemed small. Reggie and Hamish's eyes met and the walls closed in around them, not able to contain the energy that sparked in the small space. Finally, they abandoned it for the buttery swath of light warming the North Square. But instead of seeing the cracks and crevices, the soot stains, the line from the Temporary Employment Agency stretching out the office door, and the annoying children cloying for a spot in line in front of the Revere House, Hamish only saw beauty: steeples and russet brick and a place of miracles, large and small.

"I will meet you at the Flamingo tonight! I am going to bring my best mink stole."

"You had time to pack your mink stole while you were hastily planning your great runaway?" Hamish raised an eyebrow.

"Something about solving a murder makes you almost insufferable, Hamish DeLuca."

"Sorry . . . I . . .."

"No. No. I like it. Let me change. We know Johnny Wade has a weakness for women who play into his charms. You change too! So I'll meet you? Just outside the club? A date?"

A date? Of course Hamish's first official date with a girl would be her ringside seat to his inevitably poor attempt to approach his cousin about a murder. "And I'll find out why Luca was down there in the first place," Hamish said, emboldened by her enthusiasm and the thought of her in a mink stole. "Luca Valari may inspire great loyalty" — Hamish let a touch of derision slide into his voice — "but he is not above confrontation."

"Confront Luca." Reggie smiled. "It's about time."

Though her voice was light, Hamish knew she was dead serious.

"And not just about Mary's death." Hamish whistled low. "Fidget was right. Mark Suave let Luca open his club; but he won't be patient forever. He'll expect some kind of payment for Fulham."

"What kind of payment?" Reggie swallowed, deflating the buoyancy of the conversation as the sunlight hid behind a cloud.

"I guess we'll find out."

CHAPTER 25

They met at the appointed time, Reggie radiant and spinning around in her stole for his benefit.

"It's too hot for that." Hamish cleared his throat, but they both knew the nights were falling shorter — and a cool breeze was rustling over the fluorescent lights of Scollay Square, drawing the curtain on Hamish's summer of freedom.

Reggie was saying: "Tonight is the night! Where every one of the focal players in our little mystery congregates, where —"

"This isn't a picture, Reggie. It's not the end of *The Thin Man*."

"I know! I am just trying not to be nervous." She punched him in the arm playfully. "Guess some of your nerves are rubbing off on me."

"You are only as strong as the moment that finds you braver than you have ever been," Hamish quoted, not remembering where he heard it. Maisie, maybe. Or one of his father's articles. Probably his father's articles.

Then he saw it: a fluorescent emblem of a deeper secret. A flamingo jaunty and tall, brash and pink, a siren luring people to loud music.

Hamish crossed the threshold into the Deco hallway of the club. Reggie took her time at coat check to give him a head start.

Hamish took a deep breath, trying to conjure the command he'd had of the conversation in the office earlier that afternoon. He was braver than he thought. He was the only person who didn't believe himself capable. He'd change that.

"Still playing detective?" Luca fingered his cufflink. Hamish swallowed. This would be harder than he thought. It was one thing to imagine a scenario with Reggie, another to stand in front of Luca and tell him that he knew who he truly was.

"I need to talk to you." He decided to start with the name drop. "About Frank Fulham."

The lights were low. Roy Holliday and his band were running scales. They flitted over a minor key.

"What do you know about that name?" Luca's smile was pasted on for the benefit of the delivery boys and the band, preparing everything for another night. "Good job, Roy. Maybe try something a little slower tonight. Around eleven. Just when people have had a few too many cocktails and are on the lookout for a new partner."

Hamish leaned into his cousin. "The funny thing, Luca, is I do know when people are lying. Or not being candid. There is something uncomfortable about it that makes me anxious. I feel it. Except with you. A person with an incredible memory. A person who always gave me an adventure. You were having one of your own, weren't you?"

"We should go to the bar. It's quiet there." Luca's smile didn't waver. Hamish nodded.

Luca stepped behind the counter and poured himself several fingers of whiskey. He held up a bottle. "Cicero? No? More for me, then." He turned to Hamish. "Now, Hamish, it is obvious you and Reggie have been taking this rather seriously and avoiding every last thing I told you about not getting involved."

"But I am involved, Luca, because it's you — it's all you — the girl's murder is you."

"You know I didn't kill that girl."

Hamish nudged his glasses higher on his nose. "I know. But you were the indirect cause. At least my theory . . ."

Luca drained his drink. Poured another. For the first time in the half-light of the club, Hamish saw the toll of the past weeks and the endless drafts of whiskey in the lines etched into Luca's face, in the puffiness of his eyes. He was still impossibly handsome, but even Adonises weren't immune to late nights and too much liquor. It made Luca seem human, and maybe that was just the drop of courage Hamish needed to move forward.

"Why are you chuckling like that, Luca?"

"Because you were smart enough to follow my trail and I was blind enough to think that you would never put the pieces of the puzzle together." He crooked a finger under Hamish's chin. "And perhaps I will pay for underestimating my cousin."

Hamish swatted Luca's hand away. "You played us all. You played Fidget. You let those men at the Dragonfly strangle me."

"I didn't *let* them do anything. I was sick that they hurt you."

"Please. You were never really in danger at all there, were you? That night. Suave was part of it all. You needed to keep Schultze and your driver from figuring out that you had far more power than you let on. You got in too deep. Like an addiction. Like someone who gambles or drinks too much. But I can help you." Hamish nodded eagerly, convincing himself more than he assumed he convinced Luca. "Yes. I'll figure it all out. Luca, we'll do this. No one else has to know and . . ." Hamish stopped. When he spoke again, his voice had lowered. "You call me the same name as the city you stashed your old lawyer away in. Oh, I know that's a by-the-way, it happened long before any of this, but did it ever make me feel stupid. To know that the answer was staring at me and I associated it with something affectionate."

Were Luca's eyes glistening? "You are my conscience, Hamish. I could send Frank to Cicero. Somewhere safe. Unharmed. You think when directed I could order a man's death? No matter what the cad Mark Suave ordered? I have spent the past year taking care of his wife. Providing for her." Luca's big black eyes were intense and Hamish almost wavered. Ironic: Luca ever inspiring loyalty — even his own. Even while Hamish's own conscience flickered.

"She knows," Hamish said plainly.

Luca nodded. "Of course she knows. Everything she needs to know."

"And she knows where he is."

Luca cursed.

"Don't ruin another life. I put it together and Florence needs him."

"Hamish, you don't know what you've done." Luca waved to nowhere. Hamish saw his cousin maintain his usual composure through an unexpected falter. "You think that by promising to reunite him with his wife you did something good."

"He said you played him."

"Of course I played him! Played him for his own good. He had a lucky break. You realize that if the wrong people got hold of him they might have disposed him! I let him think that it wasn't safe. And it wasn't."

"Because it was easy if you stashed him away. You connect the dots. You're in the middle. And Schultze and Brian MacMillan and poor Johnny Wade thought that you were the path they needed to get to the man they needed. You *were* him." His eyes moved toward Reggie at the bar, most likely in a conversation paralleling his own. Without the personal involvement.

"People think I am too obsessed with clothes and baseball and nightclubs to take the time to run an operation."

"Does Ben Vasser know?" Hamish asked. "He's part of this, isn't he?"

"I think he suspects the level of my involvement. That's why he took me for questioning. That and to prove to his bosses that even I am not immune to suspicion. A bit of a show."

"Just give it up, Luca. Suave will have a marker on your head now. Go home to Toronto. Figure it out."

Luca shook his head, reached for the bottle and refilled his glass. "I just need to prove to Suave that I am someone to fear. That I am more powerful than he thinks I am. It's unfortunate about Frank, but we'll cross that bridge —"

"Luca! Listen to yourself!" Hamish raised his voice and people turned to look. Luca flashed him a death glare, but Hamish didn't stop. "You think you're golden. You can change. You can give this up!"

"I don't want to!" Luca's voice stirred the attention of patrons not already focused on the pair. "I want this life. I don't expect someone like you to understand."

Hamish shook his head. "No. That's not true! Luca! Think!" His conscience told him that this man — this stranger — was a criminal. He should pay and pay and pay for all that he did to steal the life of honest people. A liar. An instigator. Perhaps even an inadvertent reason that a woman was killed. But his heart saw Luca. Luca who took him to his first baseball game. Luca

436

who saw him while his parents worried about him. Luca who made him feel invincible in large crowds at the Palais Royale.

"I am above this. Above a man who would find me and threaten my secretary — yes, yes, Reggie told me. I felt sick, you know. But nothing can help that. Part and parcel of the trade."

"I have to help. I'm your cousin. I am your family."

"I am a criminal!" Hamish was surprised he said it so loudly. That he was owning up to it at all. "I am at the center of what you are trying to change."

"You have a conscience. You let Fulham go. You didn't see through what they wanted you to do."

Luca shook his head. "Think, Cicero! Think! Why do you still need to believe this of me? Why do you still need me?"

Hamish looked everywhere but at Luca. "I don't need you anymore." He saw Luca's face darken. "I can be loyal to you only through my love for you. That won't change. But I have to love myself enough to follow my gut. But, Luca, you can stop. You can change!"

"People don't change. Not that much."

"You can! You already know your first instinct is to do the right thing. Leave this behind."

"I'm not strong enough. There's something about that power" — he balled his fist — "that people will fall over themselves to do your bidding. To impress you. Even when people just thought I was an access point to this mythical file." He smiled ruefully. "You've got the brains, Cicero. And the goodness. But I've got a different kind of smarts. And a memory. A long, wonderful memory. And none of that DeLuca need to save the world that you seem to have inherited from your father."

"You saved me," Hamish said, his voice cracking a little. "You always just treated me normally. Not like I was glass or would break if you pushed me."

Luca smiled. A full smile. Not one of the smiles used to pander to a crowd. A genuine smile. Then it stopped. The room quieted with a foreboding feeling: a curtain rustling, a door closing. A feeling that things might never be the same again.

"You're in over your head." Hamish was thinking aloud. "I can help you. Yes. I'll figure it all out. Luca, we'll do this. No one else has to know. I can fix it."

"I thought they'd forget about him," Luca said after a long silence. "Fulham. Why would they care if he was alive? They asked me to take care of it. Probably assumed I would have Phil find a way to dispose of him. I have a reputation, you know, of having everyone do everything I need. But I couldn't do it. And I couldn't hurt Fidget. But I couldn't tell her either. Though she always suspected. The older I get, the more I believe an invisible line binds people together." His eyes met Hamish's. "No matter how they keep each other apart."

Hamish ran his palm over his right arm. A shaking hand was surprisingly painful. Something none of the medical studies he sought at the Toronto library would ever tell him — that his hand tremor exercised muscles near his shoulder. And then he was aware that he was tripping over his sentences. That everyone could see. His right hand had a mind of its own. For a moment, he stopped and looked around. The band was still playing, but few people were dancing. Hamish and Luca were at the center of introspective glares. Full circle: eyes on him as they had been in the courtroom at the beginning of the summer. He could retreat. Or he could plow through, regardless of his hand shaking and his words snagging like a run in a sweater. Regardless of his breaths coming in frantic gasps, hiccupping his sentences and slowing them down. Why was the Hamish so confident and assured in the North End office but hours before betraying him now?

"And then there's Mary Finn." Hamish barreled through in his shaky voice. "She's just collateral. She was close to Schultze and was going around promising Johnny she could find a way to find the center of it all. Who was controlling everything!"

"Are you sure you aren't listening to too much of that serial Reggie loves? Winchester Malone or Molly or something . . ."

"You would have heard something from where you were meeting Suave and his man."

"Arthur." Luca attempted to sound casual. "Suave's man."

"Luca, did you hear something? Did you hear a fight? An altercation?"

"Stop playing detective. It doesn't suit you."

"You know she was killed! You know she fell back on those stairs! *Your* stairs."

"I didn't hear anything," Luca said loudly. "I didn't. I swear, Hamish. I only left my meeting with Suave and Arthur and found Schultze's walking stick. I don't know what made me pick it up. But I did. Maybe in case they cornered me. What good would it do? And there she was. You were in the base-

440

ment. You know how loud the noise from upstairs gets."

"I know. But it wasn't an accident."

"You're going around in circles."

"I can fix it." Hamish looked around and heat flamed his face. Hamish couldn't even fix himself.

"There's a point, Cic . . ." Luca must have noticed the crowd's attentiveness too. His posture had changed. "When you just step off a ledge and then you fall and you fall and you can't seem to get a grip on anything. You can't seem to find a way to pull yourself back up." Luca gave a short laugh. "And I thought I could legitimize myself by making this an operation." He looked around at the carousel of the Flamingo: people spinning in and out. A few couples still dancing, mesmerized by the band. Most far more attuned to the handsome club owner. "I really wanted it to work. But I am not ashamed to say that I was meant for something more. A different lifestyle. Can you imagine me lining up at a soup kitchen? I was meant for something remarkable."

"That's what you said about me. My name —"

"I don't expect you to understand."

"I thought you had to have familial ties. To be involved in this type of . . ." Hamish waved his hand. "Crime." They both knew what he meant.

Luca reached out and straightened Hamish's tie. "A long time ago my father made some connections in Chicago. Legacies last."

Hamish straightened. Legacies did last. Even the wrong ones.

It was funny: at the beginning of the summer, Reggie was mortified that she had slapped Vaughan Vanderlaan. Nothing of that ilk had ever touched her traditionally safe life. Now she frequented a nightclub, used to the smoke and buzz of liquor around her. She watched Hamish, waiting for something — anything — to happen in his confrontation with Luca. From where she stood, she could see Hamish's hand was shaking. She wanted to approach. Instead, her eyes followed Johnny Wade arriving, then spinning a glass in his hand as he settled behind the bar, winding the wine stem in and out of his fingers with flair.

"Regina! You're a regular here!" His smile really could stop clocks if women let it. "Popular socialite. You're going to keep bringing the class here, aren't you? You haven't let me make you a Singapore sling yet. We just got pineapple juice. I'm going to try serving up a few more exotic drinks. Keep the summer going."

"Sounds tasty," Reggie said distractedly, studying Johnny's profile. She had never been close to a murderer before. "How's your band?" She wanted to keep him talking.

"I just need Mr. Valari to let me play here. But you'll see. He'll give me the shot. I will prove myself loyal to his cause."

"How loyal?" Reggie asked, tentatively sipping the drink he passed over to her. "Mmm." She closed her eyes briefly. "Sweet."

His suddenly raised shoulders emulated Luca's usual stance. His hands, shoved deep into his pockets, reminded her of how Luca circled the club, taking everything in stride. Luca, so calm and cool and collected.

"You know I found Mary," she said quietly after Johnny finished slinging a few more drinks for customers who tripped away from him as quickly as they had approached the bar a moment before.

He pocketed the tip money and looked at her. "I told you. I am a little tired of hearing about it."

Reggie pursed her lips. Hamish and Luca were still in her sight line, deep in conversation, haloed by the spotlight each time it flashed in their direction. A conversation echoing her own. That invisible strand binding them gave her the confidence she needed to move ahead. She straightened her shoulders and threw her head back a bit, with a finesse she hoped made her look a little more like Loretta Young than a startled bird. "I hear Luca likes all different sorts of shows of loyalty." She rimmed the nearly untouched drink with her fingernail the way she had seen it done in the movies once. Ginger Rogers or someone who exuded class. "You know, working for him I hear all sorts of things."

Reggie studied Johnny's face as well as she could in the club light.

"Oh." He was noncommittal.

"He talked about how Mary's death, as unfortunate as it was, God rest her soul, brought about major dividends for the Flamingo." She made up a few numbers. "The fiscal quarterly earnings" — she hoped it sounded legitimate — "were 45 percent more than anticipated."

Johnny rinsed out a glass. Hamish and Luca's voices were rising, but Reggie trained herself to focus on the conversation at hand.

"See, Hamish DeLuca and I are kind of doing an under-the-table favor for Luca. The police ruled it an accident, but Luca wants to properly thank the person who gave his club a running start. Not that he wished anyone dead. Just that collateral damage is often at the center of unanticipated gain." Who was she and where was she pulling all of these lines from? Films? The sky? She remembered her first interview with Luca and how she thought she sounded ridiculously over the top. Johnny, however, seemed to be buying it. "That's why I am talking to you."

Johnny turned from her to help a few customers, but kept looking over his shoulder in her direction even as he finagled the martini shaker.

"It was an accident, sure. And then it was an opportunity."

Reggie choked on a small sip of her drink. A confession! To a murder! She was excited. Guilty for being excited. Traumatized too. And nervous. What should she do? No one else heard it. She looked around. Then back at Johnny Wade. Then swept over to where Luca and Hamish were talking . . . talking . . . talking. Drawing a crowd with their talking. Reggie willed him to look over so she could catch his eye. Then, miraculously, he and Luca fell apart a moment. Luca combing his long fingers through his hair; Hamish looking around in that unsure way of his. With the hand not holding her drink, she looped her arm behind her back and motioned to him.

Hamish held up a finger. Luca was distracted. They were both heated. Hamish was a study in careful breathing.

"I was just telling Johnny here," Reggie said knowingly, "about the brand of loyalty Luca Valari so appreciates." She glared in Luca's direction. He was trying to patch up the scene he and Hamish had caused. "Anything that would help promote his club."

"I had no idea Luca felt so strongly about that brand of loyalty," Johnny finally said. "That . . . an accident . . . could turn into something. I mean, in the moment . . . I thought . . ."

Reggie flashed Hamish a meaningful look. Hamish's tired face lit.

"You thought that Luca would appreciate an opportunity to bring attention to his club. More press," Hamish said, cool as a cucumber. Reggie was impressed.

"I didn't know he was going to be the one who was questioned for it," Johnny said. Then another patron required his attention and he was momentarily distracted. When he turned back to Hamish and Reggie, it was with a slight conspiratorial nod to them.

"I would do anything for your cousin." He directed the remark to Hamish. Every time Reggie and Hamish locked eyes, she sensed her friend was following her line of thought in a kind of unspoken code.

"And so you pushed Mary Finn down a stairwell?" Hamish said easily. Surprisingly easily, Reggie thought. He had to have pushed through a barrier talking to Luca.

"Mary and I had an altercation," Johnny explained. "Schultze's stick was there. I have a temper. I didn't mean to push her down the stairs. I just had her and then let go and she went."

"Excuse me?" Luca appeared, stripped of his customary charm and not making eye contact with Hamish. Reggie studied the dynamic between them. If Hamish had been anyone else, Luca Valari would have had him ridden out on a rail. She supposed, at the very least, Luca's avoidance was to his credit. "Hand me a whiskey, Johnny."

"Johnny was just confessing to Mary's murder," Reggie explained, wondering where her confidence was coming from and how she might bottle it and keep it for future occasions.

"To prove I was loyal to you," Johnny added casually. "I heard of a club in Chicago where a girl was murdered and it's filled to the brim every night. I know who you are. I know your influence. Mary told me about it and I know you expect loyalty. Regina here confirmed it."

"Loyalty by way of murder?" Luca cursed. "That I would *kill* a girl?" He spun to Hamish. "Is this another one of your ideas?"

"I heard her fall," Johnny continued before Hamish could speak. "I didn't know she was dead. That's why I came back to the bar. I need this job. I have this music. I didn't mean to kill her. I got angry. She said she was staying with Schultze. We were supposed to be together." Johnny shook his head. "But she betrayed me and I saw that Luca . . . that you wanted me for your club. I heard that the club was a way you were going to keep people in your circle. That's why I up and left the Dragonfly. They've been talking about you since you arrived. And you were going to give me the opportunity to make something of myself. So I took the opportunity. I thought you would see it as a gesture of loyalty. So I let it happen. Look at the publicity you got."

"You're wrong there," Hamish said. "Luca doesn't look after anyone else. Luca's only concern is for Luca." Hamish turned his head over his shoulder. "You would think that maybe he hired you for your potential

448

or out of the goodness of his heart or to bring you closer into his circle, as you say. He's not thinking of that at all."

"Luca —" Johnny held up a hand.

"Quiet!" Luca's voice was loud enough to draw several pairs of eyes again, though the club — quickly filling to its full capacity — had returned to its normal bustle after Luca and Hamish's conversation. "Johnny, if you are telling me this, you are confessing to a murder."

"It was an accident."

"You change your pitch quickly," Reggie said.

"You led me to believe that was what he would want." Johnny seethed. He looked around frantically like a man who couldn't believe he had painted himself into this corner on account of a pretty girl. Then, regardless of Luca, of the crowd demanding drinks, of the first bars of a Roy Holliday tune, he reached behind a collection of bottles and extracted a pistol that he aimed directly at Hamish's chest.

Hamish didn't move, just took a fleeting look at the barrel, then at Johnny's uneven gaze. He was blinking, a nervous tic twitching his eyelash.

"I don't want to hurt anyone. But I can't

449

go to jail. Not for something I did for you." Johnny turned at a quick diagonal and centered the gun on Luca, clicking the bullet into place. Hamish saw a lifetime cross before his mind's eye. Luca caught Hamish's gaze. Then they both turned to Reggie, ghost white under the lights of the bar.

"Well, at least your theory turned out to be right," Reggie said drily.

Luca cursed under his breath. "You killed a young woman," he said to Johnny. "For no reason."

"For you."

"You think I have an influence I don't have and you're willing to waste a life for it?"

All three men turned at the sound of a low laugh. "This is the least of your problems." Mark Suave stood behind Luca. "And stop talking so loudly." He scowled at Johnny. "What a terrible criminal you would make."

"Mark," Luca said, a warning in his tone. "Now is not the time."

"It's always the time, Valari. Move aside." He lifted his own pistol and caught Johnny off guard by waving it at his nose. After a few gasps emitted from nearby patrons, Suave answered them with an ultimatum:

"You clear out for a breath of air, or I start shooting at random, yes? And don't think of calling the police." He narrowed his eyes at Luca while still flashing his weapon. "Vasser's men were informed of our conversation."

Hamish tried to catch Reggie's eye, but she'd turned toward the club. The band was still playing, though Suave's ultimatum rippled through the milling crowd, forcing them outside.

"Interesting, isn't it?" Suave's voice pierced Hamish's thoughts. "That people would flee rather than play hero." He turned to Johnny. "You killed that girl, didn't you? That Mary Finn girl? After Luca and I had our little meeting downstairs."

"I . . ." Johnny spluttered through a few words that only reached toward cohesion.

"Never mind. Go." He jostled the gun a little without compromising its aim.

"No!" Reggie yelled. "He murdered someone."

"Aren't you a brave little thing!" Mark Suave chuckled. "I should have kept pinning you against the wall in Luca's office when I had the chance. Be gone, Wade. Go on crowd control. Make sure the volume is loud." He tilted his head and straightened his firing arm. "Best not disturb our guests while I finish the proprietor."

Hamish felt something new and incendiary wind through his veins. But he stayed still. What could he do? An armed man was controlling the situation with a silent command he could only dream of possessing. He looked to Luca. Then hated himself. He had always looked to Luca, and now he knew he would find nothing in Luca to hold on to.

"I've had men at South and North Stations watching, you know," Suave was saying to Luca in a soft tone. "Watching every night just in case a ghost haunted the platforms. A ghost who looked surprisingly like Frank Fulham."

Hamish concentrated on his shoes. Reggie saw a lot in that study: Hamish fixating his eyes, driving his hands deep into his pockets. He watched Reggie deflate a little, her shoulders sinking. It was a new sensation: wanting to assure her before he stilled his own nerves. Wanting to convince her she was safe and life was fine before he stilled his own heartbeat.

Beside him Luca was still, save for heavy swallows pronouncing his Adam's apple. Mark was still talking but everything sounded as if they were in a tunnel, reverberating with the pulse of the club and the beat of his heart.

Luca's face was a mask of panic while a million questions blazed behind his dark eyes. "I can't be responsible for every rumor you hear," Luca was saying. "But I won't let Hamish and Reggie be a part of this. You let them leave now."

Suave shook his head. "Her . . . maybe." He slitted his eyes at Reggie before turning back to Luca and Hamish. Mostly Hamish. "But I saw your breaking point the night I first found you here at the Dragonfly: smoothing your way through a new city, thinking the past was far behind. But him —" He pointed the gun at Hamish, then took a step farther, pressing the barrel into Hamish's chest. Hamish shuddered, his nerves fizzling into a frozen moment. He knew he couldn't let that bullet hit Luca. That it was better directed at him. Better him than Reggie or Luca. His heart would beat too rapidly until it finally burst. A split second and he thought of his parents and how he would be leaving them with nothing.

"Get your filthy hand off the trigger!" Luca shouted. The patrons of the club were glaringly aware. This standoff was far more appealing than Hamish and Luca's row. Far more distracting than the rise and fall of

453

the band. Some panicked, but Suave ignored it.

"I can ruin you in this town." Luca's voice was dark, slicing through the noise. "You think you can walk out of here and point your finger at me and people will believe you? Who would take your word over mine the moment we stepped onto Salem Street? I own this city. And those I don't own, I soon will — and you would rather shrivel into oblivion by firing a bullet at my little cousin?" Luca clucked his tongue. The gun still imprinted Hamish's flesh. "If you harm one hair on Hamish's head, I will see you are blacklisted the world over. You will find every door closed to you."

"You are bartering with power you don't have." Suave pinned Hamish with his eyes. "There's always someone more powerful, Luca. Something you haven't learned."

The world buzzed and for a moment Hamish forgot where he was. The buzz hummed around him and his eyes wouldn't focus even as he tried to blink his surroundings into view. And even when he heard the click . . . a long moment before he felt it and even when he felt the sudden rush through him and the external force of metal and sudden shock and pain while someone said his name . . . he knew it was right. He was relieved. Because it couldn't be Luca or Reggie who bore the brunt of this man's rage and vindication. It had to be him. It was best this way. And even as he fell, the music in the club a void, the lights dimming dark, he wouldn't have turned back the clock or had it any other way.

"Hamish!" Luca's voice was frantic. "Hamish!"

Hamish looked through half-closed eyes. Something cold was beneath him. The floor. Cold. Luca's arms propped him up. Perspiration dripped into his eyes, but he blinked away the sting and funneled in on his cousin a moment. Luca looked terrified. Hamish looked down. His shirt was sticky and an iron pressed through him. Hamish blinked and blinked. Mark. A crowded club. The train. Fulham. Everything hurt.

"You're so stupid, Hamish. Wh-why did you do that?" Luca smoothed Hamish's hair back. "You make it so hard. I don't deserve this. Why did you do it?"

Hamish licked his dry lips, tongue cotton. He tried a slight smile but his teeth had begun chattering, clacking like crystal plates in his slackened mouth. "You're Luca." It was the only explanation he had. Through the ringing tunnel of his eardrums he heard sirens and then a woman's voice. Regina

455

was barking his name. Blurrily, he made out the scene of chaos and confusion. Acoustics usually filled with music, stale and hollow. And nearby . . . not too far . . . a ribbon of red trailing from Suave's expensive suit.

His hands shoved through the feeling of cement to grip Luca's arm with the tiniest bit of energy he still had while his brain flickered on. "You have to go. They can't find you here. Suave . . ."

"I won't leave you. Hamish, you'll be fine. I swear to you. You'll be fine. It will all be over." Luca's voice shook a little. "I got him. It's over."

But it wasn't over. To think was like pushing through the weight of water, but Hamish was strong enough to remember there were two of them: Suave and Arthur. And Fulham, the corpse who lived. Hamish's eyes were fluttering shut but he pried them open for one last pleading glimpse. Reggie's voice again, this time for someone to call the police. The real police. The police not on Luca's list.

"Go," he whispered.

"I'm not leaving you here."

Luca did a poor job of convincing either of them, his voice warbling. His eyes brushed over Hamish before he slowly detached himself, lowering Hamish's head gently to the cold tile. He leaned over and pressed his lips tightly to the top of Hamish's hair. "You know me, Cicero. There are few things in this world I truly love. But you are one of them. Reggie. Reggie, tell him I'm sorry."

Through a fog, Hamish made out Reggie's outline and her worried face. He grabbed at her skirt as she knelt over.

"Reggie! Th-they can't know. About Suave. About Luca!" Hamish had no more to lose. "P-put the gun in my hand," he whispered before the world went black.

CHAPTER 26

The Court of Miracles. He mapped it in his mind, flitting in and out of a cold, sterile room, mind tracing fragments of cobble-stone and brick and jutting little alleys that winked from age-old buildings. This little land was checkered with uneven roads and painted with banners and filled with light and music and sound. And even in its safe space, his thoughts spiraled out to a night when he let Luca get away.

The gun they found in his possession worked: heavy steel he clutched so tightly the officer had to pry it from his hand. But if he had the gun, then Luca got away. The police believed it was self-defense. The real police. Not Ben Vasser. In one of his more conscious moments, he thought he heard Reggie say that Vasser had disappeared. With Schultze and MacMillan. Maybe he had.

And it was self-defense. Hamish just

didn't offer who was defending whom. He wished he had done something heroic rather than just standing there. It might have been easier if he had been able to jump in front of Luca and take the bullet, saving him. Instead, he was just collateral. He convinced himself that it was enough he was there at all. If he hadn't come to Boston, would Suave and Luca have just reached an inevitable point without him? Maybe it was heroic enough that he was there. The unintentional hero of Luca's story as well as his own.

"Well, you can't just lie there." Nate's voice came through a far tunnel that, when Hamish blinked away drowsiness, was really just the door of his hospital room. "If you recall, we just started a chess game and you were losing abysmally and I refuse to finish it myself."

Hamish tried a smile. He was groggy and everything hurt. He blinked a few times, the world around him making more sense the longer his eyes stayed open. But Hamish's will was something stronger than what chained Luca to what he thought he had to be. If you dug a hole of your own choosing, if you were responsible for your own actions, there was a kind of grace in that.

Luca didn't think he had the will to get

out of his trap. Like Claude Frollo looking at the fly in the spider's web in the book Reggie had retrieved from the office. Hamish moved chess pieces with his good hand and tried to forget. Mrs. Leoni sent cannoli with Reggie, who didn't seem to want to move from the chair next to him.

"I'm going to be all right, Reggie."

Reggie sniffed. "I'm not crying for you," she cried.

"Then why are you crying?"

"Okay, I'm crying for you! You looked dead, and Suave's man might find Luca, and . . ."

Hamish reached out and patted her hand. "I'm not dead, and Luca is out of my control."

Reggie shot up, drying her eyes with her kerchief. "He is?"

"I can't be responsible. I can't fix everything." He said it like a mantra. Maybe he was wriggling out of that part of himself that chained him to things he couldn't change. He looked up and smiled. Maybe it was the medication. Maybe it was her presence. Whatever it was, he felt a surge of light and possibility. "More cannoli, please."

"It worked out!" Reggie's voice brightened and she dabbed her eyes dry. "Johnny Wade is being tried next week."

Hamish's brow furrowed. It hurt. Everything hurt. "What?"

"It wasn't in vain." Reggie shook her head
and her curls bounced a little. "Our murder
mystery was solved and the perpetrator . . .
No. That's not how you say it. Perpetrator?
Rats! I have to watch a few more pictures!
Our per-pe-trator . . . There! Got it!" She
smiled. "Is behind bars."

The crescent of Vaughan's thumb stopped
the tear trickling just under Reggie's bottom lash line. Hamish looked pale. He
looked dead. It wasn't a vital organ, the doctor said, just his shoulder. A sling. Time.
Healing. She hadn't left his room. Then she
did when Vaughan insisted. And when Nate
insisted. And when Vaughan *and* Nate
insisted, their voices layering in a discordant
symphony of concern. Vaughan tried to re-
assure her with a slight shake, stretching his
arm around her. She fit like a missing puzzle
piece. Like the summer hadn't wedged a
space between them. If Reggie couldn't
fathom returning to who she was, maybe
she could pull him into her present. His
broad shoulders and nearness, his smell of
New Haven. She was seeing him in a new
light, and it wasn't just the lemony tint
blessing the city as fall edged in. He was

461

relaxed here. His shoulders loose, his smile frequent. Not confined by the china and yachts and forced small talk of their parents' circles, Vaughan was as delightful as he had been . . . once . . . when they stole a boat and shoved off far from her father's estate. Or when he snuck a flask to a baseball game. Boston was changing Vaughan. It shouldn't have surprised her. Boston had changed her too.

"Vaughan, I'm exhausted." She was sticky too. Her hair was plastered to her head and the back of her neck, and she was sure she looked a sight. Vaughan's eyes, however, positively sparkled at her. They were wandering through the hospital corridor after a visit to Hamish, her heels clacking on the linoleum, her body feeling so tired it could sleep for a week.

"I was hoping we could postpone our night." She didn't want to sit through the silver cutlery and ivory linen of the Parker House restaurant.

"You need to eat, Reg. Why don't you show me where you've been all summer?"

Reggie lightened. "Really?"

Vaughan insisted on a cab from the hospital, but Reggie insisted they alight just at the rim of the neighborhood she now called home.

They walked back past the North Church and onto Salem, Reggie pointing out the little moments that made her days before tugging Vaughan in the direction of a cozy trattoria.

Inside, neat tables were covered with red-and-white checkered cloths. Candle wax stood in congealed sculptures in decorative holders, and fat little wine bottles encased in wicker shells were flowing freely.

A waiter Reggie recognized from her daily comings and goings presented them with a basket of bread and filled their water goblets.

Over large platters of homemade pasta twirled in sweet tomato sauce, Vaughan picked up where they had left off at the Flamingo's opening: with incessant small talk. She let him ramble on about the summer and his father's business and his uncle's participation in the annual regatta. Reggie was tugged back to sun-dimpled water, the brim of a wide hat sloping over her forehead, pretending interest in rigging and sails. She picked up a piece of bread and dipped it in a pool of olive oil.

And Vaughan was still talking. Her thoughts turned to Hamish until something about their earlier experience and his bout of nerves made her look up at Vaughan as if seeing him for the first time that evening. Was Vaughan waxing incessantly about home because he wanted to catch her up? Or was Vaughan nervous?

"I wanted to apologize. About the night at the Flamingo. For abandoning you. I hope you know I was only trying to do what was best."

"I know. It was a horrible night. A horrible thing."

"I thought I could make it up to you. I thought we could see a picture tonight, if you like. I checked the newspaper listings. That film you like with Loretta Young is playing. Or the other *Thin Man* film."

"*Platinum Blonde,*" Reggie said softly, watching Vaughan over the rim of her wineglass. He was handsome and he was trying. He was a perfect gentleman to her, as always, dabbing at the corners of his mouth with his starched napkin, warm and friendly to the waitstaff, not even looking up when a clang of dishes crashed in the open kitchen behind them. The fact that Vaughan Vanderlaan stepped into an establishment with an open kitchen at all told her exactly how hard he was trying. She decided to throw him a rope.

"Maybe we could skip the picture and just take a walk? We could decline dessert here

464

and find some gelato."

Vaughan's smile widened, puncturing his cheeks with semicolons of smile lines. He was a looker all right. He could have any number of girls in their circle back home. Far prettier girls. He was a study in perfect contrast to Hamish DeLuca. Strong cheekbones and chin, and just the slightest cleft in that chin. Bright hazel eyes and sunshine-kissed hair. Broad shoulders and those rower's arms, their muscles visible even now through his light cotton shirt.

Vaughan settled the bill and Reggie watched as he left a generous gratuity. More, he shook the waiter's hand with a sincere thanks before they set out into the starlight.

"The North End becomes an entirely different character at night," Reggie explained, relishing the last flicker of sun before it disappeared completely, leading Vaughan to her favorite gelato place. "Music funnels out of the windows and everything comes alive. People loiter on the fire escapes and smoke and talk and drink wine. And a guy is always whistling after his girl. And kids are finished with school so they jump rope or play hopscotch or draw on the stones in the Prado."

Vaughan watched her a moment then stole

her hand. She didn't pull away. "There's life here, Vaughan." She squeezed his hand and tugged him farther. "Life in these streets and over these stones and in the women hanging their wash to dry. There's life in that smell — you smell it? It's so fresh. Oil and basil and bread."

"And you love this life, don't you?"

"I do. And I belong here."

"But, Reggie — these people are so different from you. From your life." It was the first shade of Vaughan-ness she had experienced since he had appeared. But rather than narrow her eyes at its apparent derision, she decided to give Vaughan the benefit of the doubt.

"I know."

"But I also know that you love your new friends. And your work."

"I worry about Hamish. More than I do my work. Oh, don't look at me like that."

"Like what?"

"Don't be jealous, Vaughan. He's my friend. Ah! Here we are."

Inside the small shop, she ordered pistachio gelato for Vaughan and lemon for herself.

"What do you think?" she asked after placing a few coins on the counter and smiling at a woman who wished them good night in

Italian, brushing away a loose tendril from her sloppy gray-black bun. Vaughan flicked his tongue over the ice. "It's delightful."

Reggie swallowed a bite of lemon that melted on her tongue like a cold cloud. Once their cones were finished, Vaughan stopped her. By now, night brandished the sky with its blue-black canvas and stars overhead faded with the shine of the street-lights.

Vaughan's hand moved over the back of her neck, then down her spine. He pulled her in, his cologne, an expensive smell, immediately taking her home to her parents' parlor, to the sticky leather of his car's front seat en route to a picnic at the sea. It was a smell that transposed her to church on a Sunday morning, the heavy fabric of his suit jacket brushing her bare arm. It was a smell delectably familiar and yet oh so dangerous.

She was just learning how to cross things off in her Journal of Independence. She was just beginning to abandon all thoughts of home. But he was sincere. And he was here.

His smile. His eyes.

"I'm not the only one to blame, Reg," he said. "You know that. You are not the easiest girl to get along with. Don't flash me that look. You have a very set opinion of how people should act and react as it pertains to you. And it was hard — knowing that you wanted me to follow you in any small way you could turn away from your parents. I am not like that. I don't want that."

"I understand."

"Do you? Do you understand that I can disagree with that part of you and not go along but still care deeply about you? That my announcement that evening at the party was my way of being impulsive? Have you ever seen me do anything that rash before? I was standing to confront as much humiliation as you, and I bore the brunt of it with your slap."

Something turned over in Reggie's heart. "Honestly, Vaughan, I never thought —"

"Of me?" he said. "No. You only thought of yourself, and maybe I was in earnest. I've always wanted you."

His finger caressed her shoulder blades. And, as difficult as it was for her to admit it, she had wanted him too. She turned so that their faces were an inch apart, their noses almost touching, their collective breaths joining in the tang of late summer. Here was Vaughan out of place in the North End. Here was Vaughan trailing her over the North End.

"And you used me as an excuse, Reggie.

To run away. Don't say you came here because you were escaping the embarrassment of that day. Because you were going to run anyway. You were always going to run. It was a matter of time."

"Were you going to follow me?" she asked, tipping her face up, searching his eyes, and what she found in them was her — all her.

He answered her with a kiss, his lips over hers in a gentle butterfly brush before pressing harder. She kissed him back, rising slightly on her oxfords, feeling the carefully cut tendrils of hair over the back of his neck, just where they were downy and light beneath her fingertips.

She loved the feel of his hands on her waist and around her back. She loved the strength and breadth of him. When she finally pulled away, her face was alight with a smile that she could feel stretching her cheeks.

"I still love you, Reg." His voice was thick, in recovery as he caught his breath. "That doesn't change because you stole off to Boston for half the summer."

"I needed time," Reggie explained. "With or without you, I needed time. Away from my parents, away from our life. This" — she spread her hands out toward the tenement houses hugging each other, the road undulating with uneven stones, the church towers beginning to toll brassy bold markings of the half hour — "this is living, Vaughan."

Vaughan followed her gaze, scraping his eyes around them, then looked back to her. "Is it this Hamish fellow? Playing Nick and Nora?"

"He's a good friend," Reggie said again.

Reggie felt Vaughan straighten beside her. Then the hopefulness bubbling through her during their dinner and stroll was a bright red balloon and Vaughan the pin. "Why are you here, Vaughan?"

"I miss you, Regina. Before, we were . . ." He let the wave of his hand finish everything encompassed in their relationship: Dating. Nearly engaged. Inseparable sometimes. She heard the words even when he didn't say them: *We were always friends.*

Their friendship was often the one bright light in days of endless routine and her mother's lace teas. Her stupid pride had kept her from seeing that.

"See, Reg, not everything about home was completely insufferable."

His fingers lightly brushed hers as their arms swung with their slow stride, and she pressed their palms together, a summery dry kiss.

"I'm looking for a flat, you know."

Reggie sparked. "So you're going to stay in the city? You and Dirk got the job?"

Vaughan nodded. "It's grown on me." He squeezed her hand. "I was thinking more about our last conversation, Reg. And I was thinking that of course you took off. I was insufferable there. I can be myself here." He took a beat. Reggie drank in the familiar sights and sounds and smells of the community that clutched her heart and tugged tightly.

Reggie fell back a step, taking Vaughan with her. He looked down at her, concern filming his blue eyes. "What is it?"

"For the first time in my life, I haven't been thinking or planning. I have divided my summer into little hurdles that I had to jump. So I've been living in the moment. It's been so freeing."

"You're going to let your hair grow out and go camping at Walden Pond?"

"No." She giggled. "Vaughan, my entire life has been a series of routines. It was about time for some disruption." She bit her lip. "But I think I am a free agent."

He walked her to the elevated train, kissing her on the cheek. "I hope your friend is all right, Reg. And I hope this means we're starting over again."

Reggie smiled in lieu of a response. She

471

wasn't sure she wanted to start again. But she admitted to herself it was nice to have someone who reminded her of home.

In her room that night, she thought about her evening and how she wanted to change. She couldn't go back home. Intimidating. That's what Vaughan had called her. Funny, Hamish never seemed to be uneasy around her — other than his usual nerves. She absently fingered the pearls of her heirloom necklace, a nervous habit from the time she was a child.

"They're not a toy," her mother had scolded. "They're too expensive. Worth almost as much as some people's mortgages!"

Reggie unlatched the clasp and pulled the necklace over her head, holding it out to the light, admiring the pearls' milky sheen. And with fervent internal apologies to Great-Grandmother Euphrasia, she made up her mind to visit a pawnbroker on North Bennet Street the next day.

CHAPTER 27

Hamish stayed two more nights at the hospital, staring at the four walls around him, beating Nate at chess, lying to his parents that he fell off his bike and was temporarily hospitalized but they were not to try to see him. It was a superficial wound. Accepting the lemon jam and flowers and telegrams delivered from Toronto with a sheepish guilt. Receiving Maisie Forth's phone call and wandering through pleasantries, knowing that a return trip to Toronto wasn't enough for him anymore.

There was nothing from Luca. Hamish wondered where his cousin was, and if he was running, who he was running from. Arthur, maybe, Mark's associate. Hamish knew enough about this type of business to know that when someone disappeared, another took his place, like sharks' teeth.

Reggie broke into his thoughts on several occasions. And visited often.

"I did better than I thought," she said, just as the nurse was preparing him for departure, checking his temperature, applying a clean bandage.

"At what?"

She held up an envelope. "Pawning my nana's pearls." The envelope, he saw when he peered closely, was full of cash.

"Looks like we'll be needing a few North End detectives." Nate clapped, appearing at her shoulder. "For every crime you solve, you get cannoli."

"Even Winchester Molloy doesn't have it that good!" Reggie's excitement shone brightly.

Hamish gingerly slid off the bed, smiling at the nurse and gathering his few belongings. "The idea is ridiculous," he said.

"You look lost." Reggie's eyes were on him intently.

"I am. Do I go back to Luca's? Do I —"

"Vaughan's cleared out of his suite at the Park Plaza," Reggie said. "It's yours until you figure out what to do. I mean, soon enough we will be in booming business, but until then —"

"And I am just here to collect my chessboard," Nate said with a kind look at Hamish before gathering the board and pieces.

"Your friends take good care of you," the nurse remarked as Hamish maneuvered into his coat with his stiff shoulder.

"They do, don't they?"

"Well, William Powell?" Reggie smiled as Hamish ascended the steps to the second-floor landing. He had slept better than he had at the hospital, thanks to Vaughan's illustrious suite. Any guilt or discomfort he felt in taking the room was erased when he found a box of bruttiboni and a note from Vaughan on a slick monogrammed pad: *Any friend of Regina's is a friend of mine. Get well soon.*

There was still a sadness to Hamish's pale face, but Reggie's words twitched a smile in his cheek. "Well, Myrna Loy, I don't even know why I keep showing up here. The Flamingo isn't our problem anymore."

"True, but you are one half of my new endeavor."

"And what endeavor is that? You rented an office with your nana's stolen pearls?"

"We'll be detectives. Or legal consultants or . . . we'll basically just keep doing what we're doing. But with *our* names on the door instead of Luca's! And part of the day I will be doing pro bono work at the Temporary Employment Agency. We'll be a fixture here!"

He spread out his hand to lay imaginary type. "DeLuca and Van Buren: Consultants in Nightclubs and Crime."

Reggie giggled. "Are you kidding me?"

"Fine. Consultants in Crime?"

"Just crime?" Reggie raised an eyebrow. "Also, it's Van Buren and DeLuca."

"Alphabetically, DeLuca comes first."

"The heirloom pearls I just pawned and the money I just wired my father for with no questions asked say differently."

Hamish stretched his arms then winced at the tug on his shoulder. "Anything! Consultants in Anything! If you think your employer has cut some off the top to improve his bottom line!" Hamish flushed as he warmed to his theme. "Murder! Mayhem!"

"Kittens!" offered Nate from his open door. "Someone is bound to have a lost kitten."

"True," Reggie complied.

"And who is going to take the Flamingo anyway?" Nate's voice filtered into the hallway.

"Mr. Galbraith," Hamish explained. "The fellow whose club went under when Luca's opened. He's legitimate, Nate. He won't be using any properties here to feed into the club."

"I trust you."

"It's Van Buren and DeLuca," Reggie emphasized, framing the glass window with outstretched fingers. "It rolls easily off the tongue and I am the one with the impressive familial connections. Secondly . . ." Reggie swatted his good arm, stood back, and watched him a moment.

Hamish waited. "Secondly?"

"It's just . . ." She rose a little on the balls of her feet, then rocked backward. "It's De-Lovely, DeLuca."

"You've waited a long time to say that." Hamish grinned, the muscles in his face much looser than they had been at the beginning of the summer. His smiles came easy now.

Reggie jogged into the office.

"You'll get the girl, Hamish DeLuca." Nate joined him in the hallway, speaking near Hamish's ear just as his smile was wavering off.

"I don't know what you're talking about."

"You don't think you will, but you will," Nate said. "Patience, young DeLuca." He squeezed Hamish's shoulder and retreated to his office.

■ ■ ■ ■

Reggie licked her tongue over her bottom lip. She had tugged so much of her life into her future, she just couldn't help but keep her left foot on the ground. And maybe he needed time to learn who he was. And maybe she needed to keep flipping back the pages to see where Vaughan led her. It was confusing. More confusing still with him sitting there looking at her expectantly, the blank pages of their new adventure purchased with her pearl money still unmarked.

"We should get a plant." It was the absolute stupidest thing to say the moment he walked into the office, but it brought her down to earth and kept her eyes from tracing the shape of his lips much as she would trace around her fingers with a crayon in school.

"Oh yes." He nodded. "That would brighten the place up. Give it some life." His smile tugged at his cheek.

But the place didn't need life — it had plenty of it. She was ridiculously attracted to him but circling around expectation and fear and a bond that still tied her to Vaughan.

"I'll get one. Tomorrow."

"Good." Hamish smiled. "That sounds good." He looked toward the open door to the hallway as a messenger boy delivered a telegram across the hall. He would watch every day as the boys ran in and out on their errands, and he knew somehow, some way, one of those telegrams would be for him. It might be in code. It might be from a million worlds away. But Luca would reach him and Hamish would wait until he did. And then the final unraveled piece of the new life he was knitting would tighten into place.

Meanwhile, Reggie played with the dial on the radio.

"Hello!" Mrs. Leoni's voice chimed from the hall. Mrs. O'Connell was at her elbow. "Hamish DeLuca." She looked Hamish over, clucking her tongue like a hen. Hamish rose and greeted them both.

"We heard you were hurt," Mrs. O'Connell cooed with maternal affection, inspecting the top of Hamish's black hair and his pale face.

"And your mother is not here." Mrs. Leoni sighed, holding up a basket. "This is all you need. Soup and bruttiboni and lemon sandwiches." She lifted the checkered cloth covering the food, and Reggie could see from her vantage point that it was enough to last several men a week.

"How can I ever thank you?" Mrs. O'Connell was saying. "It was enough. Just to say that I had someone who was looking into my case. Those rats, they scurry back into their holes."

Hamish smiled. "It was my pleasure, Mrs. O'Connell." He accepted the basket from Mrs. Leoni and it nearly bowled him over. "That's too much! So heavy."

Mrs. Leoni leaned her portly figure over the desk and cupped his cheek. "You are a good boy, Hamish."

Reggie wasn't sure if it was an opportune time to peddle their services, but she seized the moment anyway. "Hamish and I are going to keep the office. Not for any nightclub business. For helping people like you. People who need mysteries solved. People who don't want to be gouged by Baskit's ridiculous prices."

Hamish wasn't sure what he was doing, signing up to return day after day to a space she inhabited, knowing that he was so in love with her it hurt to breathe when she was in his near vicinity. That sometime she would look over at him and his heart would likely burst. But what was love if not the ability to make a complete and utter fool of yourself daily just for the gift of breathing the same air as a person who made your heart sing and soar?

Reggie had the wireless playing and the familiar talk-singing of Fred Astaire spilled out the door. *"The way you wear your hat . . ."*

And nothing could take it away from him. Nothing — not Vaughan, not Luca, not circumstance could separate him from the little idiosyncrasies that pulsed through him in an irregular symphony. The quirks and qualms that made her Reggie and the sound of her indelible music: the rhythm of her heels over the creaky floorboards and the way she wrinkled her nose when she was deep in concentration. That was his — all his — a little corner of the world that Vaughan could never infiltrate. Suddenly the song he had heard a million and one times sounded as if he were hearing it for the first time. Because in a way he was. It made sense now. It was a song about her.

Hamish passed the doorman at the apartment they'd shared, then took the elevator one last time, noticing his reflection in the wall mirror as he maneuvered his belongings with his good arm, balancing others beside him on the floor. He looked different somehow. Older, maybe, but happier too. No thin lines and angles to his face or cuts of purple under his eyes. Even though he had been shot and lost Luca, he had gained . . . Yes. Gained. Nate and Reggie were waiting in the front hall to help him with his things, and as soon as the elevator dinged, they dashed over to him, laughing about something he had missed. He didn't look back.

"You're coming home with me," Nate had said. "I have a room to let. When you have money, you'll pay me. When your detective business begins to boom."

Reggie went back to the office to see if she couldn't start the business booming while Nate helped Hamish move clothes and books into his house. "You still have those fancy suits." He motioned to a few garment bags. "You can run a nightclub."

Hamish laughed. "I think I'll keep the baseball tickets. You like baseball?"

Nate nodded. "I'll let you get settled in."

Hamish followed Nate's eyes around the clean, cozy room. It had a few Harvard and Bruins pennants but was ready for Hamish to transform into home. There was a big, comfy chair by the window overlooking crisscrossing fire escapes, the music of children laughing wisping through fluttering lace curtains. The bed was cozily made with a plaid coverlet and the bookshelves were empty for Hamish to fill with books he had taken from Luca's penthouse.

"I'm going to be happy here, I think." He smiled at Nate. "It's more my style."

"Stay as long as you like."

Hamish nodded, rubbing at his stiff shoulder.

Nate disappeared a moment while Hamish clicked open the flap on his suitcase. When Nate returned, he passed an Action Comic to Hamish. "Here. This one is about Clark Kent. But Kal-El is his real name. From planet Krypton."

"That super human who can jump high?" Hamish ran his finger over the glossy cover.

"He must turn his titanic strength into channels that benefit mankind." Nate's eyes narrowed as he quoted, " 'Superman, champion of the oppressed.' " He smiled. "A little like you, Hamish DeLuca."

"Oh, I'm no —"

"A little like you." Nate lingered in the open doorway. "Now we just need Reggie to see it. If she doesn't already. You know, Reggie seemed to love the view from Old North Church. I am sure I can get Hal to forget to lock it for a few hours this evening." He clicked the door shut behind him.

Hamish flexed the hand that had set Luca free, wondering if he could live with the lie or if it would crawl under his skin and tether him tightly.

Hamish sank into the chair near the window, focusing on the new space around him, seeing it afresh. He felt lighter. And he supposed he always knew this. Knew there was another turn to the tale. But the story he'd woven in his head had so long convinced him otherwise.

He unpacked the belongings he'd shipped from Toronto and found in the trunk a package of shortbread cookies from his mother. It smelled of her — like lavender. He found a note tucked inside.

Nate had said he could use the telephone in the front hall. He asked the operator to connect him to the Toronto *Telegraph* office, and soon he was speaking to his father's secretary. A moment later, his dad picked up.

"Hi."

"Hamish."

"Listen . . ." Hamish wound the cord around his index finger. "I have to apologize to you."

"An argument takes two people, Hamish. I feel that —"

"Listen," he said more forcefully. "I think I used what happened at the court that day to stand in for my feeling inadequate in your eyes. Please don't say anything until I am finished. You always told me that I had to keep myself in check. Check my heartbeat, assess my surroundings. I always took that as your way of trying to get me to hide myself. I figured it was because you were ashamed of me." Hamish stopped a moment, sure that his father would interject. When he didn't, Hamish continued. "But I was really ashamed of myself. It took coming here, and fresh surroundings, and finding out . . ." He wasn't ready to tell his father about Luca. It wasn't his story to tell. "When I found out the truth about a murder I saw, I realized that I have something no one else has. A perspective. A natural empathy. A very wise person once told me that empathy is the greatest gift. So I am sorry that we fought. But I'm not ready to come home. Except at Thanksgiving and Christmas. And probably Easter if you buy me a ticket." Hamish stopped and waited. Silence. Had he said something wrong? Had he made things worse? He wound the cord more tightly.

"You sound different," his father finally said. Hamish had to press the receiver more closely to his ear, the voice on the other end was so low.

"I'm content here. It fits me."

"Of course you know it's rubbish that I was ashamed of you. I was trying to protect you. All of those doctors. Those studies. I edit a national newspaper, Hamish. Every time something crossed my desk, my heart stopped. I read about people with some of your . . . challenges being taken away."

"So you were scared."

"Of course I was. It sounds like you're just discovering what I knew all along."

"What's that?"

"That you're exceptional."

Later, ducking out for fresh air and a stroll to Leoni's, he thought about how his conversation with his father had ended. *Thank Luca for me,* his dad had said.

Luca. Hamish thought of him and was put in mind of a line from *Notre-Dame* about the romantic figure Phoebus, who survives while Esmeralda the gypsy girl perishes: "Men of his kind are not easily killed." Luca would start somewhere else and be fine. He would. And he had. *"Thank Luca."* Thank Luca for binding him to a terrible secret? No. Thank Luca for unfettering him and setting him free.

CHAPTER 28

The Court of Miracles glowed an incendiary orange under a sky so bright it gleamed turquoise. Mrs. Leoni's doorstep stood host to two jack-o'-lanterns. Banners for a harvest festival drooped over Hanover Street. The children who had overflowed the Prado during the summer months were buttoned and collared and sent to school in uniform lines. A solemn and hallowed quiet ushered in the colder days and shorter nights, where a harvest moon languorously spread over the crimson brick houses and crimson leaves on the trees below.

The streetlights from the square filtered into the office, bathing the staircase in gritty light. Outside, car tires screeched and dogs yelped. A mother barked at two children playing stick hockey over the shimmery stones. Reggie was probably helping Mildred Rue with paperwork. She took on quite a load each week at the Temporary Employment Agency, never expecting any type of payment and far happier, Hamish thought, for the work.

Hamish passed Leoni's and turned on Prince, following it to Hanover. He could navigate with his eyes closed now, the city wrapped so tightly around him. It was a map of Reggie: every turn and nook and alley sparked a memory they shared, and he could kick himself for not letting himself linger in every moment their shoulders brushed and they fell into step. The night cackled at him: *If you had known she would slip through your fingers, you would have slowed time down. If you had known she would turn and find her nose at the height of Vaughan Vanderlaan's broad shoulders, you would have appreciated the soft laughter hallmarking your conversations.* You would have. You should have.

Hamish's secret was tucked in his pocket with his right hand. It didn't tremble as often anymore. He was relaxed painting the office with Reggie, moving furniture, and spending his free moments curled in the overstuffed chair in his bedroom at Nate's, learning property law with the same velocity and steel-trap mind that had seen him to the top of his class at Osgoode.

A footnote cited Winslow, Winslow, and

Smythe, and Hamish's mouth turned up a little. If he hadn't come here he might still be sitting in a stuffy courtroom taking instruction from the interchangeable Winslows.

His chest was always a balloon expanding until near bursting when he caught the first sight of the regal steeple piercing up from Old North Church. It was silly to fall for a city, but he had. It was more than familiar now. It was home.

People fall in love with *people,* not cities. Not Hamish. When you weren't always comfortable with people, the silent reassurance of place was the next best thing.

His pulse raced when he swerved around a corner, or looked up in pursuit of the starlight, and caught the ornamented rim of a very old building.

He shrugged. Explaining this to Reggie made his pulse quicken, his ears redden, and the inflection of his voice rise and fall.

And then she was standing beside him. She told him she trusted him, even as he took each careful step to the top of Old North Church, whiling away the first yawn of evening. Up on top of the world. A long day it had been, yes. First, reading up on property law. Then Mrs. Leoni had arrived at the office with cannoli and vendor contracts, which Hamish examined and consulted. He and Reggie hadn't been paid in money yet. They were paid in plants and cannoli and good wishes and prayer candles lit at St. Leonard's in their name. And even while Hamish worried aloud about sustainability and how many more months of rent pearl beads would purchase, Reggie just smiled.

Just as she was smiling now after they reached the top, overlooking Boston below, the kinks of the day ironed out with the appearance of the stars. *Heartbeat, Hamish.* Reggie's index finger found the precise spot on his chest where his beat was speeding up, just under his pocket square. He swallowed.

He put his hand over hers and slowly moved it away from him.

She smiled. "And see? Just like that." He wondered if she knew how her eyes sparkled under the starlight and how when he was near her something drummed through his trembling fingers and spun through his head — something that had little to do with murder or new business ventures.

You're my adventure, he wanted to say. *I'm braver with you. I can do anything if I am with you. I don't have to hide anything. I can just be me . . . with all of my flaws.* You *steady my heartbeat, Reggie . . .* "What a surprising summer." He dipped his chin.

She nodded and gave him her content smile. The natural one that told him she was completely comfortable in the moment. "You never know, do you?"

Her hair was ribboned by starlight. Now her impish smile — so different from her coy smile or her sad smile or her reassuring smile. All the smiles he now knew by heart.

"Know what?" Hamish asked.

"When someone is going to change your life," she said.

Her chin tilted slightly. Her lips were darker with the evening, cranberry red and parted a little.

"Vaughan will be by any moment." She looked down to the street below where people were pinpricks in the darkening evening.

Hamish reached into his pocket and extracted a small parcel.

"A celebratory gift for our new business adventure. And because you pawned your pearls to make it happen."

He could feel his ears redden a little. She gave him a quizzical look and unfolded the paper, removing the locket with her delicate fingers.

"It's beautiful." She turned it over in her

palm. "Spira Spera."

"Breathe. Hope," Hamish translated. "It's from *The Hunchback of Notre-Dame.*"

"Your favorite book."

She clutched the necklace in her hand. "It's a treasure. Shines here, in the moonlight." She held it up for the North End's inspection. Yet while she spoke of the necklace, her big brown eyes stayed with him. "I have to go. You're coming with me?"

"I think I'll stay here."

"Up here, all alone?"

"I'm fine now."

"I'll see you tomorrow then." She turned and left, and Hamish wriggled out of the moment's spell.

He tried to blink her away, but her eyes were still with him and she was still there — a breath away, her dress brushing the open space of his shirt over his collarbone. He imagined her catching up to Vaughan, brown curls bouncing in the moonlight, taking his offered arm, offering a delighted laugh. Hamish swallowed.

It could have been him feeling the tendrils of her hair under his chin and brushing arms with her in the dark. He wondered if it would ever be him. She was so different from other girls. The kind of girl he could imagine a future with. But only a future with the unexpected at every turn.

Heartbeat, Hamish. He placed two fingers under his braces and counted. He looked out to Charlestown across the river, a few boats bobbing in the water, the lights winking in the dark, the Bunker Hill monument piercing the sky. Then he edged over to the other side of the steeple, to the side that looked out at Salem Street and the North End and Boston. He was sure the movement at such a height would speed his heartbeat. But it stayed the same. It didn't quicken or thrum or pulse against him. Funny, it had a mind of its own when he'd stood with Reggie under the starlight just moments before . . .

Like Quasimodo greeting his bells, he greeted the city below. The uneven roofs of the red-bricked North End, the maze of fire escapes teased by moonlight. The steeples of the Old State House, the Old South Meeting House, and Park Street Church, and the top of the Parker House, and even, yes, even a little speck of the building he and Luca had shared. Boston paid in dividends all he had believed about its possibility of home. He recalled all those moments on his bike, skidding over the cobblestones and finding the familiar in the unknown.

Just like that first day after departing South Station.

He swallowed any more thoughts of Luca down for the moment, running his hand over his wounded arm. It smarted a little with the exertion. Then he lost himself in Boston again. The symphony of rooftops and cobblestones, stories dripping from the streetlamps and heavy glass windows. It was familiar. Just as he hoped it would be.

What if home wasn't something you were born into but rather something you found and ultimately chose? Hamish's smile stretched beyond thoughts of Reggie or Luca or trembling fingers or a court case of early summer. Any of the thoughts that led to his wishing he were the Superman of Nate's comics while facing the Quasimodo of his anxious episodes. He could handle anything here.

"I'm not going back," he told Boston, assured the city heard him. "I'm not going back because this is where I belong." He flexed his still fingers, then gripped the rail before him. Several steps forward from when he and Nate and Reggie had been here before. Before he knew Luca's secret. "And I will get the girl," he promised to himself and to the night sky.

The bells marking the hour tolled. The

494

sound surprised him and he tumbled forward a little, catching onto the rail, leaning over it, the ground a long way below, shoe cap ramming into the wooden spoke partitioning him from a quick drop. He instinctively placed his palm over his heart, his fingers catching in his brace. The thrum. The pulse. The familiar beat. Not sped up or irregular from the quick bout of nerves. Just his heartbeat.

"Maybe Boston's your heartbeat, Hamish," he thought aloud as the bells continued to chime.

A NOTE FROM THE AUTHOR

If Hamish DeLuca were alive today, he would be treated for an anxiety and panic disorder. In Hamish's time, however, the world was still learning about mental illness. Primitive — and often violent — treatments were at the forefront of medical study. While I had to research how Hamish's illness would be viewed through the lens of 1930s medicine, I required no research in presenting his symptoms. I have suffered from a panic and anxiety disorder my entire life. Every symptom I have ascribed to Hamish is something I — along with millions of others — have experienced. Fortunately, with medicine and the modern strides to eliminate stigma, I have been able to live and work through what in Hamish's time could have been a debilitating illness. It was very important for me to find some way to channel what I always thought of as my greatest weakness into something empowering. In writing this series, I am dedicated to creating space for the conversation about mental illness and normalizing it in the fictional community. I want my readers to know there is help out there. Talk to someone. Let's end the stigma. There is no shame in taking the first step on a path toward help.

DISCUSSION QUESTIONS

1. Hamish's reporter father believes that often "stories are in the people whose life's pages no one thinks of turning." Can you think of someone in your family, church, or community whose inspiring story might be overlooked?

2. Reggie arrives in Boston with little clue of what she is doing or how she will make her new life work. What are the some of the ways you have adapted to the consequences of a rash decision?

3. Reggie always carries her journal of independence and writes down things (both big and small) she wants to accomplish. What are some of the things we might find if you kept a similar journal?

4. Throughout the book, several characters speak to the loyalty Luca Valari inspires. Can you think of an instance where you showed blind loyalty to someone close to you? What were the implications of letting

your love for that person get in the way of your conscience?

5. "You are only as strong as the moment that finds you braver than you have ever been." Hamish relies on his father's quote before stepping into an uncertain situation with Reggie. Can you think of a time when you have stepped completely out of your comfort zone?

6. Hamish sees the world through the lens of his favorite book, *The Hunchback of Notre Dame*. Is there a book that has influenced the way you see the world around you? Why is its influence so strong?

7. When they visit the top of the Old North Church, Nate tells Hamish and Reggie that "some sanctuaries are for all" regardless of race, ethnicity, or religion. Is there a safe haven in your community or town that reminds you of the solace they find at the church?

8. Even though Hamish and Reggie live in Boston centuries after the Revolutionary War, the history still echoes in the world around them. What are some ways you find the ghosts of the past in your city or town?

9. "Maybe Boston is your heartbeat," Hamish wonders as he settles into the home that he wasn't born into but chose. Think

of a moment in your own life where you have felt deeply connected to a place — why did it grab hold of you so tightly?

10. Vaughan Vanderlaan's influence on Reggie is partly because of his representation of the world she ran away from. Is there a person in your life who ties you to your past?

11. Even though Luca clearly loves Hamish, Luca still decides to leave him at the end. How did this action change or strengthen your view of his character?

12. Hamish spent most of his life misinterpreting his father's view of him as shame rather than the fear for his condition it actually was. Can you think of a time in your life when you have misread the actions of someone who had your best interests at heart?

13. By the end of the book, Hamish realizes that what he had always thought was his greatest weakness is actually the source of his biggest strength. Do you have a perceived weakness in your life that you could use as an opportunity for good?

ACKNOWLEDGMENTS

Hamish and Reggie's adventures would not be possible without the opportunity Daisy Hutton and the team at Thomas Nelson gave me, and I am so grateful. Thank you to Karli Ann Jackson, Kimberly Carlton, Laura Wheeler, and Kristen Golden. Working with your team is a dream come true. Sometimes I still pinch myself that this has really happened.

My agent Ruth Samsel is always in my corner. Thanks so much for your continued belief in me and my stories.

Partnering with Jamie Chavez was the best kind of brilliant challenge and an absolute joy. I learned so much and I can safely say a lot of this book's heart and soul is in her careful direction. Thank you a million.

Will Stilwell, lead educator at the Old North Church, I pestered you with so many questions about the beautiful church in Hamish's time and you were so patient. I tried to capture the essence of the magnificence of the place — and the North End — so liberties are all my own.

To the entire staff at the Massachusetts Historical Society: without your resources and patience ("Excuse me, Canadian girl, can you not lean on our almost century-old maps, please?"), the streets and world of Hamish's Boston would lack the authenticity I tried to bring to its recreation.

To the staff at Brewery Bay in Orillia, Ontario — thanks for always clearing a table with an outlet when I visit home. To the staff at my Forest Hill Starbucks in Toronto, without you I would be a zombie. I appreciate you and your little notes and your joy.

Is it strange to thank a city? Well, I don't think so. Boston, in the past years, you have snuck your way so deeply into this Toronto girl's heart. I love you and I hope this series reflects your unique flavor. If cities can be best friends, you're certainly one of mine.

Thanks to Stephen Schwartz, Katherine Reay, and Lynn Austin.

Sonja Spaetzel and Allison Pittman are always talking me off ledges and inspiring me to see more in myself than I ever thought possible. Annette Gilbert, I will never be able to think of signing this contract without you putting me on speaker and playing

Barry Manilow in the background on the piano. Not many consider their aunts dearest friends, but not many have aunts like you.

Gerry and Kathleen McMillan, you always believed that I could do anything I put my mind to. That there were no limitations for this shaking, anxious girl. You taught me to approach life with humour and courage and to turn what I found perceived weakness into my own indelible brand of strength. You've walked me through the panic attacks and medicine changes, the doctors and the long nights and you never thought I was anything but exceptional. That belief hopefully translates into my decision to serve out my vulnerability and challenges to the world at large. Hopefully in a way that shows the same resilience, aplomb, and grace I learned from growing up in your household.

ABOUT THE AUTHOR

Rachel McMillan is a history enthusiast, lifelong bibliophile, and author of the Herringford and Watts series. When not reading (or writing), Rachel can be found at the theater, traveling near and far, and watching far too many British miniseries. Rachel lives in Toronto where she works in educational publishing and is always planning her next trip to Boston.

Facebook: RachKMc1
Twitter: @RachKMc
Instagram: RachKMc

The employees of Thorndike Press hope you have enjoyed this Large Print book. All our Thorndike, Wheeler, and Kennebec Large Print titles are designed for easy reading, and all our books are made to last. Other Thorndike Press Large Print books are available at your library, through selected bookstores, or directly from us.

For information about titles, please call:
(800) 223-1244

or visit our website at:
gale.com/thorndike

To share your comments, please write:
Publisher
Thorndike Press
10 Water St., Suite 310
Waterville, ME 04901